SENTINEL'S SOUL

KRISTOPHER L. CAMPA

For my mother,
who instilled in me
a love of reading.

For my wife,
who always believed
I could make it.

Watch your thoughts, they become words;
Watch your words, they become actions;
Watch your actions, they become habits;
Watch your habits, they become character;
Watch your character, for it becomes your destiny

-Anonymous

CHAPTER 1

"Are you listening to me?" Arturo Morales stared at his latest apprentice from where he knelt at the edge of the building. In his thirty-six years in the field, he'd never come across a sentinel who lost focus so easily. How had she made it through the Academy, let alone on an accelerated track?

Lorri Preston stood next to him on the roof of the three-story brick office building. Rather than observing the people on the sidewalks below like she was supposed to, she stared out across the city skyline.

"Lorri?" Arturo snapped.

She jerked. "What?"

He took a deep breath and rubbed his temples. The smooth jazz of a street musician and his saxophone filtered through the cacophony of people and cars moving through the St. Louis streets.

"At least *try* to pay attention," Arturo said.

"I was paying attention." Lorri twisted the uppermost ring on her brow. Several piercings lined both ears and one eyebrow. With her black jeans, leather biker's jacket, and spiked scarlet hair, she was an intimidating force.

Except the façade was wasted since she wasn't ready by any means to be on her own as a field sentinel. Until she had the skills necessary, she would remain an apprentice.

Arturo stood. "If you're going to survive in the field, you're going to have to be able to identify ganastu in a crowd. It could keep you alive and, more importantly, the other sentinels you get assigned to work with."

"That's a little melodramatic, don't you think?"

"No, I don't. Even though we have the power to control the elements like ganastu, we lack their general ability to endure damage. If it ever comes to a fight with one, the best defense is to spot them long before they spot you and make sure you have the advantage. So, tell me, who is a ganastu down there? What species?"

She glared at him. "I don't know. They all look normal to me."

"Normal is a relative term. Keep watching and study them."

They scanned the people in the streets. Most wore light coats and scarves, as the weather had finally started to cool for November. Fall had lasted longer than normal, which no one was complaining about, but Arturo was ready for a nice cold winter. Tensions between the two species of ganastu, the mastem and the shedim, tended to calm down during the winter months. No one wanted to be out in the cold.

"How am I supposed to tell the difference? It's impossible."

"They're there." Arturo grabbed a silver briefcase from the ground and flicked the latches open. Inside were three small surveillance cameras and mounting brackets. "Remember your training. You were taught this already."

"Why don't you just tell me the differences so I know what to look for?"

Arturo lay on his stomach and leaned over the edge of the building. He ran his hand along the brick wall until he found a nice smooth section. "If I gave you the answers without any effort, you wouldn't learn anything. You know this. Try to remember. And hand me a bracket."

Lorri shoved one into his outstretched hand. "My instructors didn't tell us we'd have to be picking them out of crowds. This is ridiculous."

Arturo took another deep breath. Yet another complaint for the instructors at the Academy. Honestly, what was the Academy doing?

Not only did she lack the depth of knowledge a field sentinel needed, but her lack of discipline flew in the face of everything Arturo had ever seen from fresh graduates. Lorri argued with every one of his orders and challenged his authority every chance she got. While he expected a little rebelliousness, she pushed the boundaries

"Remember your lessons. Start with the shedim."

"Seriously?" Lorri set her fists on her hips and sighed. "Fine, the shedim are dedicated to chaos and control the elements of fire and earth. They're reptilian and even though both shedim and mastem can change their physical appearance to blend in with humans, we would likely be dealing with them in their natural forms."

She stopped. Maybe she'd finally noticed one of the ganastu below them.

But the silence dragged on.

He glanced up at her but she stared back at him. "That's it?"

"Yeah, pretty much."

Who in their right mind decided to strip the curriculum down? Certainly no one who'd actually operated in the field recently. Arturo would rather sentinels remain out of danger the extra two years if this was what the accelerated track produced. Three months and still she continued to surprise him with how the Academy was failing them.

"What about the mastem? Please tell me it's more than that?"

"No, just the basics. They're the opposite of the shedim and value order. They use water and air and are avian." She crossed her arms over her chest and turned back to look over the crowd.

Arturo rubbed his forehead. He would definitely be complaining up the chain of command. And he'd be checking with field sentinels in other cities as well to see if their experience with new sentinels was similar. They needed more sentinels in the field to keep ganastu in check, but this was reckless and people were bound to get killed with how little they knew.

"Watch them. Look for anything that stands out as different, anything that aligns with what makes them unique."

She huffed again but stared back out at the crowd.

Arturo turned his attention from Lorri to his work. He'd teach her what she needed to know after they finished installing this camera. He placed the bracket against the smooth section of wall.

He focused and reached within himself to where his power resided. In his mind's eye, two bright energies circled each other, one a sky blue and the other a ruddy red, each a deep pool of power that spread tendrils throughout his body. These were manifestations of his power, of his heritage as a sentinel, a mixture of human and shedim and mastem.

Arturo tapped into the red energy, the manifestation of his shedimic heritage and power and channeled it into the wall. He pressed the bracket in and the brick squished like soft clay. It spread over and around the metal. After about two inches were inside the wall, he let go and the brick solidified again. He gave it a firm tug to make sure it was secured in place.

"Now, a camera," he said.

Lorri handed him a camera much more gently than the bracket. These were far more expensive than the metal. Dropping it over the edge would cost both of them. She leaned back over to watch the people walking by. At least she made it seem like she was trying.

Arturo loosened the bolt on the camera's base and attached it to the mounting bracket, then flipped a switch on top. "Okay," he said as pulled himself back onto the rooftop. He pressed a button on a small screen in the briefcase and a picture of the street appeared, transmitted from below. The picture was clear but a little off center.

Arturo was unique among sentinels in that he had never specialized his power and thus could control every element, not just those of shedim or mastem. He liked to think it gave him an edge in the field. He reached back inside and pulled on his blue mastemic power. He focused on the air currents around the building and, with a little push, tilted the camera to the right an inch and a half to line the picture up with the full street. Much easier than leaning over the edge of the roof again.

As he released his mastemic nature, his shedimic flared up, trying to get free and overtake the mastem. Blue and red clashed for a fraction of a second before Arturo clamped down on both and pressed them back into his core. A small headache bloomed from the effort.

The only downside to keeping both natures was the constant fighting in his head that he had to control.

He latched the briefcase and stood next to Lorri. "Well. Anything?"

"No," she snapped. "But you knew that already. What's the point of me trying to figure out who's shedim and who's mastem if I don't even know what I'm looking for?"

He nodded. These outbursts of honest struggle usually meant apprentices were really trying but couldn't figure out the task. He'd rather work with this Lorri than the one who spouted snide remarks and half insults any day

"The point is you have to pay attention to the smallest of details when you work in the field. Any little change in a person's demeanor could signal they're not human." He leaned on the edge of the railing. "And you have to be ready. They've perfected camouflaging themselves."

"But I don't even know what I'm looking for!"

Arturo raised his hands. "Ease up a little and listen for a moment. There are at least two ganastu down there. One mastem and one shedim who aren't hiding what they are, not from the trained eye."

Lorri leaned over the edge and searched with an intensity Arturo rarely saw from her. A vein pulsed in her temple. "Where?"

"Look carefully. In many ways, the mastem and shedim are no different than humans. They fit themselves into human society, which means they have jobs and lives, raise families of their own to keep their individual species alive. They can't pass in their natural forms though, the forms you were taught in basic training."

The Academy should have taught this. Simple information like this was crucial to identify shedim and mastem in the field. He took a breath. It wasn't really her fault. He knew that. But he wouldn't let any sentinel he trained lack the skills needed to survive. He'd teach her what they didn't.

"Blending in has become their safety net, the way they keep themselves hidden from the world and each other. But each race still has certain tendencies they can't help but exhibit that give them away. You were taught these, even if you didn't realize it."

Lorri shrugged her shoulders and crossed her arms. She was starting to lose interest.

"Let's start with the mastem. You said they value order but it's so much more than that. Order tends to run everything they do. Everything has its place and must be in its place in the proper order. Where do you see that coming through out there?"

Lorri's eyes widened and she pointed across the street. "Him. The grocer. He's a mastem."

That was quick. Good.

"Why do you say that?"

"I'm right, aren't I?"

"Yes," Arturo said. "But why?"

Lorri glared at him but he ignored it. He wasn't going to make this easy on her just because it was new. She needed to be sure at all times in their line of work.

She put her hands on her hips. "Like you said, the little details."

"Like…"

She glanced back at the grocer. Her gaze flicked back and forth from him to the little outdoor stand he'd set up. "Like his produce displays. The vegetables are all too tidy, too ordered in each section, largest to smallest. Even the colors. The tomatoes are colored from darkest to lightest. It's too much, perfectly ordered. And look."

A woman picked a cucumber from the middle of the pile and paid for it. As she walked away, the mastem shuffled every cucumber over to close the space and maintain the uniformity.

"Good," Arturo said. "That's a mastem as sure as I've ever seen one. But you hesitated when I asked for a reason. You can't have uncertainty in the field. Always be sure. Mastem give themselves away with their unthinking dedication to order. Extreme OCD is a sign you should be aware of."

"But anyone could have similar tendencies, right? They could just be human."

Arturo smiled. "That's absolutely right." He shrugged. "You tell me though. If you saw someone like that grocer, would you just assume he was human, or would you be ready should he reveal he's a mastem?"

Lorri opened her mouth for a moment, then closed it.

"Precisely. A single clue could be all you need to be cautious enough to survive. You just have to stay aware of the possibility of an individual being ganastu."

Lorri looked over the street below. "You said you thought there was a shedim down there too?"

"Yes, I did. Can you find him?"

"I already got the mastem right. Can't you just show me the shedim?"

Arturo stared at her. Why she assumed he'd just tell her answers boggled him. He'd never made it easy on her, why would he start now.

"Fine," she said.

"The shedim should be the easiest for you to spot."

"Why?" Curiosity tinged her voice.

"Because it's the nature you embraced. You share some of the same chaotic tendencies as the shedim. Use them to find him."

Lorri studied the people below for a few more moments. "I don't see anything."

"Close your eyes."

"What?"

"Close your eyes and listen."

"Really? How could that possibly—"

"Just do as I say," Arturo said. Why couldn't she just follow orders? He was her instructor and he was trying to teach her a skill that could save her life. He was fine with questions but not when they were just to be contradictory.

Lorri hesitated, then did as she was told.

Arturo closed his eyes. "Don't just rely on your eyesight to find them. Use all your senses."

Horns honked. The dull hum of people chatting as they walked by drifted through the air. A bell at a bank on the corner rang. And then the freeform jazz of the street musician rose above the rest.

"The saxophone," Lorri said.

Arturo opened his eyes. Lorri leaned over the edge and pointed to the musician further down the street. He wore baggy clothes that were dirty and stained. But the saxophone in his hands showed the care he put into keeping it in top condition.

"What about the saxophone?"

"The man playing it. He's a shedim."

"Why?"

Lorri smiled but didn't hesitate to answer. "There's nothing orderly about that music. It's improvisation, spontaneity. He's making it up as he goes along without any kind of plan."

"Excellent."

"But that doesn't make any sense. That music is beautiful. How could a shedim be creating that?"

Arturo picked up the briefcase. "You have more to learn than you think. Shedim aren't evil. They're chaotic. And it isn't always a negative trait. A fair number of the most innovative musicians and artists were shedim. And from their chaos, entire genres have been born and expanded on by humans."

Arturo laughed at the dumbfounded look on her face. This at least wasn't new. All the sentinels he'd worked with held the same misconception. The idea that the line between good and evil was most definitely gray was a truth each came to terms with on their own. But they realized it by the time they were done training with him. He made sure of that.

Arturo's cell phone buzzed and he fished it out of his pocket. "Hello."

"Hey, what's taking you so long?" Jamaal asked. "I know you aren't having that much fun."

Jamaal Woodsman was a fellow sentinel and one of Arturo's oldest friends. He was also training Lorri's twin sister, Lydia.

"We were just finishing up."

"Good. Hurry up, then. McLeod wants to see the two of us. My place in an hour."

"All right. I'll be there."

"Don't be late," Jamaal said.

Arturo chuckled. "Bye," he said, then hung up. "Listen to me. The shedim are not all evil, just like the mastem aren't all good. Unfortunately, the mastem scored a major victory when they infiltrated the Christian church. Just because they made religions equate demons with shedim in their reptilian form, doesn't mean we have to follow those stereotypes. You'll see for yourself."

"If you say so," Lorri said with a shrug.

Arturo pursed his lips and frowned. "That's it for our lessons today. Spend some time out on the streets with Lydia. See if you can spot any mastem or shedim. But absolutely do not confront any of them."

Lorri nodded and headed for the stairs. "Sure, whatever."

Arturo looked out across the city he called home. In the distance, he could just make out the St. Louis Arch, the silver arc of metal rising above the buildings.

Other sentinels had been stubborn, had challenged him, but Lorri was going to drive him insane. He could feel it in his gut. If they didn't need every sentinel in the field they could get, he'd recommend she be sent back to the Sentinalia for further training.

He squared his shoulders. He'd never had to take that course of action with an apprentice before, and he wasn't about to start now.

CHAPTER 2

Arturo stepped up onto the porch of Jamaal's house. The two-story brick home sat squeezed between a whole row of similar simple homes. The driveway on the side led to a backyard where the two sentinels had spent many summer evenings barbecuing.

Arturo knocked on the front door, then glanced up and down the street. He waved to a neighbor a few houses down, an older woman who Jamaal regularly helped with her trash. Jamaal had grown up in a similar neighborhood to this in the heart of Memphis and when he'd been assigned to St. Louis, he wanted to live where he could get to know his neighbors, be a real part of the community.

A stillness filled the neighborhood today, the kind of stillness not from abandonment but from families curled up on the couch together with a warm blanket watching TV. With the colder weather, Arturo didn't really blame them.

He lifted his fist to knock again but the door swung open.

"It's about time," Jamaal said. Jamaal stood taller than Arturo, with broader shoulders and dreads pulled back with a hair tie. A subtle scent of cologne, nothing too overdone, surrounded him with a bright aura.

"You're one to talk. What took you so long?"

Jamaal clasped Arturo's hand, then gave him a hug. He said hugs told him more about a person than handshakes. Arturo figured it just gave someone easier access to stab him in the back.

"Sorry," Jamaal said. "I was just tidying up." He beckoned Arturo inside.

Arturo cocked his head. "Sure," he said as he closed the front door behind him.

Jamaal led him through the house and back to the kitchen. The living room was simple, with a TV and couch and a few photos on the wall. The place was spotless and clutter free, and the kitchen was no different. Arturo didn't know what kind of tidying up needed to be done.

"Where's McLeod?"

"I'm sure he'll be here before too long."

Arturo took a seat at the little dining table tucked in the corner. "Did he tell you what he wanted to talk about?"

"Nope. Not a clue." Jamaal pulled two mugs down from a perfectly organized cabinet and poured tea from a kettle. "Tea?"

"You've already served it for me, so I guess so. What kind?"

Jamaal passed him a mug. "It's a new oolong I found over on Olive."

"Then definitely sugar."

"Weak." Jamaal opened another cabinet color-coded with different flavors of teas. He grabbed two packets of sugar from the bottom shelf, careful to move more forward into their place before he shut the door.

"So what's new?" Arturo asked as he stirred the sugar into his cup. "Haven't seen you in a couple days."

"Oh, the same old, same old. Training and more training with Lydia. She's an excellent student."

"Good for you," Arturo muttered into his mug as he blew on his tea.

"That bad, huh?"

Arturo glanced up at him. Jamaal's raised his eyebrow and smirked a bit.

"And then some. You'd think twins would be similar," Arturo said. "But Lorri is nothing like Lydia."

"I'm sure she'll get better."

"Maybe. I'd probably be more understanding if she put a little more effort into learning what she should have already known. Like today, she didn't even know the signs for shedim and mastem in human form. We learned that within our first two years of basic training."

Jamaal set his mug on the table. "Yeah, Lydia struggled with it, too. We might have learned it, but we also struggled when it came to applying it in the field."

Arturo nodded. "But we at least knew what to look for. She didn't even know."

Jamaal chuckled. "It's concerning. But you know what else?"

"What?"

"We're starting to be the old men," Jamaal said. "McLeod used to complain about the things we didn't know too."

They laughed. It was too true and though Arturo looked and felt young, it really had been almost forty-six years since his power emerged, a decade less since he'd attained full field status.

A knock sounded at the door.

"That would be McLeod," Jamaal said as he stood. "Be right back."

Arturo took a hesitant sip of his tea. It was strong, with a hint of smoky wood, but all in all, it tasted better than some teas his best friend had served him over the years. Jamaal had one near addiction and that was teas. He'd buy any new tea he found just so he could try it and, if possible, force Arturo to try it.

Jamaal returned with McLeod behind him. Earl McLeod was the senior, and thus commanding, sentinel for St. Louis and had been for longer than Arturo knew. He also trained Arturo and Jamaal when they graduated from basic training and transferred to the city, Jamaal seven years after Arturo.

His skin was darker than Jamaal's and pale scars ran the length of the right side of his face, a stark contrast to his skin and hair. Sentinels rarely scarred, possessing some partial regenerative abilities and longevity passed down from their mastemic and shedimic ancestry. Whatever left the scars either happened before McLeod's powers emerged or had been excruciatingly traumatic. He refused to talk about them.

In fact, he refused to talk about his past in general unless it was relevant to the current assignment. Arturo had no idea how old his mentor really was. Gray streaked McLeod's short afro, which, with a sentinel's slower aging process put him well over two hundred years old.

"Hello, Arturo," McLeod said, a subtle southern drawl to his voice. He accepted a mug of tea from Jamaal then sat at the head of the table. "Thank you."

"Of course." Jamaal returned to his seat.

"And thank you both for meeting me on such short notice."

They held bi-weekly meetings to check in on the current state of ganastu activities in the city and so McLeod could get updates on the twins' training progress. They weren't scheduled to meet until the end of the week.

"How's the training going?"

"Lydia's great," Jamaal said. "She grasps concepts quickly and is eager to learn even more. She's studied most of our field reports and can handle herself pretty well in a fight."

Field reports? Lorri probably hadn't picked one up since joining them. Even though she had unlimited access to nearly all of them, Arturo had the feeling she was the type to learn as she went and hope for the best.

"And her control?" McLeod said, drawing Arturo's thoughts back to the conversation.

"Excellent. No problems with her mastemic nature and controls both water and air effortlessly. She lacks a bit of creativity when it comes to using them but it might just be because she hasn't seen a lot of possibilities for their uses yet. I wish I could say that was the only problem I had at her age. I'll start showing her more intricate maneuvers in the next month or so. A year, year-and-a-half, and I'm sure she'll be ready to test for full field status."

McLeod turned his attention to Arturo. "And Lorri?"

"She's just as skilled as her sister with fire and earth. I'm sure the two of them will make a pretty potent force, to say the least." Arturo took another sip of tea.

"But…" McLeod glanced at Jamaal, who only held up his hands.

Arturo set his tea on the table and crossed his arms. "But she argues with every little thing I say and loses focus too often during her lessons. It slows down what I'm trying to teach her when I have to reteach basic lessons she should have gotten at the Academy."

"Are you challenging her enough?" McLeod asked.

Arturo rubbed his neck. With how much catch up she needed to do, he didn't see how she couldn't be challenged. "As much as any other apprentice I've ever had. She's struggled with several of our lessons. It's more than the material. She thinks she already knows enough and acts like she can just wing it the rest of the way, which might have worked with the boiled-down accelerated track but won't work with real people."

"Shedim," Jamaal said as though that explained it all.

While Arturo would generally agree that a sentinel could be more rebellious because of their alignment with the shedim, this felt larger than that.

"Her choice to embrace the shedim makes her more likely to be defiant, but not to this extent. Still, I would recommend you keep a close watch on her to make sure she stays on track. Do you think they're ready for field work?"

Jamaal and Arturo glanced at each other. What was McLeod getting at? They'd worked with the twins for three months. Most apprentices didn't start to participate in fieldwork until their sixth at the earliest. The skills necessary to handle themselves just weren't developed any sooner.

"Why the rush?" Arturo said.

"They did move through the Academy on the accelerated track," McLeod said.

Arturo arched an eyebrow. "You're getting pressured to push them through field training faster, too." Arturo wasn't asking. It was exactly what the Sentinalia would do.

"No, not exactly," McLeod said. "They've already shaved two years off their training."

It made sense to anticipate what might eventually become an expectation for them. Only a handful of sentinels had made it through the new accelerated training. Not only were the graduates being tested on the viability of the program, but the instructors as well.

"I think they could be ready earlier than others have been," Arturo said. "In all honesty, they could probably handle themselves in combat well enough now if absolutely necessary. But the other skills that allow us to work individually in the field, to adapt to situations on the fly, just aren't there yet."

"I agree, maybe to a lesser extent with Lydia. She's done a lot of studying on her own to supplement what she missed at the Academy. But she doesn't have the training ingrained yet to follow orders immediately. She needs more time and experience."

Jamaal had a point. When operating in the field, a moment's hesitation could mean the difference between life and death.

Jamaal shrugged. "I would say in a couple months, they could be ready to put in the field under close observation with us, maybe shaving off a month?"

Arturo nodded as he drank more of his tea. He was near the bottom where some of the dissolved sugar had pooled and helped even further to mask the taste of the oolong.

McLeod pulled a large envelope from his pocket and removed several sheets of paper. "A case has been brought to our attention. We will need them to assist you in the field."

"You've got to be kidding," Jamaal said.

"I'm not," McLeod said. "Calm down."

Arturo shook his head. "You *did* get orders to put them in the field, didn't you?"

"It wasn't exactly an order, more a strong suggestion. Listen before you jump to conclusions. The two of you won't be able to handle this on your own."

Arturo sighed but nodded. McLeod wouldn't risk something like this on orders alone, although he was a stickler about following them.

"You've seen the news reports about the attacks in Forest Park? Supposedly gang related."

"Yeah, it's starting to make some national news as well," Jamaal said. "Saw it this morning."

"That's the problem. It's drawing too much attention. We will have official orders soon to deal with it, and I'd rather not reach that point."

Their job was keeping stuff like this out of the public view. Speed was important.

McLeod sighed. "What the media doesn't know is a woman survived the attack two nights ago. She's been kept under police guard at a local hospital. This is her official statement." He handed them each a copy of the report.

"She claims monsters beat and raped her," McLeod said.

Arturo's hand clenched into a fist as he skimmed the paperwork. It was pretty standard cop jargon, but the brutality was still there. The woman, whose name had been redacted, suffered several broken bones and bruised organs. A rape kit was performed but something went wrong with the DNA tests. The labs were looking into it.

It could be shedim, but there were always other possibilities for why the testing failed. Arturo didn't doubt the competence of whoever actually performed the kit and collected the evidence, but mistakes happened.

Jamaal shook his head as he scanned the final pages of the report. McLeod held his mug between his hands on the table.

"Her description was of scaled, horned creatures. They made the boyfriend watch as they raped her, then killed the boyfriend. It's unclear how she got away, only that someone scared them off."

"So we're thinking the shedim attacked her," Jamaal said.

Arturo nodded. Shedim thrived on the chaos they created in human souls, the passionate invocation of spontaneity. They caused it however they could – anger, ecstasy, fear. Anything they could do to sway a soul towards chaos at the moment of death allowed them to claim the soul, add it to their own personal collection and use it to become stronger. The actions of these alleged shedim fit that bill.

"It's possible," Arturo said. "Then, maybe a mastem came upon them? Scared them off?"

McLeod shrugged. "No way to know for sure. Of course, the police don't believe a word of it. They think she hallucinated the whole monster part, coping with the trauma. When our contact in the District Attorney's Office heard about it, she immediately sent it my way."

"It's pretty blatant though, even for shedim. It openly defies all the rulings from the Bosses and Lords," Arturo said.

A tenuous alliance of leaders, the Bosses controlled the shedim in the same way the Sentinalia controlled the sentinels. However, each family chose their leaders based on who was the strongest and collected the most souls. They worked together only when they needed to and only if it benefited each family involved.

The Bosses enforced the balance among their own kind, ensuring no souls were harvested before their natural maturation. And they definitely made sure their existence was kept a secret. To do anything else risked angering the mastem and the Lords that ruled them.

McLeod tapped his two index fingers on his mug. "Both species have farmed souls early before, but this is going too far. Either the Bosses don't realize it yet, or they don't know who among their kind is involved. We cannot allow it to continue."

"And you want us to stop them?" Jamaal said. "Okay, fine, but why do we need to involve the twins? Arturo and I can handle a few shedim out to snag some extra souls."

"Because the shedim's current M.O. is to attack a male and female couple. They use the violence and trauma to sway the human soul towards chaos so they can harvest it. I don't think they'll break their pattern. And I can't call in any sentinels from Chicago or Kansas City. We're spread thin in the Midwest as it is already."

"So you need one of them to pose with us as bait?" Arturo said. It made sense. Just like the shedim and mastem could hide among humans, so could the sentinels. They could appear as bait. But the twins?

"Yes," McLeod said. "The shedim responsible for the attacks have to realize fewer and fewer couples are going out since these attacks started making headlines. Let's hope they'll jump at the chance to take two more souls before they have to move on to another city."

Arturo nodded. He didn't doubt McLeod's reasoning around the motive and plan of action. His old mentor had far more experience to draw on. It was the thought of Lorri in the field that worried him.

"Look, it's the best option we have. The Sentinalia has passed word down to proceed if we think it can be pulled off." McLeod set his mug aside. "So I thought you and Lorri could pose as the bait and Jamaal and Lydia—"

"No, sir, that won't work," Arturo said. "Lorri barely gets along with me in training. She might follow orders but posing as any kind of believable couple?"

Jamaal chuckled. "Truth. Lorri would play it up horribly. Arturo and Lydia would be a better option."

"Why not you?" Arturo said. "She's your apprentice."

"I was the bait last time. Or did you forget the homeless shelter downtown already?"

"Right," Arturo said. A few overzealous mastem had opened a food kitchen and begun harvesting the souls of the homeless off the street. No one missed them at first. It was more subtle than the current attacks but no less illegal. They'd cleaned out the mastem quickly, but Jamaal had served as a homeless man for a couple weeks before they narrowed down the shelter.

"All right, fine. It's a plan," Arturo said. "But we need to clear this with Lorri and Lydia first. They need to be aware of the consequences if we fail." Arturo raised a hand to Jamaal. "I'm confident we can handle it too, but just in case. If either of them doesn't feel comfortable with the plan, we'll have to figure something else out."

Jamaal and McLeod nodded. They were risking their lives, potentially suffering the same fate as all the previous victims.

Jamaal patted him on the shoulder. "Good call. What about cops?"

"Has that stopped you before?" McLeod shrugged. "We've got a small opportunity here. The cops are going to be patrolling the northern half of the park. You'll operate in the southern half. Just make sure no evidence remains."

"Yes, sir," Arturo said. Jamaal saluted.

"Good." McLeod finished his tea and stood. "Thanks for the drink. Get ahold of the twins and let me know if we're a go." He stopped Jamaal from rising with a hand on the shoulder. "I can let myself out. It's not that hard to find the front door."

They shared a laugh as McLeod left. After the door closed, Arturo leaned back in his chair. "Well, this should be interesting."

"That's one word for it." Jamaal grabbed McLeod's mug and took it to the sink. "Hell, you never know. It might be fun."

Arturo drank his tea but couldn't help the tight ball his stomach had turned into. Lorri didn't listen to him well on the best of days. This would either go off without a hitch or be a total mess. He really hoped it was the former.

He pulled out his phone and called the twins.

CHAPTER 3

What Arturo wouldn't give for this night to be real. To be a normal human. Unfortunately, his life was anything but normal. When his sentinel powers emerged, they forced him forever out of the world of normal and into this life. His purpose now was to keep the peace and protect human souls.

The twins had both agreed to the plan for tonight, maybe a little too excitedly, despite the warning of what might happen if they failed. They wanted to be in the field, wanted to put their training into practice. Arturo remembered that feeling all too well from his early years.

There was no going back now. He and Lydia strolled through Forest Park, the romantic couple out alone after dark. With any luck, the shedim would take the bait.

A chill gust rushed by, the last remaining leaves in the park flittering across the grass like birds finally set free from their cages. Moisture hung heavy in the air. They'd have their first snow soon.

Lydia laced her arm in his with a little shiver, then leaned her head against his shoulder. Arturo took off his coat and offered it to her. She slid it on, then lifted her hair over the back. It fell against the soft leather like a golden fan.

She was a perfect copy of her twin, save for her long naturally blonde hair and the absence of the myriad piercings Lorri sported. "Thanks," she said.

"No problem." He wrapped his arm around her.

While they were the "romantic couple" for their attackers, he couldn't think of Lydia like that. If he'd been a normal human, he'd be old enough to be her father. What would it have been like to have a family, have a daughter who might be in college at this point? Maybe he'd be visiting her at college now and she'd be happy to show her father around Forest Park.

Such normalcy wasn't meant for any of them. There was no running from this life.

Arturo and Lydia stopped when a branch snapped up ahead. She stepped in closer to him and played the scared girl routine to perfection. Another snap behind them. They'd taken the bait. The gang stepped onto the path, four in front and five behind.

Lydia tensed and Arturo tightened his grip on her arm. She needed to be still, draw their attackers in closer. They needed to be certain they weren't actually human before they acted.

They wore baggy jeans, leather vests, and tattoos covered their skin from wrists to neck. All of them were stocky and their muscles bulged from overly hairy arms. A couple swung chains in tight circles. The matching clothes certainly added to the media's theory of a new gang in town.

"Stay back," Arturo said as he pulled Lydia even closer to him. He let enough of a quiver slip into his voice to make the act believable when he backed off the path. "What do you want? Take my wallet, my keys."

"Don't worry," one of them said. He stood taller than any of the others with broader shoulders. "We just want to play."

Arturo jerked his head from side to side, trying to see them all at once. Lydia shivered against him as they kept backing up. Her feet tripped on the ground and she nearly fell, but Arturo held tight to her.

A rumble of laughter rippled through the gang as their faces shifted. Their eyes gleamed crimson with the reflection of the streetlamp further along the path. Small horns sprouted from their foreheads and they leered with sharpened teeth. Dull gray and brown scales ripped through their skin as tails ending in barbs slid to the ground. They stepped in closer to Arturo and Lydia, razor sharp claws extended.

"Play?" Arturo asked, all traces of fear gone from his voice. "Is that what you shedim are calling it these days?" He stood tall and Lydia stepped away from him, squaring her shoulders.

Their attackers stopped and looked at each other. Arturo chuckled, which seemed to unsettle them more. They shifted from foot to foot and looked to their leader.

Most of them only had horns that were maybe three inches. Their leader's horns topped out just over four but still only two of them. The older shedim of the world sported dozens of horns of varying length, a reflection of the sheer volume of souls they'd collected. These shedim were so young and inexperienced they didn't even know what it meant when their victims could identify them.

"Stupid human," the biggest shedim, definitely the leader, said, squaring his shoulders. "You will be filled with fear by the time I'm finished with you."

The shedim had followed Lydia and Arturo perfectly. Two figures dressed in black dropped from the trees behind the shedim, quiet as shadows. They approached for phase two of the plan, avoiding the leaves and sticks the shedim carelessly trampled over.

"Shedim, cease and desist all aggression towards humans and leave this city in peace," Arturo said. Standard procedure required him to give some kind of formal warning.

The leader bellowed a deep laugh but Arturo heard the doubt underneath. Arturo and Lydia didn't act like humans who'd never seen a shedim. Humans didn't stand up for themselves. They screamed. They ran.

"Why should we leave?" the shedim asked. "Just because you know what we are? No, we like it here far too much."

Pretty much the response Arturo expected.

"You are in violation of the balance and guilty of illegal soul trafficking, punishable by death," Arturo said. "Leave now or we will be forced to deal with you accordingly. This is your last warning."

One of the smaller shedim leaned over. "What if they're sentinels?"

The leader tensed, then shoved him away. "I don't care if they're sentinels. Those half-breed mutts just wish they were as strong as us." He lunged forward, clawed hand raised.

And the shedim called *Arturo* stupid?

Lydia was already moving, putting space between them. Arturo focused on the air around his hands. With a quick pluck, he pulled a bit of his mastemic power and drew the moisture from the damp night air. It condensed into a single shard of ice in his hand.

He threw as the shedim closed within a few feet of him.

The shedim slammed to a stop, his hand outstretched. His gaze drifted down to his chest as a second shard from Lydia knocked him onto his back. He gasped for air, then stilled. His chest steamed and bubbled as the ice burned through him.

Water was a shedim's negative element. Their natural ability to heal themselves kept them safe from the occasional splash of water or light rain, but frozen water of any kind acted like the most potent of acids on their bodies. And that made it the best way to dispatch them.

Silence filled the air. For half a second, it looked like the other shedim would flee. Maybe they only needed to kill this one to shake their resolve.

"Sentinels!" the little shedim shrieked.

"Kill them!" another shouted.

So much for an easy out.

Lorri and Jamaal each grabbed a shedim from behind before they could move, and with a flash of silver and a quick jerk, two shedim fell with slit throats. The coppery scent of blood tinged the air. The other shedim scattered as the attackers became the attacked.

Lydia launched two more shards of ice in rapid succession into the shedim charging her. He dodged one but took the other in his shoulder. The water steamed, but with a grunt, the shedim kept on. Lydia threw again as the shedim leapt forward and caught him in the chest, the force of the blow throwing him backward across the ground.

Jamaal was right. She certainly could handle herself well enough. Arturo hoped Lorri did as well supporting his friend.

The temperature soared around Arturo and he flung his hands up.

A wall of solid rock shot from the ground as flames surged towards him. They slammed into the wall and split a moment before they could engulf him.

A shedim charged through the flames and around the wall, his innate tolerance keeping him unharmed. He swung a chain at Arturo's head.

Arturo ducked and the chain rushed by an inch above. The wind of its passage ruffled his hair and bits of rock sprinkled over him as it slammed into the wall. He punched out into the shedim's gut, and he grunted and doubled over at the waist.

Arturo yanked a knife from a wrist sheath and jammed it up under the shedim's jaw. The blade rammed through the roof of his mouth into his brain and sprayed bright red blood. He twisted and let go, leaving the blade embedded to the hilt.

The creature clutched at his throat, the body not realizing it was already dead. His knees gave out and he crumpled.

Shedim healed fast but they couldn't heal around foreign objects. With the blade still lodged in his skull, he'd stay down.

Arturo's hand was sticky with blood. Shedim blood. A cold thrill spread through him. More. He wanted these shedim to pay more for the innocent lives they took in his city. No one broke the balance in his city.

A shriek from the other side of the rock wall brought him back to the moment as the flames disappeared. With a conscious effort, he shoved away his own desire to kill and stepped around the wall.

Jamaal stood behind the last shedim with a long knife stuck through the creature's chest. He held it in place until the shedim finally fell limp. All the others lay dead on the ground. The air was silent save for Arturo and his fellow sentinels' heavy breathing.

A shedim leapt to his feet, a claw poised to strike Jamaal from behind. Arturo threw his arm out and without the slightest thought, another shard of ice launched through the air. It smacked into the shedim's head and his neck snapped with a loud pop.

Jamaal glanced over his shoulder as the shedim jerked on the ground. "Nice shot." He dropped the dead shedim he still held, leaving his knife firmly fixed in its spine.

Another shedim, one of the ones with a slashed throat from Jamaal or Lorri, dragged himself across the grass away from the fight. Arturo pulled another knife and kicked him over. The muscles in his neck inched closed. He was young, too young to heal with the speed of the other shedim.

"Please. I have a family. Don't kill me." The shedim's voice was garbled and a slight whistle of air accompanied each breath, like only part of his larynx had healed.

The rush of death cleared from Arturo's vision and he looked at the shedim. Did he need to kill this shedim? He didn't make the decisions, just followed his orders. Most grunts like him did as they were told or risked pain and even death. The sentinels weren't the Bosses. Mercy could be an option for them.

Arturo sheathed his knife. "All right. It's okay." He knelt by the shedim. "I won't—"

The shedim slashed out with his claws.

Arturo leapt back but not before the claws drew four thin lines of blood down his arm. The shedim cackled as he fell back to the ground, a cackle that quickly became a cough of inhaled blood from his still open throat.

Arturo looked at his arm, then at the shedim. Why? He had been willing to show this shedim mercy.

The cold anger seeped up from his stomach.

The creature could have gone home, told the rest of his family the consequences for breaking the balance, breaking the countless treaties between shedim and mastem meant to prevent all this death.

Arturo's fists clenched and he grit his teeth.

Instead, the shedim was so focused on destruction and chaos. It didn't think about anything beyond its own petty cruelty.

Arturo raised his hands over his head and a shard of ice appeared in each.

The shedim flinched as Arturo threw the shards down. Again and again, shard after shard smacked into the shedim's chest, arms, and legs. The scent of blood, faint before, now saturated the air.

"Arturo. Arturo!" Jamaal grabbed his arm and spun him around.

It took a moment to focus. Everything seemed brighter around him, like the lights on the path had been replaced with little suns. He took a deep breath and dropped the last shard of ice to the ground.

"I think he's dead," Jamaal said, a half-hearted smirk on his face.

All that remained of the shedim's chest was bloodied pulp, pinned to the ground by two dozen shards of bubbling, steaming ice. The shards had grown larger and more jagged as his anger built.

"Right, I'm all right. Give me a second."

He hadn't lost control like that in a long time. Early in his career, before he'd had the experience and discipline, bloodlust had overwhelmed him in the field. But McLeod had taught him to control himself and, more importantly, his natures. He couldn't regress, couldn't lose it, especially not in front of the twins. Lydia and Lorri stared at him but kept their distance.

"Let's clean up," he finally said after a few deep breaths.

Jamaal motioned for Lydia to follow him to a body while Lorri knelt at the closest one to her.

Arturo waved a hand at his rock wall and it melted back into the ground. The only sign it ever existed was a bare spot in the grass and a bit of charred earth. Then he joined Lorri as she sawed at the neck of her shedim.

"Why do we remove the heads?" Arturo asked, still calming his breathing. Focusing on Lorri and training helped a bit to center himself back in the moment.

Lorri worked the serrated edge of the knife back and forth. "Because if we don't, then ganastu will heal their wounds. They'll come back to life and keep causing trouble." She glanced over at the shedim Arturo had lost it on. "I doubt that one will, though."

Most of the body was gone. All that remained was a bubbling mass with two legs.

He ignored her jab and focused on her cutting. "Now watch carefully." He pointed at the neck. "You want to get right below the base of the skull, where the vertebrae join it, and cut between the two. Otherwise, you'll hit bone and double the time it takes to cut through. And you don't want to cut slower than the flesh heals. Trust me."

He'd done that once when he was an apprentice and the shedim revived part way through. He was forced to kill it again, then recut everything he'd worked on.

Lorri shifted her angle and sawed upwards under the skull. Her knife moved more smoothly as she kept away from bone.

Satisfied with her progress, he moved to another shedim and built up a sweat as he tried to lose himself in the repetitive motion of his blade sliding back and forth. The repetition worked for a few seconds but he couldn't shake the sheer satisfaction of punishing these shedim.

They chose to disregard the balance and the rules. They took souls before their time and death was what they deserved. But did he have to execute that last one like that?

He served as the instrument trained to keep the peace. Sentinels had existed for thousands of years with the sole purpose of making sure the two races didn't harm humanity, didn't overstep their bounds. But there was a right way and a wrong way to do his job.

With a pull and a tear of skin, he ripped the head from the body and moved to another shedim. What he'd done was definitely the wrong way. He knew better than to let his emotions ride so high and give in to his bloodlust.

Lorri pulled the head off her shedim and stood. "Finally." She held it by one of its horns and let the blood drip onto the ground.

"Gross," Lydia said as the shedim blinked in her sister's hands.

"What?" Lorri swung the head up in front of her. "Awesome." She moved it around and its eyes followed her.

"Stop that. It's weird."

"Oh, toughen up." Lorri threw the head at her twin's feet. "It's cool and you know it. Besides, you just cut your first head, too."

Lydia kicked the head over so it would stop looking at her. "Why can't the brain just stop working, like a human's?"

"Enough," Jamaal said. "Stay focused."

"He's right," Arturo tossed his second head down on the ground. "We don't have time to fool around. Anyone could walk up."

A few minutes later, Arturo stood with his third head and stretched his back. Jamaal worked on the last body.

"What's next, you two?"

"We need to dispose of the bodies," Lydia said from where she knelt on the ground. "So humans don't find them."

"And what's the best way to do that?" Jamaal asked. He tossed the last head next to Arturo's pile of three.

Lorri beat her sister to the answer. "Submerge them in water."

"And if they heal?" Arturo asked.

"Not gonna happen," Lydia said. "Now that the central nervous system has been severed, they lose the ability to heal. We don't even need ice anymore. Any water will do. It'll dissolve the bodies in a few hours and take all evidence of their existence with them."

At least they knew that much. "Let's get to it then," Arturo said.

They each grabbed a shedim by its legs and dragged it along the path to a nearby pond. Arturo and his team slid the bodies out into the water, where they sank to the bottom. After another trip and a few tosses, the bodies and heads were lost in the murky depths of the pond. Bubbles rose where the flesh had already started to break down.

Arturo surveyed the area. Nothing could remain that would indicate a fight had taken place, that anything supernatural existed. Jamaal instructed Lydia on how to call water up from the pond and use it to wash the blood off the ground. The blood sizzled as the water ran over it and dissolved back into the earth. A slight breeze helped ease the pungent odor of freshly spilled blood. By morning, nothing would remain.

"Do you *really* think this'll stop any other attacks?" Lorri asked.

"McLeod will make sure word gets back to the Bosses that we cleaned up their mess. This'll reinforce the rules against illegal soul trafficking for any other shedim."

She shook her head. "You hope."

He took a deep breath. "Is there a problem?"

She hesitated for only a moment before she spoke. "Souls are the most powerful resource on the planet. These shedim were willing to break the rules just to collect a handful extra. You really think others will stop just because we killed a few of them?"

"And what do you think we should do? Hunt them down and kill them all?"

"Whatever it takes," Lorri said.

Arturo scoffed. "We are not exterminators. We cannot hold the entire race responsible for the actions of a select few. True, there are those who break the rules to get ahead, but they exist on both sides of the line. When they do, we keep the peace, the balance. That's all."

Lorri crossed her arms and glared at him. She was stubborn, that was for sure.

Arturo glanced back to Jamaal and Lydia as they washed the last bits of blood away.

"How did it feel?"

Arturo frowned. "What?"

"You know," Lorri said as she met his gaze. "Killing the shedim like that. How did it feel?"

Arturo clenched his fists. "It was unnecessary. It's not the way our jobs are meant to be done."

"It looked like you were enjoying it."

"I wasn't."

"Who are you trying to convince?" she asked.

Arturo opened his mouth, then closed it. He wouldn't admit it to her but on some level, he did enjoy killing the shedim and it turned his stomach.

"I got lost in the moment. We all do from time to time. It doesn't make it right."

"We're all clear," Jamaal said before Lorri could respond. "Not a trace left."

"All right," Arturo said, turning his attention to both twins. "Excellent job. You handled yourselves well for your first night in the field. Go home and get some rest. We'll debrief at McLeod's at eight tomorrow morning."

"And hope no other shedim attack anyone," Lorri muttered.

"What was that?" Warmth spread through Arturo's cheeks.

Lydia glared at Lorri and shook her head.

Lorri ignored her and pressed on. "You're basing all of this on the hope that no other shedim will attack. They're raping and murdering humans."

Lydia bumped her sister's elbow.

"I'm just saying what we're all thinking," Lorri said.

"Enough! I'm your instructor and you're my apprentice. Not the other way around. Jamaal and I have been doing this a hell of a lot longer than you. The shedim will back down. They always do. Do you understand?"

"Sure, whatever." Lorri walked off without being dismissed.

Arturo stepped after her but Jamaal grabbed his arm.

"Lydia," Jamaal said. "You're dismissed for the night as well. Go with your sister."

Lydia glanced from Jamaal to Arturo, then ran to catch up with her sister. They moved off into the night, leaving their instructors standing on the edge of the pond. A few feet off, little bubbles continued to rise from the disintegrating bodies of the shedim with little popping sounds.

Jamaal let go of Arturo's arm. "Let it go. These crimes are terrible. She's just letting that emotion get to her. It's her shedim."

"I know. But her constant questioning is starting to wear on me."

"It'll pass with time. Remember, she's only been a sentinel for a few years. And only in the field a few months. Think about how you were at her age."

"I was nothing like that," Arturo said. "I listened to everything McLeod tried to teach me. I wanted to learn."

"Bullshit," Jamaal said. "I distinctly remember stories of the trouble you caused for him. She'll realize you have plenty still to teach her, too. Just lighten up a little, okay?"

A strong gust of wind blew through the park, scattering leaves. Arturo took a deep breath. "Yeah, all right."

"What I really want to know," Jamaal said, "is what happened with that shedim?"

Arturo took another breath and stared over the water. "I don't know. One minute I was ready to spare his life and the next he attacked me. I couldn't think of anything other than killing him."

"That was a bit more than killing, don't you think?"

"Yeah." He knelt at the edge of the pond and dipped his hands in. It was cold but a warm tingling sensation covered his skin as the last of the shedimic blood broke down and drifted away. After a few moments, they were spotless. At least physically.

"I haven't lost control like that in years," Arturo said.

Jamaal opened his mouth to say something, then stopped, then pushed ahead. "Do you think it might be time to make a decision? Maybe pick a nature?"

"That's got nothing to do with it," Arturo snapped.

Jamaal raised his hands. "Hey, I'm just asking. It looked like your shedim might have gotten the better of you."

Arturo took a few breaths. "I'm sorry. I didn't mean to snap. But I'm fine with using both natures. I've mastered them."

"Okay, but it's so much easier if you just embrace one. Then you can use your power without worrying about controlling it or it trying to control you. It's just different when you don't have to stay on your guard."

"I'm fine the way I am," Arturo said. Most sentinels embraced a nature early in their lives, relying on a single set of elements to use in the field. Instructors had encouraged him to do the same for years, but he enjoyed the freedom he had.

"Maybe this is a sign for which way you might choose? The violence might be pointing to the shedim."

"I doubt it. It doesn't matter," Arturo said. He'd lived his entire sentinel life controlling both natures equally. It made him more versatile in the field, able to adapt to any situation. He couldn't imagine giving up half of his power just for some off chance it might be easier to control a single nature.

"If you say so," Jamaal said. "Just shooting out ideas."

"I know. Thanks."

Jamaal patted him on the shoulder. "You heading home?"

"Soon. I think I'll take a walk first. Enjoy some of this night air. It'll be too cold for it pretty soon."

"All right. Just stay out of trouble." Jamaal headed off into the trees. "And try not to kill anyone else," he shouted over his shoulder.

Arturo picked up a couple stones as another breeze rippled the surface of the water. Why had he lost control? He always stayed composed in the field. He yawned. Maybe he was just tired from all this training with Lorri.

He threw the rocks out into the middle of the pond. Should he have told Jamaal the full truth? Usually he would, but this was different. It wasn't his shedim that flared up and filled him with rage.

He'd been consumed by an ice-cold desire for blood. His mastem had craved the death of that shedim.

He walked off down the path and rubbed his arms. Lydia still had his coat. He'd have to remember to get it back tomorrow. He checked his watch. 11:47. He needed a drink.

CHAPTER 4

The Loop was usually a busy hangout on the weekends, with several bars and concert halls crowded along the entire length of the street. Normally, college students, adults of all ages, and a fair share of shedim and mastem strolled the sidewalks and enjoyed themselves, but not tonight.

The street was subdued. The proximity to Forest Park curtailed a lot of business for the Loop. Hopefully, after the negative press from the attacks died down, patrons would return.

A lone trumpeter played outside an old record shop but the few people on the sidewalks paid him little mind. The distinct aroma of fried food wafted from the few bars that kept their kitchens open this late.

Arturo emerged from an alley that stank of piss and beer and crossed the street, making for a bar on the other side. The Trolley was written in bright green neon over the door. Decommissioned trolley tracks ran down the center of the street, left over from an experiment to bring back actual trolley cars. Arturo remembered the excitement to have them up and running and the inevitable disappointment their failure had been for all involved. The bar profited off their return though and still lobbied to have the trolleys reinstalled. Arturo didn't have much faith in that.

He entered the bar and stopped as a burly bouncer stood from a stool inside the door. The man's stomach bulged from too much beer, too little exercise, or – most likely – a combination of both.

"ID?" he asked. His voice was gruff and had a bit of a drawl to it.

It never failed. Even though Arturo was almost sixty, he still physically looked less than half that. The fact that he aged slower than humans certainly had its advantages, but times like this, when he just wanted a drink without a hassle, could be a real pain.

He dug a license out of his pocket that said he was twenty-two. The bouncer studied it for a few moments before he handed it back. Of course it was a fake, but the sentinels perfected the art of counterfeiting ages ago. American driver's licenses were among the easiest to forge.

"Have a nice night," the bouncer said as he let Arturo pass.

Arturo approached the counter to order a beer. The bar was nearly empty. A middle-aged couple danced near the jukebox to a country song released fifty years earlier. Arturo had listened to it in the car with his parents when he was a kid, before they'd died. His mother had been a huge fan of country, to his father's dismay. His dad had been a fan of rock and roll, which had rubbed off on his eldest son.

In another corner, a few guys threw darts. They laughed and spewed beer as one of them missed by nearly a foot. Several empty pitchers and plastic cups lay scattered on a table, and the guy who missed the board hollered for another round. Like they needed it.

Arturo turned back around as the bartender set his beer down and scooped up his money. Thankfully, no one else sat at the bar near him. He was tired and just wanted to be alone for a while.

He took a large swig and closed his eyes. Hints of stale hops and roasted peanuts filled his nose but he didn't mind. The normalcy of the bar surrounded him and for a few precious moments, he was a regular guy out for a drink on a Friday night. No shedim, no deaths, no decapitated heads.

To be normal, what that must be like. To never have become a sentinel in the first place.

The stench of flames and burning flesh flashed through his mind before he opened his eyes. No, he was here to drift from his reality, not relive those memories. He didn't want to worry about the past or the future. He took a deep breath and kept his focus on the present – a cold beer and really bad country music.

But his mind wouldn't stay put.

Why had he lost control like that in the park? His shoulders tightened again. Inside, his mastemic and shedimic natures lounged peacefully, separated as far from each other as they could be but well under his control. And yet, despite that, his mastem had risen and influenced him with such subtle ease. He needed to pay attention to them more, keep an eye on them both to make sure they didn't try anything like that again.

"We need you to come outside with us," a deep voice whispered in Arturo's ear.

Arturo's focus jerked from his internal natures to the bar around him. He opened his eyes and looked in the mirror behind the bar. Three men dressed in biker gear stood behind him. Tattoos covered their arms. The center guy was larger than the other two, with a tattoo of a flaming snake covering the top of his shaved head down to his brow.

Sloppy. He shouldn't have zoned out like that, not this close to the park. With as quiet as the Trolley was tonight, he should have noticed them approach.

"And why would you want me to do that? Do I know you?" Arturo took another drink from his beer, then laid his hands flat on the countertop. His fingertips rubbed against the wood, chipped and scarred from countless patrons over the years.

"Because, sentinel, if you don't, we'll have to *persuade* you to come with us." He slipped enough inflection for Arturo to understand just how persuasive they were willing to be. "You wouldn't want that display in front of your precious humans."

Arturo glanced over to the bouncer at the door. The man watched them, his muscles bunched under his shirt. His hand hung at his side within easy reach of a bat. If trouble started, he would jump in to stop it. But that bat would do next to nothing to these shedim.

The shedim grabbed Arturo's shoulder. "What's it going to be?"

There were too many innocents in the bar. Arturo gripped the wood harder. He wouldn't risk a fight that would expose these humans to the power of three shedim.

Why hadn't he noticed them sooner? At least then he could have led them out of the bar and to a fight of his own choosing. He still had his knives and outside, he could take them on. But not if they kept the upper hand. McLeod's voice echoed in his head.

"Adapt." McLeod had drilled that singular lesson into his head first. Things changed quickly in the field and if you didn't adapt to them, you didn't survive.

"All right, let's go." Arturo swallowed the last of his beer and stood.

The shedim gave him a slight push towards the door, then followed. Arturo nodded to the bouncer with a half-hearted smile. Just a friendly chat outside, nothing to concern himself with. The bouncer met Arturo's eyes for a moment before he looked away.

Arturo understood. It was obvious this wasn't going to be friendly in any way but the bouncer didn't really care as long as it was taken off the bar's property.

As they stepped onto the sidewalk, the shedim turned Arturo down an alley and out of earshot of any passersby.

Arturo pretended to stumble a few steps, then spun to face his opponents with a knife drawn. "Listen to me. Just drop this. Leave St. Louis now."

They circled like sharks, smiles spread across their faces. "You sentinels just killed six of our youngest and you want us to leave," their leader said.

"They violated the balance, murdered and raped so they could harvest souls before their time," Arturo said. "You know the rules."

"So you murdered them? An eye for an eye, huh?" The shedim's shoulders shook and he spit out every word. "Well, you're all alone now, aren't you? I'm going to take my time tearing you to pieces."

There was no talking his way out of this one. Arturo snapped his hand out and launched a shard of ice at the leader.

The shedim doubled over, his hand held to his gut.

The two flanking him glanced at each other, their eyes wide. They couldn't have expected that. Arturo stepped forward with a smile and they flinched.

Then the leader straightened and raised his closed fist. The ice sizzled and steamed against his skin. Arturo's smile faded as the shedim smirked and tossed the shard away. His hand was red and blistered but already beginning to scar over.

"You'll have to do better than that." He looked down at his hand. "But thank you for the scars. I want to remember this." Six horns sprouted from his forehead and curved back over his scalp.

Arturo swiped with his knife but his attacker was quick. Too quick.

He blocked Arturo's forearm and punched him in the face. Light sparked in his vision. The shedim grabbed his wrist and flung him back against the wall. His knife clanged to the concrete. The other two shedim rushed in, grabbed his arms, and pinned them back against the brick.

He struggled against their grip, but he might as well have fought against solid steel. Another fist collided with his stomach and he gasped as the air rushed from his lungs. His mouth opened and closed like a fish as he struggled to catch his breath.

"You killed my cousin." The shedim punched him again, and the two holding his arms cackled. "I promise you, this is going to hurt." Another punch.

Arturo coughed and tried to catch his breath. He refused to die in some back alley surrounded by trash and piss.

The shedim grabbed Arturo's chin and yanked his head up. "Look me in the eye, sentinel." Ember-red eyes flared. "We may not be able to take your soul, but we will kill you… slowly. My name is Anzu, and I'm going to be the last face you ever see."

Arturo reached down to his mastem. If he could just focus for a moment, he could do something.

Anzu punched him in the face and broke whatever concentration he could have formed.

"You know, I never understood why you sentinels thought you could police us. You're nothing but filthy mutts. We should have wiped all of you away when you first became a thorn in our sides." He raised a hand and a flame the size of a marble appeared in it. "I think we'll start with one of your eyes. Right? Or left?"

"Get the hell away from him!" someone shouted from the mouth of the alley.

A gust of wind rushed between the buildings and knocked Anzu away from Arturo. His flame disappeared as he crashed into a dumpster. The other two shedim loosened their grips on his arms.

He kicked out and down at one of them, wrenching the creature's kneecap to the side.

The shedim screeched in pain and half leapt, half fell away from him. The last shedim let go of Arturo, picked up his comrade, and ran. Their leader scrambled to his feet and hesitated only a moment before following them.

Jamaal ran to Arturo and propped him against the wall. "Are you all right?"

He spat coppery-tasting blood out and wiped his mouth. "Yeah, I'm good now. I had the situation under control."

He met Jamaal's gaze and they chuckled. Arturo had never been more glad to see his friend than in that moment.

Jamaal patted him on the back. "Oh, yeah, I could tell. Nice job with that. Didn't I tell you to stay out of trouble?"

"Well, I didn't go looking for it. They found me in The Trolley." He picked up his knife and sheathed it. "I thought you were heading home?"

Jamaal shrugged. "Luckily, I thought it might be good for you to have some company. Otherwise who knows what you would have let them do to you."

Arturo rubbed the back of his head where he'd hit the brick wall.

"What's really wrong?"

Arturo glanced at his friend. Jamaal stood with his arms crossed over his chest, the smile gone.

"I told you I'm fine. Will you stop that?"

"You may be able to fool the twins. They don't know you yet. Maybe you can fool McLeod. But you know better than to try and fool me, old friend. If you didn't just notice, you let three shedim get the drop on you, something you definitely wouldn't let happen if you were fine. Now spill it."

Maybe Jamaal was right. But he couldn't explain everything that had happened. He didn't even fully understand it himself. "Look, I don't know. I'm a little off. I haven't been sleeping well and with all the time we're spending training the twins... I've just been having a little trouble with my natures. I'll be fine, though, okay?"

Jamaal raised his hands. "I get it. But if that's the case, you need to tell McLeod. You can take a break from training to get some rest. No point in working yourself to exhaustion."

"Yeah, I planned to get some sleep after a drink."

"You need more than sleep. A few days off would be better."

"I'll be fine."

Jamaal nodded. "Look, we could all use some time off, a little vacation. You could ask for all of us, yeah?"

Arturo could do that. See if McLeod might give them all a break. "Sure. And hey, thanks for the save."

"Anytime," Jamaal said. "Come on, I'll let you buy me a drink."

They started back up the alley towards the Loop, but Arturo stopped as they reached the street.

"You know what bugs me the most?"

Jamaal shrugged. "How bad those shedim smelled?"

"No. I'm fifty-nine and I can't even get into a bar without being carded."

"Yeah, our lives suck," Jamaal said.

CHAPTER 5

Lydia poured her chamomile tea in the kitchen of the house she shared with her sister. It was a little two bedroom twenty minutes from McLeod's. He'd found it for them when they were assigned to St. Louis and bought it outright from his funding. They'd slowly made it feel like a home, somewhere they'd be comfortable with for the next few years.

She entered the living room with a bounce in her step and a towel wrapped around her head to help dry her hair. The fresh smell of lavender from a candle filled the room. Energy still rushed through her, the adrenaline sticking around from their successful mission.

"I can't even think about sleeping now. I mean, we've been trained to kill shedim but to actually be in the field with two sentinels who have spent decades keeping the balance was... it was..."

Lorri sat on the leather couch. She was still dressed in her combat gear but at least she'd washed her face and hands. She sipped a glass of scotch, and a half empty bottle stood on the coffee table. "Let me guess, awesome?"

"Yeah." Lydia took a drink of tea and sat in a matching chair across from her. "Awesome. Exactly. You know what I mean?"

"Well, you know, I don't think I got it the first time you said it, but the fifth time definitely did the trick." Lorri put her boots on the table and Lydia shoved them back off.

"Feet on the floor. You know better. Why are your boots even still on?" Her sister was such a slob. She always had been, at the Academy in the dorm room they shared and before they became sentinels.

Lorri shrugged. "Didn't take them off."

"Well, next time you'll vacuum and I'll just sit around."

"Yeah, right."

Lydia shook her head. Typical response. "Anyways, I'm learning so much from Jamaal. Way more than we did at the Academy. And it's all practical skills we'll use too. Not just boring history." As much as she loved learning the real history of the world, getting more real world experience had always been her goal.

"Well, I'm glad you're learning." Lorri drained her scotch and poured another glass.

Lydia stared at the sour look on her sister's face. "Come on, Lorri. What's that supposed to mean? You can't tell me you aren't learning anything from Arturo."

Lorri stared right back at her.

Lydia's smile faded. "You know, if you'd give him a chance—"

"What do you mean give him a chance? I have given him a chance." She swung her arm out wide, sloshing a bit of her scotch.

Was she starting to get drunk? "Oh, really? That's why you don't listen to anything he has to say."

"I don't know what you're talking about." Lorri leaned back and crossed her arms.

"You know exactly what I'm talking about. Arturo is your instructor just like Jamaal's mine. You can't question his orders, especially while we're in the field."

"So I challenged him. Look, the shedim aren't going to stop because we killed a couple of them. Trust me, I know how they think. It's one of the advantages of having chosen my shedimic nature. I can think like they do."

"And there's your problem." Lydia sat back in her chair. "You let it run you."

Lorri was too impulsive. She didn't take the time to think before she opened her mouth. It got her in trouble at the Academy and it was still getting her in trouble here.

"Now you sound like a mastem."

"No. I control my nature, not the other way around. Ever since we were transferred here, you've done nothing but question Arturo."

"Why shouldn't I? Why does he deserve to be an instructor?"

"How about the fact that he's been doing this longer than we've been alive? He's a very accomplished field sentinel. Besides, you were the one excited to get assigned here, remember?"

The population of non-humans in St. Louis had grown steadily over the past decade and their instructors constantly referenced that expansion during basic training. This city was well on its way to becoming one of the most densely populated in the country. This was where the action was and where they'd get the most experience. Lorri had made the argument for St. Louis, begged the headmasters at the Academy to post them here for their apprenticeship.

Lorri slammed her glass on the table. "They didn't tell us everything. He doesn't even know what nature he wants to follow."

Lydia stared at her, dumbfounded. What did that have to do with anything?

Lorri pursed her lips and glared at Lydia.

Arturo hadn't chosen a nature. Lydia remembered finding that out after a couple days here in St. Louis but hadn't put a whole lot of weight on it.

"So that's what this is all about, isn't it? You don't think he can teach you because he hasn't chosen his shedim like you."

"You get to have a teacher with the same nature as you. One who has mastered his mastemic side and let the other fade away. But me, I get a guy who's juggling both of his. There's no way he knows half of what he could learn from his shedim."

"It shouldn't matter. If anything, he might know more."

"Forget it," Lorri said. "You're going to do what you always do, make nice with the instructors and be just fine."

Lydia scoffed. "Make nice? Are you kidding me? I follow orders, do as I'm told and learn as much as I can along the way."

"You suck up!" Lorri spat.

Heat rose in Lydia's cheeks and she stood. She headed for the kitchen as Lorri's boots hit the floor behind her. She set her cup in the sink and leaned against the counter.

"I'm sorry," Lorri whispered from the door.

Lydia glanced at her as Lorri entered the kitchen and set her glass on the island. At times, she felt so different from her sister. Having chosen opposing natures made for terrible fights and awkward make-ups. But in the end they were sentinels and, more importantly, family.

"I'm just... I'm just frustrated."

"Look, Arturo is a good sentinel and teacher. Remember, the instructors at the Academy all said so. Even Headmaster Neyens said so and he hates everyone."

Lorri nodded and opened her mouth to speak, but Lydia wanted to finish her point.

"Sure, he hasn't chosen a nature. I thought it was weird too at first. But he's your instructor. We've had worse sentinels teach us before. You can't deny that."

Lorri nodded ever so slightly.

"And he's second-in-command to McLeod here. McLeod wouldn't just pick anyone for that."

Lorri shrugged. "You're probably right. But do you at least see where I'm coming from? I need to learn as much as I can to be the best. This life has always come so easy to you."

Lydia walked over to her twin and bumped shoulders with her. "Come on. You're a great sentinel too. Maybe just ease up a bit. Try to hear what Arturo has to teach you. Get through the last of our training so we can both be field sentinels together, just like we always talked about."

Lorri grinned. "I'll try."

"Good," Lydia said. "Come on, let's get some rest. We've got to be at McLeod's early tomorrow."

Lorri swirled her glass of scotch. "Yeah, okay."

CHAPTER 6

Arturo shut his car door as Jamaal whipped up in his own and parked on the street. He checked his watch. 8:05 a.m. They were officially late for the debriefing. He leaned against the trunk and wiped a smudge of dirt off the taillight. He needed to wash it soon, get the dirt and grime of the city off.

"A Mustang should shine," his father had said when he was a kid. Arturo's '72 Mustang was no different.

Jamaal jogged up the driveway, an unlit cigarette between his lips. He snapped his fingers and a puff of smoke rose from the tip. It was about all he could do with fire after embracing his mastemic nature, but he never needed or wanted more than that.

"We're late," Jamaal said. He drew deep on the cigarette.

"Only five minutes. We'll be fine. Why are you late though? You hate being late." For Arturo never could seem to get anywhere quite on time, but for Jamaal, being on time was late, being early was on time.

"The radio said some idiot was going too slow on the highway and got in an accident. Traffic was backed up for a couple miles."

"That's why I tell you to take the side streets. Too much traffic on the highway."

"Yeah, yeah," Jamaal said.

They started up the slight slope leading to McLeod's three-story colonial-style brick home. It had been built in the early twentieth century. A wooden porch wrapped around the front and several empty flowerbeds ran along the driveway. In the spring, McLeod made sure they were in full bloom with the most beautiful flowers.

They reminded Arturo of his mom's garden when he was a kid, before he became a sentinel and…

He shied away from that memory. "You know, being late is good for you every once in a while?"

Jamaal took another puff of his cigarette. "Says who? No, I don't want to make a habit of it."

"Like smoking?" Arturo said.

"Hey, it's not like it's gonna kill me. Besides, I still hope it'll rub off on you. It'd help settle your nerves."

"I don't think so."

"Your loss."

They walked around the side of the house. Old oak trees, older than the house itself, surrounded the yard. When McLeod bought his home, it was still brand new and the city was relatively young. He made sure to buy a chunk of land around the house so he could keep the trees. He said he liked being surrounded by nature.

It also helped make their jobs easier. No nosy neighbors to peek over the fence at the wrong time.

A large patio with a built-in grill sat directly off the back door, surrounded by more flowerbeds. A small garden plot took up part of the yard.

They stopped by an old storm cellar door propped open along the wall.

Jamaal finished his cigarette and handed it to Arturo, who incinerated it with a burst of shedim.

"Well, it looks like your face healed nicely. You had a nice shiner last night." Jamaal turned Arturo's face to the side. "It's a shame. Might have made you look better."

Arturo shoved his hand away. "You just wish you looked this good."

"You don't know what you're talking about."

"It was gone by this morning." Arturo held his arm up where the shedim had clawed him. "All healed up."

"Ah, the joys of being a sentinel," Jamaal said. "The brochure said it all – calling the elements, extended life, and rapid healing. We take a licking and keep on ticking."

"Come on," Arturo said. "Let's get inside before your jokes get any worse."

They descended the short set of stairs in the storm cellar and stopped before an iron door. There was no handle, just smooth cold metal.

Arturo placed both of his hands on the center of the door and closed his eyes. Inside the metal frame, samples of all four elements in individual tubes called to him. Each held a distinct flavor in his mind.

The door could only be unlocked by calling on two opposing elements and expanding them. Normally this meant two sentinels had to be present to enter this way—one who'd chosen the mastemic nature and one who'd chosen the shedimic. It was a safety precaution to keep non-sentinels from entering their base of operations.

Since Arturo controlled all four elements equally, he was free to come and go on his own. He gripped his mastem and his shedim and pulled one up through each arm as he'd done countless times over the decades. They resisted, though, bucking his hold off and flaring up at each other.

"You okay?"

"Yeah," Arturo said. "Still a little tired."

"I told you, you need some time off."

"Yeah, yeah," he said, echoing Jamaal's tone.

He took a firmer grip on each and forced them up his arms and into the wall. They fought back only for a moment longer then rushed to the surface. With his mastem, he sent the water in its tube to the top and pressed a button there. With his right, he heated the flame until it glowed white hot in his mind. The internal thermometer measured the temperature and, with a soft click, the door swung inwards.

Arturo released his power and his natures settled back into their usual places. That was odd. They didn't usually fight him that hard.

"Well, hopefully we can slow down our training regimen and get some rest," Jamaal said.

Arturo nodded. Maybe his body knew something he didn't. Maybe they'd just worked too hard getting the twins through this ridiculous accelerated training and it was finally taking its toll.

They stepped into their base of operations for the region, a large multi-roomed bunker that ran under McLeod's house. Here, the sentinels could train and maintain a constant watch over the activities in the city and surrounding areas. Most major cities had at least one similar base, home for the sentinels posted there.

The first room they entered held a sparring ring. Rows and rows of swords, knives, spears, and all manner of hand-to-hand weapons lined two of the walls. The room stored enough blades to supply an army, let alone the five sentinels currently responsible for St. Louis. McLeod asked for a stronger force year after year but his requests had always been denied. The best they got were apprentices, never fully trained field sentinels.

Anything else the sentinels might need in the field could be found on the third wall. Explosives, first aid, combat armor, cleaning supplies for their weapons. They had it all, and between McLeod and Jamaal, they kept it in pristine condition. The familiar aroma of oil and lacquer tinged the air and relaxed Arturo's shoulders. He was more tired than he thought if even that was helping.

They continued through the basement to the next room. A wall of monitors displayed different views of major areas around St. Louis. Arturo spotted the street where he and Lorri installed one of their newest cameras the day before.

The entire surveillance network was part of a new initiative McLeod had designed to monitor ganastu movements in the city. It was the next best thing to more sentinels. But the equipment they needed was expensive, both to purchase and to maintain, and with the funds they received every year, they could only install cameras in a small percentage of the city. As usual, they were forced to work with the little they were given.

McLeod stood at the front of the room, his arms crossed over his chest. Lydia and Lorri sat at the boardroom table that ran down the center, playing cards as they waited for their instructors.

Lydia smiled as she revealed a full house.

"Wow," Lorri said.

"I know. I never do this well." Lydia reached for the ten bucks in the center of the table.

Lorri grabbed her hand. "It's pretty good, but not good enough." She showed her hand, four kings. "Better luck next time."

Lydia threw the money at her, then brushed her bangs out of her face. "You couldn't even let me win once, could you?"

"Of course not," Jamaal said as he sat across from the twins. "It's in her nature." He threw a five on the table, then shuffled the cards. "Another?"

"Sure, I could use some more cash."

Arturo leaned against the wall next to McLeod as the hand played out. "Sorry we're late."

"It's all right," McLeod said, his voice neutral as he watched the game.

McLeod's emotions were as hard to read now as they had been the first day they'd met thirty-eight years earlier. He controlled them perfectly, a trait normally associated with sentinels who embraced their mastem, not shedim. Arturo chalked it up to age.

"Besides, this is quite amusing to watch."

"Yeah," Arturo said.

Jamaal was in for it now.

Lorri laid down her hand. A royal flush in diamonds. Jamaal flipped his cards, a simple pair of tens. Another win for Lorri.

Arturo had to give it to her. She was unbelievable when it came to gambling. She was either extremely lucky or she was cheating. If it was the latter, he hadn't figured out how. And he'd tried to figure it out, playing occasionally as a way to maybe get her respect. He sat down next to Jamaal as McLeod approached the head of the table.

"Remind me never to bet anything I'm afraid of losing," Jamaal said.

Everyone laughed, then turned their attention to McLeod. "All right," he said. "Let's get down to it. Tell me how the op went last night."

Lorri and Lydia looked to their instructors but all they did was stare back. Silence filled the room as the apprentices waited for their instructors to take the lead. But Arturo had no intention of speaking up. Jamaal and he had agreed over drinks that they'd let the twins debrief McLeod. That's what they did with any apprentice for their first field operation. The twins were just unlucky enough to be thrown into a field operation early.

"Well, come on ladies. Part of taking on any action is reporting back on the success of it, or lack thereof, if necessary," McLeod said.

The twins glanced at each other. With Lorri's insubordination and lack of discipline, Arturo had been hesitant to follow what they'd always done with other apprentices. But Jamaal had won him over. They needed to see how comfortable the twins were doing it on their own. And the best way to learn was to dive right in.

"We were successful," Lydia finally said. "The intelligence you provided us with was accurate and the shedim took the bait as we expected."

"And what was their reaction, Lorri?"

Lorri scooped up her cards and shuffled again. "They attacked with the overconfidence of their race. When they refused to back down and leave peacefully, we dealt with them according to regulations. Death was quick and the bodies were disposed of without any witnesses."

McLeod checked with Jamaal and Arturo. They each nodded. Their summary was accurate, if a little abbreviated.

"Well done, then. So there weren't any problems?"

Lydia shook her head but Lorri only stared at her cards.

"Something to say?" McLeod asked.

Arturo bit his cheek. Lorri could take this anywhere, and with her outburst last night, he had a pretty good idea what she was thinking. But he and Jamaal had agreed to let them speak. It was the risk of letting them lead the debriefing. If she let her shedimic nature get the best of her, maybe McLeod could put her in her place.

"I don't believe this is the end of their hostilities," Lorri said.

"Of course not," McLeod said. "If it were, we'd be out of a job."

"That's not what I meant. If there are more shedim connected to these, they'll only keep attacking and killing humans, if for no other reason than revenge."

"That may be true," McLeod said. "It's a risk we run every time we interfere. Other members of their family are likely to be upset by our actions. However, in this case and many where we're forced to act, the human media has gotten wind of the attacks and the Bosses did not keep their families in check. Our intervention is a reminder to them that they need to do better."

"And what does that guarantee us?" Lorri demanded, her voice growing louder. "You're willing to put your trust in the Bosses? We cleaned up their mess this time. Why would they do anything next time? Just let us do the dirty work, risk our lives. And with Arturo calling the shots—"

"That's quite enough," McLeod said. His voice, quiet yet firm, sliced through Lorri's yelling and silenced her.

Arturo recognized that tone, had experienced it several times in his life. It was the closest McLeod ever came to losing control of his emotions and letting his shedim out. Arturo did his very best to minimize being on the receiving end of those emotions.

Lorri leaned back in her chair, simmering but quiet.

"Watch the way you speak to me," McLeod said. "You are young and learning but that gives you no right to question the validity of the orders I give you, no matter how much you disagree with them. Nor the orders of your instructor. There's a time and place for questions. You are an apprentice and will remember your place. Do you understand?"

"Yes," Lorri mumbled.

"I said, do you understand?" McLeod asked again.

"Yes, sir," she said, matching his gaze.

She might have her flaws, but Arturo had to applaud the steel will that bolstered her.

"Don't think we didn't discuss the best course of action," McLeod said. "This isn't the first time we've dealt with shedim or mastem, not by a long shot. Your concerns are real and valid." Lorri perked up at this. "It's a risk we run every time we get involved in the ganastu's struggle. But we spilled just enough blood to encourage the Bosses to take care of themselves so we wouldn't have to be involved again. It's a cycle and sometimes the Bosses and the Lords need a reminder. Neither side wants full on confrontation with each other, so it is in their best interest to keep the balance."

Lorri nodded her head.

McLeod folded his arms and sighed. "Next time, use the head on your shoulders instead of the shedim inside of you when you want to question your orders. Chaos isn't always the answer. Believe me, I know. But as a sentinel, you are better than your shedim alone."

"Yes, sir," Lorri said again, but the anger was gone.

"Good." McLeod looked around the table. "For now, we'll wait and let the shedim make the next move. If there are any others who were involved in the attacks, the Bosses will take care of them rather than allow the attacks to continue. Keep your contacts open and listen for any more disturbances."

Arturo nodded. Standard protocol. Whatever family the attackers were a part of would realize what had occurred. Even the shedim that had attacked him last night would cool off a bit and realize what had been done was necessary and inevitable. It had only been a matter of time before the sentinels or the Bosses themselves stepped in. And if their Boss had been forced to step in, things would have been much worse for them and their family. It was quite possible Anzu would be killed by whatever Boss led his family for instigating further violence against the sentinels, if word got out.

"Anything else?" McLeod asked.

"Any more assignments coming down the pipe from the Sentinalia we need to be aware of?" Jamaal asked.

"No," McLeod said. "They aren't due to convene again for a couple weeks. Until they do, we'll keep the peace like normal unless I hear further from our representative.

Lydia raised her hand. "You mean you know someone on the Sentinalia?"

"Yes," McLeod said. "And no, I won't tell you who."

The identities of the thirteen oldest and most experienced sentinels who dictated operations world-wide was strictly kept on a need-to-know basis. Arturo had never met one either.

"Maybe it's McLeod," Jamaal said.

They all chuckled.

"I'm not that old, thank you," McLeod said. "Suffice it to say, I'll let you know if I hear anything."

"So our orders then?" Arturo asked.

"For now, take some time to relax and celebrate your first successful mission. You have all been going hard these past few months to get field ready, and the progress seems to be going well. You can resume training in a few days, whenever you feel ready."

Arturo smiled. True, they'd worked non-stop since the twins transferred to St. Louis. Arturo would enjoy a few days of sleep and relaxation, a chance to recharge and re-center himself, get his natures back under control. It was exactly what he needed. And better, he didn't have to ask for the vacation for his team.

But what else would they do with a bit of free time to themselves? Three solid months of training made it difficult to have any kind of life.

"Now, get out of here," McLeod said. "The forecast says today is supposed to be the last warm day before winter sets in. You should enjoy it."

The team stood and headed for the door.

"Arturo," McLeod said. "Stay for a few minutes. I'd like to talk with you alone."

Arturo hesitated. What was he in for now? Memories of McLeod scolding him as an apprentice surged in his mind. He hadn't gotten in trouble very often, but when he did, it was always severe. He sat again as the rest of his team left.

McLeod laced his fingers on the table. "How did Lorri really do last night?"

Arturo opened his mouth, then closed it. It was his responsibility to train her correctly, to get her ready. As an instructor, he could focus on her flaws or he could adapt to her learning style and support her growth. He'd been trying to do the latter, but she made it rather difficult.

"She and Lydia are definitely capable fighters, better than many sentinels their age. There's no doubt there. She handled herself quite well and stuck to her training."

"I didn't doubt she would, and I'm sure you didn't either." He stared at Arturo.

Arturo sighed. "Like I told you, she's rebellious. You saw it for yourself today. She questioned my orders last night as well."

"And you reprimanded her, of course?" McLeod tapped his index fingers together.

"As I would with any other sentinel. Jamaal and I knew it would be possible she'd bring it back up today."

"And she did. These are the kinds of insubordination you've told me about?"

Arturo nodded. "I think her shedim is driving her to act out and challenge authority every chance she gets. While physically she's trained well, I don't know that she's had the proper time to get herself under control."

"I disagree. We all have shedimic blood in us, but it doesn't mean we aren't disciplined. The Sentinalia would not have allowed her to be placed here if she couldn't control herself. We aren't in that desperate need of sentinels yet. And she did graduate with flying colors and was well recommended by her instructors. Something else is causing these outbursts."

Arturo ran a hand over his head. "I'd love to know what it is then. She even listens to Jamaal better than she does to me."

McLeod crossed his arms. "Why do you think that is?"

Arturo clenched his teeth. McLeod was trying to teach him something, using his questions to guide Arturo's thinking. But if he knew the answer to the question, they wouldn't be having this discussion. He would have worked it out with Lorri and they would be able to train on much more solid terms. Yet no matter how much he racked his brain, nothing came to mind.

"I'm trying everything I can think of to help her along. I've changed my approaches to our lessons, tried to develop a better relationship with her, help her really control herself."

"And yet it doesn't appear to be working. Maybe she isn't the problem."

"Then what?"

McLeod cocked an eyebrow up. "Have you had any luck choosing a nature to follow?"

"What?"

"Have you thought about choosing a nature?"

Arturo shook his head. Jamaal pushed him to choose a nature fairly regularly but McLeod hadn't said anything about it in years. They'd worked out long ago that he would pick when he was ready, if that time ever came.

"Sir, I'm trying to figure out how to train Lorri. What does my own nature have to do…" Arturo stopped and his jaw dropped open. Surely it wasn't that.

McLeod nodded. "Yes, go on."

"I haven't chosen a nature," Arturo said.

"Every sentinel they've ever met is aligned with one nature or the other. From the beginning of their training, they're encouraged to explore which is best for them and embrace it. You remember that."

"Yeah. And since I haven't chosen one to follow, she doesn't think I'm a worthy teacher." Arturo hesitated to put words in anyone's mouth, but it made sense. Lorri had been fine and respectful when she'd arrived, until she found out he still used both natures equally. But why was that such a problem?

"It's the only reason that fits," McLeod said. "This choice is one of the single most important decisions a sentinel will make in their lifetime. Our mastemic and shedimic lineages are constantly at war inside each of us until one is allowed to win. The longer you resist them, the more violent the war. You know what I'm talking about, don't you?"

Arturo stared into McLeod's eyes. Images of the night before flashed through his eyes. His bloodlust. His desire to kill the shedim. His actions as he repeatedly impaled the creature.

It was only one mistake. He slipped with his focus because he was tired. Exhausted. He'd experienced it before but he knew how to control them.

"If you don't choose, not only will Lorri continue to rebel against you as her superior, but I fear what will happen to your mind. Our natures are powerful forces in their own right with wills of their own. Denying them both can drive a sentinel mad."

McLeod couldn't be serious. But he wasn't exactly the joking type. "Mad?"

"Yes, mad. Each sentinel is the product of human, mastem, and shedim bloodlines mixing through the centuries. We get our gifts from them, but if one nature isn't allowed to have control, well, let's just say I've seen horrible things happen."

"Why haven't you ever said anything? We talked through this when I first got here." The worst McLeod had ever said was he'd have more mental exhaustion from the drain of controlling both.

McLeod raised his hands. "You seemed to be doing fine, and you still do. A few sentinels have waited to choose, but inevitably they naturally figure out where they'll align themselves. And honestly, I assumed you would have by now too. Besides, there are usually signs when the mind begins to slip – mistakes in the field, emotional fluctuations, trouble controlling the elements. Eventually it leads to black out and total eruptions of powers, similar to when you became a sentinel only much more destructive."

Smoke and flames jabbed through his memory with the stench of burning flesh. Was he losing control? No, that was just a slip up. He was tired. Arturo pushed the memory away.

Arturo nodded. "And you've seen this happen before?"

"Only a couple times. The Sentinalia always moves quickly to cover them up before anyone finds out. But you remember Chernobyl? The nuclear reactor did go critical but only after a sentinel lost control inside while hunting down a mastem. Are you all right?"

"Yeah, I'm fine." What if that happened to him? He couldn't lose it like when he was a kid. He squeezed his trembling hands into fists. "How can I choose a nature? I haven't been able to yet and I've always been comfortable controlling both."

"I know that. You've been strong. But you will have to figure it out on your own. I can't tell you one way or the other. But do it sooner rather than later."

"Why?"

"The onset can be sudden. If you choose, I'd be willing to bet Lorri will start listening better."

Arturo nodded. Should he choose just to get Lorri to listen? Or because things could get exponentially worse? He needed time to think about this. This single decision had the potential to change who he was, how he did his job.

"Also, the Sentinalia has begun to ask about you."

That got Arturo's attention and he sat up straighter. "About what?"

"They've noticed how well you've performed over the past decade, both in the field and as an instructor. There has been talk of several promotions, leading a city, and your name has come up. They're concerned though about the fact you haven't chosen."

"I'll try to choose. Now that I know what will happen, I'll choose." He hoped he could, at least.

"Good," McLeod said. "Do you want to talk about anything else?"

"No, sir."

"Nothing at all?"

Arturo shook his head. "Not that I can think of."

McLeod stood. "All right. If you need anything, let me know. I'll contact you if new orders come in."

CHAPTER 7

Arturo rounded the side of McLeod's house and stopped at the sight of his team. Jamaal, Lydia, and Lorri leaned against his car and chatted. Jamaal's shoulders were relaxed and he laughed with an ease Arturo hadn't seen since before they started training the twins.

Even they looked so relaxed and at ease. And why shouldn't they? The night's mission had been a milestone of sorts, a true moment where their lives had been on the line in service to humanity. They all deserved a break for the accomplishment.

Lorri glanced over and caught sight of him. Her smile faded. "So, what was that all about? Throwing me under the bus?"

Arturo sighed as he joined them. He wasn't going to take her bait, no matter how much he really wanted to chew her out for her actions inside. "No. We just needed to discuss some personal matters."

"Sure, I bet."

"So, what are we going to do with our mini-vacation?" Lydia asked before the awkward silence could grow too long. She shot a glare at her sister, begging her not to make any sarcastic retort. Arturo silently applauded her for even trying. "You know, we haven't actually seen what St. Louis has to offer since we got here and I, for one, would love to go up in the Arch."

"Why would you want to take your feet off the ground?" Lorri said. "Being that high up just isn't right."

Jamaal chuckled. "The Arch is pretty awesome, but not for everyone." He clapped Arturo on the shoulder. "It's weird getting time to ourselves again. We haven't had a true break for longer than you all have been here."

"I wouldn't plan for anything big," Lorri said as she crossed her arms over her chest. "The shedim could strike back at any point and then we're back to work."

"Will you back off already?" Arturo snapped. Heat rose in his chest. "I swear, Lorri, I've had it with your constant questioning. I'm your instructor whether you like it or not and I'll be damned if you won't listen and follow orders without questioning me every thirty seconds. That little stunt you pulled in there was disgraceful, and if you learn nothing else from me, you will learn to respect your superiors no matter what your shedim feels. You won't go disrespecting McLeod or any other sentinel again, do you understand?"

Lorri stared at him for a moment, stunned silence written across her slack face. Arturo didn't like that he snapped at her. It worked in the beginning, while a sentinel was still at the Academy, but once they got older, it grew less effective.

Lorri's face darkened as she clenched her jaws. The muscles in her cheek twitched, but she held Arturo's gaze.

"Something you want to say, sentinel?"

Lorri pursed her lips as her shoulders shook. "No, sir," she finally said.

"Very well," Arturo said. "I will see you for training tomorrow morning at nine o'clock, the roof of my apartment building."

"But McLeod said…" Lorri pleaded to Jamaal.

"Don't look at him," Arturo said. "I'm your instructor and I will tell you when we will train. McLeod said to resume when we were ready, and you clearly need to spend more time on your discipline. I will see you at nine."

Lorri opened her mouth to speak again but Arturo cut her off. "That will be all. Dismissed."

Lorri closed her mouth, spun on her heel, and stomped to her car.

Her entire body shook but Arturo didn't care how angry she was. He'd had enough. She yanked the door open and climbed in, starting the engine.

"I'll call you later," Jamaal told Lydia. "Let's let everyone's nerves calm down just a bit."

"Yes, sir," Lydia said. She got into the car and Lorri peeled out of McLeod's driveway. They tore down the street with a screech of tires.

"That was awfully harsh, don't you think?" Jamaal asked.

"She needs to learn some respect. Just because I haven't chosen a nature doesn't mean she can act like that, especially not to McLeod. It's not how an apprentice should behave."

"What does choosing a nature have to do with her behavior?"

"That's why she won't listen to me," Arturo shouted.

"Oh, come on…" Jamaal stopped and stared at him. "Wow, that actually makes sense."

Arturo leaned against his car. "Yeah, that's pretty much what I said." He took a deep breath and focused.

His shedim raged inside him, incited by Lorri. He willed it to be still, to calm itself, but it refused to let go, drawing on his emotions. It grew with each surge of raw anger and soon, his mastem would start to fight back. Arturo took more breaths and brought his emotion back into check. Without his anger to draw on, the shedim withdrew and simmered away in a corner.

"All good?" Jamaal asked.

"Yeah. She just pisses me off."

Jamaal nodded. "I get that. It's a petty reason to act like that. But I do think she's trying to be realistic about the shedim."

"I know," Arturo said. "She needs to trust us a bit more. We always have that to worry about. But the mastem could easily get angry about the attacks and do something of their own to get a few more souls."

"It's the constant struggle. So is that what McLeod wanted to talk to you about?"

"Yeah," Arturo said. He didn't fill Jamaal in on the last part of the conversation. It wasn't the time to talk about the dangers of not choosing a nature. He needed more time on his own to think about it first.

"Okay..." Jamaal said.

Arturo could hear the doubt in his friend's voice but he didn't say anything, and after a moment, Jamaal continued.

"Well, what do you want to do tonight?"

"I don't know," Arturo said. "Sleep sounds like a pretty nice plan right now."

Jamaal slung his arm over Arturo's shoulders. "Oh, come on. We've got a few days. You can sleep tomorrow. I heard there's a new club downtown. The Moonlight. Just opened last month. Let's go check it out."

"A club?" Arturo said. "You know that's not my scene."

"It'll be refreshing for you to get out. Don't be such an old man."

"Who are you calling old?" Arturo said. "You're not that much younger than me."

"Yeah, but I don't act old," Jamaal said. They laughed. "Seriously, though, it'll be good for you."

"We were just at a bar last night," Arturo argued.

"That doesn't count and you know it. A drink is one thing, but going out and blowing off some steam dancing, that's completely different."

Arturo hesitated, then nodded.

"Excellent. I'll call the twins and have them meet us around ten."

Arturo threw his hands up. "Hold up, really? We're their instructors, not their friends."

"Stop that," Jamaal said. "We've hung out with apprentices before. Just because you and Lorri aren't getting along doesn't mean we should treat them any differently than any others we've had."

It wasn't just that. Lorri could easily try and start something in public and Arturo wouldn't be able to say anything to reprimand her, at least not without drawing attention to them.

"Besides," Jamaal said as he walked down to his car. "If they're with us, then they can't really get into any kind of trouble." He stopped as he opened his car door. "I'll pick you up tonight."

"Yeah, yeah," Arturo said. He got into his car and backed onto the street. Just what he wanted to do, go to a club which he hated in the first place, and go with Lorri and Lydia. This was going to be a great night.

***

The Moonlight, a massive three-story dance club with bars and high-tech sound systems on every floor, took up a whole city block. The majority of the ground floor consisted of the self-proclaimed "largest dance floor in St. Louis," with balconies on each of the next two floors for patrons to sit or stand and watch the dancers below. The entire place was done up in a starry night theme, with artificial light in the ceiling meant to mimic the night sky. A single large orb floodlight hung suspended in the air, pocked and colored like a full moon.

The building was packed to overfilling, great for a business whose doors opened only a couple weeks earlier. It took Arturo and Jamaal standing in line for thirty minutes to get in the door, and now they had no idea where Lorri and Lydia were. Cell phone reception was nonexistent, probably due to all the iron beams built into the walls and ceiling.

Once inside, Arturo and Jamaal shoved their way through the crowd to the bar. Jamaal relaxed against the edge and nodded in time with the music. He appeared completely comfortable in his pressed shirt and jeans. Even with embracing his inner mastem, Jamaal had always been comfortable in crowds like this. It helped that after a lifetime with a body in its prime, he could dance circles around anyone in the club.

Why couldn't it be that easy for Arturo?

While Jamaal had helped him pick his outfit for the night, it did nothing to make him any more comfortable. He stood with a hand in his pocket clutched around a knife hidden in the seam of his dark jeans. A red silk shirt covered a knife strapped to his back, just in case. Despite Jamaal's assurance that he looked fine, Arturo couldn't help feeling exposed, probably because the clothes he had on really offered no protection.

"Here you go," the bartender said. He handed them their beers and took their money. Arturo took a large swig and Jamaal laughed.

"Relax," Jamaal shouted over the music. He took a much smaller drink of his own beer.

"Easy for you to say. For all we know, any number of these people could be ganastu." Arturo didn't like crowds on a good day, and after getting jumped last night, he was especially observant of everyone around him. There were too many people and they all shouted and gyrated along with the music, the mixed scent of sweat and perfume thick in the air. He'd never be able to sense an attack in time.

Jamaal patted him on the shoulder. "Yeah, true, but it's the world we live in. You can't let not knowing who is and isn't human hold you back. Loosen up and have a little fun with the vacation we're getting."

Arturo let go of the knife in his pocket. Jamaal was probably right. He needed to relax a bit. Even with the packed club, it wouldn't be like the night before. He had back up with him if he needed it. Although that wouldn't make much difference if he got stabbed in the back. He leaned against the bar to prevent that option. The music, a techno track the DJ appeared to be mixing himself, kept up a steady bass beat and lulled his focus and anxiety away from the crowd.

"Looking for us?" Lorri asked.

The twins walked up from the entrance, arms laced so they wouldn't get separated in the crowd. Both wore mid-thigh skirts and matching black tops. If their hair hadn't been styled differently and Lorri didn't have her myriad piercings, they'd be truly identical. Lorri sipped from a glass of amber liquid, probably a whiskey or scotch.

"This place is crazy," Lydia shouted over the music.

Jamaal raised his beer. "Tell me about it. Glad to see you all got in."

"The line was ridiculous," Lydia said. "Luckily, Lorri can be pretty persuasive."

"Bouncers are easy." Lorri took a sip of her drink. "I didn't expect to see the both of you. What's wrong with you?" she asked Arturo. "Expecting a fight?"

Arturo's jaw clenched. "I don't like large crowds."

"Your loss," Lorri said as she swayed with the music. "This is a great club."

The DJ changed the song to one with an upbeat and distinctly Latin flare. The crowd cycled around as those standing on the edges moved in to dance and those who'd been on the floor for a while left to buy drinks.

"Care for a dance?" Lorri extended her hand to Jamaal.

"It would be my pleasure." He barely had a chance to pass his beer to Arturo before she dragged him into the crowd.

Arturo and Lydia stared at each other for a moment before they leaned against the bar. She held her arms close to her chest and scanned the crowd as Arturo had been doing.

"Do you want a drink?" Arturo asked.

"No," Lydia said. "I won't be twenty-one for another year."

"Oh, right." He forgot just how much younger Lydia and her sister were than him and Jamaal when they were apprentices. The accelerated basic training didn't help the matter. Neither did the fact that Lorri drank already.

He stared back into the crowd. The club clicked on a fog machine and as the fog spread, it gave the dance floor an eerie ambience, like ghostly figures dancing in a cemetery. What a dismal thought. He really needed to loosen up a bit.

The crowd stepped back as Jamaal swung Lorri through a complex salsa. Arturo smiled. The look of shock on Lorri's face told the entire club that she didn't expect Jamaal to be able to move as he did. But after a moment, a smile lit up her face and she caught up with him.

"Wow," Lydia said. "He can dance."

"Yes, he can," Arturo said. Jamaal was as smooth as ever. Arturo might have been older and in the field longer, but Jamaal had always been the more comfortable of the two. A voice at the back of his mind argued that maybe it was because Jamaal had chosen the mastem. Arturo pushed it away.

"So have you enjoyed living in St. Louis?" he asked Lydia.

She nodded. "I guess. We haven't really explored much, but I know it's a great place for our first assignments. Lorri and I are learning a lot."

"Really? Lorri says she's learning?"

Lydia looked up at him and then quickly away.

Arturo got it. "It's all right. I know she has a problem with me."

"It's not that. She just needs time to appreciate what a good instructor you are," Lydia said.

Arturo nodded. Perhaps. Their conversation faltered and Arturo stumbled to think of what to say next. He really hadn't gotten the chance to interact with Lydia as much as Lorri. He and Jamaal had trained them together regularly, but Arturo had always focused on Lorri. It made it easier. He opened his mouth to say something.

"Excuse me," a tall guy said as he stepped up next to Lydia. "I'm Mark. I couldn't help but notice you were standing over here by yourself. Would you like to dance?"

Lydia glanced over to Arturo. He lifted his beer and smiled. He didn't take any offense at the young man, whether Mark had known he was talking to Lydia or not.

She smiled back at Arturo, then focused on Mark. "Sure, why not." She followed him onto the dance floor.

Arturo drank his beer and set the bottle on the bar next to Jamaal's, then disappeared into the foggy crowd.

CHAPTER 8

The table was piled high as a mountain with beautifully wrapped presents. The sun shone down on his family and friends as his mom brought out his birthday cake with thirteen candles stuck in the top.

His little brother Ramon climbed up into their father's lap as everyone joined together to sing 'Happy Birthday.'

No, this couldn't be happening, not again. They were all dead. Why did he have to relive this?

He had to stop them. He tried to move, to shout at them to get the hell away from him. But all his body did was remain still, a ridiculously innocent smile plastered on his face.

Then it began. Deep down in his belly, a pain like when he got a stomachache, small but very much present. It spread through his entire abdomen, building layer upon layer. He clamped his hands over his belly and moaned.

The pain surged harder and he fell from his chair. Tears beaded in his eyes as his chest and legs tingled. Heat filled his veins as his muscles spasmed.

"My God, he's burning up," his mom said.

"Call 9-1-1," his father ordered.

Get away from me, Arturo tried to shout, but he couldn't get any words out through the pain.

His father grabbed his arm and he screamed all the louder. He yanked his arm away. His body tensed and his jaws snapped shut. Blood seeped into his mouth as part of his cheek caught between his teeth.

His body arced and flames exploded from every pore. His little brother screamed—

Arturo gasped and bolted straight up in his bed. Sweat covered his bare chest and arms. The yin and yang tattoo on his chest glistened in what little light filtered through the window.

He searched his room for his family, his gaze darting to every corner where they might still be hiding. They weren't there though. He took a deep breath. They'd been dead for decades. He knew that. He'd killed them the day his powers emerged.

All sentinels gained their power in violent ways. The energy stored up for thirteen years burst out and awakened the shedimic and mastemic natures inside each and every one of them. Unfortunately, those violent outbursts almost always destroyed whatever families the newly formed sentinels had.

Lorri and Lydia were among the very few who hadn't lost everyone they loved, something he hoped they cherished.

He climbed out of bed and slipped on a pair of boxers before he padded to the bathroom to wipe his face and chest off. Just another nightmare of a memory long since passed. He'd dreamt that same day more times than he cared to count, relived the moments leading up to killing his parents and little brother over and over again.

It never got any easier. He always awoke from the dream with the same nauseous feeling in his stomach, the rolling guilt that he could never ever escape, no matter how many humans or ganastu he saved. It was the price he'd unwillingly paid to enter this life.

The clock in the living room read 3:23 a.m. as he walked to the floor-to-ceiling window that took up one wall. He peered out from his high-rise apartment over downtown St. Louis. A few blocks away, the Arch loomed over the skyline, lit from below by floodlights.

He leaned his forehead against the cold glass and clasped his father's medallion. It had somehow survived the blast from his power. Evidently his flames had been hot enough to kill his family, not melt metal.

He returned to his bedroom and sat on the edge of the bed. A framed photo of his family stood on his nightstand, the only other physical reminder that he ever had a normal life. They were all so happy together, before he messed it up. He flipped the photo down so he didn't have to see their accusing smiles.

He grabbed his cell phone off the nightstand and dialed a number listed as "O" in his contacts. It rang twice.

"Arturo?" a male voice answered.

Arturo sighed. "Oriphiel, sorry to wake you." He was glad Oriphiel was awake.

"No, it is quite all right," Oriphiel said. "I was already up. What's wrong?"

"Nothing," Arturo lied. "Can we meet?"

"Now?" Oriphiel paused. "Yes, of course. The usual place?"

"That'd be great."

"Can you give me ten minutes?"

"Of course." Arturo hung up the phone, then got dressed.

There was his opening. The wind whipped his hair and chilled his breath as he stabbed forward with his knife.

But Oriphiel was already there and blocked with a deft parry of his own knife, the curved tip catching the end of Arturo's knife. Then he forced Arturo's wrist out and landed a restrained punch on his chin.

Arturo backpedaled a few steps and set his feet a few inches from the edge. He glanced down at the six hundred foot drop from the top of the St. Louis Arch to the empty park below.

"Stay focused," Oriphiel said.

Arturo rolled his wrist. "Easy for you to say." He attacked, swiping and slashing to probe Oriphiel's defenses. He needed another opening before he committed to his next attack.

Oriphiel kept his movements consistent and blocked each incoming strike. But he didn't take the offensive. Arturo sidestepped and pushed him closer and closer to the other side of the Arch. When Oriphiel was nearly to the edge, Arturo called on the elements around him and launched a pea-sized fireball at his chest.

Oriphiel leapt straight into the air. Sapphire-blue feathered wings sprouted from his shoulders and snapped down with enough force to launch him over the flame. He flipped in the air and landed behind Arturo.

Arturo spun with his knife at the ready, elated to catch the mastem off balance as he landed, but froze as the cold, gentle edge of a blade settled on his neck. He lowered his arms to his side and took several deep breaths.

"Not bad," Oriphiel said, hardly winded. He lowered his knife and folded his wings along his back.

Arturo stared into his eyes for a moment, eyes that seemed to suck him in and hold him in the deepest, clearest pond.

"Not bad yourself," Arturo said. "But I think the wings gave you an unfair advantage."

"Perhaps. Although we all do what we must to survive with what we are given."

"True. And I almost had you."

"Only in your dreams, my friend." Oriphiel ran a hand over the fine gray silk shirt he wore over long pants. "Although, I wish you wouldn't have used flames. You almost scorched my shirt."

"So I did catch you off guard, then?"

Oriphiel inclined his head with a slight smile. "Perhaps."

'Perhaps' was Oriphiel's go-to word, meaning anything from agreement to displeasure. "Yet you still should not tempt your shedim. It encourages it to override your mastemic nature."

Arturo sat on the edge of the Arch and dangled his legs over the side. The metal structure swayed in the early morning breeze, cool against his skin. He pulled the hood up on his sweatshirt.

Oriphiel joined him as his wings receded into his back and disappeared. He stared across the Mississippi River into East St. Louis as he rubbed a smooth blue pendant shaped like a water droplet that he always wore around his neck.

They sat in silence, mastem and sentinel, breathing the fresh morning air.

"So is there a reason you called me this early in the morning? Or did you just feel like sparring?"

"We found the shedim responsible for the attacks in Forest Park and killed them a couple nights ago."

"Excellent," Oriphiel said. He patted Arturo on the shoulder. "They deserved their punishment for harming innocents."

"Yes," Arturo said halfheartedly as the memory of the rage he'd felt resurfaced. "Our only concern now is whether or not any like-minded shedim will retaliate. I never know with the shedim. A few might want to, but the Bosses have always kept them in line."

Lorri had raised the concern repeatedly now, and he couldn't help but give it some credence. It was unlikely, but not unheard of.

"A fair assumption. They are a fickle and cowardly race. Your actions will scare them off for a little while. Their leaders will keep the peace until some other miscreant decides they want to steal a few more souls. But I'm assuming you want me to keep an ear open just in case?"

"Yes."

Oriphiel nodded. "It has always been my pleasure to assist your kind when I can," Oriphiel said. "There are mastem who do not trust your kind, but I am certainly not one of them. I will inform you if I hear anything."

"Thank you," Arturo said.

The silence grew again. The screams of his family, particularly his younger brother, echoed in his mind but were drowned out as an ambulance and firetruck rushed by on the highway, sirens blaring. As they faded into the distance, Oriphiel spoke again.

"You could have easily called me to ask for help. Why were you really up at three-thirty in the morning?"

Arturo sighed. "I had the dream again."

"Ah. Of your birthday?" Oriphiel squeezed Arturo's shoulder. "You cannot keep blaming yourself for your family's deaths. Most of your kind lose those nearest them when their powers emerge. When the mastem and shedim lineages from either side of your heritage collide, disaster ensues. You couldn't have known or prevented it. There would have been no indicator that either of your parents had ganastu DNA."

"I know that," Arturo said. "I keep telling myself that. But I still have the dreams. I still see the horror on their faces as I burned them alive." Arturo looked away and wiped his face on his sleeve.

"I know how hard that was for you. When I found you that day, you were a thirteen-year-old boy lost in his grief. But you certainly were not afraid of me nor anyone else. Do you remember trying to kill me because you thought I'd hurt them?"

When he had woken up and seen the destruction, the charred corpses and burnt house, his eyes had immediately been drawn to Oriphiel crouched in full mastem form, covered in feathers with a razor-sharp beak and talons outstretched over one of the bodies. Oriphiel had been collecting their souls, and Arturo immediately assumed this creature had been the one who had destroyed everything.

"The fact that you didn't just fall into shock but rather picked up a stick and tried to beat me with it showed the immense strength you possess. A strength you will use to do great things for the sentinels and for humanity."

"Thanks," Arturo said, a small smile perking up.

He wasn't always sure what strength Oriphiel meant. Oriphiel had taken him from his childhood home that day to the nearest sentinels to begin his training. But he'd kept in contact and always offered his advice and support. Through the years, Arturo had grown close to the ancient mastem and trusted in his wisdom. But it was hard to believe him, especially in the hours after waking from one of those dreams.

"Perhaps you should try to embrace your mastemic nature. It would calm your mind and allow you to release the grief you still hold from your family's deaths."

"Perhaps," Arturo said and Oriphiel laughed. Arturo wondered... "Why do you push me so hard to choose the mastemic?" Unlike McLeod, Oriphiel constantly brought up choosing a nature. Never obnoxiously, but still consistently.

Oriphiel stared at him. "The mastemic nature is all you will ever need. It is pure and ordered, not tainted by the chaos that shedim embrace. I have told you that for as long as I have known you."

"And you know what will happen if I don't choose either nature? Do you know what will happen to my mind?" Part of him knew the answer he would get but he needed to ask.

"Ah." Oriphiel laced his fingers together in his lap. "Yes. Yes, I do."

Of course, Oriphiel knew. He was over a thousand years old, much older than McLeod or any other sentinel.

"Why haven't you ever said anything?" he shouted. He took a deep breath to try to calm himself, then whispered, "You could have made me choose."

Oriphiel stared at Arturo for a moment, then shook his head. "No. I wouldn't do that to you. The same rules of influence apply to mastem as to shedim, even with you sentinels. I cannot force you into choosing the mastemic any more than a shedim could force you, than we could force humans to order or chaos. Even if it was to protect you, I can only serve as a guide."

"You still could have told me about the consequences of not choosing, the destruction that I could cause again," Arturo's voice grew louder again with each word. Why hadn't anyone warned him sooner?

"I could have," Oriphiel said. "To be quite honest, I thought you already knew. I thought your superiors surely would have told you when you were young."

"They didn't," Arturo said. "I don't know what to choose. I've never known or thought I needed to know."

Oriphiel patted him on the thigh. "You sentinels are neutral in disputes between my kind and the shedim, but you can admit the mastemic is by far the better of the two."

"I don't know that, though. Sometimes my shedimic nature feels just as right as my mastemic. And I have met shedim who are not evil like you claim they are."

Oriphiel scoffed. "That is a ruse. They are fooling you so they can use you. I've seen it before. Your shedimic nature is no different than them. It will make you reckless and undisciplined and get you killed."

He paused and clenched his fists. "I don't want to see that happen to you."

The first signs of dawn worked their ways across the horizon. Beautiful shades of red and purple bled through the night sky.

"I have to go. I have a busy day today." Oriphiel stood. "I'm sorry I didn't tell you sooner. Truly I am. Think about this decision, Arturo. Now that you know what can happen if you wait much longer, you must choose. There will always be a struggle for souls, and your part in it is yet to be revealed. We will need you to be strong."

Arturo nodded and stared at the sunrise.

"If you need me, you have only to call," Oriphiel said.

"And you'll answer?"

"Perhaps. If not, I will call back," he said as he stepped over the edge. His wings snapped out in a flash of blue that sparkled in the morning light. With a flap and an updraft, he launched himself higher into the air and away from the Arch.

Oriphiel listened whenever he could and Arturo appreciated that, even if the mastem was prejudiced against the shedim. Somehow, him listening now didn't necessarily bring him any closer to a decision, but it still calmed his mind. It was a step.

He dropped himself over the edge of the Arch as well. Wind rushed past his face as he free fell for a second. He gripped his mastem and called on the air to slow his descent. He gently touched down on the grass below, buoyed by the air around him. Only then did the thought that the mastem might have resisted him, refused to allow him control over the air, occur to him. But he shrugged it off and walked back to his apartment. The mastem might be resisting him but it wouldn't survive if anything happened to him.

He pushed those thoughts away. He could control both his natures still. He shifted his focus to Lorri and the long day of training he had planned.

CHAPTER 9

Arturo sat cross-legged on the pebble-covered roof of his apartment building, with his assortment of knives and a pair of short swords spread out on a sheet of canvas in front of him. The knives' blades ranged from six to fifteen inches but were all made of quality steel.

Each bore an engraving of four overlapping circles, the symbol of the sentinels. Each circle represented one of the elements sentinels could control, fire in opposition to water, earth in opposition to air, but all interwoven as the sentinels themselves were.

Armed with a cleaning cloth and oil, he worked at each one while he waited for Lorri.

He could understand being a few minutes late. He'd been late to plenty of meetings in his lifetime. It was only natural that someone who embraced their shedim would consistently arrive late. But it was already ten o'clock. An hour late was unacceptable.

A cool breeze blew across the rooftop, softer than earlier when he'd sat on the Arch. But it still promised the ever-approaching winter close at hand. Moisture hung in the air, a strong indicator that snow was right around the corner, coming quicker than anyone anticipated. Gray clouds blotted out the sun and cast the skyline in a pale light. It wasn't as magnificent as the sunrise, but the gray held its own beauty.

The lock on the stairwell door clicked and then eased open. Only he and his apprentices had keys to the rooftop. Arturo paid the super for the building a nice lump of money for his privacy.

Lorri strolled onto the rooftop with her usual arrogant swagger. A standard issue duffel, designed to carry the supplies a sentinel needed to train and work in the field, was slung over her shoulder. She wore a light denim jacket over a black shirt and a pair of jeans. Not exactly workout clothes.

"You're late," Arturo snapped.

Lorri yawned and stretched her arm up. "Yeah, well, I was out late last night."

"I don't care how late you stayed out. I don't like to have my time wasted."

"Well, McLeod gave us a vacation," Lorri said with a shrug. "Maybe you shouldn't have assigned training during it."

"His orders were to resume when we were ready." Arturo stared at her over his knives, his muscles frozen. Her attitude, her entitlement, her blatant disrespect astounded him. But now he knew where that disrespect was coming from.

"Now, sit down," he said.

"I'll stand."

Arturo set his rag and the knife he was cleaning on the canvas. Enough was enough. "I've had it with your defiance," he said, clipping each word off. "Sit down."

She smirked and stayed where she was.

A cold calm spread over Arturo. If she wanted to push him, so be it.

"Very well, as it seems talking isn't getting us anywhere." Arturo stood in one fluid motion, his feet spread shoulder width.

Lorri dropped her bag and her hand jerked to the edge of her jacket, no doubt where she had a knife hidden. Arturo stored her reaction away for later. Yet another lesson he'd need to teach her that should have been covered. Never reveal where your weapons were until you drew them.

"If you have a problem with me, then let's get it out in the open and settled. Just you and me."

He kept his tone even and enunciated each word. It wouldn't do him any good to give in to the anger boiling underneath the surface. That's what got young sentinels like Lorri into trouble. He needed to maintain calm. His mind flashed to Oriphiel and the calm the old mastern always held. His formal speech was a natural way to keep his emotions regulated.

Lorri stared at him but said nothing. Her jaw twitched. She wanted to respond; Arturo could tell that at the very least. She held back though. That wouldn't do, not now. He needed her to open up.

"Not so talkative now?" Heat rose in his cheeks and his shedim twitched inside like a tiger ready to be unleashed. He pushed it away with a deep breath. "I know why you don't respect me. You think because I haven't embraced my shedim, I'm not a worthy teacher, right?"

Lorri's face reddened. He'd hit the nail on the head. "How can you teach me the skills I need to know when you don't even know them yourself?"

"I've fought over three decades using both of my natures equally. I know far more than you think."

"But you haven't mastered them," Lorri said.

"And you think you're better than me because of that?"

Lorri crossed her arms over her chest, but still kept a hand close to the knife hidden in her jacket. "Yeah, I do."

Arturo stopped. He hadn't thought she'd so readily agree. To think that any sentinel ever truly mastered anything was naïve at the least, potentially dangerous. He hesitated for only a moment. He'd started down this path and couldn't stop now. He'd see this through to the end.

"I've trained many sentinels and never seen such arrogance. If you think you're better than me, then prove it."

"What?" Lorri said.

"Prove you don't need an instructor and I will report your apprenticeship as finished," Arturo said, his voice still calm, composed. "I assure you, it would be the fastest anyone has progressed through the training process... ever." He met her gaze and held it.

Her shedim wouldn't resist the opportunity for such quick advancement. She'd made it abundantly clear that whatever she thought of Arturo's mastery of his own natures, she was nowhere near in control of her own. It swayed her reactions far too easily.

Her gaze drifted down to his hands. Her weight shifted to her left foot and her opposite shoulder tensed. The muscle in her forearm twitched half a second before she moved.

Arturo rolled out of the way in that moment as flames rushed through the air from her extended hand. Heat washed over his back as the flames flew past him and smashed into the wall, fizzling to nothingness.

Arturo grabbed a long knife from his pile before he rolled to his feet in a dead sprint for her. She drew the blade from under her jacket and met his head on. Their knives collided and weaved a pattern of lunge, block, and counter.

Arturo stabbed straight forward and Lorri pulled her blade up to block. She reversed her momentum to bring the knife back across at him.

But Arturo stepped aside a second before she could connect and slashed again with his own knife. Yet again, though, she recovered in time to deflect him. They circled each other and waited for a weak point. Lorri held her own and matched Arturo blow for blow, block for block.

"We both know you can handle your knife well enough. But it takes more than a blade in the field."

Arturo called on the moisture in the air to form a swirling orb of water in hand. He lobbed it at Lorri but she twisted her body out of the way. It flew past her and splattered against the wall. Water droplets dripped down onto the rooftop.

"What was—"

She backpedaled as he took advantage of her distraction and attacked harder. He swung his blade up and under hers and she twisted to get her knife in line for a block. He was already there though. His knife nicked the back of her wrist. She jerked her arm back.

Arturo disengaged. "You must manage multiple forms and approaches of attacks while in the field. Neither shedim nor mastem will attack you one at a time. And to believe they will is childish and naïve."

She glared at him and the heat on the rooftop rose. The insult had hit home, good. But could she control her anger, channel it? He held his knife at the ready and taunted her to attack.

Lorri snarled and charged him. She swiped in rapid succession – down, across, up.

He dodged each attack, only blocking when absolutely necessary.

"Do you still think you can beat me?" He taunted her with each missed strike. "You'll have to do much better than that. I've seen children with stronger attacks than you."

Lorri screamed and quickened her pace. She was fast, there was no doubt. But losing herself in her anger made her careless. Each swipe slid a little wider, each lunge threw her a hair further off balance. She would overcommit herself. All he had to do was wait and stay ahead of her.

Lorri lunged and stumbled as her momentum pulled her forward. Arturo spun away beside her and called another ball of water to his hand.

As he completed his spin, he smacked his hand onto the back of her neck. The water popped with a loud, wet clap and threw her to the rocks. Her knife clattered out of her reach.

She stayed still, her breathing heavy and the muscles along her back tensed.

"Your anger isn't your weakness. Giving in to it is." He picked up her knife. "You speak of my mastery of my natures, yet you let your shedim control you. It makes you careless and overconfident. It's that same overconfidence we exploit in them in the field."

Lorri pushed herself to her hands and knees as water dripped off her neck and shoulders.

"You have skill," Arturo said. "No one denies you that. But you are not nearly as prepared for the field as you might think." He knelt and held out her knife hilt first. "You may not like me being your instructor but you'll accept it. And you *will* respect me. You have too much to learn and I won't pass you until I know you'll survive on your own. Do you understand?"

She glared at him, the fire in her eyes dimmed but certainly not extinguished. She nodded as she took her knife. "Fine."

He held her gaze. Her jaw clenched and unclenched and she firmly stared back at him. He may have beaten her for the moment but he was still far from gaining her respect.

"Good enough for now," he said.

Arturo offered his hand to help her up but she brushed him away and stood on her own. He shook his head as he returned to his knives. He took what small victories he could get. But he couldn't keep fighting her for another two years to get her through her training.

Lorri stood and watched him pick up his knife and rags. "I thought we were going to train," she asked as she wiped water from her neck.

"You were late. I said I didn't like my time to be wasted so I started another project. You can wait until I'm done."

"And do what?" Lorri asked.

"Sit," he said.

Lorri stared at him. She sheathed her knife and sat across from him, hands in her lap. "Now what?"

"Be quiet."

He worked at each knife, diligently removing every piece of dirt and grime they collected from the field. He hadn't had much time to clean more than the knives he used on a regular basis, what with the constant training. He did now though.

He also watched Lorri. She twitched and fidgeted, tapped her fingers on her thigh. Patience was a lesson she needed to learn, especially since the shedim held such a strong hold on her. If she couldn't bring it under her control, it would get her or someone else hurt. Arturo wouldn't let that happen.

Control was the first step of what was going to be a very long process. But they had to start somewhere.

Arturo sat across from Lorri. His weapons lay neatly next to him, all polished to a perfect sheen and ordered for easy placement in the various sheaths and pockets on his combat gear. Lorri had stayed quiet through the entire process, eventually calming down and stilling. Now she sat cross legged across from him.

"Close your eyes and breathe in," Arturo said. They inhaled together. "And out." They exhaled.

"Continue breathing while I speak," Arturo said.

Lorri nodded. Her breathing matched his perfectly.

"You were taught to meditate," Arturo said between breaths, "so you could focus your energy, and call on the elements. Without focus they wouldn't hear your call, let alone answer it."

"This is basic," Lorri said.

"I said breathe, not talk."

Lorri shut her mouth and took another breath through her nose.

"While meditation can be used to focus your energy, it is also necessary to learn control. Just because you have chosen to follow your shedim doesn't mean it will happily do what you tell it. You must control it, not let it control you."

They took a couple more breaths together.

"Now focus on your shedim and the chaotic nature it represents inside of you. Do you see it?"

Lorri nodded again.

Arturo closed his eyes and focused on the shedim residing inside himself. The bulk of it lay in the recesses of his mind like a dark red river, subtly pressing at every possible moment against his mastem, a bright blue river of its own. Each nature spread out smaller channels and rivulets throughout his body, filling him evenly but staying separate from each other.

He drew upon the main river to control the elements around him and often thought of them as forces located in his center, but in reality they filled every aspect of his body. Both natures had cohabitated for so long in him, he couldn't imagine either losing so much real estate.

"Now, grasp your shedim firmly in your mind's grip." Arturo imagined a hand in his mind, an extension of his own will power. He flexed it, then grabbed the red river.

"Maintain your hold and compress the shedim. It won't affect how much power you can draw. Nothing can change that. But it will allow you to control it better and more efficiently."

Her breathing smoothed out as she fell deeper into the meditation, into the exercise of control.

Arturo pressed on his own shedim and pulled its tributaries from the different sections of his body. They clung like roots on a tree but he maintained his grip and one-by-one they relinquished their hold. However, as the red of the shedim drew back, blue rushed in to lay claim to his body. This the shedim wouldn't allow and it knocked Arturo's hold away.

He took another breath and grasped hold of both rivers simultaneously. He'd worked for years on his own meditation and control in order to keep both natures in check and separate from each other. But neither had ever liked it.

Both bucked and thrashed against him. They pressed outwards and for a moment his skin felt like it would explode. Each wanted to gain control of him and become his sole nature. Even with McLeod's warning to choose, though, he wasn't ready and he wouldn't be forced into it by either nature.

He breathed deeper and squeezed each a little tighter to seal the leaks they were creating in his hold, the blue and red waters that were dripping out. Little by little, he shored up the dam that was his control over them. Another breath and the leaks were gone.

Something still felt off. The pressure inside his control was growing too quickly.

His natures flared and simultaneously shattered his hold on them. They collided with each other and swirled around in his mind. Sparks flew where they struck each other, accompanied by white hot bursts of pain in his head. A screeching like metal scraping against metal sent shivers down his spine as each fought for dominance, no longer caring what his choice might be.

Arturo drew another breath and threw up a mental barrier to block the pain their war caused for him, then dove between the two natures. Inch by inch, tendril by tendril he pulled them apart from each other until they were finally separated in his mind. He pushed them down and rather than hold them in place, he set release valves and allowed them to unspool out into their usual territory. They refilled their channels.

Each simmered and still struck at each other, although in much smaller, more regular bursts, bursts he was used to.

"Arturo," Jamaal said as he squeezed his shoulder.

Arturo opened his eyes. Jamaal stood over him, his face drawn tight in concern. Lorri and Lydia stood to the side and watched them.

"Jamaal," Arturo croaked. His throat was dry. "What are you doing here?"

"When I couldn't wake you up, I called him," Lorri said. She handed him a bottle of water. "I didn't know who else to call."

Arturo coughed on the first drink of water. "What? It's only been five minutes."

"No," Jamaal said. "You've been under for almost two hours."

Arturo swallowed, then checked his watch. It was one thirty in the afternoon. That couldn't be right. He couldn't have meditated that long. How could he have lost track of time like that?

"What were you doing?" Jamaal asked.

"Meditating."

"Yeah, we got that from Lorri," Lydia said. "That wasn't normal."

Arturo had to agree there. "I was focusing on my natures like I was teaching Lorri to do. I was working to compartmentalize both of them separately from each other, like I've always done."

"And yet you went so deep, you were barely breathing," Jamaal said.

"For two hours," Lorri added.

"Is that even possible?" Lydia asked.

"Yes," Jamaal said. "Some of the older sentinels can do it. Monks, too, I've heard. But you're the youngest sentinel I've ever seen do it."

Arturo couldn't really believe it either. One of his instructors at the Academy, an ancient sentinel older than McLeod, had told him about the concept. He'd even helped Arturo develop a stronger grip on his own dual natures, but in all honesty, he'd always thought the idea of going that deep to be exaggeration.

He stretched out his right leg and pain lanced through him as blood flowed back to his foot.

"Oh, God, that stings."

He rubbed first one leg, then the other, but the tingling persisted.

He focused and pulled a little of his mastem up to push the water in his blood through his system, increasing the blood flow and circulation.

The pain intensified to become nearly unbearable, then receded as Jamaal helped Arturo to his feet. It certainly wasn't the most comfortable way to wake up a sleeping limb but it was the quickest. He hobbled around for a second and let the blood flow return to normal.

"You really scared us," Lydia said.

"Sorry. I didn't realize I could lose myself like that."

"It's all right," Jamaal said. "Since we know you can actually pull it off, we won't freak out the next time you do it."

Arturo limped a couple loops around the rooftop. Someone had picked up his knives and put them in his duffel bag, probably Lydia. Lord knew Lorri wouldn't have done it. As he reached the edge of the roof, he looked west over the city and pulled his legs up one at a time to stretch them.

Jamaal joined him. "Are you okay? Why did you go that deep?"

Arturo glanced over his shoulder. Lorri and Lydia whispered to one another on the other side of the roof. "I'm fine, really. And it's not like I was trying to. It just sort of happened. I didn't even know time was passing at all."

"Wild," Jamaal said. "Please, if you decide you want to go under like that again, let me know first, okay?"

"You've got it." He turned back to look out at the city. The sky was gray with the approach of winter and possible snow.

"So, what did you see? God?" Jamaal asked.

"Come on," Arturo said. He didn't have time for fanciful thoughts like that.

Jamaal chuckled. "Fine. But seriously, what did you focus on that could keep you under like that?"

Arturo shook his head. How much should he say?

Then his gaze caught on black smoke rising several miles in the distance. But from that far away, that had to mean it was thousands of feet high. What could cause that?

"What is that?" Jamaal said, his question lost as he saw it as well.

Lydia and Lorri joined them at the edge.

"Smoke?" Lydia said.

"Obviously," Lorri added but without her usual sarcasm. "But from what?"

Arturo's cell phone buzzed in his pocket and he answered without taking his eyes off the smoke. "Hello?"

"Arturo," McLeod said. "Are you with Jamaal?"

His tone was deadly serious, focused in a way Arturo had never heard before. "Yes, sir. What's going on?"

"There's been an attack at the airport."

"Attack?" Arturo said.

"Yes, the first fires erupted about twenty minutes ago."

"Shedim?" Arturo asked. His team turned their attention from the smoke to him.

"That's my assumption. A couple calls were made out to the authorities about monsters tearing through the airport. There's a lot of fire and reports of explosions throughout the terminal before all communication was lost inside."

"We're at my apartment and can see the smoke. It must be a thousand feet high."

"There isn't a soul in the entire city who can't see it," McLeod said. "I'm sorry, but I've got to cut your vacation short."

"Who cares about vacation, sir. What are your orders?"

"You're our response team. I need you and Jamaal inside that terminal to figure out what is happening and, if any shedim are still in there, get rid of them."

"And Lorri and Lydia?"

"Dammit," McLeod said. "Take them with you. They did well enough in the field once, this will be more practice. I'm sure the Sentinalia will love them getting more field experience. And from what I'm hearing over the scanners, you two might need the backup."

"Yes, sir." He wasn't the most thrilled with it, but now wasn't the time to argue. Who knew how many lives had been lost already. "Law enforcement?"

"Local PD and fire department are already on site but they've been ordered to wait outside until the FBI arrive. You won't have a lot of time... Hang on a second."

A police scanner in the background crackled. *"Terrorists have stated they'll kill hostages if anyone attempts to enter the terminal. They have everyone gathered in the baggage claims. It's unclear how many people they have,"* the dispatcher said.

"Did you catch that?"

"Yes. If these are shedim attacking, then they're only buying time to kill off the hostages and harvest their souls."

"I agree," McLeod said. "I'll try to stall the FBI from storming the entrance but there's not a lot I can do at this point. Get your team in there now. I'll send the schematics to you en route."

"Yes, sir." Arturo hung up the phone.

"Shedim?" Lorri asked. Her eyes asked if this had anything to do with the shedim they killed in Forest Park. And he couldn't help but wonder the same himself.

"Looks that way."

Lorri's face grew paler than usual. She might act tough every time she challenged him about the shedim, but she wouldn't have asked for this to prove him wrong.

Arturo looked at Jamaal. "You've got your gear?"

"Of course," Jamaal said. "I had Lydia bring hers, too, in case we decided to train today."

"Good. Then we'll suit up on the way," Arturo said. "We're going to figure out what's happened and stop anyone from doing more harm."

The team sprinted for the stairs. Arturo grabbed his bag and followed them down. He prayed they would get there in time. That there would be someone left to save. But he didn't hold out hope.

It was going to be a long day.

CHAPTER 10

"Where are we?" Arturo asked.

He and his team advanced single file through a narrow maintenance tunnel, each with a short sword drawn. Pale red emergency lights lit the tunnel every dozen feet. Pipes hissed and squealed around them. Water dripped down the walls and through the grated floor.

"Not there yet." Jamaal said.

Arturo raised his eyebrow but ignored him. They needed to get to the terminal and they'd already spent far too long in the tunnels. They reached another intersection. How many tunnels were there?

"We should have gotten there already," Arturo said.

"Let's check." Lydia slid her sword into a sheath sewn diagonally along the back of her vest and pulled a tablet from a pocket. They all wore similar black vests and pants filled with their various knives and other field gear. Lydia powered the tablet up and a 3-D hologram appeared above it of the entire tunnel network and airport above.

"What's that?" Jamaal asked.

Lydia typed a few commands into the tablet and it zoomed in on their location. "Holographic mapping. You don't use these?"

"We're old school," Arturo said. "Technology isn't our strongest suit."

"Everyone who graduates from the Academy is taught to use these," Lorri said. "Maybe they should think about training *you* some more."

Arturo glared at her but didn't say anything. They had a job to do. They could discuss his comfort with technology, or rather lack of comfort, later.

"We're close to the main terminal," Lydia said. "According to the reports McLeod sent, that's where the attacks were clustered."

"And where the hostages were being held," Lorri added.

Arturo beckoned. "Lead the way."

Lydia studied her map a second longer and then pointed. "This way." She headed off down the tunnel and the others followed.

They took a left at the next junction and after a few more minutes reached a simple gray door. Lydia nodded and Arturo waved her away. Jamaal stepped forward, glanced back, then threw the door open.

Arturo rushed in, Jamaal right behind him.

Thick black smoke swirled around him and stung his eyes. He could barely see his own sword held in front of him. His team spread out, swords held at the ready and hands poised to call on the elements at the slightest signs of movement.

"Jamaal, Lydia," Arturo said. He coughed as he breathed more of the smoke. It stank of burnt sheetrock with a tinge of something fouler, like singed hair. "Clear this smoke."

Jamaal and Lydia each waved a hand and a breeze moved around them. It pushed the smoke away and created a bubble of fresh air ten feet in each direction. Arturo breathed in the cleaner air and tried unsuccessfully to clear the taste from the back of his throat.

"What *is* that?" Lorri asked as she sniffed the air.

Jamaal and Arturo looked at each other. The smell wasn't strong yet, but it would be. He knew it all too well from his years of fighting with fire. A sickly-sweet smell, not all dissimilar from a spoiled steak left on a grill for too long. It was the stench of burnt flesh.

"Come on," Jamaal said. "Keep your eyes open and your voices down."

They headed for the baggage claim area. It was eerily quiet in the hallway. Their bubble of fresh air followed them but only showed a small portion of the wrecked terminal. Scorched rubble and smashed glass littered the floor. Sections of wall were blown out and the wiring inside sparked and cracked. The odor grew stronger and stronger as they drew closer to the center of the terminal.

"At least the power is still on," Lorri said.

Jamaal stepped over a cart of discarded luggage. "Probably a backup generator feeding juice. FBI protocol would have been to cut the power on arrival."

"Stay away from it anyways," Arturo said. "All we need is for one of us to get electrocuted."

They advanced through the silence. The smoke hung thick in the air. Shapes surprised them as they appeared out of the smoke with little to no warning. But they were only plants or stacked chairs.

"Why hasn't all this cleared out yet?" Lydia whispered.

"Nowhere for it to go if the hallway is still intact," Arturo said. The terminal was so quiet and with this much smoke, Arturo couldn't help but wonder how anyone could be left alive. Were they too late to save even one soul?

A figure appeared in the smoke with horns protruding from its head. Lydia reacted first and threw her fist forward. A shard of ice slammed into its center and sent it clattering to the ground.

The team rushed it only to find a cardboard advertisement of a man in a business suit. It had been leaned against a coat rack that conveniently looked like horns in the smoke. Now, Lydia's shard of ice protruded from its center.

"Well," Lorri said with a chuckle. "You got him."

"Shut up," Lydia said.

"Both of you, quiet," Arturo ordered.

A slow, irregular tapping came from ahead of them.

They crept into the baggage area. The smoke had partially dissipated but still clung like a fog in the air. The stench in the smoke, subdued before now, nearly overwhelmed them and they covered their noses with their hands.

Arturo's stomach knotted. "Clear the area," he said.

He and Lorri spread out and watched for movement while Jamaal and Lydia worked. They pushed as much of the smoke out of the room and down the halls as possible. When the room cleared, they found the source of the horrid stench.

Too many bodies to count lay piled around the central carousel in the room, all burned to various degrees. Smoke still rose from the more severely scorched ones. A pyramid of decapitated but mostly unburned heads from men, women and children were stacked on top of the carousel itself. A wristwatch on a severed arm hung over the edge and tapped against the side as a few pieces of luggage circled round and round.

Lydia's face drained of all color and she crumpled to her knees, hacking and vomiting.

Lorri's face was as pale as her sister's. She met Arturo's gaze and swallowed, clenching her jaw. Then she took a deep breath. Wrong move. Lorri gagged on the taste and threw up by a pile of discarded luggage.

Arturo and Jamaal walked around the carousel but watched the two entrances to the baggage claim area for any signs of shedim. While the sight of the dead bodies was certainly one of the most gruesome Arturo had ever seen, he pushed aside his body's instinctual response to vomit or run screaming.

He didn't blame Lorri and Lydia for throwing up. He'd done the same thing the first time he'd smelled what fire did to humans. In those moments after he'd awoken from the emergence of his power, he'd been surrounded by the burnt and charred corpses of his entire family and his childhood friends. He'd thrown up the birthday lunch his mother had prepared for the party.

He gritted his teeth and focused on the task at hand.

As they reached the other side of the carousel without any sign of shedim, Arturo glanced up at the wall. Two lines of runes were painted in drying blood.

"Can you read those?" Jamaal asked.

Arturo studied the message, then shook his head. "No. Whatever it's written in, it's not a common dialect." It was familiar though. He just couldn't place his finger on how. A character here and there had features of both species' written language, but nothing coherent.

"Well, whoever did this isn't here anymore," Jamaal said.

"Whoever?" Lydia said. She wiped her mouth with a rag and tied her hair back in a ponytail. "Isn't it obvious this was done by shedim?"

Jamaal nodded. "It does look like their handiwork."

"Did this have to do with the gang members we killed? Maybe the Bosses themselves?" Lorri said as she rejoined the group.

"No," Arturo replied. "This isn't a simple play for a couple souls. This is a large scale attack meant to send a message."

"Exactly," Lorri said. "They're the only ones who could have organized an attack like this, right?"

"Perhaps," Arturo said. "This takes time to plan, time to execute. We just killed those shedim two days ago." Arturo shook his head. "We won't figure anything out by standing around. Get pictures of the message and the bodies. Eliminate any obvious traces of ganastu you find. McLeod will make sure anything the forensics teams get is taken care of."

Jamaal and Lydia nodded. They each pulled out a camera. Lydia rushed to the wall to take pictures of the writing, which left Jamaal with the bodies.

Lorri and Arturo searched around the floor between the carousel and the tunnels. Blood smeared the tiles but Arturo saw nothing beyond normal human remains and bits of clothing and scattered luggage. The shedim who did this had done it correctly and destroyed any evidence of themselves.

If they did it, he chided himself. It was too early to jump to any conclusions.

The silence in the terminal was deafening. This was the only commercial airport around. It was a busy place with a usual roar of voices and squeaking luggage.

But this, this was something else entirely. Only the occasional crack of flames and the steady clicking of the watch filled the air.

Jamaal walked over to the arm as another piece of luggage tapped into it and kicked it back. He shrugged at Arturo, then resumed taking pictures.

"We need to hurry," Lydia said. "How long will the FBI stay outside?"

Overhead, the sound of several approaching helicopters echoed into the terminal.

"Way to jinx us," Lorri said.

"I guess they're done waiting," Jamaal said.

"Come on. Let's get out of here."

Arturo took off down the hallway towards the maintenance access tunnel, his team right behind him. Several small detonations behind them signaled the authorities forcing their way through the exits. Arturo ran faster.

They couldn't get caught, not now. As far as the police would know, he and his team were the terrorists. And no matter what standard protocol said, Arturo wouldn't attack humans to get themselves out of trouble. They needed to get out of the airport before the authorities saw them.

They were halfway down the hall when Arturo threw up his fist. Everyone drew to a halt. Boots pounded on the tiled floor from further ahead. He motioned and they squeezed into a small alcove.

Jamaal raised his hands and the air shifted around them. Smoke pooled in front of the alcove in a dense layer that hid them from view. A moment later, the SWAT team rushed by towards the baggage claims, shadowy silhouettes in armored gear toting assault rifles and shields.

"Okay," Arturo said after they had passed. "Let's go."

They burst through the smoke screen and continued down the hall, moving as quickly and quietly as possible. The door lay just ahead around the next corner.

"Freeze!" a voice shouted.

Arturo stopped and cursed under his breath. A group of police led by a woman in an FBI bulletproof vest entered from an adjoining hallway. He and his team raised their hands and backed up against the wall.

"Drop the... swords," the woman shouted. She aimed her gun at Arturo.

He watched her for a moment. She had long brown hair and sharp eyes that assessed each of them before focusing back on Arturo. There was confidence there but also deep-seated concern.

"Thoughts?" Lorri asked.

More police approached from behind them. Lorri flexed her grip on her sword and her right hand twitched closer to a knife. Why had she drawn her blades? Swords weren't really going to be much good against bullets.

"I said drop them," the woman said. She activated a laser and a small red dot appeared on Arturo's chest.

She knew what she was doing. She must have seen Lorri tense and reach toward a knife. Taking out the leader first would make it easier to take out the rest of the team.

"Do it," Arturo told her. He raised his hands as metal clanged on tile.

An officer rushed up from the hall that led to the baggage claims, a line of vomit running down his chin. "Ma'am, we found the hostages. They're... they're all dead."

The FBI agent glared at Arturo and his team. A fire lit in her eyes and her finger inched closer to the trigger. He needed to deescalate the situation. None of them were fast enough to stop a bullet.

"We had nothing to do with that," he said. "They were already dead."

In a quick motion, she holstered her gun, stepped forward, and twisted his arm behind his back. Pain arced through his shoulder but he held his tongue. Handcuffs snapped onto first one wrist and then the other.

"You're going to tell me everything," she said. She motioned to the other officers. "Arrest them all and get them out of here. We'll question them downtown."

CHAPTER 11

Handcuffed to a table wasn't exactly how Arturo envisioned the day ending up. Much less in an FBI field office. Far from it actually. Sure, he'd been held against his will before, but it was always by shedim or mastem. And usually part of whatever mission he or Jamaal were assigned. He had work to do and the humans were letting the trail grow colder by the minute.

They'd transported him separately from his team but protocol would have dictated they all be brought down for interrogation. A single large mirror lined one wall. Like all the classic cop shows, he had no doubt the agents watched and assessed him through it. The camera in the corner of the room blinked red, just another form of surveillance as they waited for him to crack.

In all his years, Arturo had been lucky enough never to get arrested. This was bound to happen sooner or later. Luckily, the mild interrogation the FBI would be allowed to do would be nothing in comparison to what he'd been trained to withstand, much less the time he'd been captured by mastem for infiltrating a cult they'd set up outside the city. They'd used some rather colorful methods with water and electricity for a few hours before Jamaal busted him out.

It shouldn't be a problem for his team either. At least he hoped it wouldn't. He assumed new sentinels were still taught to keep their mouths shut, but Lorri and Lydia were young. And quite a bit had already evidently changed from his own days at the Academy. All they had to do was keep quiet until McLeod could bail them out. But how long would that take?

Arturo twiddled his thumbs and waited. They might attribute his nerves to guilt but that wasn't it at all. Whoever was responsible for the attack on the airport would already be covering their trail or worse – preparing for their next attack. This was a waste of his time.

The door opened and the woman who arrested him entered. She'd pulled her brown hair back into a ponytail but she still wore her tactical vest even though they were safely inside. A little over cautious but he didn't fault her. If she could extract information from him, maybe she thought she'd be headed right back out into the city.

She pulled out the chair opposite him and sat, setting a thin file folder in front of her. Arturo's lip curled up and she crossed her arms. The cold look on her face told him everything he needed to know. She'd made up her mind about him, even though she'd found very little if anything out about him or his team. The thin file in her hand was evidence enough of that.

"My name is Special Agent Kelly Nickolaus," she said.

"It's a pleasure to meet you, Special Agent. I'm Arturo Morales. But you already know that, I'm sure." He nodded to the file.

"I don't believe it's your real name. Your prints didn't show up in any of our databases and your name isn't registered with any of the usual government organizations. No birth certificates, no driver's licenses, no tax forms, nothing." She tossed his ID down on the table. "That's clearly a fake, albeit a really good one."

Of course he wasn't registered. None of his team were. No sentinel was. It was far too much of a hassle when they got older and had to adjust their birthdates or change lives, becoming some distant relative. Human attempts to track other humans simply got in the way of their work.

"Well, you'll just have to take my word for it," he said.

Agent Nickolaus stared at him and he stared back. Up close, he could see the beginnings of crows' feet at the edges of her eyes. She had to be mid-thirties, maybe early-forties, to be in charge of this big of an investigation. She'd also probably been stationed here in St. Louis for a while and this was the most she'd ever had to deal with.

"Tell me, kid, why did you kill all those people?" she asked after he refused to break eye contact.

Arturo sighed internally. The kid remark was a bit much, even if he did look young. "We didn't kill them."

"Then why were you inside when we breached the terminal?" Nickolaus asked.

"We were investigating the terrorist attack." It wasn't a lie, just not a full truth. Arturo didn't know if she'd be able to tell if he was lying, but it was better to play it safe than sorry. Something about her ease in questioning him gave the impression she was good at her job.

"I was the senior agent in charge of the situation. I don't remember you asking for permission to enter the airport ahead of us."

"That's because we didn't ask," he said, spreading his hands out before him as far as the cuffs would allow. "We didn't need it." He hated to be an ass about this but he really didn't have the time to waste.

Red seeped into her cheeks. "Well, then you'll understand why I can't take you at your word."

"Completely understand, but it's the truth nonetheless."

She tilted her head, like a cat that's found an interesting little mouse that it just isn't quite sure what to do with. Or maybe she thought she knew exactly what he was and how to deal with him. She had to be confident she could intimidate him, especially if she believed he was far younger than her.

"And what organization are you with that would give you authorization above mine? NSA? DOD?" He didn't say anything and Agent Nickolaus leaned forward. "You know what I think? I think you and your friends were with the terrorists. I think you helped kill all those people and were trying to escape but were just a little too late."

Arturo leaned forward as well. "You're mistaken."

"Okay, you weren't late then. Maybe you were left behind on purpose. Did you piss off your bosses and get left with the bill?"

If only she knew how close she might have been to the truth with that bosses comment.

"Or is it a religious thing? Wanting to be martyrs for the cause?"

Arturo leaned back in his chair. "You've got it all wrong."

Agent Nickolaus' face softened and her shoulders relaxed. "Listen, if you tell me what happened in there, I can work out some kind of deal for you. You don't want the death penalty, right?"

He admired her persistence. She was pulling out all the stops to get him to talk, give her something to work with. But she had no clue what actually happened in that terminal. No human did. Arturo wasn't entirely sure himself yet.

"There are a lot of dead people," she continued. "If you tell us who you were working with, maybe we can reduce your sentence to life in prison. But you need to talk to me before someone else walks through that door who isn't as nice as me."

Arturo shook his head. She was good, but the way she watched every move he made, the way she'd threatened him in the terminal, her emotions were roiling just below the surface. He needed her to stay off balance. Angry humans were easier to manipulate, especially in law enforcement.

"Agent Nickolaus, I appreciate that you're just doing your job. And you're doing quite well, a true testament to the FBI. But you've arrested the wrong people. And I assure you that the next person who walks through that door is going to have you release us."

Agent Nickolaus opened her mouth to respond but a knock on the door stopped her. A tall, bulky man entered. He wore a suit and Agent Nickolaus tensed when she saw him. Her superior? "Agent Nickolaus, may I have a word with you outside?"

She nodded and stood. "Think about your options," she said before she closed the door.

Arturo smiled. It was only a matter of time now. He closed his eyes.

Images from the airport flashed through his memory. The violent deaths of all those people. The fire and destruction. All of that certainly pointed to the shedim. That much destruction and mayhem would have twisted any soul toward the chaotic, earning some shedim a healthy number of souls.

But what about the message on the wall? What did it mean? If it was meant to be a warning, why not just write it in modern shedimic?

The bigger question of course was why leave so much carnage in the eyes of humans?

Arturo opened his eyes as the door opened.

Agent Nickolaus dropped a duffel on the table with a clang of metal on metal, then slapped a thicker file down next to it. The muscles in her neck were tensed and her cheeks flushed with color. She must not have gotten good news.

He flipped open the file. Looked like copies of all the evidence the FBI had collected so far. McLeod had gotten them out.

"Everything all right?" he asked.

Agent Nickolaus yanked his hands forward and unlocked the cuffs. He rubbed his wrists, then unzipped the duffel. His weapons were piled inside.

"You're free to go," she said. "An agent will escort you out of the building."

"Thank you," Arturo said. He did mean it. He stood and zipped the bag. "This information will be very helpful.

Agent Nickolaus leaned on the table as he headed for the door. "Listen to me, punk. I don't know who you work for but if I find out you had anything to do with this attack, I'll make sure the electric chair is the best part of the rest of your life."

Arturo stopped and glanced over his shoulder. Off balance, unnerved. That had been accomplished for sure. "Agent Nickolaus, I assure you we're on the same side. Trust me on this. Leave it alone."

"Why should I?" she asked. "Who do you work for?"

"It's better if you don't know," Arturo said. And he meant it too. Humans weren't built for the conflicts of shedim and mastem. The door eased shut behind him.

Arturo exited the FBI building through a rear door, free and clear. And yet, it wasn't exactly how he'd imagined it might feel to get out of the hands of a human agency. He expected more elation, like what he saw on the crime shows. Instead, all he felt was worry and the nagging sense his day was just getting started. He shrugged and glanced around.

A chill breeze blew over his skin, a reflection of the slate gray clouds blanketing the sky. Winter had arrived at last. Before too long, they'd have snow on the ground. Maybe even later that day. It was always hard to tell. The city's weather was more chaotic than most shedim.

Several cops and FBI agents stood at the foot of the stairs smoking and rubbing their hands together against the cold. They quit talking as he emerged and glared at him. He slung his duffel bag over his shoulders and descended the steps, nodding at them congenially.

"Arturo," Jamaal shouted. He waved from the driver's side window of a blue cargo van parked across the street. "Over here."

Arturo jogged over to the van and slid into the backseat. McLeod sat up front and Lydia and Lorri were in the back, focused on a computer and monitoring station. The display screen flashed news coverage of the attack.

"Thanks for the bailout," Arturo said.

"I shouldn't have needed to," McLeod said.

That stung a bit and Arturo couldn't help but wince.

Jamaal pulled onto the street and took a left, heading back towards McLeod's house.

"It wasn't our fault," Lorri said. "Just bad timing."

"How did you manage to get us released so quickly?" Lydia asked. "I figured we'd be there for a while."

McLeod turned in his seat. "The Sentinalia have protocols in place should something like this happen," McLeod said. "We're able to operate in the United States as a covert branch of the military investigating terrorist activity. Of course, they can't trace our legitimacy to any concrete division, so it works. In this case, though, because of the high-profile nature of this attack, I had to call in a favor to the deputy director of the FBI, a favor I had hoped to save a little while longer."

Arturo met his mentor's gaze and nodded. "Thanks."

McLeod returned the nod. "You and Jamaal have never been

arrested. I suppose I should be thankful it took this long. So tell me, what happened in the airport?"

"Death," Jamaal said. "A lot of death. Oh, yeah, and we got caught."

"I know that already." He smacked Jamaal on the back of the head. "I didn't have to wait for you all to find that out. How about something more concrete? Maybe related to the attack?"

McLeod was being testy. It meant the Sentinalia had already been in contact with him, likely chewed him from one end to the other.

"It was horrible," Lydia said. There was a quiver to her voice that she quickly swallowed.

Lorri unmuted one of the news reports.

"In what's being called the worst attack since 9/11, we have confirmed 188 passengers and workers have been killed, with dozens more missing and damage reaching into the millions. Local and federal law enforcement are combing through the Lambert Airport, searching for survivors or evidence pointing who could be behind this act of terror."

She cut the volume again. "The humans haven't got the first clue."

Arturo shook his head. That was the best they could hope for at this point. "Agent Nickolaus gave me a file with everything the FBI has so far," Arturo said. "I'm assuming you did more than just get us out."

"Yes," McLeod said as they merged onto the highway. "The FBI has been instructed to share all evidence every step of the way.

"I'm sure they loved getting that order," Jamaal said.

"Our friend Agent Nickolaus certainly wasn't pleased," Arturo said. "I don't know how cooperative she'll actually be."

"It doesn't matter," McLeod said. "I doubt they'll actually be able to connect any dots. But if I was calling in a favor to get you all out, I was getting everything we might need, including access to any remaining evidence they might find."

True. The FBI would be searching for human criminals. They wouldn't likely be able to make heads or tails of any important evidence. Or they'd find it and write it off as a mistake.

"Better safe than sorry," Lorri said.

"Indeed. So, anything we can use?"

Arturo opened the file and handed a large stack of pictures to McLeod. "We saw all this ourselves. Dead bodies, carnage." He flipped several printed pages, with various preliminary theories and reports. "Their theory is a set of explosives were placed around the terminal to isolate the hostages inside. After the explosions, the terrorists killed everyone and set up their display."

McLeod held up a picture of the pile of bodies and heads. "Shedim, then?"

"Yes," Jamaal said. "That's definitely my vote."

"Why?" Lydia asked.

McLeod and Arturo turned to her.

"What?" she said. "You tell us to ask questions. Why rule out the mastem?"

Arturo nodded. She had a point. He just figured she'd know this already. "Bosses use this method when they eliminate a rival. It's their normal execution method. Mastem wouldn't kill in this manner. They don't usually involve human casualties.

"Bosses don't either, though," Jamaal said.

Arturo nodded. "True." He handed another photo to McLeod, this one showing the two lines of runes written on the wall. "There was also this message on the wall."

McLeod held it up to the light shining in from the window. "I don't recognize the script. It has elements of both shedimic and mastemic though."

"I thought the same thing," Arturo said.

They needed someone who could decipher the text. Someone with an extensive knowledge of the languages of both races currently and in the past.

"The Sentinalia has declared this a top priority," McLeod said. "We are to find the perpetrators of the attack and deal with them swiftly. We have authorization to use whatever means necessary."

"Backup?" Arturo asked. More boots on the ground searching the city would help.

"No," McLeod said. "The Sentinalia doesn't want to move anyone in case this isn't an isolated incident. We might need damage control in other cities."

It wasn't an ideal situation by any means but he understood their concerns.

"It's obviously the Bosses," Lorri asserted. "Let's just take them out."

Silence filled the van.

"That is a serious accusation with no concrete evidence to back it up," Jamaal said. "It's one thing to know that shedim are behind this, maybe a single Boss. It's another to jump to their whole ruling caste."

"Besides, this is far out of character for them," Arturo added. "They would never risk exposure like this." At least they never had before.

"I agree," McLeod said. "Of course, we can't rule it out. If it was all the Bosses, or a power struggle between some of them, then we need one hundred percent confirmation before we make any moves. If this isn't handled the right way and through the proper channels, we could start a fight we're nowhere near prepared to deal with."

McLeod handed him back the photo of the runes and Arturo studied it for a moment. This was the key. He needed someone ancient, with an interest in both races' history. Only one option, then.

"Okay, I think I know someone who can read this."

Jamaal glanced in the rearview mirror. "You're thinking of asking *him*, aren't you?"

Arturo smiled.

He'd cultivated several contacts among both species that he could tap for information from time to time. Jamaal had his own. Every sentinel built their own networks of informants in the field. It was how they got any real work done.

Jamaal had clearly already thought of the shedim Arturo wanted to use. His friend just wasn't willing to trust the old creature.

"Who is it?" Lorri asked.

Arturo ignored her. She'd see soon enough. "He's our best option, no matter where his allegiance lies. Drop me and Lorri off at Limbo."

"It's a good first step," McLeod said. "He's probably the oldest ganastu in the city. If anyone can decipher this, it'll be him."

Jamaal sighed. "Fine. Lydia and I will see what we can dig up with the mastem then."

"Good. Move quickly and be back at my place by this evening," McLeod said. "We can decide next steps from there."

"Who are we going to see?" Lorri asked again.

"An old acquaintance," Arturo said. He pulled knives out of his duffel and slid them back into his vest. "You better suit up."

CHAPTER 12

"Hurry up," Arturo said.

"But where are we going?" Lorri said as Jamaal drove off in the van.

He pointed to a pool hall across the street. "There." Limbo was written in bold script over the door. Tinted windows covered the front of the building but several neon signs advertising beer, pool, and darts flashed on and off.

"You said that already," Lorri said. "That doesn't tell me anything. Who's going to help us in there?"

"A shedim."

Lorri stopped. "Why? If it's a shedim, why would it tell us anything? Wouldn't it want to protect its own kind?"

"*He* isn't quite like other shedim. You know, you might learn a few things today."

Lorri scoffed. Yet another reason why Arturo hadn't said anything about where they were going.

"Just trust me," Arturo said. He walked across the street.

"Right," Lorri said before she stepped off the sidewalk and fell in line beside him.

She may have been firmly set in her beliefs about him, but he was going to show her a side of the world that would shake her views about ganastu. It always did when he brought an apprentice to Limbo. If not for the looming pressure to find those responsible for the airport attack, he would likely enjoy these next few minutes.

"Now, listen," he said. "When we get in here, don't draw any weapons or make any threats. This is a place of peace and you will respect that. There are rules here. Do you understand?"

Lorri nodded.

Arturo opened the front door and beckoned her to follow. They entered a short hallway that led to the main room. This level was open to the general human public, but was empty save for a few patrons who sat at a bar and watched the news. A set of stairs descended into a basement to their left and a large man with tattooed arms barred anyone's descent.

Arturo waved a hand and engulfed a fingertip in flame for a heartbeat before he shook his wrist to extinguish it. To any humans in the room, it would've looked like he'd flicked a lighter. But the bouncer saw what he had really done. It was his job.

He stepped aside and allowed Arturo and Lorri to pass.

"Shedim only down here?" Lorri said, as she lifted her hand to a knife.

"Not quite. And I said don't draw a weapon."

"Why not? We could be walking into an ambush for all I know."

"We're not," Arturo said. "Now control yourself or go back outside. Can you do that?"

Lorri lowered her hands back to her side. "Of course."

"Good," Arturo said. "Welcome to Limbo."

They reached the bottom of the stairs and emerged in a room nearly as large as the upstairs with several more pool tables and a bar along the back wall. A seating area with plush red couches and chairs was set to the left side. Several incense burners hung around the room and the smoke clouded the pale overhead lighting.

Shedim and mastem sat on the couches or shot pool in their natural forms among one another. A pair arm-wrestled at a table, cheered on by members of both races. Feathers and scales of every color of the rainbow shimmered in the smoke.

The air was charged with good-natured competition and comradery. Arturo sighed as the comfort in the room eased a bit of the tension of the day.

Lorri, on the other hand, froze as her gaze took in the mixed company. "What the..."

Arturo pulled her towards the bar. "Come on." She reacted as all of his apprentices did after getting a glimpse of Limbo's patrons. It was kind of nice to see her speechless.

"Arturo Morales," the bartender said. He was a shedim with dark red scales. Four horns sprouted from his head and intertwined down his neck like a braided ponytail.

Arturo shook the shedim's clawed hand. "Farrier, it's good to see you. So you finally decided to form them?"

Farrier ran a hand down his horns. "Yeah, and the barbed wire hurt like hell. But it was definitely worth it."

Shedim's horns grew naturally like any other animals. But for the sake of style, a shedim could repeatedly cut them and then use metals to coax them back into certain patterns. The only problem was how excruciatingly painful it could be. Farrier had talked about doing his for years.

"Well, it looks great," Arturo said.

"Thanks. So what brings the sentinels down here today?"

A few nearby patrons glanced at them, then moved to seats farther away down the bar. Even here, sentinels were uncommon and a little frightening. They were the boogeymen used to scare children of both races. If they didn't follow the rules, the sentinels would come in the night and take their heads.

"I need to see Raum as soon as possible."

"About the attack, huh?" Farrier asked.

Arturo nodded.

"Horrible, absolutely horrible. Think it's shedim?"

Arturo shrugged.

Farrier chuckled. "No, you wouldn't be here if you didn't think ganastu were involved. But I'm telling you, no ganastu would make a scene like that. It's just another attack of hate from one group of humans on their own kind." He waved his hand, as if swatting a fly.

Then he pulled a pair of glasses out from under the bar. "Sometimes, they're worse than we ever were. You're wasting your time here." He sighed. "Raum's in a meeting at the moment but it shouldn't be too much longer. Can I get you a drink while you wait?"

"No, thank you," Arturo said.

"How about for the lady?"

Lorri stared at a shedim kissing a mastem's neck in a corner booth. He ran his hand over her feathers and she giggled. She playfully pushed him away but he flicked out a forked tongue and licked her collarbone.

Arturo tapped Lorri on the shoulder.

"What?" she said as she looked away, red creeping into her cheeks.

"Something to drink?" Arturo said.

"Oh, sorry, no, nothing for me."

Farrier laughed. "Fresh graduate?"

"Yeah," Arturo said.

"Well, I'm glad to see you're showing another sentinel the real world. Holler if you need anything." He moved away to help a couple other patrons who had just entered.

Lorri leaned her back against the bar. "I don't understand. I thought they hated each other."

Arturo studied the mastem and shedim as well. "It's not all so black and white. There are a handful of neutral zones like this scattered around the world, places where ganastu who believe in peace can gather and not worry about fighting over souls or pretending to be human. They can just be themselves."

"They didn't mention any of this at the Academy."

"No, I don't imagine they would have. It's not exactly the most common example of life in the real world." Arturo still remembered learning this lesson. McLeod introduced him to a small band of rogues after about a year of training. Until that point, Arturo held the same belief as Lorri and many other sentinels, that the two races could never get along. That a sentinel's single purpose was to keep them in check since they couldn't do so themselves.

"But we were taught that chaos and order couldn't mix," Lorri said. "That's why the shedim and mastem fight."

"Of course they can mix. Humans make it work every day. We do when we partner with sentinels who embrace different natures. You and your sister are prime examples. If others can, why can't these people make it work?"

"Why fight at all then?"

It was the age-old question, the same one Arturo had asked himself and many others over the years. "Unfortunately, there aren't that many who believe as these do. One day, perhaps there will be peace, but it'll be a long time before they coexist on a regular basis. The prejudices still run too strong in them."

A shedim entered the basement, shifted to her scaled self, and hugged a mastem sitting near the stairs. Together, arm in arm, they headed for the bar to order from Farrier.

"This is weird," Lorri said.

"You'll get used to it." Arturo nudged her with his elbow. "See, I told you I had more to teach you."

Lorri glared at him with a slight smirk, then stared back at the crowd. "You said we were here to see a shedim. How is he going to help us?"

"Well, that would depend on what you needed help with," a man said behind them.

Arturo and Lorri turned as the shedim approached. He was halfway between his shedim and human appearances, with a head full of horns and a neatly trimmed gray beard. Scars covered his forehead and his right eye was clouded.

"Raum, thank you for seeing us," Arturo said.

"Certainly, certainly. Farrier said it was important." Raum beckoned to them. "Come on back to my office where it's quieter."

The patrons scattered around the basement had grown silent as the owner of Limbo and the sentinels talked. 'Quieter' wasn't the problem. Back in the office, there would at least be fewer eavesdroppers.

Arturo and Lorri followed Raum through a side door behind the bar and into his office. A large mahogany desk sat at the back of the long room with a wingback chair behind it. A painting of a yin and yang symbol made from fire and water hung on the wall above the desk. Two chairs sat opposite the wingback, no less plush and luxuriant.

A woman sat on top of Raum's desk, her legs crossed under a blue sundress and her hands clasped over her knees. Long white hair framed bright blue eyes, with skin the color of fresh cream. Raum leaned against the desk next to her as Lorri and Arturo sat in the two chairs.

As soon as the door shut, all sounds from the bar ceased.

"You remember my wife Elise?" Raum asked.

"Of course," Arturo said. "It's good to see you again." He meant it. Elise was a kind woman and had treated Arturo well through the years, better than most ganastu did.

"Likewise," Elise said. She held out her hand and Arturo gently kissed it. She'd always been a bit old fashioned. She wrapped her arms around Raum's shoulders. "It's always a pleasure to entertain the man who saved my dear husband. But tell me, who is this beautiful young sentinel?" Her eyes turned to Lorri.

"I'm Lorri," she said. "You said Arturo saved him? How?"

Raum raised an eyebrow. "Well, I'm glad to see you can speak for yourself. Most first-time visitors can barely stammer a hello." He chuckled. "To answer your question, though, it was a long time ago, when I first renounced my life as a Boss. The others didn't take too kindly to my decision and ordered my execution by ice down on the riverfront. That's how I got these lovely scars." He pointed to his face. "Luckily for me, Arturo was walking by and heard my screams."

"Well, I couldn't just stand by and watch," he said.

He'd nearly gotten himself killed that night, almost twenty years earlier. He'd been alone and young, not all that different from Lorri. He'd surprised the three Bosses carrying out the execution and in the confusion, he'd pulled Raum out of there and tucked him away to recover. In all honesty, they'd been more than lucky to both get away with their lives.

"We're both very glad you felt that way," Elise said. She pecked Raum on the cheek.

"Why stop being a Boss? Isn't that the point?" Lorri asked.

"For most, maybe. But when you live as long as I do." Raum shook his head. "I stopped taking souls because they weren't filling the hole in my soul. The constant struggle and fighting, the full embrace of chaos. There's so much more to the world. So much more to fill that hole with."

Lorri nodded, then stared at Elise. Elise met her gaze and held it. Raum and Arturo glanced at each other but Raum shook his head before Arturo could say anything.

"Something else to ask, dear?" Elise finally said.

Lorri hesitated for a heartbeat. "Are you a shedim, too?"

"Lorri," Arturo snapped. It was a rude question to ask here. She didn't know any better, of course, but did she have to be so blunt?

"It's quite all right," Elise said. "She's still young and curious. No, I'm not shedim."

Three sets of the palest turquoise wings slid from her shoulder blades and draped lightly over the back of the desk. Raum reached up and caressed them. She batted his hand away, a little giggle escaping her lips.

"Oh." Lorri bit her lower lip.

"You really do have a fresh one, don't you?" Raum said.

"Yeah. Today's her first time seeing rogues."

"Rogues?" Lorri asked.

"It's what the others call us," Raum said. "We don't subscribe to the molds our kin press themselves into in this day and age. We admire a human's ability to choose his or her own path and only seek to have the same opportunity for ourselves. That's how I met my lovely wife. And because of our so called heretical desires, our belief that we don't have to fight, we are declared rogues."

"It's hard to swallow," Elise said. "Trust me, I know. When I first desired to remove myself from the eternal struggle, I thought I must be losing my mind, betraying everyone and everything I knew. But I was only embracing a far better way of life."

Lorri looked from one to the other and back again. Arturo smirked. She took it better than some sentinels, but the shock would settle sooner or later and she'd never look at a shedim or mastem in the field the same way again. He certainly didn't. If enough ganastu could believe like these ones did, then the constant fighting could be put to an end.

He doubted he'd ever see it in his lifetime, but maybe one day.

"Give it time to process." Raum moved around the desk and sat in his chair. "But I know you didn't come to me just so you could draw the veil aside for your latest apprentice. That usually doesn't come until much later in the process. You've only been together, what, three months or so?"

Lorri gasped but Arturo shook his head. How the old shedim knew how long he'd been training Lorri, he'd never know. Raum's network of informants put any sentinel's to shame. Very little happened in St. Louis that he didn't learn about in time.

"Unfortunately, no," Arturo said. "We're here because of the attack at the airport. You know that, though."

Raum nodded. "Indeed. Well, I assure you I know nothing about it. It was as much a surprise to me as it was for the rest of the world. And from what I've heard, it was humans killing humans again."

Arturo pulled a few pictures from his vest. "Not quite. We believe the shedim were behind the attack, perhaps the Bosses."

Raum scrunched up his forehead. "And why would you think that?"

Arturo handed the stack of photos to Raum.

"My God," Elise said. She turned away.

Arturo wished she didn't have to see them. Like most mastem, this amount of chaotic violence was sickening for her. "It's the way a Boss takes out a rival and his or her legion," Arturo said, focusing on Raum. "You know that."

Raum nodded, his lips pursed. "Well, I can understand why you would think this was done by my kind. I'm ashamed to say I've done this very thing to upstart rivals in the past and witnessed the same executions used by others. I don't think a mastem would do this."

"No, it's too brutal for us," Elise said. "Even the most zealous of our kind."

"But we are never allowed to kill humans. Only a rival Boss and his soldiers. To do so would lead to exactly what we've witnessed today."

Raum raised his good eyebrow. "This isn't everything you found, though."

"No. The real reason we came to you was this." Arturo handed Raum the photo of the message on the wall.

Raum glanced at the image with a hiss of breath. He handed the picture to Elise, his hand shaking ever so slightly. Lorri straightened in her chair at the same moment Arturo did. Good, she'd caught it too. Something about it had shaken the usually steady shedim.

"Where did you see this?" A muscle in Elise's neck twitched and her eyes darted between the two sentinels like a skittish rabbit.

"In the main terminal," Arturo said. "It was painted on the wall in the blood of the victims. We can't read it though."

"There are few still alive who can," Raum said. "This language hasn't been spoken for several millennia, let alone written down. Elise and I were still young the last time we saw it."

"What does it mean?"

"And why are you afraid of it?" Lorri added.

Arturo nodded to her. Very good. If she worked with him like this all the time, finishing her training would be a breeze.

Raum leaned back in his chair. The wrinkles on his face seemed to deepen and his shoulders sagged a bit further down. "I'm getting too old for this."

"For what?" Arturo said.

"I..." Raum began, then hesitated. "I wish I could tell you."

Arturo shook his head. "What do you mean? What can't you tell me?"

Elise held up a hand. "You have to understand something. There are some things that are forbidden, even for us as rogues. This is one of them."

That wasn't good enough. "No, I won't accept that. There are almost two hundred people dead, murdered. You are rogues. You gave up the struggle for souls and declared neutrality. You have to help us figure this out."

Raum looked up to Elise and she patted his hand. "All right. But you didn't learn this from us." He rubbed his brow. "This is a declaration of war written in the universal language spoken by shedim and mastem alike before the Divide."

"The Divide?" Lorri asked before Arturo could.

Elise took a deep breath. "Yes. Both species originally lived in peace. We shared our knowledge and worked together to build a beautiful society. But then came the Divide. This was long before I was born. Perhaps there are some who remember what caused it, but I was never told."

Arturo sat on the edge of his seat. He'd heard rumors, theories from instructors, about the history of the ganastu and their hatred. But no confirmations.

"It doesn't really matter though," Raum said, taking up the thread. "We devolved after that, fought and drove each other to the brinks of extinction. Our numbers were so drastically diminished, the world so changed, that humans were finally able to assume dominance on the earth. When the balance was struck, any who remembered the time before the Divide were ordered to remain silent or they would be silenced."

"I was never taught about that," Lorri said.

"Nor I," Arturo agreed. They were taught that this struggle between them was just how it had always been, how it would always be.

"No," Raum said. "This was long before the first sentinels were born. Besides, the Sentinalia don't really care why we fight each other, only how to keep us in check and protect the humans. And not many of our kind care either."

"And the message?" Arturo asked.

"Yes, the message," Raum said. He met Arturo's gaze. "It says: *The day has come at last when we shall emerge as sole inheritors of the earth.* It was a mantra used by both sides during the war, usually as an indicator of a major confrontation to come. And believe me, we had many of those."

War? Arturo furrowed his brow as his stomach somersaulted. All out war between the races had never happened, not once during the history of the sentinels. They made sure of it.

But if the shedim were trying to start another war, if they could spark that, no one would be safe. Tensions would escalate further and in the present state of the world, keeping it secret from humanity would be impossible.

"It doesn't make any sense," Raum said. "Granted, I haven't been a Boss in two decades now, but they always knew a war could only end in destruction for everyone. That's why the balance was agreed to and you sentinels were encouraged to help us maintain it."

Raum slid the photos back across the desk to Arturo. He echoed Arturo's own thoughts. But there had to be a reason to launch an attack like this in front of the world.

"Could it be Boss-on-Boss violence?" Lorri asked.

Raum shook his head. "No, if that were the case, the Boss would have followed the normal path to take out a rival, kept it secret then cleaned up their message. It's how things have always been done, again to keep out of sight of humans."

"This is a sign for every shedim and mastem to see," Elise said. "It's a call to arms. And I'd say it's good the media hasn't gotten access to the message yet. The Lords and Bosses would be able to read this and it would cause panic on both sides."

Arturo nodded and stood. "Thank you for the information."

"For what it's worth, you're welcome," Raum said. He moved around the desk and opened the door for them. Laughter echoed in from the bar.

Lorri smiled as she passed by Raum.

"Take care of yourself, young one," Raum said. She nodded and left. "Arturo, I'll keep my ears open for any more information. Trust me, a war is the last thing I want. If I hear anything, you'll be the first to know."

"Thank you," Arturo said as he followed Lorri out. The weight on his shoulders pressed heavier now. This attack suddenly had much further reaching implications. They needed to move quickly if they were going to stop this from erupting across the globe.

CHAPTER 13

Lydia followed Jamaal up the stairs to the main campus of Washington University. The school sat nestled in the heart of the city on the western edge of Forest Park. Collegiate Gothic style buildings soared above them as they climbed the stairs, like an ancient castle's keep. As they passed through an archway, they entered the empty main quad. A stillness lay on the campus, not exactly what Lydia expected of a college.

"Where is everyone?" she asked. It was only about 4:30 but surely students would still be around.

"Probably inside watching the reports on the attacks," Jamaal said.

A couple of students walked by, their textbooks held tight to their chests. Lydia pulled her coat closer around her to hide the weapons stored within easy reach on her vest. Or rather, Arturo's coat from the other night in Forest Park. She needed to invest in a good one for herself.

She glanced back at the students. What would it be like to go to college? What would she have studied? They continued down the sidewalk as squirrels chased each other across the path, collecting the last few nuts and discarded French fries before winter set in.

Bells chimed to a simple tune ahead of them from a chapel in the center of campus. Lydia picked up her pace to catch back up with Jamaal.

"So, Arturo and Lorri were going to see a shedim, weren't they?"

"Yeah," Jamaal said. "His name is Raum."

"Raum?" She'd seen his name before, but where? She stopped as the memory flashed back to her, then hurried to catch up with Jamaal again. "The same Raum who helped you with the shedim-human cage fighting?"

"That'd be him," Jamaal said. "You weren't kidding when you said you'd read all our field reports, were you?"

Warmth spread to her cheeks. She'd reviewed every report she could find in the sentinel database after they found out they'd been assigned to St. Louis. "They were pretty interesting. But you guys really didn't say much about Raum beyond that he was the informant."

"No, we generally try to leave our contacts out of reports. If the information got into the wrong hands, it'd make them targets just for helping us."

It made sense. Shedim and mastem generally distrusted the sentinels. They were the police for ganastu. Or perhaps more like the spooks. The ones who were there to stop you the moment you stepped out of line. Helping sentinels wouldn't be the most advantageous of situations.

"If he's like other informants, why didn't you want them going to see him? Because he's a shedim?"

Jamaal ran his hand through his dreads. "It's not that. Raum is different than most shedim. He's a rogue."

"Rogue?" She hadn't heard the term before, not applied to ganastu.

"It means he betrayed his kind and vowed to stop taking souls. He was formerly the most powerful Boss in the city but when he left, the other Bosses ordered him executed. Arturo stopped the assassination. He's been Arturo's informant ever since."

Arturo went against protocol then. Jamaal hadn't said it, but Lydia knew it as well as anyone else. Sentinels were mandated to protect humans, not to interfere with the inner politics of the shedim or the mastem. But Arturo did it anyways, even though the Bosses wanted to kill Raum.

These were the kinds of acts that had convinced her she wanted to be in St. Louis. Arturo and Jamaal both had consistently gone against the norm, bent the rules and risked their lives to save others and not just humans. It was the kind of sentinel she hoped to be one day.

"Sounds like Raum should owe us then," Lydia said.

"True. For all intents and purposes, he tries to repay his debt with information whenever Arturo asks. His intel is usually solid but I don't know. I just can't trust him like Arturo does."

Jamaal had never struck her as the prejudiced type. Why the hesitance to trust Raum?

They continued across campus along a sidewalk bordered by tall oak trees. The last of their leaves barely clung to the branches. But the grounds were cleared. Whoever took care of the landscaping did a good job collecting the leaves.

"You still think he's taking souls?" Lydia said.

"I don't know that. But what would cause a shedim to stop desiring more power? It's in their nature."

"You could say that for the mastem, too," Lydia said.

"Yeah, you could. But Raum has collected more souls than most, not always through the permitted methods. He has real power, so much that he makes most Bosses look like children. Anyone who's tasted that much won't just want to stop."

Lydia shrugged. She didn't know enough about the politics of shedim or mastem at this point. And she certainly didn't know what either species was really like in their normal lives. At the Academy, their focus was on how to deal with the ones who tipped the balance and broke the rules.

"So who are we here to see?" she asked.

Jamaal opened the door to the university's main library. "I have my own informants among the mastem."

She followed Jamaal to the front desk.

"I'm looking for Kaya," he said.

The woman pointed to a stairwell. "She's re-shelving in the B stacks."

"Of course she is," Jamaal said with a smile. "Thanks."

They descended two floors to a subbasement. More books than she could count or ever hope to have time to read filled the shelves. And this was only one floor of the five-level library. It would have been impressive to most. But she'd spent hours and hours in the Grand Library at the Academy, a library that dwarfed this one so many times over.

Jamaal led them through the maze of shelves as she stared up. Each shelf reached from floor to ceiling, creating book-lined tunnels through the basement. The distinct smell of old paper and worn leather filled the air and warmed her with an odd sense of comfort. This was a place she could get lost in for hours. It might not be as awesome as the library she'd grown up with, but she would be coming back.

They rounded a shelf to find an old woman sitting on a stool. Her back was to them and stark white hair fell to the middle of her shoulders. A black cane with a blue stone set in the top leaned against a cart while she sorted and shelved books from it.

"It always aggravates me when students rearrange these books," she said as she worked. "Each has a place and should be left there. Wouldn't you agree, Jamaal?"

He laughed. "Yes, I do."

Kaya glanced over her shoulder and smiled, the wrinkles around her eyes softening as she peered over her thick glasses. "Well, you look like you are doing well. Staying healthy, I hope."

"Of course," he said.

"Excellent." She returned to shelving books. "You sentinels are so young. You're stronger than humans, but you're not indestructible. You still need to take care of yourselves. It's not like there are a whole lot of you left in the world."

Lydia found herself smiling at the mastem. She had a glow around her that immediately reminded Lydia of her grandmother, who she hadn't seen since before she became a sentinel. Something about the mastem radiated a genuine care for Jamaal, one that he reflected back to her from the smile on his face. She hoped Jamaal would introduce them but stayed silent for the moment. It would be rude to interject. And mastem didn't take kindly to rudeness.

Kaya reached to the bottom of her cart and grabbed a yellow package. "This will be what you are wanting."

"How did you—" Lydia stopped as Kaya locked her gaze on her. Her eyes sparkled with icy anger just below the surface. Lydia froze as the warmth she'd felt from Kaya drained away. She'd just told herself to stay quiet. What was she thinking?

"How did I know?" Kaya said. She glanced at Jamaal as she handed him the package. "Jamaal, dear, your apprentice has much to learn still."

Jamaal frowned. "She's still curious, a trait I encourage."

Kaya raised a brow. "I see. Well, child, to answer your question, when I heard of the attack today, I knew it would only be a matter of time until the sentinels came to me for information. So I thought I would just gather it. Save you all the wait. And I had a feeling Jamaal would be quick to get here."

Lydia nodded.

"And we thank you for it," Jamaal said as he slid the package into his coat.

"Of course. Everything I could find about the activities of the shedim in the city is in there, as well as any unusual chatter we've overheard." She turned back to the shelves. "Now, take your apprentice and let an old mastem get back to work."

Jamaal beckoned with his chin and they backed away. Lydia glanced back at her as they turned a corner. Such a strange creature. And that stare. It held so much power behind it, so much more than she'd ever experienced.

As they reached the stairs, she spoke up. "I'm sorry if I offended her."

"It's fine," Jamaal said. "Kaya's very set in her ways. She believes in perfect order, or as close to it as possible, and that means only speaking when you've been spoken to. I, on the other hand, would much rather have you ask questions and offend someone than not and be thought dull."

Lydia nodded. At least he supported her. "So how do sentinels get informants?"

"Now that's a good question." He paused in the stairwell.

"Shedim and mastem don't generally cooperate with our investigations, especially if they don't think it will benefit their own species. However, there are those who get to know us a little better and are willing to help. Take Kaya, for example. I've known her most of my time here in St. Louis and helped her get connected to some resources to help her younger descendants. And with this attack, I'm sure she thinks if we catch the shedim, it will give her kind an advantage in controlling the collection of souls in St. Louis when humans die.

"To really answer your question, though, it just takes time in the field. I will introduce you to several of my contacts and in turn, when you are ready, you will engage in solo missions. You'll start interacting with mastem, they'll start to owe you favors, and you'll develop your own few who are more likely to talk to you."

Lydia could deal with that. She was patient and still young, especially for sentinels. Plenty of time to meet more mastem. "You said the mastem. Why not the shedim?"

Jamaal shrugged. "Well, the shedim tend to trust sentinels who embrace that side of themselves. Same for the mastem. They think whatever nature you choose influences your actions and decisions in the field."

Lydia thought about her sister's rash attitude. "I could see that."

"It's one line of thinking. But you control your nature, not the other way around. It's why we focus so much on meditation. But don't worry about the shedim. Lorri'll get them. The two of you together are gonna make quite the team."

Lydia nodded. She loved her sister and the fact that she still had family alive and with her. It wasn't something most sentinels could enjoy.

"What about Arturo?"

Jamaal smiled. "Yeah, Arturo's always the exception. Since he hasn't chosen a nature, several of his contacts probably think they can swing him to their sides. But he uses both races to get information rather well."

Jamaal kept climbing the stairs and Lydia followed. Maybe it wasn't such a bad thing that Arturo hadn't chosen a nature. Or at least not as bad as Lorri made it out to be. Lorri should appreciate the unique opportunity she had to train with him.

They exited the library into the chill wind. Large snowflakes fell, blanketing the ground. Just what they needed. Snow in addition to everything else. They needed to be able to get around the city easily if they were going to find the attackers.

Jamaal grabbed her shoulder and turned her. "Follow me, but act normal."

Lydia kept pace with Jamaal and resisted the urge to glance over her shoulder. "What's wrong?"

"We're being followed," Jamaal said. "Look at the reflection in this window."

As they passed the building, Lydia looked through the reflection behind them. Two men in black suits followed a hundred feet back. One of them had his wrist held to his mouth and was speaking into his cuff.

"Who are they?" she asked. "FBI?"

"Probably," Jamaal said. "This complicates things. We'll have to lose them before we go back to McLeod's."

Protocol stated no one could know where their headquarters were located. And McLeod really didn't seem like the type to bend or break that particular rule.

"What about Arturo and Lorri?"

They reached the stairs leading down to where they'd parked.

"Arturo can handle himself. No worries there."

They climbed into the cargo van. They'd dropped McLeod off earlier at his car in a local park. He was always paranoid of being followed and this time, it proved true.

The FBI agents following them climbed into a black car parked a few spaces away.

Jamaal checked his rearview mirror. "Any ideas?"

Jamaal knew what to do, she was sure of it. But he liked to test her like this, push her to be creative. She liked the challenge.

Lydia rolled down her window and looked out the side mirror. The snow continued to fall but melted on the pavement. "Yeah, actually."

She focused on the water on the ground and called on her mastem.

She pushed the moisture under the tires of the FBI car and urged it to rapidly cool. Ice spread across the street and up the tires.

Jamaal chuckled. "Very nice." He put the van in gear and pulled out of the parking space.

The FBI's car engine rumbled but the vehicle didn't move. Lydia glanced out her mirror as they threw open their doors and stepped out, only to immediately slip and slide on the ice.

"Not bad," Jamaal said. "Not bad at all." They turned onto the street and sped off.

CHAPTER 14

"Well, that was…"

"Enlightening?" Arturo finished for Lorri.

They emerged from the front doors of Limbo. Half an inch of snow coated the ground as more continued to fall. An icy wind whipped along the sidewalk as a plow truck drove past. Salt scattered across the road from a feeder attached to its tailgate.

"I was going to say strange. But sure, that, too." She glanced up and down the street. "Shedim and mastem peaceably together in one place. It just seems weird and, I guess, kind of unnatural."

"You have to look past what you know of ganastu. They can get along just like humans. Besides, like Raum said, they used to get along."

At least until the Divide. He needed to come back and ask Raum more about that. No one in all his time as a sentinel had spoken of it. But from what Raum said, it was before sentinels were even a thing. Maybe that was why the first rogues were older. They remembered a time when peace was the norm.

"The next thing you know, cats and mice will be shacking up together." Lorri rubbed her arms. Neither of them had a jacket for this weather. "What do we do now? It's freezing out here."

Arturo flipped open his cell phone and dialed. "Use your shedim to heat the air around your skin. It'll help. I'll see if Jamaal's found any leads."

Lorri did as she was told and stopped rubbing her arms. "Neat trick."

Arturo smiled. "I do know a few."

Jamaal picked up after the third ring. "Hello."

"It's me. Anything yet?"

"Yeah. I got a file from one of my contacts. She's done some extensive research for us. This might be worse than we thought. You've got to see these figures."

Arturo's stomach tightened. How much worse could it get? Almost two hundred people had died at the airport. "All right. Can you come pick us up at Limbo?"

"What, you don't like a little snow?" Arturo could hear the smile in Jamaal's voice. Lydia laughed in the background.

"Arturo," Lorri said, tapping him on the shoulder. She nodded to a couple men in suits getting out of a car across the street.

Great. What did the FBI want now? "Actually, Jamaal, just head back to McLeod's. We'll meet you there."

"Got a tail, too?"

"Looks like it."

"We shook ours pretty quick. Shouldn't be a problem for you. See you soon."

Arturo closed his cell and stepped from under the awning over the door of Limbo. "Come on."

Lorri fell in line beside him as they headed away from the men. "What do you want to do?"

The snow crunched behind them as the agents crossed to their side of the street.

"Stay calm," Arturo said. "This doesn't need to get out of hand."

They kept walking and the men followed. One talked on a cell phone but Arturo couldn't catch what he was saying. They needed to lose these guys before they wasted any more time.

"Mr. Morales," Agent Nickolaus said as she rounded the corner ahead of them.

They skidded to a stop on the slick sidewalk. So much for losing them. He had to admit, he was impressed with her tenacity. She no doubt had been ordered to stay out of their way. McLeod would have ensured that.

Better to play the authority figure now. A little bluffing could still get them away from her and her bureau.

"Agent Nickolaus. Twice in one day. To what do we owe this pleasure? I thought we were free to go."

She smirked. "Of course you are. But I was told to share any new information we found with you."

McLeod had mentioned that. But typically information was transferred remotely. "A simple email would have sufficed. We didn't need a tail."

She feigned ignorance. "We weren't tailing you. Our agents are just patrolling more heavily now." An open lie if he'd ever heard one.

"What do you have then?" Arturo said. She was trying his patience now, but she'd tipped her hand that they were being followed. It was an extra measure that he really didn't want to deal with but humans could be stubborn at times, especially law enforcement. He needed to deal with this now.

"Let's take a ride down to the city morgue."

"The morgue?" Arturo said. What did she need them down there for? Or more specifically, what had they found? "Just tell me what you've learned and we'll be on our way. We don't have time to go to the morgue."

"Make time." Ice filled her tone as she placed her hands on her hip, her right hand close to her gun. A forty-five by the look of it, not a small gun by any means. Enough to put a human or sentinel down for good, but just annoy a ganastu.

Arturo was pretty sure he and Lorri could incapacitate Nickolaus and the two agents at their backs before any of them could draw. But this wasn't the time or place for that. And it would only make things more complicated in the long run. "All right. You driving?"

"Of course. We're not going to walk and we're the only ones here with vehicles."

The two agents behind Arturo and Lorri grabbed each of their arms to usher them forward.

Lorri glared at them. "Don't touch me," she snapped and the temperature rose a few degrees. Light puffs of steam rose from the snow but the agents didn't seem to notice.

"I'd do as the lady asks," Arturo said.

The men glanced at Agent Nickolaus, who nodded, and then let Lorri go.

Arturo shrugged as Nickolaus turned her glare on him, then beckoned for her. "After you."

The morgue was nearly as cold as outside in the snow but Arturo just shrugged it off. Several bodies lay on gurneys in various stages of autopsies. The pungent smell of antiseptic mixed with the charred remains from the airport burned Arturo's nostrils. Several people in scrubs worked on the bodies. It looked like they'd called in extra coroners to help with the sheer number of victims.

A short woman with brown hair pulled back in a ponytail and dressed in scrubs walked over to them. "Kelly, are these the agents you needed to view the body?" She spoke with a bit of an accent but Arturo couldn't place where. Central America maybe?

"Yes. Mr. Morales, Ms. Preston, this is Dr. Cifuentes, the medical examiner."

Arturo shook her hand. "A pleasure."

"Nice to meet you," Lorri said.

"Likewise." Dr. Cifuentes turned on her heel and led them down the row of gurneys. Apparently, she wasn't one for idle chitchat. "The body's right over here. But I have to warn you, it's pretty gruesome."

"Oh, I don't doubt it," Lorri said.

Dr. Cifuentes cocked her head. Her eyes scoured into Lorri like a hawk's, searching for the meaning behind her off-handed comment.

"She means we've seen this already," Arturo said. He shook his head at Lorri. She talked tough for someone who'd thrown up when she saw the carnage for the first time. "We were at the airport before the bodies were brought in."

"Well, the rest of these, sure. But you didn't see this." Dr. Cifuentes pulled the sheet back on the body at the end of the row.

Nearly every inch of skin was burned and blistered. What little skin remained was a dark brown. Raw muscle and tissue peeked through where the skin peeled away from flesh. However, unlike the other bodies in the morgue, nothing was charred and no soot marked this body. It was like this person was burned by acid instead of fire. Or water.

Arturo and Lorri both exchanged glances before bending to examine the damage. Arturo had seen these kinds of burns many times over. Raum had been in a similar state when he'd saved his life years earlier. And as of a few nights ago, Lorri had seen similar in Forest Park.

"His wounds are similar to the victims from the airport," Lorri said, pointing to the severed neck and missing head.

"He came in with all the rest." Dr. Cifuentes pulled on a pair of gloves. "But he didn't look like this when I began the autopsy."

"What do you mean?" Arturo said. He knew exactly what she meant but Agent Nickolaus was watching.

"His skin was only mildly burned and appeared to be caused post-mortem. Cause of death was definitely beheading. I did my preliminary investigation as usual. But when I went to wash him down, his skin started to steam. The water reacted like acid. I dried him as quickly as I could but by the time I got all the water off, the damage was done."

"Something in your water?" Lorri tilted the nozzle over the table and rubbed a drop of water between her fingertips.

"That was my first guess. I even removed all my clothes just in case. But another body had been washed at this station before and plenty of it was splashed around. Nothing happened."

Arturo rubbed his jaw. "Interesting. But why exactly did we need to see this?"

Nickolaus crossed her arms and leaned against the wall. "I hoped you could tell me why the body reacted like this?"

"And how would we know?" She was smart, Arturo didn't have any doubts about that. He needed to keep her from growing any more suspicious of them than she already was.

Nickolaus frowned. "Call it a hunch."

"I'm sorry to tell you I don't know why the body did this. Do you, Lorri?"

"No," Lorri said as she continued to stare at the body. "It's definitely strange."

"Did you identify him, yet?" Arturo said.

"Yes." Dr. Cifuentes brought over a large metal pan covered in a towel. She pulled the towel away to reveal a man's head, badly disfigured by a pink scar that ran down the right side of his face. The dark skin matched the body. Thankfully, the brain had finally died and stopped moving the eyes.

"His name is Seth Duodu. Recognize him?"

Lorri shrugged but Arturo kept his face neutral.

"The name's familiar," he said.

"I'm not surprised. If you work in any kind of law enforcement here in St. Louis, you've probably heard the name Seth Duodu. He was believed to be connected to all kinds of criminal activities. Drugs, extortion, money laundering, even murder. But no one's been able to make any charges stick."

Seth Duodu wasn't any normal criminal though. He was one of the Bosses of St. Louis, known among his kind as Dueden. Arturo's heartbeat spiked. Was this Boss the target of the attacks? He was the most powerful Boss they knew of in St. Louis. Who could take him out?

"I'm assuming that means you have a theory then?" Arturo said, doing his best to keep his voice calm.

Nickolaus smirked. "Yes. I think whoever did this was trying to kill him and make us think it was a terrorist attack to keep us off the scent."

Lorri laughed and shook her head. "So you think this was what, some kind of mob hit?"

"Disagree?" Nickolaus said.

Lorri crossed her arms over her chest and stared Nickolaus down.

"It seems like a lot of trouble to kill one man, no matter what kind of illegal activities he was into."

Arturo agreed, but to kill a Boss like Dueden, it might just have been necessary. A rival shedim, maybe even someone within his own family? It really didn't matter. They'd have to pull out all the stops to pull off his death. And even then there would have been no guarantee.

Arturo pulled the sheet back over the body, careful not to touch him. "I think what my colleague is trying to say is, what evidence points to your conclusion? For all we know, he was just in the wrong airport at the wrong time."

"That's bullshit and I think you know it," Nickolaus said. She glared at him. "You all are hiding something. And dammit I don't have time to be stabbing blindly in the dark. You need to share what you know so we can figure this out."

Arturo raised an eyebrow. "You're reaching here and it's quite unprofessional, especially for the FBI."

Nickolaus' face reddened. He was pushing her, he knew that. But she needed to stay out of this.

"We're still following up with our leads," Arturo continued. "But they point to a terrorist attack, not a conspiracy to assassinate one man. Now, when you have found something more concrete, feel free to contact us."

Agent Nickolaus practically leapt from the wall and planted her feet in front of Arturo as he turned to leave. "How about filling me in on some of those leads then? The bureau has plenty of resources that could help."

"No, agent. I don't think so."

"Why the hell not? We're on the same side, you said so yourself." She grabbed the front of his shirt and pushed him towards the wall, but his feet were set and he didn't move. Another reason she couldn't get involved with their side of the investigation. Humans literally didn't have the strength that sentinels did.

"Please, let go," Arturo said.

Nickolaus' eyes widened at something she saw in his gaze and she released him.

Arturo took a deep breath and pressed both his natures back down.

They didn't like the threat Nickolaus had offered. "We will follow up on our own leads, and if we need you, we'll let you know. Now, please, don't interfere with us again."

Arturo walked past her, Lorri right behind him. Her heart was in the right place, but she had no idea what was going on. And if Arturo did his job right, she never would.

"That was a shedim, right?" Lorri whispered as they got on the elevator.

"Yes," Arturo said. His mind bounced around the implications a dead Boss raised. It had originally looked like the kind of assassination Bosses would commit against one another. But the message on the wall had pointed to mastem as the targets. He had been ready to follow that lead down the rabbit hole as some kind of all-out attack on the mastem. But now Dueden's body threw a wrench in that hypothesis. This was turning into a giant circle.

"Well, what does it all mean?" Lorri asked.

"It means we need to make another stop."

Arturo wanted another set of eyes on this.

Arturo paid the taxi for the short ride from the city morgue to the St. Louis Basilica. The cabbie thanked him for the cash and sped off.

"An Uber would have been cheaper," Lorri said.

Arturo nodded. "Yes, but cash can't be traced. And we have enough issues just with being followed." He waved to the two FBI agents as they parked their black car in a metered space down the street.

Lorri craned her head back to stare up at the massive cathedral. A large stained glass window hung over the main archway and two ornately carved towers flanked the dome. Pristine snow clung to the many crosses and gargoyles, uncontaminated for now by the grime of the city that seemed to coat the snow just outside the Basilica's property.

"This is gorgeous," Lorri said. "I didn't know St. Louis had a church this big."

"It was built back in the early twentieth century." Arturo climbed the stairs and Lorri followed. "The old one's still down by the river but this one is the larger of the two.

They entered the church and candles flickered as a chill wind slipped in with them. Arturo stretched his shoulders and released the heat he'd held around his body. The warmth inside was much more comfortable than the snowy weather. Beautiful mosaics and religious statues surrounded the main vestibule.

"Wait here," Arturo whispered. "This'll only take a few minutes."

"Why?" Lorri demanded.

"Because the mastem who lives here doesn't like shedim and really doesn't care too much for sentinels who've chosen that nature."

Lorri crossed her arms. "Fine."

She wanted to be helpful. Arturo remembered that feeling at her age well enough. "Okay, listen, I need you to do something else."

Lorri lifted an eye, careful not to seem too excited, but Arturo could tell from her attention alone she was.

"Call McLeod. Tell him about the body and that it needs to be removed ASAP. The FBI can't hold onto it any longer."

"Yeah, okay," she said. She fished her cell phone out of a pocket and moved off to one of the side rooms.

Arturo smiled. It was a simple enough task but it made her feel like she was contributing. And it really was helpful. Maybe that was his ticket to working well with her. He tucked that thought away for later and walked into the main sanctuary. Pews filled the enormous room. The domed ceiling was decorated with a dozen different mosaics depicting stories from the Bible and Catholic history. This room alone could easily hold a thousand people not counting the large choir and church staff.

A priest approached him from one of the pews. "Hello, my son. What may I do for you today?"

Arturo nodded to the priest. "Hello, Father. I was wondering if I might speak with Mr. Ortiz. It's important." Ortiz was the name Oriphiel used in human society.

"Certainly," the priest said with a smile. He clasped his hands together. "Please follow me. He's in the middle of a lecture for the young men of the congregation but I'm sure they could use a break."

He followed the priest through a side wing of the basilica to a set of double doors. The priest held them open. Oriphiel's voice echoed out as Arturo entered. He nodded his thanks as the priest eased the doors shut.

"In this section of the gospel of Mark, we see Jesus casting out Legion into a herd of pigs," Oriphiel said. "After which, the herd of pigs plunges into the sea and to their deaths."

Arturo stepped around the corner of the room as Oriphiel continued his lecture. Oriphiel paced the front of the room, a Bible held open in one hand and a piece of chalk in the other. He was dressed simply in a pair of gray slacks and an open collared white shirt. A suit jacket was hung neatly on a hanger next to the blackboard.

The young men all looked like they were in high school or early college. Most of them hung onto their teacher's words like parched desert wanderers who'd found an oasis, their eyes following him back and forth.

Arturo couldn't blame them. The old mastem was an excellent teacher and public speaker. He spoke a couple times during Arturo's time at the Academy and always enthralled his classmates. Arturo had grown comfortable with the mastem, so wasn't as engrossed, but he still enjoyed the lectures.

Oriphiel halted and scanned the room. His gaze stopped on Arturo and he nodded slightly.

"Well, class, I think it might be time for a little break." He shut his Bible. "Let's take ten minutes to stretch our legs and use the restroom. While you're gone, think about what lessons we can glean from this particular passage."

The class stood and filtered out the back of the room, whispered discussions about Oriphiel's words springing up.

Arturo walked to the front of the classroom, shaking his head. "I thought you didn't believe in Heaven?"

Oriphiel held up his worn leather Bible. "True. I do not believe there is a heaven. But these humans have great faith in this man Jesus. And the teachings in this book are actually quite close to our own, maybe even inspired by a mastem. So I make a few concessions to keep the humans on the ordered path."

"Ah, of course," Arturo said. "There's the ulterior motive."

Oriphiel scoffed. "You make it sound like a bad thing."

Arturo smirked at Oriphiel, who chuckled.

"You're teasing me?" Oriphiel said.

"Of course," Arturo replied. "I'll say though, I'm surprised to find you teaching when there have been attacks in our city. Surely the Lords would request a meeting with you."

Oriphiel laced his fingers together and bowed his head for a moment. "I am deeply saddened by the loss of life today. But I will not let my own life be disrupted by these acts of terrorism. I doubt the Lords will either. We trust the sentinels to find the real culprits. Since you are here, I'm assuming you suspect the shedim were involved?"

"It looks that way, but I'm not sure. Something doesn't feel right."

Oriphiel arched his eyebrows. "Meaning?"

"A Boss was killed in the attacks. Dueden. Why would the shedim kill one of their Bosses in the attack?"

Oriphiel stroked his chin. "Vile creatures, the lot of them. Who knows why they do anything? But honestly, it's not the strangest thing I've seen them do. If a shedim had the opportunity to take out a Boss as powerful as Dueden and make it look like something else entirely, it is exactly the kind of treachery they'd engage in."

"I don't think I'll ever understand ganastu politics," Arturo said. Oriphiel's prejudices aside, the shedim were indeed ruthless in their dispatching of their rivals. But they also knew to keep their violence out of human sight. "A violent attack with human casualties to kill a Boss might make sense, especially one as powerful as Dueden, but why leave his body where humans could get it?"

Oriphiel's mouth hung open for a fraction of a second. "I must have misheard you. Did you say the humans have a shedim body?"

"Yeah, down at the morgue."

Oriphiel slammed his fist on the lectern and the wood creaked. "I cannot believe they would do that. It goes against everything we've taught, everything we've lived by. The continuance of either of our species depends on staying out of the spotlight."

"Don't worry," Arturo said. "McLeod's already been made aware of it. He'll have the body taken care of within a few hours."

"Good." Oriphiel wrote a note for himself, then slipped it in a pocket. "I will speak with the Lords as soon as my class is over. Perhaps someone will have a lead that you can use to find the shedim responsible for this blatant breach of conduct."

"Thanks."

Oriphiel eyed him. "Something else is on your mind. What else did you find?"

Arturo hesitated. "What can you tell me about the Divide?"

Oriphiel dropped his pen. It bounced off the lectern but Arturo caught it before it could hit the floor. He set it down.

"How did you learn about that?" Oriphiel whispered.

"One of my contacts mentioned it while deciphering this." Arturo slid the picture of the message out of his pocket. "We found it at the airport terminal."

Oriphiel sucked in a breath, then met Arturo's gaze. "The Divide is the root of our struggle today. The shedim wanted more power, as they always have. They started to search out more ways to get that power and rule all life on this planet. They found the souls of fledgling man to be the perfect source and began to harvest without regard for the well-being of the latest sentient race to inhabit our planet. We wouldn't allow that, so we went to war."

The story didn't line up exactly with Raum's, but the gist was the same.

"And now it's happening again," Arturo said.

"Perhaps. But the death of Dueden makes no sense. Unless Dueden stood against the Bosses decision to start another war. But as you said, to have the power to kill him, that would mean someone else was here in St. Louis, someone older." Oriphiel shook his head. "It doesn't matter, though. If this is the start of another war, then the Lords must be notified. We must prepare to strike back should the shedim move against us in force."

Things were escalating too quickly. "Just hang on," Arturo said. "We need time to figure this out. We need to understand what is going on and see if we can stop it. All out war won't end well for anyone, ganastu or human."

Oriphiel opened his mouth to speak but stopped as students entered the room. He leaned in close to Arturo. "You must be swift in apprehending the shedim responsible for the attacks. If word spreads that the Bosses want to start a war, then things will go to hell quickly. None of us wants that. I will find what information I can from the Lords and pass it along."

"Thank you," Arturo said. He turned and headed up the aisle as the last of the students took their seats.

"One lesson we can glean from this story is to never believe demons," Oriphiel said as he resumed his lecture. "You can let them go, but make sure they take a dive off a cliff into the sea to stop them for good."

CHAPTER 15

Arturo cringed as McLeod's shouts echoed out of his office. He let Lorri move past him, then shut the door to the basement.

"I've been petitioning you for more funding for years! This is hardly our fault."

They continued into the conference room. Jamaal and Lydia sat at a table, sharpening their knives. A single file lay on the table. No one was trying to eavesdrop, but it was hard to ignore when McLeod's shouts reverberated around the room.

"It was bound to happen without the proper equipment to keep track of the populations here, not the way they've all been expanding. I'd be shocked if the numbers of both populations haven't tripled!"

Most of the monitors along the back wall showed different news channels' coverage of the attacks on the airport. Several stations were interviewing experts on terrorist attacks while others replayed video of smoke rising from the main terminal and the air traffic control tower. A couple monitors in the lower corner showed surveillance footage from a couple of the busier intersections in the city, areas they'd installed cameras to capture ganastu activity.

Lorri sat next to her sister. "What's going on in there?" she whispered.

Lydia glanced at McLeod's closed door. "The Sentinalia called to chew him out."

Arturo sat and called two marble-size elements to his fingertips, one of flame and one of water. He pushed them along the back of his knuckles like a coin, one chasing after the other. They disappeared under his hand and reappeared on the other side, round and round.

"I'm not surprised," he said. "The Sentinalia needs a scapegoat in case we don't figure out who's behind this."

The Sentinalia placing all the blame on them was the last thing they needed, but it was a typical response from bureaucrats. Just one more level of stress that did nothing to help solve anything. The punishments could be severe. In the old days, it meant a temporary exile, cut off from all sentinel connections and resources. Given how few sentinels there were, reassignment to a rougher city was the more likely.

Granted, if war broke out, punishment might be the least of his worries.

"But to blame McLeod when there wasn't anything else he could have done?" Lorri crossed her arms. "It's ridiculous."

"The Sentinalia have the final say in everything we do. Remember that," Jamaal said. He ran a cloth over a six-inch knife with a hook at the end, then sheathed it. "But I agree. They haven't been in the field for a long time. They probably don't even remember what it's like in the real world."

Arturo agreed. Most of the Sentinalia were rumored to be over two hundred years old. They hadn't seen combat in so long, they were more politicians than warriors. Arturo wished McLeod could have a seat among the council. He would bring a little more common sense to them and remind them what it really meant to be a sentinel.

The crack of the phone slamming onto its receiver echoed from the office. Jamaal and Lydia put their knives away while Arturo smashed his two elements together with a puff of steam.

McLeod emerged from his office, rubbing his temples as he joined them.

Lydia stood. "Drink, sir?"

He rubbed his eyes next. "That would be wonderful."

He sat silent with his hand over his mouth, his eyes shut. Jamaal and Arturo looked at each other and waited. Arturo could count on one hand the number of times he'd seen McLeod this stressed.

Lorri opened her mouth to speak but Arturo shook his head and she stopped. McLeod would tell them about the conversation after he'd gathered his thoughts. To rush him would only bring the anger he was fighting to control back to the surface.

Lydia returned with a tumbler full of amber liquid and handed it to him.

"Thank you." He took a large drink, then sighed. "I'm assuming you all heard most of that."

"Oh, yeah," Jamaal said. "I can't believe you're still using a landline. You know we have cell phones now, right?"

McLeod chuckled. "Yes, I know that. But my phone doesn't need a battery to run."

"Well—"

"Actually, Lorri and I just got here," Arturo said, cutting Jamaal's attempts at humor off. "But we got the gist of it. They're putting the blame on us, huh?"

"Yes, they are. Specifically our region's representative on the council is. She expects us to fix this with a snap of our fingers, too. If we'd just been given the funding we originally asked for, we'd be able to keep better tabs on the city." He took another drink. "But there's nothing we can do about that now."

"Maybe this'll convince them to give us more money?"

Lydia sounded so hopeful, which only made Arturo cringe all the harder. During basic, the Sentinalia were portrayed in a positive light, as supportive leaders of the sentinels in the field. Arturo had felt just like she did when he'd graduated. It didn't take long for him to learn that wasn't always the case.

"I wouldn't count on it," McLeod said. "Of course, we can hope. We don't have enough personnel in the field to match the growth in ganastu populations and the Sentinalia puts more funding towards cities with higher concentrations. New York, Beijing, London. We're small potatoes in comparison." He finished off his drink. "All right, let's keep moving. What did you all find out at Limbo?"

Arturo leaned forward in his chair. "We met with Raum. He doesn't know anything about the attacks but he was able to translate true message on the wall. It said: *the day has come at last, when we shall emerge as sole inheritors of the earth*. It was written in a language that used to be spoken universally between both species."

"That means it could be either species responsible then," Lydia said.

"It's always possible," Lorri replied. "Just like it's possible pigs could fly. Raum told us the brutal deaths are an indicator the shedim were behind this."

Lydia glared at her. "If that's the case, why leave the message? What purpose does it serve?"

"According to Raum, it's a declaration of war," Arturo said. McLeod side-eyed him but didn't say anything. They sat in silence for a moment. They'd stopped many individuals or small groups over the years from taking souls. It was the most common threat. But this? They'd never encountered any ganastu bent on starting all-out war. Even the shedim, arguably more prone to violence, never pushed for exposure.

"We won't let it escalate that far. What else do we have?"

Jamaal opened the file laying on the table and passed a few sheets to McLeod. "I think I've got something. My contact among the mastem has documented a large influx of shedim into St. Louis. From what she was able to gather, their population has nearly doubled in the last three months."

Arturo snapped his gaze to Jamaal. They couldn't put all the blame on a fully functioning monitoring system, not with those numbers. They should have seen this kind of growth, gotten some kind of sense their population was on the rise.

"Shouldn't we have noticed that?" Lorri said, echoing Arturo's thoughts.

McLeod sighed. "We don't have the numbers to keep up with ganastu. I imagine with the training we've focused on you two and the recent attacks in Forest Park, we haven't seen the larger picture."

"My thoughts as well," Jamaal said. "The park attacks might've even been a distraction to keep us off the scent of the shedim's true plans." Jamaal flipped a page. "My contact also found a shedim named Marut who works as a clerk at a convenience store in the Central West End. Evidently he was blabbering about how powerful the shedim are and how they were going to 'blow the mastem away'. I've got the address for the store."

"That's something concrete we can work with. It'll at least keep the rep off my back a little longer. Get what information you can from the shedim before this gets any worse. With any luck, this'll be over soon and the Sentinalia will be happy."

Arturo couldn't agree more. He just wished it would be that easy. "We have another problem."

"The shedim at the morgue?" McLeod asked. "I've already taken care of it. It'll be destroyed in a couple hours."

"It wasn't just any shedim," Arturo said. "It was Seth Duodu, better known to us as Dueden."

Everyone around the table was silent, the muffled voices of the newscasters on the monitors mixing with each other to create a dull rumble.

"Shit," Jamaal said.

McLeod set the empty glass he'd been rolling in his palms down on the table. "The Boss?"

"Yes, sir," Arturo said.

"What did the FBI have to say?" McLeod asked, ever the practical thinker.

"They don't have a clue yet," Lorri said.

Arturo agreed. "When the body started to dissolve during the autopsy, it set off all kinds of red flags. And Agent Nickolaus brought us in to check it out. She's still in the dark but she's sniffing real close. We had to shake a tail to get back here."

"Us too. Real pain in the ass." Jamaal laughed. "Ass, tail, get it?"

"Not now," Arturo said.

"Do I need to have her removed from the case?" McLeod asked.

Arturo considered it. She had the potential to get in the way, but removing her from the case completely? It might ruin her career. Or it could lead to her digging even deeper. Arturo didn't want to explore either option.

"No, not yet. She's suspicious but it's only a mild inconvenience."

"All right. A dead Boss. This adds a whole new level to this. Oh, the Sentinalia won't be happy at all. Could this damned day get any better?"

Arturo winced.

"What else?" McLeod said, rubbing his temple.

"Well, to kill a Boss isn't easy," Arturo said.

McLeod nodded, then stopped.

"Yeah," Arturo said, figuring McLeod had reached the same conclusion he had. " And to kill this particular Boss is even worse. Whoever is responsible for the attacks had to be strong enough to overpower Dueden."

"Meaning another Boss," Lorri finished. "Or all of them."

McLeod raised a hand. "Don't jump to conclusions. I've said it before."

"She might be right though," Arturo said. Lorri and McLeod both looked to him. "Only the oldest of either race can read that message. So it's likely either a new Boss in town who's fed up with the balance or a concerted effort from all of them."

McLeod sighed. "I really don't need this. All right, we need to move quickly. Talk to this shedim immediately. Find out what he knows and see just how high up this goes. And pray that we aren't as screwed as this looks."

Arturo and his team stood. "We'll let you know as soon as we have anything."

For all their sakes, he hoped the shedim had information worth telling them. They couldn't afford to let the lid boil over on this.

CHAPTER 16

A tin bell jingled above the door as Arturo and Jamaal entered the little convenience store. Shelves were packed to overfilling with chips, sodas, and household items. But rather than an organized display, this felt like a crane poured the items in from the ceiling and Arturo couldn't help but enjoy the pure disgust on his friend's face as they picked their way down an aisle. Decorations from several different Middle Eastern countries hung on the walls, including a couple of prayer rugs and a poster for the UAE soccer team.

Behind a small counter tucked at the back of the store between a haphazard magazine rack and candy displays, a little brown man watched a soccer match on a tiny television set. A doorway behind the counter was strung with beads that clacked back and forth slightly from a heater that blew on the floor.

"Good evening," the man said without taking his eyes off the TV screen. He had a thick Arabic accent. Cheers erupted from the television as a team scored a goal and the man cursed.

Jamaal raised his eyebrows.

Was this the shedim? It certainly made sense with the mess. Arturo led the way to the counter at the back of the store. He drew a single knife and laid it down with a clank of metal on wood.

The shedim glanced down at it and then his customers. He jerked out of his chair and raised his hands. "I don't want any trouble. The money's in the cash register. Take whatever you want and leave."

"What we want is information," Arturo said.

Jamaal waved a hand and a breeze ruffled the magazines on its way to the door, where it flipped the open sign to closed.

"Oh, shit." The shedim bolted through the back door. The beads snapped and rattled like a pit of snakes.

Arturo glanced at Jamaal, who just shook his head, then sheathed his knife.

Jamaal snatched two chocolate bars from the candy displays, which only caused another dozen to clatter to the ground. He pulled a few quarters from his pocket and stacked them neatly on the counter.

"Really?" Arturo asked.

"What? They're buy one, get one free."

Jamaal, ever the honest one.

The beads clacked again as the shedim backed into the storefront. Lorri and Lydia entered after him, each with a knife held at the ready.

The shedim darted around the counter but Lorri moved faster. She grabbed him by the back of the head and pressed her knife to his throat. "Give me a reason and I'll gladly take your head."

"That's enough." Arturo stepped forward. "I think our friend here understands us."

She let the shedim go but kept her knife ready.

Marut wiped away a single drop of blood where Lorri's knife had nicked him. "Mastem would've killed me on the spot for being what I am." He rubbed his throat and glared at them. "Which means you're half-breed sentinels." He spat on the ground.

"That's right," Arturo said. This had to be their number one fan.

"I've done nothing wrong. I've never collected a soul before its timely death and I follow all the rules. Now get the hell out of my shop." He inched away from Lorri and Arturo both.

"I'm glad to hear that," Arturo said. "But no."

Jamaal stepped around to Marut's far side as he unwrapped one of his chocolate bars. "The attack on the airport. What do you know about it?"

Marut stopped and stared at the sentinels. "I don't know anything." He wrung his hands together and shifted from one foot to the other.

Lorri spun her knife in her hand. "Don't lie to us."

The shedim squared his shoulders. "I'm not lying. I swear. I had nothing to do with the attack."

"Then why did you run?" Lydia asked.

Marut glared at her. "I thought you were mastem at first. You would've run, too."

Arturo shook his head. This shedim was lying about something. The way he danced about showed as much. But why? How much did he actually know?

"We have it on good authority you were at a local bar several nights ago claiming the mastem were going to get blown away," Jamaal said.

"Look, I was drunk," Marut blurted. "I didn't know what I was saying. I must have just gotten a little carried away."

More lies. Cold rage seeped into Arturo's bones and he clenched his fists.

"Most of us spout off like that sometimes."

"Awfully suspicious considering the attack today," Lydia said.

"You can't be serious?" the shedim said, glancing back and forth between the sentinels and the door, his chance for freedom.

Jamaal stepped further into his way. "Just tell us what you know about it all."

"I don't know anything about anything. I'm telling you the truth."

They didn't have time for this. If all the Bosses were behind this, then they could very well be planning a larger attack.

"Enough." Arturo rushed forward, grabbed Marut by the back of the head and slammed him forward onto the countertop. Jamaal's quarters scattered across the floor. A crack echoed inside the shop as Marut's nose broke and he screamed.

"Tell us the truth! What do you know about the attack?"

"Nothing, I swear." The shedim sputtered and spat as blood from his nose drained into his mouth and onto the countertop. He tried to lift his head but Arturo smacked it back down, holding him in place.

He drew a knife and plunged it into the counter an inch from Marut's face. The cold chill that had worked its way into his bones crept up his spine and steadied his nerves. This was only a shedim, and not even a powerful one at that. It would answer his questions.

"Answer me, shedim. I won't ask you twice." He pulled the knife out of the counter and lifted it.

"Please, don't hurt me," Marut begged.

Arturo tensed and Jamaal stepped forward. "Stop it, Arturo. He doesn't know anything."

"No. He's protecting whoever was responsible for the attacks. He knows something." He pressed the knife to Marut's cheek. "Were you with them? How many children did you kill?"

"None, I swear."

"You're lying." Arturo raised his knife higher, ready to bring it down. Jamaal shouted in protest.

"Okay, all right," Marut screamed.

Arturo lowered his knife.

"I don't know anything about the attack. I wasn't there. But the Bosses are having a gathering tonight. Many of our kind were summoned. They want everyone to know what's going on, where we go from here."

"The Bosses are planning the next attack?" Lorri asked.

"My family wasn't responsible for the attack," Marut said. "I don't know about the other families though."

"Where?" Lydia said.

"Down on the Landing... at the old bottle works factory. Nine-thirty. That's all I know, I swear."

"See, that wasn't too difficult," Arturo said.

He eased his grip but stopped before he let go. What if this shedim *was* one of the attackers? Arturo could stop him here and now and the creature would never take another soul again. It would be as easy as plunging his knife into the back of the shedim's skull.

No. That wasn't his way. The cool desire to destroy the shedim fought back against him as his mastemic nature urged violence. Arturo shuddered, then slammed his mastem to the side like he had Marut's head. It settled back into the recesses of his mind, snapping at his shedim. It had come so close to ruling him.

Arturo's hand shook as he let go of Marut. The shedim collapsed by the counter.

Arturo stared at the knife in his hand. How close had he come to staining that blade forever, murdering the shedim in cold blood without a second thought? He sheathed the knife and walked out of the store, not meeting anyone's eyes.

The cold wind swept across his skin but he didn't warm himself. The chill was refreshing, far different from the ice that had crept through him and urged him to kill. The street lamps provided only a pale glow that reflected off the snow.

How did his mastem take over so subtly? He hadn't even noticed it until it was almost too late. What would he have done if he hadn't?

The tin bell jingled and he shoved his still shaking hands in his pockets.

Jamaal stepped up beside him on the sidewalk. "Want to explain that?"

"I don't know," he said. "My mastemic nature... it filled me up. And all I wanted to do was beat the information out of him, then kill him."

"Just like in the park. Arturo, you're losing control."

His heart beat faster and his breathing shuddered, like a giant hand squeezed his chest. "I'm not." He set his jaw. "I just need to get my mind straight, keep focused. We've been going for hours straight now with no rest. I'll be fine."

"Seriously?" Jamaal spun him around and Arturo met his gaze. "You're running the risk of losing it every minute. Pick one and be done with it."

"It's not that easy. Not for me. I know McLeod said eventually I wouldn't be able to control it but I can right now. I don't need... I can't choose right now."

Arturo meant it. Neither option was the right one for him, not right now. Both scared him to no end, felt like a betrayal to who he was as a person.

"Look, I've known you for decades and that's the only reason I've let this slide. But you can't keep going like this. When this is over and we're done, you need to choose. If you don't, I swear I will get you pulled from active duty."

Arturo stared at him. How could he say that? Being a sentinel was his life. It's all he knew. Jamaal couldn't, wouldn't report him.

"You're going to get someone killed," Jamaal said. "I won't let that happen. Not to my friend." Jamaal grabbed Arturo's shoulder and squeezed. "Keep it together, then take the time you need to make the right decision."

Arturo hesitated. He just needed to hold out until after they found who was responsible for the attacks. Then he could take the time to weigh the options, decide and commit to one of his natures. It was a good plan.

"All right."

Jamaal lowered his hand as Lorri and Lydia walked out of the shop.

"How is he?" Arturo asked.

"Fine," Lorri replied almost casually. "You broke the nose clean so it should heal in no time. You know, though. I thought I was pissed at the shedim. That was a whole other level."

"Ease up a little," Jamaal said. "It was an accident. We all get a little heated in the moment now and then, especially when we've got a lot riding on an investigation."

Lorri shrugged. "Sure."

Jamaal met Arturo's stare and nodded. "Let's go. We know where the shedim will be. And we don't have a lot of time."

The Landing, one of downtown St. Louis' most historic areas, had originally been the village that started the whole city. Over two hundred and fifty years later, it was still the center of entertainment, with bars, nightclubs, and fancy restaurants. The Mississippi River ran along the eastern length of the district, dividing Missouri from Illinois.

It was also home to one of the original beer bottling factories for the region.

Arturo and his team waited in a side alley across the street from the factory. It was only 9:15 and since the factory was located off the main street, it was still relatively quiet. They'd changed into civilian clothes to better blend in with the human population, but each of them carried at least half a dozen knives hidden in the pockets of their jackets and pants.

Lorri and Lydia watched the front of the factory as a hulking man with arms the size of tree trunks and a chest like a large barrel lumbered up the steps and inside.

Jamaal and Arturo hung further back down the alley. Arturo leaned against the brick side of a building and relaxed, taking several deep breaths. They were going into a meeting of well over a hundred shedim, some of whom might be responsible for the attacks. He needed to get his head on straight. His two natures lay at the base of his mind, quiet and still. If he could maintain this calm, he could get through this easily.

"Are you good?" Jamaal asked.

Did he have any option otherwise? "Yeah, I think so."

"Good, because this won't end well for any of us if you don't stay in control."

Arturo crossed his arms. "I'm sure. I've got a hold on them for now."

Jamaal cocked an eyebrow. "Listen, if you can't—"

"No," Arturo said with a quick shake of his head. "I know you're worried. But Lorri can't go in there alone. And you certainly can't go with her. You couldn't pass for a shedim to save your life. I'll be fine for a little longer."

"All right." Jamaal checked his watch. "It's almost time. Let's get this over with."

They joined the twins at the mouth of the alley.

"So how are we doing this?" Lorri asked as she cleaned under her nails with a knife.

"You and Arturo will go in and pose as shedim," Jamaal said. "You're the only two who can possibly pass for them if you have to."

"Except for the having no horns or scales part?" Lorri said.

"Let's just hope they'll be satisfied with a little power instead,"

Arturo said. "We need any information we can get at this point. We'll just have to linger at the back where the Bosses won't see us."

"What about us?" Lydia said. "We're just supposed to wait outside?" She put her hands on her hips like a child who'd been told she couldn't ride the rollercoaster.

"We'll watch the perimeter," Jamaal said. "If they need us, there will be plenty of screaming."

"We'll try to make sure it doesn't come to that, but be ready for anything," Arturo said. He looked at Lorri. "Are you ready?"

"Are you?"

Silence hung in the air but Arturo let it go. He had enough to worry about at the moment. "Come on."

Lorri held her hand out for him to go first and Arturo stepped out onto the street. A couple shedim ascended the stairs and entered the factory ahead of them. He and Lorri hurried to catch up.

The shedim looked normal enough, if a little mismatched. The man had long blond dreadlocks and wore baggy jeans. The woman was dressed in a business suit and her heels clacked on the concrete inside the factory.

They all stopped in front of a set of double doors. A pair of lumbering, muscled shedim in full form stood guard. Two horns sprouted from each of their heads and curved up like a bull's. Their scaled fingers ended in razor sharp talons and they watched the entrance with burning red eyes. Each had a tail that swished back and forth on the ground.

The couple in front of them each raised a hand and called flames to them. The flames swirled in the air a couple times, then disappeared.

Arturo's shoulders eased. They weren't going to have to do anything more than control a bit of flame. Easy enough.

The couple walked between the guards and it was his and Lorri's turn. They each called flames and were waved through the doors without a second glance from the guards.

The doorway opened onto the main factory floor, a large room with several assembly lines where the bottles had been filled. Empty bottles were stacked along one wall and boxes of blank labels were piled on shelves. The factory closed almost twenty years earlier and clearly hadn't seen much traffic since. A thick layer of dust covered all the supplies and old machinery.

The room echoed with the dull roar of what had to be close to two hundred shedim, all still in human disguises that ranged from bums to bakers to businessmen. Every shade of skin color and hairstyle was scattered among the crowd. Arturo and Lorri moved off to the side but stayed near the back of the room, blending in as best they could to wait for the meeting to start.

"So what do you think about the attack?" a female shedim with gauged ears and a nose ring said to another woman.

The other, dressed in jeans and a hoodie, slammed her fist into her hand. "It was too risky. It puts all of us in danger, especially if war breaks out. Something needs to be done."

Similar conversations circled around the room. Tension filled the air and thrummed, like a low cord struck on a bass. Goosebumps prickled on Arturo's arms and the hair on his neck stood on end, but he couldn't quite place the feeling. Was it anticipation? Fear?

"Haven't seen you two around before."

A short male shedim approached them. He had a crooked nose and long, greasy hair. The putrid odor of rotting garbage wafted off him and his tattered, dirty clothes. He smiled with a mouthful of crooked teeth and held his hand out.

Arturo took it and shook. "We're new in town. Just got in today. My cousin Marut said we should show up here tonight."

"Marut?" the shedim said. "How is the rascally devil?"

"Not too bad," Lorri said. She side-eyed Arturo. "All things considered."

"Indeed. Well, you certainly picked a hell of a time to come to our fair city." The shedim waved to everyone else in the room. "This is the biggest gathering we've had in years. I hope we decide to wipe them bloody mastem out once and for all for what they've done."

"What do you mean?" Lorri said.

The shedim snorted. "You mean you haven't heard about the mastem's attack on the airport? Don't you watch TV?"

Lorri's faced showed exactly what Arturo felt. What was going on? Why did this shedim think the mastem attacked the airport?

The bum shook his head. "You guys must've lived under rocks, huh? Welcome to the fun." He walked off, shouting to another woman as she walked in.

Lorri stepped closer to Arturo. "Was that guy crazy?"

"I don't know. I think he might actually have believed what he was saying."

The shedim wrapped the woman in a hug, then started up a conversation.

What if he was playing them? What if their cover was blown already? Or what if the Bosses hadn't actually been behind the attacks?

"They aren't telling everyone the whole truth," Lorri said.

"It's a possibility," Arturo said.

A hush spread over the crowd as a door opened on a catwalk along the edge of the factory floor. Five shedim emerged, and Arturo sucked in a breath as raw power filled the room, more concentrated power in one place than he'd ever felt.

It ran along his skin like little insects, and it took a great deal of control not to rub them away. His shedim lifted its head as the power permeated him. Arturo pressed it back, and it reluctantly receded, but the power of the five shedim continued to ripple across his body.

The shedim each stood in their true forms, with heads full of long, curved horns. Each wore their horns in a different fashion, but Arturo counted no less than fifteen on the least adorned of them.

These were the Bosses of St. Louis. The distinct urge to run and not look back washed over Arturo. If they were discovered, there wouldn't be much of a fight for Jamaal and Lydia to help them with. The Bosses would wipe them out.

The center shedim stepped forward. He had so many horns that they had melded together to wrap around his head and neck like a helmet of armor plating. Deep maroon eyes peered over the crowd.

"Welcome," he said in a baritone voice. "I am pleased to see that so many have come. Tonight, we mourn the loss of one of our leaders, Dueden." Many in the crowd looked down and offered a moment of silence, likely members of his family. "His death shall not be in vain if we remain strong. I will take any from his family that wish to join with mine. The other Bosses have agreed to do the same."

Several shedim smiled and a few even cheered. It was a generous offer for any shedimic family to take members of another's with no questions asked. If the offer hadn't been extended, they would have been outcasts and had to earn their way into a family. That, or find a new Boss amongst themselves strong enough to be accepted by the leadership in the city, a process that could prove destructive for the entire family.

The shedim raised his hands and silence quickly returned. "We have much to discuss this evening. But first, I want to welcome some very special guests. Arturo Morales of the sentinels, would you and any of your companions be so kind as to show yourselves?"

CHAPTER 17

Gasps and whispers spread through the crowd. Shedim glanced at each other and several crossed their arms to make themselves as small as possible in case a sentinel stood next to them.

Arturo tensed and crossed his own arms, grasping a knife inside his jacket sleeve. So much for getting in and out without anyone knowing they were there. He studied the other shedim with as much suspicion as they gave him.

Lorri glanced at him and arched an eyebrow.

He raised a single finger. They'd stay calm and be ready. They couldn't reveal themselves yet but if they didn't move, maybe the Boss would think they weren't even there. Then they could just slip out unnoticed.

"I'm sure you believe we are responsible for the attack on the airport this morning. But I assure you, it was not sanctioned by the Bosses."

Arturo held still. They weren't safe, even if what the Boss said was true.

"I promise no harm will come to you," the Boss said.

Arturo focused on the shedim. Maybe...

The shedim sighed.

"You have my word and my protection on this night," the Boss continued. "I swear it to you by my power and those of my family. Please, come forward, we have much to discuss."

The Boss's words were so formulaic Arturo almost didn't process their meaning. The knot in his stomach loosened and he let go of the knife.

Shedim, by nature, were chaotic, but they held one principle above all others. Family. It meant everything to them. And if a shedim gave his word on his family's honor, he would do anything and everything in his power to ensure it wasn't broken. To not would result in the shedim being outcast from all shedimic society, with no chance of ever returning. It was the closest thing to a guarantee any sentinel could get from them.

Arturo squeezed between two large shedim who looked down at him and then gasped. They jumped back like he'd burned them and the domino effect began. Shedim bumped and jostled away and an instant later, a path had cleared. Arturo caught a glimpse of the bum who'd spoken with them. His face was full of horror and fear.

Arturo walked forward, head held high. The numbers in the room, maybe even the Bosses alone could kill them, but if he could play on the sentinels' reputation as enforcers, he'd take it. Lorri stared at him for a moment longer and then fell in step behind him.

The Boss smiled and, with a lithe twist of his body, flipped over the railing. He landed on the concrete floor, which almost seemed to ripple with the impact but Arturo was sure it was just his power softening his fall. He opened his arms wide to Arturo and Lorri as they passed to the front of the crowd.

"Arturo, we meet at last. I've heard so many tales of your deeds over these past few decades. Although, from the stories, I imagined you to be a hulking monster of a sentinel. A sentinel who wields the power of both shedim and mastem simultaneously. You've managed to kill many from both species, and yet many of us still think they can sway you to our side. So... curious."

Arturo bowed low and Lorri followed suit, which only made the shedim smile all the wider.

"I did what had to be done to maintain peace for all," Arturo said.

He needed to be careful. No doubt there were family members of shedim he'd killed in this room, and the Boss had just brought those memories to the surface. "We thank you for your welcome and your protection. We are honored by it."

"Such excellent manners." The shedim bowed in return. "But stand, we don't really have time for such pleasantries."

Arturo nodded. "You know my name, but I'm afraid I don't know yours."

He laughed. "Oh, I'm sure you do. You just don't know it belongs to me. I am Belial."

Lorri gasped and Arturo's gut tensed even tighter than it had before.

Belial chuckled. "You've heard of me then, young sentinel? Tell me, what did your instructors say about me?"

Lorri glanced at Arturo, then spoke. "They said you're one of the oldest shedim in known existence. One who's been responsible for countless deaths and atrocities through the ages."

Arturo had always heard the same. Belial was believed to be responsible for Pompeii. It was rumored he played a significant role in World War Two, although which side was unclear. But Arturo had never seen the shedim before and had no idea he was even in St. Louis. His location had been unknown for years.

Belial was ancient and had collected thousands, if not millions, of souls. No one else in the room came close to his power, save maybe some of the Bosses still up on the railing. Here was a Boss capable of killing Dueden. Arturo scanned the crowd for any sudden movements.

"Such exaggerations. I have instigated maybe half of the *atrocities* you were taught. I merely finished the rest." Several chuckles spread through the crowd. "Regardless, I don't think you snuck into our meeting tonight to learn about my past. And from the looks on your face, you didn't even know I was here."

Arturo snapped his eyes up to meet Belial's. The shedim read him far too easily for comfort. He relaxed the muscles in his face and buried his emotions.

"War is coming to this world, sentinels," Belial said. "As I'm sure you've realized by now."

"A war *you* started," Lorri said.

Arturo glared at her as shedim throughout the factory cried out. Several even hissed, a strange sound emerging from human mouths. She needed to be quiet before she angered Belial. He may have given his word tonight but that wouldn't guarantee anything for tomorrow.

Belial called his people to silence once again. "No, not us. As I said, we weren't responsible for the attack."

"We saw the destruction you—"

"Enough, Lorri," Arturo snapped. He shook his head once, then turned to Belial. "We have evidence that points to the shedim. The fire and chaos, the massacred bodies. Even Dueden's death. All very similar to the conflicts between rival Bosses."

Belial crossed his arms. "And I am the only one with enough power to kill Dueden. I know your line of thinking, yet I'm telling you it is a lie. A setup. We're being framed for crimes we have not committed. But if it's truly war the mastem want, perhaps it is time we answered them with our full might." Cheers rose in the crowd, although Arturo noted not from everyone. They weren't in agreement on this.

"Mastem wouldn't commit such a horrible attack on a human population," Lorri said. This was met by more hisses from the shedim.

"Ah, wouldn't they?" Belial said as he raised a hand to his people. "If they wanted it to seem like we were responsible, what wouldn't they do? Young one, I will attribute your naivety to your age. You haven't lived long enough to see how similar our two races truly are. But you, Arturo, you have. Do you not think the mastem could create this elaborate a ruse? Is genocide beyond them?"

Arturo nodded. He'd seen mastem inflict cruel tortures on shedim and humans alike. He'd also seen shedim show the greatest of mercies. Raum and his fellow rogues were living proof nothing was constant with either species. There was the possibility the mastem could be behind this, but it seemed unlikely. Too much evidence pointed the other direction.

"And the death of Dueden?"

Belial lowered his head. "I mourn his loss. He was one of my oldest friends. But his death only confirms for me that mastem were responsible. No human could have killed him and you've said yourself, I am the only shedim in St. Louis strong enough to overpower him."

The story made sense. But it also made sense for Belial to kill Dueden over a dispute of power. Just because he said differently didn't make it so. His word could hardly be taken at face value.

Belial lifted his head and met Arturo's gaze. Arturo stared deeply into the shedim's eyes, past the power that brimmed there, to the pain that roiled underneath. Real pain at the loss. Arturo imagined what he'd feel if he lost Jamaal or McLeod.

"Say we believed you," Arturo said. "What proof do you have that your kind weren't responsible?"

"Unfortunately, only very little. But tell me, what good would a war serve the shedim? Yes, it is true we thrive on chaos. But we learned long ago that the best chaos comes from subtlety. If we come to light for all to see, it will be our undoing. The mastem had done a fine job seeing to it that humans would fear us as demons."

There was truth there as well, more truth than Arturo expected from Belial. "You don't expect us to just believe you though?"

Belial laughed, a deep baritone that resounded around the room. "Hardly. In fact, I'm glad you don't. You wouldn't be living up to your reputation if you believed every word that came out of my mouth, no matter how truthful. Yet I give you my oath it's the truth."

Belial motioned to one of the other Bosses on the balcony. Horns protruded from her head in every direction and twisted around each other, a tangled, natural mass of bone. She tossed a flash drive down to Belial, who in turn handed it to Arturo.

"What's this?"

"The only proof we have of our innocence. Watch it and make up your own mind."

Arturo slid the drive into his jacket pocket. "If what you say is true, then you need to keep your people under control. Give us the time to find who is responsible. We can't have fighting in the streets."

"We thought as much, thus the other reason for our meeting tonight. If that is what's needed to ensure the sentinels do not jump to conclusions, we'll keep the peace for now." He beckoned to the other Bosses. "But if you don't find the mastem responsible for this, we'll take matters into our own hands and there will be war." He bowed his head ever so slightly. "Now, we still have much to discuss on our own."

Arturo recognized the dismissal and bowed. "Thank you for speaking with us."

"Thank you, sentinel, for listening."

Belial raised his hand and the crowd split down the middle again. Arturo and Lorri turned and strode through the shedim, all eyes trained on them. They'd gotten more information than he'd actually expected to get. But rather than answers or confirmation of his suspicions, he only had more questions.

CHAPTER 18

Arturo and Lorri crossed the street and entered the alley, silent. Arturo was actually thankful for that for the moment. Too many thoughts echoed in his mind, probably the same for her. Where did they go from here? Belial had just shattered their hypothesis that the shedim had been behind the attack. But what if he'd lied?

"How'd it go?" Jamaal asked. He and Lydia walked up from the other end of the alley.

"Great," Lorri said. "Considering Belial knew we were there."

"*The* Belial?" Lydia asked, her face pale. "Seriously?"

"Yeah. You wouldn't believe—"

Arturo cut Lorri off before she could continue. "My guess is Marut told the Bosses about our visit earlier."

"And I'd have thought he knew better after the lesson you taught him," Lorri said.

"Enough, already," Jamaal said with a stern glare. "Now you're starting to get on my nerves."

Lorri stopped, then nodded.

Arturo took a deep breath before he spoke. "Belial claims the shedim weren't responsible for the attack. And he said he had proof for us." He pulled out the flash drive.

Jamaal raised an eyebrow. "You think he was telling the truth?"

"I don't know. If they attacked the airport, why not go ahead and kill us in there? Why let us walk away unharmed?"

"They definitely could have done it, too," Lorri said, rubbing her arms.

The power still lightly brushed over Arturo's arms, but it had begun to fade.

"It looks good for them." Lydia leaned against the wall. "And it could throw us off."

"I'm not so sure," Arturo said. "You didn't see Belial. He's either a very good liar or he's truly hurt by the death of Dueden."

Jamaal stared at him, then shrugged. "I find it hard to believe the mastem would be responsible. They wouldn't run the risk of exposing themselves."

"And the shedim would?" Lorri asked. "After all this time keeping both species hidden, why would either risk it all?"

"That's the question, isn't it?" Arturo said. "The Bosses have at least said—"

"Everything okay down here?" Agent Nickolaus shouted as she stepped around the corner of the alley.

"Shit," Lorri said.

Arturo slid the flash drive into his pocket. "Agent Nickolaus? Really? Following us again?" Damn she was persistent.

Arturo backed down the street and his team followed suit.

"I was just out for a stroll. Total coincidence bumping into you."

She wasn't fooling anyone and she knew it. Maybe McLeod had been right to want her removed from the case.

"So what were you all up to in there?" She pointed over her shoulder towards the factory across the street.

"Just following up on some leads," Arturo said.

Nickolaus arched an eyebrow. "Care to share some information?"

"We've had this conversation already," Arturo said. "The answer is still the same."

Nickolaus shook her head. "I don't believe you. I think you were in there with the terrorists, plotting your next attack. Why else aren't you sharing what you know?"

"Agent Nickolaus—"

"Dammit, no." Nickolaus drew her gun. "I'm tired of it." She shifted her aim towards Arturo.

He lifted his hands.

"You're going to tell me everything and you're not going anywhere until you do!" Agent Nickolaus shouted.

"No one is going anywhere."

She spun as half a dozen shedim entered the alley.

Anzu, the shedim who'd attacked Arturo at The Trolley two nights earlier, stood at the head of the group. Six horns curved back along his head. His scales reflected a dull red and his tail flicked back and forth, barbed at the tip. The other shedim all sported several horns apiece and were varying shades of red and orange. Anzu had come prepared for a fight this time. The temperature in the alley rose and the snow sizzled on the pavement.

"Oh, this couldn't possibly get any better," Lorri said.

Arturo gestured to her and the others and they spread out a bit, arms at the ready.

"Wh... What..." Agent Nickolaus' voice quavered and she swallowed. "What the hell are you?"

Anzu stepped towards her.

"Stay back!"

"Silence, human!"

Anzu lifted his fist and Nickolaus fired two shots into his chest. Two circles of blood bloomed on his silk shirt as he lunged forward and grabbed her wrist. His talons drew blood and she whimpered. He drew her close, wrenched the gun from her, and sniffed her face. "Your soul is strong. I'll enjoy warping it before you die."

Anzu barked a laugh, then backhanded Nickolaus into the wall. She smashed into it head first and slid to the slushed snow. Anzu tossed her gun on the ground and glared at her limp form.

"What a waste," Anzu said as he pulled his blood stained shirt off. Already the wounds were closing up, stitching back together.

"We were given Belial's protection tonight," Arturo said as the shedim stepped closer. While technically this might be true, it was more likely that the Boss meant during their time inside. But it was worth the bluff.

"We don't give a rat's ass what Belial promised you," Anzu said.

The other shedim glanced at each other but didn't speak up. They might not have agreed with that, but they weren't going to challenge Anzu.

"You killed our kind," Anzu said. "Now, we're going to return the favor."

"Arturo," Jamaal said.

Footsteps echoed from behind them and he didn't have to look back to know more shedim had boxed them in. This night definitely wasn't working out the way he hoped. Arturo's natures perked up. Violence was coming and they both shared a sudden bloodlust and desire to be used.

"Well, Lorri, I guess you were right." Arturo grinned. "We do have to kill them."

Lorri's eyes sparkled as she drew a knife and twirled it in her hand.

Arturo turned as Anzu rushed him. But this time, he was ready. Anzu swung his clawed hand at Arturo's face and he ducked under it. With a quick draw, he slammed a knife into his opponent's forearm.

Anzu recoiled and held his arm close. "Kill them!" he shouted as he wrenched the knife out.

Lydia and Jamaal spun to face the shedim at their backs while Arturo and Lorri took the front. Lorri's knife was already embedded in a shedim's skull as Arturo drew another.

Arturo hoped the twins could keep themselves alive as the shedim swarmed and eliminated all rational thought.

He swiped at his first attacker, who dodged to the side. The shedim kicked at his gut but he blocked with his foot and swung again. He hit nothing but air as the shedim spun away towards Lorri, replaced by another of its kind.

This one charged forward with her head down, four sharpened horns aimed straight for his chest.

Arturo threw himself out of the way but not before a horn sliced a gash up his bicep and he dropped his knife. He spun mid-fall and called a shard of ice. With a flick of his wrist, the ice slammed into the shedim's neck as she ran past.

The creature shrieked and flailed, and the ice burned her neck from the inside out. Acrid smoke filled his nostrils.

Her shrieks faded away as her larynx dissolved.

Arturo slammed onto the ground hard and slid along the wet concrete. As he slowed, a shedim yanked him up and threw him against the wall. His head bounced back hard and for a moment his vision blurred. As he refocused, Anzu stepped in front of him with his fist raised.

"Time to die, sentinel," Anzu said.

Arturo ducked and the shedim punched his fist through the brick wall. He howled. Dust and little pieces of brick sprinkled down Arturo's neck and the back of his shirt.

Another shedim pulled Anzu aside and grabbed Arturo by the neck, grinning with a mouth full of sharpened teeth. He lifted Arturo off the ground and squeezed.

Arturo hit the shedim's arms to dislodge them but it was like smacking a steel beam. His chest tightened as his breaths grew smaller and smaller. His natures surged and roared, sparking white hot where they collided with each other.

The sharp clap of gunfire echoed in the alley and the shedim who held him jerked to the side, blood splattering from his shoulder. His grip on Arturo's neck loosened and precious air rushed into his lungs. The bullet wouldn't kill the shedim but it distracted him.

Arturo drew another knife from his jacket and jammed it up under the creature's jaw.

The shedim fell backwards on the ground and the melting snow steamed against his skin.

Arturo collapsed to his knees for a moment, drawing deep breaths. That was too close for comfort. His natures retracted now that the immediate threat to his life had gone. He stood and looked down the alley. Agent Nickolaus was on one knee with her gun held in both hands. She pivoted and fired on a shedim Lydia fought further down the alley.

Not bad for a human. Not bad at all. Arturo stood.

Anzu roared behind him and Arturo spun, his foot leading. His kicked landed solidly on the shedim's chest and sent him flying backwards out of the alley. Arturo moved to follow him but stopped as Lorri yelped.

He ran to her as she ducked and dodged two shedim. But she limped on her right leg, wet with blood. Arturo threw a shard of ice dead center into one of the shedim's backs.

He screeched as he tried to pull it out. But the ice was just outside his grip. He spun on Arturo, face red like campfire coals.

Arturo called another shard and threw it but the shedim raised his hand and flames engulfed the ice in mid-flight with a puff of dark steam.

Not good. A punch flew through the steam and clipped his jaw. He stumbled back.

The shedim punched again and Arturo blocked with his forearm. He grabbed the shedim's wrist and locked it under his own arm, then pulled. The shedim screamed as the arm popped out of socket.

Arturo pushed his opponent face first against the wall and in one swift motion pinned him through the neck with his last knife. The shedim twitched for a moment, then hung limp as the ice in his back continued to eat away at him.

Lorri took the other shedim down with a knife to the middle of the forehead, then stumbled back against the wall. She pulled a bandage from her pocket and pressed it against her leg. She waved him away.

Jamaal and Lydia were finishing the last shedim further down the alley.

Where was Anzu, though?

Arturo stalked out of the alley. Anzu was just rising to his feet from where he'd slammed into a couple trashcans. He glanced at Arturo, then took off.

Arturo launched a shard but the shedim ducked and it barely skimmed his shoulder. Anzu darted around the corner onto the main street.

"Damn it."

First the attack on the Loop and now this. He clenched his fists and stepped back into the alley. After they found whoever was responsible for the airport attack, he would hunt Anzu down.

One problem at a time.

Scratches and cuts lined Jamaal and Lydia's arms and faces. A bruise was already swelling on Lorri's cheek and she still pressed the bandage to her thigh. But they'd survived. Jamaal gathered their knives and started to remove heads.

Nickolaus still knelt in the slush, her gun held loosely in her hands.

"Agent Nickolaus," Arturo said. No response. "Kelly?"

Lydia knelt beside her and gently touched her shoulder. Nickolaus jerked her gun up and aimed it at the sentinels. "What the hell are you people?" Her pupils were dilated and her focus darted from Arturo to Lydia and then to Jamaal as he sawed at the neck of a shedim. "What's going on?"

Arturo held his hands up and stepped closer, careful to keep his voice soft and as soothing as possible. "Kelly, put the gun down. I'll explain everything to you."

Her hands shook and she took short, quick breaths. Her finger shifted closer to the trigger.

"Please," Arturo said.

Agent Nickolaus looked past him as Jamaal ripped a shedim's head from its body.

Her face paled and her eyes rolled back in her head. Arturo rushed forward and caught her just before she hit the ground. With Lydia's help, he rolled her over. He brushed her hair to the side and felt her pulse. Steady.

Lydia held Nickolaus' eyelids open and shone a penlight in each for a moment. "She might have a concussion after that hit. We can try to treat her or take her to a hospital."

"Arturo Morales," Belial said.

They couldn't get any breaks tonight.

Belial stood at the mouth of the alley, a dozen other shedim with him. His forces watched their Boss, ready no doubt to follow his orders without hesitation.

Jamaal dropped the head he'd just pulled and Lorri limped closer. They couldn't fight again. Anzu and his cronies were tough but taking on Belial and shedim who were likely the strongest in his family was suicide.

Arturo eased Agent Nickolaus into Lydia's arms and stood. He had to play this right. "Belial, we meant no disrespect. Anzu attacked us and—"

Belial raised a hand and Arturo stopped. "You don't need to explain. It was only a matter of time before the sentinels killed him or we had to."

Not exactly the reaction Arturo expected. The Boss had every right to be angry with them.

"They broke my word to you," Belial said, probably reading Arturo's emotions again. "He was present inside and heard my promise to you. I guaranteed your safety for the night. I only apologize I wasn't here to help. Is there anything I can do to make amends?"

Arturo couldn't believe what he was hearing. Belial was keeping his word to the letter. Perhaps not every story told about this Boss was accurate.

And maybe there was something he could do to help.

"Anzu ran."

Belial's lips tightened. "A bounty will be put on his head immediately. He won't live long. When I have his head, I will inform you. Unless you would like the honor for yourself?"

Arturo's shedim reared its head, hungry for vengeance, and he entertained the idea for a moment before he pressed it back down. "No, just make sure he doesn't harm anyone else."

Belial bowed his head. "We'll take care of the bodies. Go, and take the human with you."

Arturo lifted Agent Nickolaus in his arms and followed Lydia down the alley. Jamaal helped Lorri hobble along behind him.

"Get these filth into the river," Belial ordered behind them.

CHAPTER 19

Jamaal pushed the needle through Arturo's skin and he squeezed the counter with a hiss of breath. Jamaal smacked his arm. "Relax."

Easy for him to say. He took a deep breath. Jamaal could have used hot wire to close the gash in his arm and it wouldn't have hurt as bad.

They'd returned to his apartment without incident and now, Agent Nickolaus slept on his couch. She'd been out like a light since they'd gotten back. But Lydia assured them rest was best. And she was the one with the most medical training.

"What are we gonna do about her?" Lorri asked, standing in the doorframe from his kitchen to the living room. The bruise on her cheek had faded to a pale yellow and her thigh had stopped bleeding. Jamaal's scratches were already scabbed over. Their sentinel blood made healing much faster and easier. Unfortunately, the gash in Arturo's arm needed a little more help.

"Well, we can't convince her it wasn't real," Jamaal said. He pulled the needle through the last stitch, then clipped the thread. "She's seen too much. We won't be able to just explain it away."

Arturo pressed a bandage to the stitches while Jamaal threw the excess thread in the trash and handed the needle to Lorri. She engulfed it in a quick burst of flame to sterilize it.

"Let's see what she remembers first," Arturo said. "She may have blocked it all out. It's happened before with humans who were suddenly shown the truth."

He hoped it would be that easy. But nothing about the past day had been easy.

Jamaal taped the bandage to Arturo's arm and patted him on the shoulder. "All right. You should be fine in the morning. I can cut the stitches out then."

Lydia slipped past her sister with a warm washcloth and a bottle of pills. "Can one of you grab a glass of water for her? She's going to wake up with a major headache."

Jamaal pulled one out of the cabinet and filled it, then followed Lydia out to the couch, water in one hand and a cup of tea in the other.

This whole mess would throw a wrench in their investigation. One of the Sentinalia's first rules was to avoid involving a human in the politics of the shedim and mastem. Only after intense screening and prior approval could a human be told the truth, and only if it would be beneficial in the long run. Select government officials like the director of the FBI for example. The conversation with McLeod wouldn't be pretty.

Lorri watched her sister for a moment, then put the needle back in the first aid kit on the kitchen island.

"You did well tonight," Arturo said. He found he actually meant it, too. She'd used her training well and held her own against the shedim. Even in the meeting, she hadn't reacted to terribly when Belial introduced himself.

"Of course I did," she said as she opened a cabinet beneath the sink.

Couldn't she just take a compliment?

"What are you doing?" Arturo asked.

Lorri pulled out a bottle of scotch. "What does it look like? I'm getting a drink." She met Arturo's gaze. "Is that a problem?" She examined the bottle, then frowned. "You've got cheap tastes."

Arturo took the bottle from her and put it back in the cabinet. "Show some respect. I paid you a compliment but don't let it go to your head. And this is my apartment and my scotch. If you want a drink, ask first."

Lorri leaned against the counter with a smirk on her face. "Fine. May I have a drink?"

"See, that wasn't too hard, was it?" He reached into the back of another cabinet and pulled out a thirty-year-old scotch. "Grab two glasses. I'm going to need one for this conversation."

Lorri pulled the glasses from the dishwasher and Arturo poured.

"Cheers," she said.

"*Salud.*"

Lorri took a sip, then whistled. "Wow. That's really good."

"And you thought I was cheap." He took a drink and enjoyed the warmth that spread through his throat to his chest. Maybe this would serve as a peace offering, at least for a little while.

"Arturo," Lydia said from the other room.

Arturo took another drink. "Let's get this started." He grabbed the bottle and walked to the living room.

The washcloth lay across Agent Nickolaus' forehead. Lydia'd already wrapped a bandage around her wrist where Anzu had clawed her. "She's coming to."

Agent Nickolaus' eyelids fluttered, then snapped open. She peered around. Her gaze caught sight of his team and she jerked up to a sitting position. She moaned and grabbed her head as Lydia pressed her back onto the couch.

"Easy there. You took a pretty nasty blow to the head." Lydia held out a couple white pills and the glass of water. "Take these. They'll help."

She hesitated as she reached for them and Lydia held up the bottle.

"Tylenol."

She took the pills, her hands shaking ever so slightly, and drank them down. She held her hand to her head and took deep breaths. "What happened? How did I get here?"

"What do you remember?" Arturo said. This was the moment of truth.

The agent took a deep breath. "I remember..." She reached to the holster on her waist but her gun wasn't there.

Well, that meant she remembered trying to arrest them.

"Don't get too hasty, now," Jamaal said, blowing on his tea.

"Where's my gun?"

"Safe," Jamaal replied.

Agent Nickolaus clenched her first. "What are you going to do to me?"

Arturo sat in a chair across from the couch. Having everyone standing around her probably felt like an interrogation.

"Nothing," he said as Jamaal perched on the arm of the chair and Lorri flopped into another chair and slung her leg over the side. "We just want to know what you remember from earlier."

"You're working with the terrorists."

Lorri chuckled, then sipped her scotch. "Sorry, you're a little off on that assumption."

She shook her head and winced again. "No, I remember. You two were inside talking to the other terrorists. When you came out, I tried to arrest you. And then..."

Arturo glanced up at Jamaal, then back to Nickolaus. This was it. "Then what?"

Her gaze darted around the room, eyes wide. Her hands trembled harder as she remembered.

Arturo set the bottle of scotch and his glass on the coffee table. There it was. She hadn't forgotten. A part of him knew she wouldn't, her mind was too strong for that. And no matter how much she tried to deny it, she wouldn't be able to make herself forget now. But would her mind break? Or could she handle the truth?

"You remember seeing them," Arturo said. "The shedim."

The color drained from her face. "The what? No, one of the terrorists must have hit me while I was trying to arrest you. I must have dreamt it."

Denial wouldn't help her now. Denying what she fundamentally knew to be true would only drive her mad. She needed to take the plunge and accept.

Arturo raised his hand and called a ball of flame. The fire crackled and spit for a moment in his palm while Agent Nickolaus stared at it, her mouth slack. "I assure you that what you saw was real." He released the flame with a flick of his wrist and it sputtered out.

She looked at each of the sentinels. "What's going on? What are you?"

"Well, that'll take a bit of explaining." Arturo picked up his glass and began.

Two hours later, Arturo walked his team to the door. "Get some rest. I'll call you guys in a few hours and we can decide what to do next."

"Okay. I'll update McLeod. Just call if you need anything for her," Jamaal said.

"Thanks."

Agent Nickolaus had shared her doubts, her questions, but all in all, she seemed to be taking it pretty well. But anything could happen. Humans had certainly gone mad, even committed suicide, after learning about the existence of the ganastu. He doubted that'd be the case here though.

His team headed out the door but not before Arturo grabbed his bottle of scotch from Lorri. She shrugged her shoulders. "Can't blame me for trying."

He laughed as he eased the door shut.

Nickolaus was on her cell phone when he got back to the living room. "Really, I'm fine. I'm sorry about the false alarm. I thought I had a lead but it ended up being a dead end."

Arturo sat back in his chair and finished off his scotch. A few more glasses of tea, scotch, and water had made their way to the table during their conversation.

"I know," she said. "I should have called sooner but I was meeting with Mr. Morales and his team..." She hesitated for a moment and looked over at him. "Yeah, I think they're finally going to cooperate with us... Yes, I'll debrief you in the morning... You, too, sir." She hung up and leaned her head back. Her face was still pale, but not as bad as before.

"How about a drink?" Arturo lifted the bottle.

"That'd be great." She rubbed her eyes with the heels of her hands. "But I don't think alcohol and a potential concussion is a good idea."

"Ah," Arturo said. He hadn't considered that. Sentinels healed so much quicker than humans. "Then maybe you just stick with water."

"Good idea."

Arturo nodded.

"I lied to my boss for you guys," she said as she picked up her glass.

"Thanks for that," he said. "Trust me, it's easier this way. People would think you were crazy."

"I'm not sure I'm not." She took a drink.

Arturo sipped his scotch. At least she was honest. That was a good sign. When humans started subduing their feelings or covering them up, that's when sentinels had to worry. Being exposed to reality was hard for anyone to take, especially if you reached adulthood still believing humans were alone on the planet. The quicker she accepted it, the better off she'd be.

"Any way I could get my gun back?" she asked.

Arturo smiled. She'd be fine. "Sure, Agent Nickolaus." He stood.

"Please, call me Kelly. You're making me feel old."

Arturo smiled, then nodded and grabbed her gun from a bag by the wall. He handed it to her grip first. "You're going to stay here tonight," he said as she reached for it.

Her grip tightened on her gun but he didn't let go.

"Anzu, the shedim who attacked us, is still out there. And he got a good look at you. At least for tonight, you'll stay here."

"I can take care of myself," she said.

"Against humans, I have no doubt. But he's responsible for the attacks in Forest Park lately, which I'm sure you've heard about. A bounty is on his head now, so he won't be a problem for long." Arturo paused. "Just for tonight."

Kelly met his gaze, then nodded. Arturo let go of her gun and she holstered it as he returned to his chair.

"So, you're not human then." She stated it more so than asked, as if she needed to solidify the idea in her own head.

"Not completely, no. We're a combination of all three races. My mother had shedimic blood in her and my father had mastemic. Or vice versa. I don't really know. I'm sure they didn't either. The point is, when the bloodlines mixed in me, the results created a sentinel. It's how we're formed."

"And what does your family think of all this?"

Arturo clenched his fists as a knife stabbed through his heart. He blinked a couple tears back. "My family's dead. When I became a sentinel, the powers exploded out of me and killed them all. It happens that way to most sentinels." It was the truth but that didn't make it any easier to say. In fact it was the opposite, far harder than he expected.

Nickolaus looked down and twisted the glass in her hands. "I'm sorry."

They sat in silence. Arturo took a few deep breaths and rubbed his father's medallion. Sentinels never talked about the deaths they caused when their powers emerged. It was a deeply personal and traumatic moment in each of their lives. He could count on one hand the number of people he'd actually told.

"So, how long have the sentinels been around?"

"Since ancient times."

She smirked. "Well, that explains how you got the director of the FBI to release you so quickly. You probably have connections way up in the government."

"More than you could know." He watched Kelly and noticed the slight quiver in her hands, the consciously controlled breathing in and out on counts of five. "How are you doing with all of this?"

"Well, considering the fact that I just learned my priest was basically right and there really are creatures fighting over human souls, not too shabby." She took a larger drink. "What about God? You've got a saint necklace on. Does that mean He's real, too?"

He laughed. He hadn't expected her to get religious so quickly. "I don't know the answer to that. I don't believe in God or the Devil. Most of us don't. And neither race has ever admitted to the existence of either deity. As for this?" He held out his necklace. "This was my father's. It's all I have left."

"But you're not sure?"

"No, I'm not. I only have what I've seen all these years." He had his own beliefs but who was he to shatter someone else's?

"You sound like you've been at this a long time, like an old man."

Arturo smiled. "Well, I've been in the field for almost forty years now, so—"

Kelly choked on her water. "What?" She coughed again, clearing her windpipe. "Forty years in the field? But... You can't even be thirty."

"That's too kind, I think," Arturo said. "I'll actually be sixty next May. Sentinels age slower than humans."

"My God." She chuckled. "Well, you know what I mean."

Silence filled the room. Arturo wasn't sure what to say next. He'd never been allowed to talk about his life with anyone who wasn't a sentinel or a ganastu. And he really didn't have to say much to them. They already knew everything about his experience and the world around them.

"So, the attack on the airport? They were the, what did you call them?"

"The shedim. That was our original thought at least. Their chaotic nature and inherent brutality made them our prime suspects at first."

"But not anymore?" Kelly's face lit up. "The factory down at the Landing."

"Yeah. We were there to infiltrate a meeting of the shedim and their Bosses. It didn't go exactly as planned, but they did tell us they weren't responsible for the attack. They blamed the mastem."

"And you believe them?" The skepticism was more than clear on her face. "Aren't they evil?"

"The first thing you need to accept is neither species are all that different from humans. Although neither side would admit it, they're both capable of terrible and wonderful acts."

"But what proof do you actually have? If a member of Al Qaeda told me they weren't a terrorist, I'd want proof before I trusted them."

Al Qaeda. If she only knew that shedim and mastem could both be found among their ranks, she probably wouldn't believe anything any of them said. But that was another issue entirely. Her logic was sound.

The first thing they needed was proof that the shedim weren't behind the attacks. Then they could get on with finding a lead on who really was responsible.

"Proof," he said, then stood. In the chaos of Anzu attacking them and bringing Kelly up to speed, he'd totally forgotten the flash drive. He grabbed his jacket from the kitchen and his laptop off the counter. As he sat back in the chair, he pulled the drive from his pocket. "The leader of the shedim gave me this."

He plugged the drive into the laptop and accessed it. It held one file, a video. He opened it and an image popped onto the screen. It showed a hallway filled with people carrying luggage.

Kelly scooted closer. "That's the airport. How did they get that footage?"

Arturo glanced at her. "I'm assuming you've already seen this then."

"Yeah, I was supposed to send you a copy earlier," she said with a shrug.

"But you didn't."

Kelly took a drink and avoided making eye contact.

"Well, I've got it now." He pushed play.

The footage played what one would expect in a terminal. People milling about, walking to their flights. Men, women, children of all ages. Then flames erupted from one of the shops at the end of the terminal. People dropped their luggage and scattered.

A moment later another explosion, this one closer to the camera. People and luggage were blown around the hallway like discarded trash.

Finally, an explosion took out the camera and left static.

"You didn't send this over because you still thought I was responsible?" Arturo asked.

Kelly nodded.

Arturo started the video over. He didn't blame her, not really. As the explosions started up again, he felt his own blood start to boil. Shedim or mastem, it didn't really matter. Whoever had done this was going to pay.

"How does this prove the shedim weren't responsible? Didn't you say they can control fire?"

Arturo didn't answer. He just restarted the video and watched it again from beginning to end. It was the same thing. People running, screaming. Three explosions before static. What did Belial want him to see?"

He pushed play again and turned the video down to half speed. The explosions erupted but a man in the crowd stood out from the others.

"What is it?"

Arturo rewound the video and paused it before the first explosion. "There."

Kelly squinted at the man he pointed at. An ugly scar ran down the right side of his face. "I know him. That's Seth Duodu, the crime lord."

"That's Dueden, formerly the second most powerful shedim in St. Louis." Arturo rubbed his chin.

"Wait, you're saying we have a shedim down in the morgue? Is that why the body basically melted on the coroner?"

"A shedim is naturally weak against the element of water. While they're alive, only the coldest forms can harm them. But when they die, any water will react like acid to their flesh, which is what happened when Dr. Cifuentes washed him." He hesitated a moment. "But you don't have the body anymore."

"What?" Kelly scrunched her forehead.

"The sentinels took possession of him this evening and destroyed the body. We have to keep their existence a secret."

Kelly grinned. "Payback for the tape?"

"Just protocol." He pressed play again. "Watch what he does during the explosions."

The first detonation went off again and Dueden spun away. He looked back towards the camera and down the hallway. His mouth opened and his fists clenched. The second explosion erupted and just before the final explosion, he ran away from the camera and into the flames.

"I don't understand."

Arturo leaned back in his chair. Why did he run? If the shedim had launched the attacks, he wouldn't need to run. He could overpower any of his people save Belial, right?

"Arturo, what are you thinking?"

"I think I might believe them." There were far too many possibilities though to be certain.

"Really?" Kelly said. "From this alone."

"Not just this. But something has felt off about this from the beginning." He played the video again and paused it on Dueden's face after the first explosion. "That's not to say a rogue element within the shedim population can't be responsible. But if the Bosses were behind it, Dueden wouldn't have run. He had nothing to fear from any of the other shedim."

"What do you mean?"

This was going to get tedious telling her everything she needed to know about the politics of both races.

"He was the second most powerful shedim in St. Louis. No one could have taken him. Only Belial. And they're supposed to be quite close."

"That's your reasoning?" Kelly arched an eyebrow.

"Yes. If the attackers were mastem, then he'd have a reason to run. They were killing humans. Even if he wasn't the target, they wouldn't hesitate to kill him too."

Kelly shrugged. "If you say so. But why kill everyone in there and not just Dueden?"

Arturo shut the laptop. "That's the million dollar question, isn't it?"

The look on Dueden's face when the first explosion detonated played again in his mind. At first, the Boss had been shocked by what was happening. But whatever he saw on the other side of the camera hadn't just shocked him.

The second strongest Boss in St. Louis was terrified.

CHAPTER 20

Arturo stood in a long hallway with little diners and shops along its length. Seating was scattered here and there, but not comfortable seating by any means. Rather, they were rigid chairs with thin black padding. People walked around him, wheeling luggage, talking on cell phones or to each other. A golf cart passed by with luggage in the back and an elderly man in the passenger seat. A woman stood at a podium and spoke into a microphone while a line of people waited with their baggage. A family of four sat at a small table, sharing burgers and fries.

All this passed around Arturo, and yet despite the hustle and bustle, not a single sound reached his ears. Absolute silence reigned, like someone had pressed mute on the world. No squeak of sneakers on tile or the squeal of wheels on luggage. No voices from the people around him. The televisions in the diners flashed images alone.

The people spread around him like water flowed around a rock. They walked by without even noticing him, yet avoided him.

"Where am I?" he asked. But no sound emerged from his voice. Not even the vibration he would have expected from his vocal cords. His mouth moved but nothing emerged.

What was going on?

A man walked towards him with a terrible scar running down the side of his face, a scar that rippled like a living creature. Dueden?

The shedim spoke on a cell phone but paid no mind to Arturo as he passed by.

Arturo shuddered. He was in the airport. All these people were about to die.

No, he had to stop this. He couldn't let it happen again.

He rushed to Dueden and grabbed his sleeve, but the shedim ignored him. He ran in front of him and pressed against his chest but it was like fighting a freight train. Dueden kept walking. Arturo put all of his weight into knocking him over but just bounced off and landed on the ground. He would've had better luck trying to knock down a tree.

Fine, if the shedim wouldn't physically pay attention to him, maybe he'd pay attention to a little ice. Arturo focused and threw his hands out, calling on his power.

But nothing happened. He turned his attention to his natures but they weren't there. He was completely empty. No shedim, no mastem fighting for dominance. Just a dull ache where they used to reside.

He stared at the families around him, happy and oblivious.

He had no way of stopping what was coming.

Arturo scooted out of the way as another person nearly stepped on him. He stared down the hall at Dueden's back as he kept walking.

Pain erupted in his stomach and spread through him, pain he'd felt before. Pain he knew all too well from countless nightmares.

The first explosion erupted from his body with a sound that deafened him.

Arturo bolted upright. His head pounded and sweat covered his chest and face. But he sat in his own bed, in his own apartment. The clock on his nightstand read 5:30 a.m. He laid back and stared at the ceiling, taking deep breaths.

Couldn't he get one night's sleep without a nightmare?

It had felt so vivid as he replayed it in his head.

He swung his legs out of the bed and sat up. Going back to sleep was out of the question now. If he kept laying there, he'd never get his mind off the fire that roared out of him and killed all those people. He wasn't responsible for the attack on the airport.

It would be his fault, though, if he couldn't find whoever was behind the attack. And whoever died next would fall on his shoulders.

Arturo got dressed. Maybe he could check with Oriphiel. Surely he had some information now, especially if mastem were disobeying the Lords of St. Louis and exposing the humans to their struggle. The attacks could have been orchestrated by the Lords though. In which case, would Oriphiel tell him?

He hoped he would. Oriphiel would do what was best for everyone. He grabbed his jacket but stopped.

What about Kelly? He couldn't leave her alone in his apartment. Not just because she was human, but because who knew what she might do if she woke up and found herself alone here.

Arturo tossed his jacket back on a chair and instead grabbed a file from the top of his dresser. It was the folder Kelly had given them. He needed to figure out who was behind these attacks. He hadn't spent much time with the evidence. Maybe he'd missed something.

He sat on the floor with his back to his bed and opened the file, spreading documents around him.

He stacked the pictures of the bodies and the displayed heads on one side. He'd gotten a fine look at them in person already. Next were the pictures of the message on the wall. The message of war. Those went above the stack of bodies.

The next few images were shots of the different explosion sites around the terminal. He examined these more closely. He hadn't had time to get a good look at them in the moment.

Rubble and debris were scattered everywhere, burnt and scorched. Wires snapped and sparked. The FBI must've taken the shots while the emergency generators still ran. Each explosion had blasted away a large chunk of wall or ceiling.

Whoever had attacked had gone in and used fire to blow the airport to pieces, then murdered everyone inside.

Arturo held up two different explosions side by side. Something was definitely off about this whole thing, something he hadn't even come close to noticing in the moment.

The explosions were clean and efficient, evidence of a tremendous amount of focused power. If it had been the shedim behind this, it would have to have been some very strong shedim. But also shedim who were nearly identical in strength.

Arturo spread out several images of explosions. The blasts were all relatively the same size and shape. Like the same shedim had blasted away at the walls. Or maybe—

His cell phone buzzed on his nightstand and he grabbed it, flipping it open as he sat back on the floor. "Hello?"

"Hello, my friend," Oriphiel said.

Arturo smiled. "Great timing. I was just thinking I wanted to talk to you."

"Well, perhaps I'm a psychic." Oriphiel chuckled. "Unfortunately, this is about the attack on the airport. Have you found the shedim responsible?"

Arturo ran a hand through his hair and shook his head, then remembered Oriphiel couldn't see him. "No. But we're not entirely sure the shedim were responsible."

"What?" Oriphiel snapped. "What do you mean?"

"Nothing about this is clear. We're still gathering all of the evidence so we can find who is really responsible."

"Don't be a fool. The shedim were behind this. If you don't find the ones responsible soon, emotions will only continue to spiral out of anyone's control."

Arturo scrunched his forehead. Oriphiel wasn't one to exaggerate about anything. "What's going on?" Arturo said.

The mastem paused and Arturo held his breath. "We're preparing to pay them back for the attack on the airport. Several mastem were killed in the blasts."

Arturo hissed in a breath. "We didn't find any mastem."

Oriphiel scoffed. "Think. You wouldn't find our bodies after the fires burned them to ash, would you? I'm telling you, the Lords are far more angry than I've ever seen them. They are not willing to let these attacks slide. Plans are being put in place to strike back."

"You can't let that happen. I'm sorry for the losses but I have Belial's word they won't start any fights during our investigation."

"And you believe him? He's not just any normal shedim, but rather a cobra among snakes."

"Yes, I do believe him. We've got to keep the streets as peaceful as possible so we can do our jobs. If the Lords aren't behind this and the Bosses aren't either, then someone is trying to start a fight, trying to force the ganastu to go to war. We can find who they are but we need more time."

Oriphiel wasn't a Lord but he still held a lot of pull among them. He'd been a liaison to the Sentinalia on many occasions and knew how the sentinels operated. Arturo needed him to help them.

"Oriphiel, are you still there?"

"Yes," he said. "I have always had faith in you. But events are being set in motion that could change this world. I will try to buy you more time to find the shedim. But you need to find them, my friend. And quickly."

The line clicked as Oriphiel hung up. Arturo flung his phone on the bed and leaned his head back. Things were moving quicker, growing out of hand faster than they could control. They convinced the Bosses to calm down and now the Lords were riled up. Both claimed to have had people killed in the attacks. But if both lost people, who was really responsible?

A light knock resounded on the door, drawing Arturo back from his thoughts.

"Come in," he said.

Kelly eased the door open. Her hair was frizzy and knotted where she'd slept on the couch but her eyes were alert as she studied Arturo.

"Is everything okay? Sounded kind of heated in here."

"Yeah, it's fine. One of the mastem called. He's convinced the shedim were responsible for the attack."

Kelly nodded as she sat on the floor with him. "Sounds like everyone's blaming each other. They're squabbling and hoping one side will give in and take responsibility."

"Yeah, except that I don't think either side is really behind it. Some other player is causing this, some element that wants them to fight. But it could be anyone." Arturo rubbed his eyes with his palms.

"I've seen it happen before in other countries," Kelly said.

"Someone who wants to rule but doesn't have the power base. Get those in charge to fight and weaken their position. The hard part is always figuring out who that person is."

Arturo waved his hand at all the pictures. "This isn't any easier. It could have been shedim or mastem here." He shook his head. "Something's wrong, something none of us are seeing."

Kelly craned her neck to study the different images and Arturo found himself envying her. She may have just been drawn into his world but she was still human. After this was said and done, she'd still have a normal life to return to, a life outside the struggle for souls.

"What else can we do?" she asked. "This is all I've got so far. The techs might have more soon, but no promises."

Arturo pushed his jealousy aside. There was no point hoping for what he couldn't have. His gaze slid back to the pictures of the explosions. "I want to get a better look at the airport. I was a little rushed last time. Can you get me in?"

Kelly crossed her arms. "Yeah, I think we could manage that. But our forensics team went over the entire place with a fine tooth comb. I don't think we'll find anything else that we didn't already collect as evidence."

Arturo stood and she followed suit. "I wouldn't be so sure. You were searching for a human culprit. I'm not."

Kelly shrugged as they walked back to the living room. She combed her hair with her hands before she grabbed her badge and gun off the coffee table.

Arturo stepped up to a mirror and pressed a button along its rim. It slid to the side and revealed rows of knives and swords.

"Overcompensating?"

Arturo chuckled. "Very funny."

He selected an assortment and slid them into sheaths sewn into his jacket and jeans. He grabbed a short sword and slid it into a sheath built diagonally into the back of his jacket, covering the hilt with his hood.

Kelly pulled back the chamber on her gun, checked the safety, then holstered it. "Why didn't my bullets work on Anzu? Do they need to be silver or something?"

A very human question. "Nothing like that. The high-caliber bullets used nowadays just pass through the body and the flesh immediately heals."

"What about shotguns?"

Arturo nodded. "Buckshot would probably lodge inside, cause a little trouble, but it'd be minimal. You might drop a shedim with the hole you'd blow in them, but they'll start healing pretty quick."

Arturo drew his sword and held it at the ready. "A well-placed knife or sword will stay put and keep the flesh from sealing back up. You can't heal through solid metal." Arturo swung his sword. "The only real way to put them down, though, is to take off their head." He sheathed the blade.

"Oh," Kelly said. "In that case." She pulled a knife from the display, a small six-inch blade, and slid it into her waistband. "Thanks."

"No worries." He slid a final knife into a wrist sheath and headed for the door.

Tensions were escalating quickly in his home city. If they didn't find some kind of evidence pointing to the true attackers soon, Oriphiel would be right. The powder keg was ready and this city would blow up in all their faces.

CHAPTER 21

The terminal looked worse without all the smoke that had filled the air the day before. Rubble and broken glass littered the floor. The bodies and decapitated heads had thankfully been removed by the FBI but the tiles underneath were stained brown with dried blood. The overwhelming odor of smoke wafted through the air with the slightest tinge of burnt flesh.

Until the FBI had deemed they'd gotten every bit of evidence they could from the terminal, repairs would be delayed. It had the potential to economically cripple the city for years to come, especially being so close to the holidays. All air travel had been temporarily rerouted to the second, smaller terminal, but without the main terminal and the air traffic control tower, the number of flights had been drastically cut.

Arturo stood in the center of the baggage claim area and scanned the room.

Kelly watched him. "What do you expect to find?"

He glanced at her. "I'm not sure yet. I'm hoping I'll know it when I see it."

She put her hands on her hips and waited. At least she was quiet. Lorri would have peppered him with questions.

Now that he wasn't pressed for time, he examined the terminal in more detail. Brown trail marks ran across the tile where the attackers had dragged the bodies from both wings of the terminal to the central carousel. The carousel itself was covered with flaking rust-colored blood. The soft tap of the wristwatch on metal echoed in his mind.

The message still inscribed on the wall drew Arturo's attention. Like the tiles and the carousel, the blood on the wall was dried to a dull brown. It had probably soaked into the drywall. The airport would have to tear it down and replace it all.

"We've had dozens of people trying to crack that and still nothing," Kelly said. "Do you know what it means?"

"It's a declaration of war."

"In what language?"

Arturo shook his head. "That's the problem. It's a language both species spoke millennia ago. If it was written in a modern dialect, it'd at least point to a species."

Kelly's cell phone rang and she stepped away to answer it.

Arturo read the message one more time, then headed down the hall. He wanted a closer look at the explosion sites.

The power to the building had been cut and the backup generators drained, so none of the wiring sparked anymore. It also meant that where there weren't any skylights or blown out chunks of ceiling, the hall was pitch black.

He pulled a flashlight out of a pocket and shone it around. More of the same. More rubble, more destruction, more blood.

After a few feet, the wall ended at a hole ten feet wide revealing an adjoining room, what might have been a storage area. It was hard to tell. The edges were scorched, flash burned by immense heat. It definitely could have been the shedim. A few of the stronger ones could produce flames easily hot enough to deal this kind of damage.

Arturo walked on. Ahead of him, a section of ceiling had collapsed and a chill wind whistled through the hall. Little snowdrifts pooled in on the floor and the wind swirled them into mini-tornadoes. Jamaal would have made a horrible joke, probably calling them snow-devils or something else ridiculous.

He smirked but kept walking. He'd spent entirely too many years in the field if he could find jokes amongst all this chaos. He stopped under the hole in the ceiling. Above and in the distance, he could make out the air traffic control tower. News channels still played footage of the burning tower nonstop, even though the bulk of the killing had happened down in the terminal.

"Find anything?" Kelly said.

He jerked at her voice but disguised it by continuing to walk. "Not yet. Was that your boss?"

"No," Kelly said as she matched his pace. "The forensics team. They just finished analyzing some of the recovered shrapnel we found embedded in the walls and a few of the victims."

"Shrapnel?"

They reached another blown out section of hallway and Arturo looked at the next explosion about a hundred meters further. It was another section of ceiling. Back up the hall was the collapsed ceiling and then the first explosion in the wall. He wrinkled his forehead.

"Yeah," Kelly continued. "Several bodies had them. And they weren't parts of the wall or any of the metal around the terminal. The techs think there were at least a dozen high explosive devices."

Arturo shook his head. "That doesn't make sense. Shedim create and control fire on their own. They wouldn't need bombs if they were attacking."

"But the mastem might?" Kelly said, nearly identical to Arturo's own thoughts.

"Perhaps."

"Well, according to forensics, the devices were homemade materials that could have been bought nearly anywhere around the city, which doesn't give us a lot to go on. They did say the metal was rather unique, but couldn't identify it. They're checking around though."

"It's something at least," Arturo said as he looked back and forth along the hallway. Something was there. His own words from his lesson with Lorri a few days earlier came back to him.

Look for anything that stands out as different, anything that aligns with what makes them unique.

Arturo counted the number of tiles in the ceiling between each detonation site. "Maybe..." he mumbled.

"What is it?" Kelly asked.

Arturo glanced at her. He needed to be sure. He needed a better view. "Can we get into the control tower?"

"Sure," she said. "It's a bit difficult towards the top but we shouldn't have too much trouble. Why?"

Arturo headed for one of the gates so they could get out on the runway. "I need to check something."

"Are you going to tell me what it is?"

He kept walking and Kelly jogged to catch up with him.

Arturo helped Kelly over a steel beam that partially blocked the stairs up to the top level of the tower. The destruction had grown steadily worse the higher they climbed and at the top, it was absolute chaos. Bits of electronics and metal stuck out of the walls. Smashed drywall and concrete coated the ground like little pebbles, making the climb interesting to say the least.

Here at the top of the tower, a gust of wind rushed through a gaping hole in the side of the tower and Kelly shivered next to him.

"Aren't you cold?" she asked. "Or is that another benefit of being a sentinel?"

"Something like that," he said. True, he generally withstood the elements better than humans. But right now, raw emotion kept him warm. His cheeks and hands heated as he took in the destruction. He was growing more and more sure that the shedim weren't responsible for the attack. This was a setup and a very good one at that, but the signs were coming together. The pit in his stomach grew tighter.

He moved through the control deck, taking everything in. Blood splattered across the keyboards and screens. Outlines of bodies were taped out on the floor, minus their heads.

"They left them up here. We figure they didn't have the time to drag them down with the others so they just took the heads."

They did more than that. They lined them up neatly to take the heads.

Arturo stepped to the edge of the tower. The center of the terminal, where the heads and bodies had been displayed, was directly below them and the two wings extended in either direction along the runway. A black hole punched through the roof every hundred meters.

He slapped the side of the wall. "Damn."

"What?" Kelly joined him on the ledge.

Belial had been right. The shedim weren't responsible for the attacks. They embraced their chaotic natures without even thinking about it and that translated through to their displays of power.

This was not chaotic.

"Do you see the pattern?" he said.

Kelly studied the explosion sites along the roof. Then she gasped and leaned forward.

Arturo nodded. "I almost missed it myself. The explosions are spaced out exactly fifty tiles apart inside the terminal. That makes about a hundred meters between each explosion in the roof. No variance, no straying from the pattern."

"So they were methodical in their placement. What exactly does that mean?"

Arturo stepped back into the tower and leaned against the wall. "It's the most definitive evidence we've had so far. The shedim weren't responsible for the attack."

Kelly pointed at the terminal. "Because of where the explosions were? That's a bit of a stretch, isn't it? It could be just a coincidence."

"No. It's because of how ordered it was. I told you, the shedim are ruled by chaos. For the most part, they keep away from anything that bears any semblance of order. They wouldn't place bombs in such a strict fashion."

"And mastem would?"

"Absolutely."

Arturo walked back into the center of the tower. They'd all moved too quickly, hadn't stepped back and really assessed the evidence. It was a mistake. He was teaching Lorri to look for the patterns that gave away ganastu, yet when they'd gotten going on this, he'd thrown that to the wind. They'd jumped to conclusions and missed this.

"You think it was a setup?"

"Why else would you have found evidence of explosives and shrapnel? The mastem used the explosives to make us think the shedim were responsible. But the explosions themselves are too similar, like each explosive was identically manufactured. And the people in the terminal, assuming it was the victims who made the calls in the first place, said the attackers were monsters. Of course we would jump to the shedim, especially when they did everything they could to make it look like a feud between Bosses."

It was a perfect plan, except the mastem hadn't realized how they would subconsciously order the explosives. Why would they? It was just who they were. They couldn't fight a quality so inherent to their natures.

"Okay, I could buy all that but doesn't it seem a bit evil for how you've described the mastem? I mean, they're supposed to be good."

"Not good, just ordered," Arturo said.

She did have a point though. He was almost positive the mastem were connected with this but it couldn't have been a unified effort, not in the way the Bosses could have organized.

"You're not totally wrong," he said. "Most of them wouldn't have had the stomach to do this. But a select group that was more zealous could have pulled this off. Once everyone thought the shedim were responsible, they could rally the rest of the mastem to fight."

Oriphiel said the Lords were preparing to strike back. That reports had come in that mastem were killed in the blasts. If none of them realized it was fabricated, then they'd have no choice but to counter attack.

Kelly's phone dinged and she checked it. "Forensics emailed me photos of the shrapnel. Want to take a look?"

Arturo nodded as he took the phone from her but his mind raced to too many possibilities. He needed to report the information to the Sentinalia, let Oriphiel know what they'd found. The old mastem wasn't going to be happy to learn that his kind had been responsible for the attacks.

He glanced down at the phone. The shrapnel was scorched metal that held a slight blue tinge. He flipped through the individual pictures, then arrived at photos of the pieces still embedded in the victims. The devices had detonated and shattered to deal the most damage possible. Like a sentinel's knife, no shedim could have healed around those pieces of metal. It was a good chance Dueden had been put down this way.

He stopped mid-swipe as something caught his attention in one of the images. A blue reflection glimmered next to a victim's body. He expanded the image but it just grew more distorted.

"Do you have pictures of personal effects from everyone who died? Jewelry and that kind of stuff?"

"Yeah, I think some of it has been sorted and uploaded." She grabbed the phone and opened another file. "Why?"

Arturo snatched the phone out of her hand with a hand of his own that shook like a leaf and scanned the pictures. *Please let me be wrong.* Watches, necklaces, earrings, cell phones. All normal for humans. He stopped halfway through the pictures on a shot of some random items.

His knees buckled and he collapsed to the floor.

"Arturo?" Kelly crouched next to him. "Are you okay?"

"It can't be," he whispered. In the center of the pile sat a blue teardrop gem. Arturo's stomach twisted like it was locked in a pair of vice grips.

"What is it?"

He'd seen that gem hundreds of times throughout his life, ever since he became a sentinel. "Oriphiel, how could you do this?"

"Oriphiel? Who are you talking about?"

Arturo clenched his fist around the phone. Oriphiel always wore that gem. He'd worn it the day they met, the day Arturo killed his family. Was he wearing it when they'd met at the Basilica? Arturo wracked his memory but couldn't remember. "He's a friend." Arturo swallowed. "A mastem."

"He was one of the terrorists?"

The way she said it cut into him like a fire-heated knife plunging into his gut. Oriphiel was one of the attackers all along. He'd met with Arturo a few hours before the first explosion went off, when they sparred on the Arch. They met at the Basilica and he'd lied to Arturo's face. Every word he'd said since the attack had just been to throw him off the scent.

A rumbling like thunder spread through the ground and shook the tower. Dust sifted into the control room. Arturo leapt to his feet and rushed to the edge of the tower, Kelly right beside him.

Flames and smoke rose into the air in a line around a neighborhood a few miles away.

"Another attack?"

Arturo clenched his fists. His pain at Oriphiel's betrayal ignited into rage and his two natures swirled around each other.

"No. War."

CHAPTER 22

"Come on, pick up, pick up." Arturo held his cell phone between his ear and shoulder as he weaved his car in and out of traffic. He slammed on his horn as a car started to veer into his lane. It jerked back and Arturo sped past it.

Jamaal answered after the third ring.

"Where are you guys?" Arturo said.

"We're on our way," Jamaal shouted. "Traffic is a little crazy downtown but we'll be there soon. You?"

"On 40. Almost on site. Kelly's with me."

"Kelly? So you're on a first name basis, eh?" Jamaal snickered.

Of course he was joking. "Not now." Arturo switched lanes to get around a station wagon. "It looks like they hit Dogtown."

"The shedim neighborhood? Why would the shedim attack their own people?"

"They aren't behind this. No shedim are." Arturo sighed. The rage had subsided to a dull throb, now pressurized with anxiety at what they would find. "It was Oriphiel."

"What? That's not possible."

"It is," Arturo said. "There's no denying it. The evidence is clear."

"But mastem don't kill like—"

"It was staged," Arturo said. "Oriphiel built bombs to make it look like the shedim were responsible. And they're using them now in Dogtown."

Jamaal didn't say a word for a few heartbeats. "Arturo, I'm sorry. I know you and him are—"

"It's fine." He'd accepted the truth of it all already and didn't have time to feel hurt by it.

"Okay," Jamaal said. "Are you going to be okay in there?"

Arturo glanced inside at his natures. They swirled with contained power, but they didn't fight each other. His emotions were running high and they had to know they'd be used soon.

"I'll be fine. Just get there as soon as you can. The shedim are going to need our help."

Arturo hung up and tossed his phone in the cup holder.

Kelly was on her own cell phone and yelling at whoever was on the other end of the line.

"This is Agent Nickolaus. I need to speak with Roberts... Yes, I do realize there's an emergency! That's why I'm calling. I'll be on scene in less than five minutes... Get him on the phone now!"

She rolled her eyes before listening again. "Roberts? Yes, sir, I'm heading to Dogtown now. I'm with Mr. Morales... Yes, sir, we can. How soon will you be on site... All right. We'll update you when we arrive."

She hung up and tightened her ponytail. "They'll be there in thirty minutes with a full SWAT unit. Local PD and fire are en route. The National Guard has been notified but won't be mobilized for another hour. Until then, we're on our own."

"All the better," Arturo said.

"What?"

Arturo looked at her. "Only sentinels need to be in there. If word gets out to the human population that mastem and shedim are fighting in the streets, people are going to panic. Trust me, there's a reason we keep their existence a secret."

"And what do you expect the FBI to do? Sit outside and wait?"

"That's exactly what they have to do. Humans will only get slaughtered if they get in the way."

Kelly flung her hands on the dashboard. "Arturo!"

Arturo flicked his gaze to the road and yanked the wheel hard to the right. He swung around the semi-truck crawling at fifty mile an hour in front of them and clipped the side mirror off his car.

"Dammit," he said as they sailed past the semi. Lucky it was only the mirror. Pay attention, he chided himself. "Look, my team and I are the only ones in the city who can handle this situation. With this level of possible exposure, McLeod will follow protocol and call in extra sentinels from Chicago and Kansas City, but until they get here, we're on damage control. We have to stop the fighting."

"All right."

Arturo slid between two cars to take the exit ramp. They raced through quiet neighborhoods. The houses stood deserted, front doors flung open with discarded luggage and clothes scattered in yards. Not a single car was parked in any driveway, which explained the awful traffic out on the highway. Everyone was getting as far away from the explosions as they could.

Arturo turned the corner and screeched to a halt.

"Oh, God," Kelly said.

A wall of flames bisected the street a block ahead of them. It ran in either direction as far as Arturo could see, likely encompassing the entire neighborhood. Arturo opened his door and heat washed over him like a suffocating blanket. All of the snow had melted from the strength of the flames, and steam rose from the concrete.

"What are you doing?" Kelly said.

"I've got to figure out how to get through," he said as he stepped out.

Kelly hesitated before she got out too.

The flames roared thirty feet in the air, with smoke going thousands of feet higher. The perfect cover to keep humans out while mastem launched a genocidal attack on the shedim. And if the shedim tried to escape through the fire, they'd probably reveal themselves to the humans. And they wouldn't do that. That was a death sentence from their Bosses.

No one was walking out, and that was how the mastem wanted it. A part of Arturo admired the intricacies of Oriphiel's plan and it sickened him, likely because he knew the mastem was capable of coming up with something like this. He just never imagined Oriphiel would do it.

Arturo reached within himself, grasped his power, and focused. If he could control the fire, he could get inside. His shedim leapt toward the wall of flame, its complimentary element, and he wrapped his will around it. But the heat fought like it possessed a mind of its own. It threw off his power with a surge of energy and he stumbled back, his stomach rolling and his shedim hissing as it returned to him.

The flames were too hot, too widespread. Definitely more than he could control. Hell, there weren't many shedim who could master that much power. Whatever the mastem had used to build these bombs was powerful stuff to burn like this.

"Are you okay?"

"Yeah," he said as he wiped sweat from his brow. "There's too much for me to control, but I've got to get in there."

The roof of a house collapsed inwards along the wall of flames. Arturo looked from the fire to the house then over to Kelly. He couldn't help but smile.

"You've got to be kidding me!"

Arturo got back in his car and buckled his seatbelt. "Stay here."

"Like hell." She yanked open the door. "I'm coming in with you."

Sirens from a fire engine filled the air.

"No, I need you on the outside keeping other humans from entering the neighborhood. We need time to get the fighting sorted out before you all come barging in. And to be quite honest, I'm not going to be able to do that and protect you in there."

"I don't need protecting!"

Arturo stared at her for a moment. They both remembered the alley on the Landing.

Kelly slammed the door. "Fine. What do you need me to do?"

"Coordinate the first responders. Keep the fires from spreading. Once you have the perimeter secure and the fires under control, then come in. But not before. Hopefully we're done by then."

She hesitated half a heartbeat, then stepped back. "Good luck."

"Thanks."

Arturo backed down the street. A fire engine careened around the corner as he lined his car up with the collapsed roof. They were about to get quite the show.

He took a deep breath. This was a bad idea. He felt it in his gut. But if the flames wouldn't obey him, then he didn't have another choice.

He floored the gas and sped straight for the roof. His front wheels jumped the curb into the yard, sliding in the damp grass before gaining traction. A moment later, he was at the house and then on the collapsed roof. Heat rose around the car as he was engulfed in flames.

He reached inside and simultaneously grabbed his shedim and mastem, doing his best to keep the flames from roasting him or igniting the fuel tank on the bottom of the car while spreading moisture across the surface of the vehicle. The car bucked as he launched off the edge and soared through the air. The flames cleared from the windshield to reveal the side of another brick house.

"Oh, shit!"

The car smashed through a second floor window. Brick and debris flew everywhere and the car's windshield shattered in a spider web of cracks but held. He slammed through a little girl's pink bedroom and into the hallway, shuddering to a halt against a support beam in the wall. Smoke rose from the crumpled hood.

Losing his mirror on the highway didn't seem so bad anymore.

Arturo shook his head, trying to clear the ringing sensation away. He wiped blood from a cut on his forehead and flexed his arms and legs. Everything still worked, despite the cuts and bruises he'd probably have for a few days.

Not the worst landing he'd ever made.

He tried to open his door but it wouldn't budge, not even with all his weight behind it. He glanced over the window to see he'd firmly wedged himself in a hallway that wasn't meant to hold a vehicle by any means.

Not his best landing either.

He took a few deep breaths. The shakiness from the crash faded, and he focused on the air in the car. With a mental prod, he blew the front windshield out. Arturo grabbed his sword from the back seat where it had miraculously stayed put and climbed through his car into hell.

CHAPTER 23

Fire stretched through the backyard as Arturo stumbled out of the house. He coughed on the smoke and spat on the ground, trying to clear the clingy taste from his mouth. The wall of flames soared up in front of him and blocked any view of the outside world. The shedim were locked inside the neighborhood and now, so was he.

Screams rang out from somewhere nearby, followed by the clash of metal against metal. Some of the shedim must be fighting back. He took off across the yard and leapt a fence into the next, listening for the screams over the crackle of flame.

He rounded a house in a cul-de-sac and dove behind a bush, hoping he hadn't been spotted. He crawled forward and peeked through the branches.

In the street, half a dozen mastem guarded a group of shedim. The mastem stood in full form. Wings of brilliant oranges and gold shifted and twitched as they watched over their captives with bird's eyes and sharp beaks. Like the shedim with their horns, a mastem's strength and power could be gauged in their coloring and number of wings.

These were all lower ranking mastem, with only two wings a piece. Each wore silver plated armor with gold runes etched around the edges. Armed with a sword and shield that matched their armor, they were truly birds of prey.

Arturo couldn't deny it any longer. This wasn't a random attack, an unorganized act of perceived retribution for the attack at the airport. This was an act of war.

A larger mastem shouted, and the others each grabbed shedim. They jerked them around and lined them up, pushing them to their knees. Another pair of mastem dragged a woman from a house while a third yanked a child by her arm. Both sobbed, tears running down their faces.

Why didn't they fight back? There were easily twice as many shedim as mastem and even the weakest of them could control basic flames.

"That's the last ones," the mastem with the child told the leader. The child pulled out of his grasp and rushed to her mother.

"Please," the woman said. She pulled her child to her. "We haven't done anything to you."

Two small horns pushed forward from the child's hair as she whimpered in her mother's arms.

"You might not have," the leader said. "But that doesn't matter. Every shedim is a threat. But no longer." He glared at the woman, his eyes filled with an intensity bred from centuries of hatred.

Arturo shook his head. His hands itched to rush out and stop this. But he was one sentinel against nine mastem. And if the shedim wouldn't fight either, any rash attack would end rather quickly.

The mastem grabbed the woman's child by the back of her hair and ripped her from her grasp.

"Alia!" the woman shouted but stopped as the mastem held his sword to her daughter's throat.

He dragged her away towards the next yard and everything became clearer. In the adjacent yard, two mastem watched several children, shards of ice held at the ready. They were using the children to ensure the adults did as they were told. It was low to say the least, no matter how effective. Family mattered to the shedim and they'd do anything to protect their young.

The mastem tossed the child in among the rest. "We will spare your children, but you must pay for the sins of your race." He pumped his fist in the air.

At the end of the line of shedim, a mastem raised her sword. With a quick chop, she severed the first shedim's head from her body. The vertebrae popped as the blade sliced cleanly between them. The head tumbled down the street as the children screamed all the louder. The body collapsed sideways onto the next shedim, who screamed and pushed it away.

Arturo couldn't just stand by and watch this. He pulled a knife from a sheath on his shoulder and flipped it in his hand.

He needed to be accurate.

He very much doubted the mastem would spare the children. They were bent on genocide here.

He took a deep breath.

Surprise was his best friend at the moment. The executioner moved to the next shedim in line, a girl who couldn't be much older than eighteen. Another mastem kicked the dead body to the side and grabbed her shoulder to hold her in place. Tears ran down her face.

Arturo took steady aim and as the executioner lifted her sword, he threw. The blade spun through the air and buried itself to the hilt in the mastem's forehead with a thud. Everyone on the street froze as her sword clattered to the concrete and she fell backwards.

Arturo didn't wait for their shock to fade.

He rushed into the street, his sword drawn and at the ready. With a quick slash, the closest mastem's head fell to the ground. Arturo threw his left hand out and called on his power. Flames leapt from his fingertips and smashed into one of the mastem guarding the children. They spread across his skin like he was tissue paper.

The other mastem recovered and rushed toward him, leaving the shedim behind. He threw another fireball at two of them but they dodged and it smashed into a house. He didn't have time for another shot as a mastem drew within striking range.

Arturo blocked her attack and pushed outwards, deflecting her sword away. He drew a knife and slashed from the other side, but she pulled her shield in to block. The knife bounced off with a resounding clang.

He backpedaled as she swiped across at his chest. The blade missed by a fraction of an inch. A second mastem drew closer to his side and he blocked both as he retreated. He could beat them but only if the others didn't surround him as well.

The second mastem, covered in bright orange feathers, clacked his razor sharp beak and raised his sword, but screeched as fire brighter than his feathers spread over his body. Arturo charged back against the first mastem but glanced behind her to see one of the shedim with her arms outstretched.

"Fight!" she shouted at her fellow shedim.

The others leapt to their feet and roared in outrage as they found their courage and attacked the mastem, who at this point were even further outnumbered.

Arturo swung hard at the mastem in front of him but she blocked again with her shield. He side stepped and twisted his blade back to slide behind her defense. She lifted her arm higher and he had her. With his other arm, he brought the knife up through the opening under her shield and slammed through a gap in her armor into her heart.

She gasped and dropped her sword, her shield arm hanging limp at her side. With a flick of his own sword, he took her head as well. He glanced around. The last mastem burned on the ground, but three more shedim lay dead on the street. The children who'd been sequestered away rushed to their family.

The woman who'd rallied her people walked over to Arturo as he collected his two knives and chopped off heads. She was older, maybe in her early fifties which equated to several centuries if not more, with salt and pepper hair. But she only had a short pair of horns, which meant she hadn't collected many souls in her time.

"You're a sentinel?" she asked. She wheezed as she spoke.

She definitely wasn't strong. He reevaluated her age to be much younger. Shedim maintained their youthful appearance with the number of souls they'd collected.

"Yes," he said. "My name is Arturo."

"I'm Kaniel." She bowed. "Thank you for saving us."

"You helped," Arturo said as he wiped his knives on a piece of mastem's clothing, then sheathed them.

She swallowed and wiped tears from her eyes. "I wouldn't have if you hadn't shown up. I don't have any real power. And they stormed in, took the children..."

Arturo understood fear. The sentinels used it on the shedim and mastem regularly. He squeezed her shoulder. "You still fought for your family in the end."

She nodded and he smiled.

"We need to get you all off the street," he said. "Is there anywhere you can hide?"

She pointed down the street. "There's a storm cellar three houses down. I'd just gotten the families together when they ambushed us. It's well stocked and defensible in case of an attack."

"I'll escort you. But we need to move quickly."

More mastem could show up. These weren't all of them by far. If they got ambushed out in the open, he'd only be able to do so much.

Kaniel helped an elderly woman to her feet. Arturo flicked his wrist and lit each of the mastem up with a little fireball. For the shedim, he flung a few shards of ice into each and their bodies sizzled from the inside out. There wouldn't be any evidence left of either species.

He rushed up to Kaniel and picked up the child who clung to her leg while she helped an elderly woman along. The child tried to get away from him until Kaniel hushed her.

They ran down the street together, Arturo staying alert for any fighting or signs of movement.

"Right up here," she said as they stopped before an old two-story brick house. The house hadn't been touched yet by the flames but smoke filled the area along with the stench of burning wood and death.

Just off the back porch of the house, two doors led down to a storm shelter. Arturo set the child down and opened the doors, ushering the shedim inside.

Kaniel stopped beside him. "Will you stay with us?"

"No. My team will be here soon and we've got to fight off the mastem still in the neighborhood." To punctuate his point, a scream cut through the air.

"Then I'll come with you."

Arturo shook his head. "Your people need your protection. And I'll be sending any other survivors to you. Keep them safe."

She was brave for such a weak shedim. He gave her that much credit. But out on the streets, she'd be even more of a burden than Kelly would have been.

Kaniel bowed again. "Very well. A couple of Bosses live here in Dogtown. They always planned to rally their legions on Dale Avenue if we were ever attacked."

"Thanks."

Kaniel descended into the shelter and Arturo slammed the door shut.

Another scream pierced the air. He tightened his grip on his sword. They hadn't won yet. Not by a long shot.

Arturo found three other households of shedim, all frightened to the point that they thought he was a mastem come to kill them. They were mostly weak or children. From them, he managed to piece together what had happened.

The explosions had taken everyone by surprise. The heat and fire had been strong enough that even the shedim's natural affinity for fire hadn't been enough to keep them safe. Many weaker shedim had been killed in the blast. And before anyone could react, mastem had landed in force and begun killing whoever was left without mercy.

The Bosses had rallied any shedim with power to fight for their homes though and they'd put aside any familial differences to defend their species.

Arturo urged the survivors to carefully head for the storm shelter where they would be safer. But he hadn't seen any sign of the mastem. Or his team.

He crept through a back alley towards Dale Avenue. If he remembered his geography right, it was a couple more buildings away.

What he would've given for one of the GPS contraptions Lorri and Lydia were trained to use. Or even a smartphone. His flip phone just didn't cut it when he needed directions.

His duties hadn't brought him down to Dogtown in years. It was the most peaceful of all the shedimic neighborhoods, rivaling even those of the mastem. Families lived here, families who wanted their children raised in a safe environment away from the soul collecting their kind engaged in.

He reached the end of the alley and inched his way forward. Feet stomped on glass out on the street and from the sound of it, there were many of them. But were they shedim or mastem? If he could get a peek at who they were, he could decide to fight or go around.

The cool tip of a blade settled on the side of his neck. "Don't move," a voice he recognized said from behind him. "Drop your sword."

He lifted his hands but didn't put his weapon down. "I'd rather not, Belial."

The blade withdrew from his neck and he turned around. The Boss stood in full form, a long curved scimitar in his right hand and blood speckled across his scales and clothes. A crimson cloak hung over one shoulder, a stark contrast to the white horn armor on his head. Six other shedim stood behind the Boss. "Arturo, what are you doing here?"

"Helping. I saw the explosions."

Belial narrowed his eyes. "Yes, it seems you stopped us only so the mastem could attack again. Scores have fallen already."

Arturo cringed. In a way Belial was right. He had urged the shedim to wait, to not strike back. "I didn't think they'd be this bold. I was told they thought you all were responsible for the attack, but would wait to make any further attack until we found who was responsible in the first place."

"And have you?"

Arturo nodded. "I think so."

"And?"

Before Arturo could answer, shouts and the sound of battle erupted on the street. Belial ran past him, followed by his shedim. Arturo followed them out into the chaos.

All elements flew amidst the clang of swords and knives. Dozens of each race crowded into the street. The concrete cracked in some places from the heat of fire while remaining slick and coated in ice in other areas. Whirlwinds and rubble flew through the air, shattering windows and denting cars.

Arturo stopped in awe of the power and ferocity of all-out conflict between the races. He'd never seen anything like it before. This level of violence between them was never allowed.

"If you're here to help us, then help," Belial said as he ran into the fray. He flung four flames the size of quarters from his fingertips. They each collided with a mastem and detonated like mini-bombs. The mastems' bodies were thrown across the street, spreading ash over everyone.

The shedim held their own but they were outnumbered at least two-to-one. Even with the few reinforcements and a Boss, this didn't look promising. Arturo's body cooled and he looked inside. His natures swirled around each other, almost peaceful. Ready to be used.

He smiled. He'd come to defend the shedim and their homes. He was going to do it. And it appeared his natures agreed. He waded in.

He sliced at the first mastem he found. Their blades met and bounced off each other. The mastem threw a shard of ice at him. Arturo raised a hand and called a chunk of concrete up. It collided with the shard and shattered both elements in a cloud of dust and vapor.

Arturo stepped up to attack again, but the mastem was already dead. Its head rolled to stop at the feet of Anzu. The shedim glared at him and tightened his grip on his sword. He raised a hand and threw a fireball, but Arturo rolled to the side.

The fireball smashed into the head of a mastem right behind Arturo who had her sword held high to cut him down. She lit up like a feathered candle and her screams quickly died away. Arturo glanced from her burning corpse to Anzu.

"We'll finish this later," Anzu said. The shedim crossed the street to a trio of mastem who'd ganged up on another shedim.

Great, now he owed Anzu. What else could go wrong today?

Arturo blocked a blow from a mastem. He cut the mastem's wrist and the creature dropped its sword. He quickly reversed his momentum and cut its head off.

Another twenty mastem poured onto the street and he cursed. They couldn't hold this position. They were going to be overwhelmed by numbers alone. They needed to retreat.

Further down the block, Belial fought a large mastem with six wings of vivid green. The mastem somehow held his own blow for blow against the Boss.

Arturo joined the duo and sliced at the mastem's side. But the creature spun and parried the blow. He backed away from the sentinel and the Boss, watching both. Belial glanced at him and nodded.

Belial charged and Arturo followed. The mastem blocked as Belial and Arturo each slashed and stabbed. They gained more speed though as they fell into a mutual rhythm of attack and block, each compensating for the other's natural cadence.

The mastem dipped his sword a little too low to block a strike from Belial and Arturo struck. He plunged his sword into the mastem's chest before he could recover and Belial brought his scimitar across to remove the creature's head.

Belial started to move on, but Arturo grabbed his arm.

"We can't stay here," he said. "We need to fall back."

"No, we can't lose this street." Belial's eyes met his with a challenge to disagree.

The stubbornness of shedim. That's where Lorri got it from. "Look around you. We've already lost it."

Belial glanced up and down the street. His forces desperately fought, but they'd lost too many of their numbers. He opened his mouth and then closed it.

"Fall back!" he shouted.

Belial and Arturo ran to an alley that led further into Dogtown and ushered the retreating shedim down it. The mastem still on the street didn't follow for the moment, instead organizing themselves into formation. Their sense of order could be the defenders' only saving grace.

Two shedim stopped by Belial and Arturo recognized them as

two of the six that had followed him on the other side of the street. They shouted at him in shedimic but Arturo couldn't keep up with it.

Belial argued with them but their mouths were set as the last of their force ran past. The Boss hesitated a moment, then laid a hand on each of their shoulders and nodded. A shout rose up from the mastem and they swarmed forward toward the alley. Belial pushed Arturo ahead of him into the alley.

Arturo glanced back as the two shedim met the oncoming mastem head on, using the alley to bottleneck them. They were sacrificing themselves to give the rest of the force a chance to escape.

"Where does this go?" Arturo asked.

"Another street like the last. I don't know which."

"And if there are more mastem?"

Belial met his gaze. Nothing needed to be said. If there were more mastem, it would be a slaughter. There weren't enough of them left. The shedim would be killed for what they were and Arturo for helping them.

A bright flash erupted from behind them and Arturo and Belial spun around. A wall of flames blocked off the alley from any further pursuit.

"Where did that come from?" Belial asked.

The flames grew and roared up the alley toward them and Belial threw his hands up. The flames deflected upwards and over them, like a canopy of fire, but not before two figures jumped over the edge of the building next to the alley and landed in front of them.

"Thought you could use a hand," Lorri said. She and Lydia bowed to the Boss. Arturo smiled. He was glad to see them.

Belial waved a hand. "Bah, none of that. You don't have to bow after saving our skins."

"Your two shedim had just fallen when we reached the street," Lydia said. "I'm sorry."

Belial nodded. "They were good lads."

"How did you do that?" Arturo asked Lorri. "That was a lot of power."

Lorri shrugged. "I'm just that good."

Arturo raised an eyebrow, but Lydia answered. "We found an explosive that hadn't detonated. Lorri tinkered with it."

"Didn't want to leave it laying around. A kid could have found it."

Belial laughed. "Well, you picked a good time to use it."

"Indeed," Arturo said. "Thanks for the save. Where's Jamaal?"

Lorri took a drink from a canteen, then handed it to Lydia. "We heard battle from two different locations when we got inside the wall. Jamaal went to one and sent us here."

"Where was the other battle?" Belial asked.

"North of here, about three blocks," Lydia said.

The other shedim circled around and waited for Belial's orders. "Raysiel was gathering her forces north of here," he said. "We need to join her, rally together, and drive these mastem from our homes. Death to the mastem!"

"Death to the mastem!" his forces shouted.

Arturo certainly hoped so. The alternative didn't sound too appealing.

CHAPTER 24

Smoke filtered through the buildings as Arturo followed the shedim. Lorri and Lydia flanked him on either side, swords drawn and at the ready. They'd run for three blocks and reached the end of an alley that opened onto another main street where battle raged.

Belial charged out with a war cry, his shedim following closely behind and echoing him. The combination of volume and power chilled Arturo's spine and made the hairs on his arms stand on end. The shedim forces surged out onto the street around him and the twins.

He blocked Lydia and Lorri before they got caught up with the charge. He'd decided already to help the shedim as best he could, but he wasn't about to lead his team into a suicidal fight. His top priority was to find Jamaal first and make sure they all survived this.

Arturo surveyed the street before they moved. It was packed even tighter than the last battle, with at least a couple hundred ganastu in the fray and almost a third as many already dead or dying.

A large plume of smoke rose into the air as a shedim launched a fireball at a clump of mastem and blew them to pieces. A mastem across the street froze two shedim in place and shattered them with a mace. Above it all, screams rose and fell of both victory and pain.

A woman with a head full of tangled horns, who had to be the Boss Raysiel, threw her hands in the air and raised a sheet of concrete up to shield the shedim around her from a volley of ice shards. After the volley landed, she pressed her hands forward and the concrete exploded and peppered the attacking mastem.

Jamaal fought two mastem a couple storefronts down on the opposite sidewalk. Several shedim supported him and they held firm, bolstered by his presence. From their vantage, they likely thought they could withstand any attackers. Their backs were covered by the bulk of the shedim forces and the storefronts.

But from where Arturo stood at a slightly higher elevation, it was obvious they'd be overrun soon. Mastem continued to pour from an alley down the street. Already, they were massing together, like a giant hive preparing to launch its fighters.

"There," Arturo said, pointing to Jamaal.

They waded forward to their teammate. They needed to get him out of there.

Arturo slashed a mastem as they leapt towards him. They, he couldn't tell the gender because of their helmet, fell to the side while their wrist spurted blood. Lorri sliced crossways between their helmet and armor to separate their head from their orange feathered body.

Arturo cut down two more mastem in their mad charge, then he was at Jamaal. He threw a fireball over Jamaal's shoulder into a mastem who'd gotten a little too close. The flame caught and the mastem fell backwards, forcing his comrades out of the way. He rolled around for a few heartbeats before finally laying still.

"Thanks for showing up." Jamaal stabbed another mastem in the chest, then kicked him away. He had a couple cuts on his arms but otherwise looked unharmed.

"Sorry, got a little caught up. How long have you been here?"

"Twenty minutes or so."

Arturo glanced at him. He hadn't noticed from a distance, but up close, the early signs of fatigue were already setting in. Jamaal's arms moved slower than normal and his strikes didn't reach as far. Twenty minutes of fighting without any rest were taking their toll.

Arturo parried a blow, then pulled a knife and stabbed into a mastem's side. The creature screeched.

Jamaal grunted as another bashed her shield into him and knocked him into Arturo. The two stumbled but Jamaal recovered and stabbed forward. Not quick enough though as the mastem got her shield up to block.

Arturo spun to throw a fireball at her but stopped as a shedim rushed past them and launched himself through the air. He was unarmed save for his talons, but that didn't stop him as he landed on top of her shield and raked over it at the mastem's throat.

Her shriek turned to a gurgle as the shedim climbed closer, latched his jaw onto her head and, with a jerk, ripped it off before he leapt to another mastem. Arturo stared for a moment, then jerked back to reality.

"There are going to be at least thirty more mastem on us soon," Arturo yelled. "We can't fight them all. We don't have the numbers."

"Any suggestions?" Jamaal shouted.

All the fighting in Dogtown had to be converging here, especially with the sheer number of ganastu on the street. And the shedim weren't the majority by any means. They couldn't keep this up and Belial had to know it too. They had to fall back and save as many lives as they could.

The mastem before them parted and a familiar form stepped forward. Brilliant sapphire feathers coated him and his wings hung behind him like a regal cloak.

"Oriphiel," Arturo whispered.

Oriphiel stopped as his gaze fell on Arturo and his sentinels, his face blank. He radiated authority in his pristine armor. Gold filigree covered his breastplate in intricate, symmetrical designs. His sword was sheathed at his side and its jeweled hilt glinted in the sun.

He stepped forward with his empty talons held at his side. His forces spread around them but left Arturo, his sentinels, and the shedim nearest them untouched.

Arturo pointed his sword at his friend and Oriphiel stopped. "You were behind this all along. Why?"

Oriphiel met his glare with pain-filled eyes, orbs the size of saucers and deep as a crystal clear pool. "You know why. The shedim are a plague on this world. We are here to eradicate them."

The closest of Oriphiel's forces watched them but didn't attack yet, instead spreading out to shedim behind them.

Arturo shook his head. "I can't let you."

Tears welled in his eyes as Oriphiel took a step closer. "Yes, you can. This will make the world better for all of us. No more chaos to disrupt society. No more lives destroyed by shedimic greed. It's the only way, and you know this is true."

The mastemic nature inside him shifted from its smooth circling and lifted its head. Without the shedim in the world, order would rule. But did that make it right?

His mastemic nature rose higher and flexed its power. But his shedim wouldn't let go easily. It leapt up atop the mastem and the two roared as they sparked off each other.

Arturo winced as he separated them, then set his jaw. "No. You don't have the right. Killing them like this is wrong."

Oriphiel snarled. "Wrong? What these shedim do each and every day is wrong. They kill and spread their chaos to this city, to the world. They lead the souls of men from the ordered path and *that* is wrong. We're correcting all those wrongs."

The position where Oriphiel spoke from was an extremist view, order taken to the furthest. True, the shedim did sew chaos. But they weren't evil. The mastem wanted order but the means did not justify the end. "These shedim are innocents. I won't let you massacre them."

His shedimic and mastemic natures slipped out of his grip and smashed into each other. Each spread its power like a fast-creeping vine to snag as much dominance as possible, filling every fiber of his body. Arturo pressed his temple as pain beat like a hundred drums. Where his natures flexed out, his skin itched like power would sprout out of his pores.

"None of them are innocent. Now stand aside." The lines around Oriphiel's eyes softened. "Please. Don't force my hand."

Arturo shook his head. "No."

Oriphiel nodded and something inside him darkened. "Fine."

In a heartbeat, Oriphiel drew his sword and lunged forward. As

Arturo blocked, his natures collided again with renewed vigor. He blinked the spots in his vision away and barely kept Oriphiel's sword at bay. The crowd around them, held back by the short exchange, swarmed.

Oriphiel chopped again, and Arturo almost lost his sword from the ferocity of the blow. Oriphiel's full strength was like a sledgehammer on Arturo's arm and he prayed his own strength would hold. He parried Oriphiel's next two jabs, then slashed forward.

The mastem knocked him wide and slid his blade along Arturo's to the hilt. With a quick twist of his wrist, he cut the sentinel's forearm. Arturo pulled back so he didn't drop his sword.

"Join us, Arturo. Choose now. Choose the mastem."

Arturo slashed across and Oriphiel stepped back.

"Accept the mastemic. Do what is right. I'm begging you."

Arturo's mastem pressed forward harder than ever and the shedim responded in kind. They collided with a flash of light and a sharp pain ripped through his head.

"Stay out of my head," Arturo said.

"Don't die for this filth," Oriphiel said. "They aren't worth it."

"No!" Arturo grit his way through the white hot pain and struck forward blindly.

Oriphiel slapped the blade aside and out of Arturo's grip. Then he spun and kicked Arturo in the chest. Arturo fell backwards as his natures continued to gnaw at each other, sending bolts of lightning through his skull no matter how hard he tried to pull them apart.

As he hit the ground, a moment of clarity filled him. This was how it ended. Years of fighting for human souls, protecting life and enforcing the balance, only to die at the hands of his oldest mentor. He closed his eyes, and waited for the inevitable strike that would hit soon.

Metal clashed against metal and Lydia screamed, cutting through the pain in his head. His shedim and mastem leapt away from each other and the pain vanished.

He opened his eyes. Jamaal stood over him with Oriphiel's sword plunged through his gut and out his back, blood dripping from the tip.

Oriphiel withdrew his blade with a wet squelch and stepped back. Jamaal fell with a groan.

Oriphiel looked from Jamaal's body to Arturo. His arm bled where Jamaal must have scored a hit. But it wasn't enough.

An animalistic roar grew in Arturo's chest. He flung his hands up and threw a burst of flame at Oriphiel's face, but the mastem rolled out of the way. Arturo slid forward and pulled Jamaal over, cradling his head in one hand while applying pressure to his stomach with the other.

"Jamaal?"

Jamaal's eyes focused on him for a moment, then rolled back in his head.

"No, no, no…"

Oriphiel stood a few yards away and didn't try to get closer. "I didn't mean for any of you to get hurt. I never wanted that." He focused on Lorri and Lydia, who held their swords at the ready. "Think about the side each of you has chosen and what it's going to cost you. I will give you one day."

Oriphiel pulled a long silver whistle from a side pouch and blew three sharp trills. The mastem around the battlefield disengaged, leapt into the air, and soared straight into the smoke.

"One day," Oriphiel said before he took flight.

Lydia and Lorri rushed to Arturo and Jamaal. Lydia immediately pulled bandages from her pockets and pressed them into Jamaal's gut. They soaked through in seconds.

Tears streaked her cheeks. "He's bleeding too fast. I… I can't do anything. I don't know what to do."

Arturo glanced at the twins, then to Jamaal. This was his best friend. They'd stood together all these years. He'd always been there for Arturo. Memories flashed of the first time they met, the countless hours they'd trained and sparred together. His obsession with awful teas and the pranks they'd pulled on each other.

All of that was gone because he couldn't choose a nature sooner and it had finally caught up with him.

No. Jamaal couldn't die, not like this. Arturo wouldn't let him.

"Cool his body down. We'll take him to a hospital."

"A human hospital?" Lorri said.

Lydia wiped her cheeks. "We can't do that. The humans can't know we exist. You'd expose us all."

"I don't give a damn! He needs a doctor or he's going to die. Now do it!" He shook with anger and fear and sorrow. He'd do it himself, but his natures still sparked off one another. He couldn't guarantee he'd even be able to draw them now.

Lydia nodded and laid her hands on Jamaal's chest. She closed her eyes. Frost spread across his skin as she lowered his body temperature. His bleeding slowed but didn't completely stop. He couldn't stay like this for long but maybe, maybe it'd be long enough.

Belial rushed up with several shedim. Blood splattered his face and chest and chunks of bone were chipped from his armor. "St. Erin's. It's the closest hospital. Take him there. They'll take care of him." He yanked his cloak from his shoulders and helped Arturo roll Jamaal onto it. "My shedim will help you."

"Thank you."

Belial nodded. "No, thank you. We couldn't have survived any other way. Now go. And good luck."

Arturo nodded and together, the sentinels and shedim lifted Jamaal and ran.

CHAPTER 25

"Don't you dare die on me!" Arturo pressed on Jamaal's chest over and over again, tears streaming down his face.

They were almost there, practically on the doorstep of the hospital and he'd seized up and stopped breathing. Arturo leaned his ear to Jamaal's mouth. His friend sucked in a ragged breath.

"Better, better."

He couldn't die. Not when they were so close. They'd practically flown through the neighborhood. When they'd reached the still-burning wall, Belial had shifted the earth to create a tunnel beneath it to the outside world. And again, they'd run, never stopping until they reached the hospital.

He glanced up. The shedim who'd helped carry Jamaal were gone, probably back to Dogtown. He didn't blame them. They had their own families to check on. Lorri was gone, too, hopefully inside getting some help.

Lydia leaned down and felt Jamaal's pulse. "Still there," she whispered.

Jamaal was almost gray with blood loss. A normal human would have died far sooner, either from the loss of blood or the near freezing state Lydia had put him in.

"Over here," Lorri shouted. She ran through the emergency room doors, nurses and a doctor on her heels. The nurses wheeled a gurney between them and the doctor knelt next to Arturo.

The doctor, an older black woman with close cropped gray hair, listened to Jamaal's breathing with a stethoscope. "What happened? Why's he freezing?"

Arturo opened his mouth to speak but couldn't get the words to form.

"He was stabbed in the abdomen about ten minutes ago," Lydia said. "He's lost a lot of blood and just stopped breathing. His pulse is all over the place. But his body temperature is low enough to slow the bleeding somewhat."

"What was he stabbed with? A sword?"

"Yes," Arturo said. They'd brought Jamaal to human doctors, something he most definitely wasn't supposed to do. But Jamaal was in no condition for Arturo to withhold information that could help her treat him.

The doctor stared at him for half a heartbeat, no doubt taking in his blood-soaked gear and weapons. "Okay, let's get him inside." The nurses gathered around and grabbed the cloak. "Lift on three. One, two, three."

They laid Jamaal on the gurney and rolled him into the hospital. It was quiet in the ER, like the parking lot outside, surprising considering the explosions were only a handful of blocks away. Humans must not have been caught in the blast, otherwise the ER would be packed.

Jamaal convulsed, his arms and legs shaking. The nurses grabbed him and held on. His body bucked and thrashed and then he went limp. He exhaled and didn't take another breath.

"He's crashing!" The doctor jumped on the gurney and straddled Jamaal, pressing on his chest. "Let's get an IV running and some more blood in him. I want him in surgery now!"

"Jamaal!" Arturo shouted. He tried to stay next to the gurney as it passed through a set of double doors but a couple nurses blocked his way.

"I'm sorry, sir," one of them said. "You have to stay out here."

Arturo looked from the nurses past the doors. They swung shut and blocked his view of the gurney, the doctor still performing CPR. Was this the last time he'd see Jamaal alive? His stomach flipped and his heart felt like it would leap out of his throat.

He leaned against the wall and ran a hand over his head. Lorri and Lydia stood together, almost supporting each other from falling down.

Another doctor approached them. He glanced at their knives and swords sheathed on their arms and backs. "Do I need to call security?"

Lorri laughed, which, by the way he jerked, unsettled the man more.

"Sorry," Lydia said for her sister. "We won't cause any trouble. You have our word."

The doctor bit his lip. "Are any of you hurt? That's a lot of blood."

"A few scratches but we'll be fine. It's mostly not ours," Lorri said. She glared at Arturo. "We're the lucky ones." She shook her head and walked to the bathroom.

She blamed him, Arturo was sure of it. And she had every reason to. Hell, it was his fault. Jamaal jumped in front of Oriphiel's sword to protect him. But he shouldn't have had to. He wouldn't have if Arturo hadn't fooled himself into thinking he could control himself.

His shedim and mastem circled each other in the depths of his mind, two leviathans ready to assert their own dominance. Each had come so close to defeating the other. They'd gotten so powerful so fast. Or had they always been like this?

Whatever the case, they'd cost him. And would continue to fight harder than ever now that they'd had a taste of the potential to extend their power throughout his body and gain control.

He realized he stood alone outside the doors. Lydia must have gone off to the bathroom too. The doctor whispered into a phone behind the check-in desk. Probably talking to security. Arturo didn't care.

He fished his cell phone out of his pocket and stared at it. Normally, he'd call Oriphiel when anything horrible happened. It wasn't often, but he'd lost allies in the field before. Oriphiel had always been there to listen. But now? Now that was out of the question.

His second choice was usually Jamaal, but that might not ever happen again. He jerked his mind from that thought. No, Jamaal would be fine.

McLeod then. He needed to report in anyways. He hit dial as he sat in an uncomfortable chair in the waiting room and leaned his head against the wall.

McLeod answered after the second ring. "Where are you?"

"St. Erin's Hospital, right outside of Dogtown."

Silence echoed across the line before McLeod spoke. "Why are you at a human hospital? What happened?"

"Jamaal got hurt." Arturo swallowed the lump in his throat. "They've got him in surgery."

"What were you thinking, taking him to a human hospital? You know this risks all of our covers."

Of course he knew. He knew it as well as anyone. He'd willingly gone against every rule written to keep humans in the dark. And he'd do it again if it gave Jamaal a fighting chance.

The room blurred and he wiped his tears. "I wasn't going to let Jamaal die. It's my fault. I couldn't control myself and he got hurt saving me."

"Arturo, take a breath. It wasn't your fault."

McLeod's voice held a tone he hadn't heard him use before. Blame? No, this wasn't angry enough. Pity? McLeod warned him what would happen if he lost control, but he couldn't have imagined it would hurt his best friend.

"Are you there?" McLeod said.

"Yeah, I'm here." Arturo pulled his father's medallion from his shirt and rubbed it.

"All right. Keep me posted on Jamaal. How's everything else in Dogtown?"

Arturo sat up and focused. He still had his duties. He wiped his eyes again with a clean spot on his shirt, one of the only clean spots actually. "The attack was an initial act of war by the mastem and will be seen as such by the Bosses. We were able to repel it but only because Oriphiel called off his troops after stabbing Jamaal."

"Oriphiel led the attack?" McLeod's voice was tight.

"Yeah," Arturo said. He quickly explained everything he'd discovered at the airport and how Oriphiel had been connected. Arturo's history with Oriphiel wouldn't look good. McLeod knew how close they were. The Sentinalia did too. They'd ask questions, or use him as a scapegoat for the whole attack.

"Well, at least we have a little more time. I'll be on my way to the hospital soon. We'll deal with the humans later."

"Okay."

Arturo hung up and leaned back in his chair, staring up at the ceiling and beyond. He didn't believe in God. He never had. There was never a reason he needed to call on some deity who might not even be real. But in that moment, what did he stand to lose? Jamaal needed any and all the help he could get. Arturo bowed his head and prayed.

Lydia stared at herself in the bathroom mirror. Bags hung under her eyes. A cut under one cheek had already scabbed over. She didn't even remember getting cut. Blood was stuck in her hair and smeared and speckled across her face. She took several deep breaths, steadying herself.

From the stall behind her, the sound of heaving echoed as Lorri threw up again. This was hell, far from what she had ever hoped or wanted as a sentinel. Only a few days ago, they'd been celebrating a victory. Now...

The sounds of the battle echoed in her mind. The moment when Oriphiel rammed his blade into her teacher, into Jamaal, flashed through her mind. Someone had screamed and that scream had pierced through all the sounds of the battle. Only now did she realize it had been her scream.

She clenched her fists to try to stop them from shaking. As she glanced down, she noticed more blood covered them. It wasn't blood from the battle either. It was Jamaal's blood.

The intense, overwhelming desire to be completely clean seized her. She flung the hot water on and started scrubbing, grabbing a handful of paper towels and furiously pumping the soap dispenser again and again. She started with her hands, then moved up her forearms to her upper arms, her neck and face.

She scrubbed and scrubbed and scrubbed, until her pale skin glowed red.

"Hey, calm down," Lorri whispered. She squeezed Lydia's shoulder.

Lydia froze mid-swipe at her face again. Her breathing was ragged as the room stretched and shrank around her. She took a few deep breaths and everything settled back into place. The tile floor, the pink stalls, the smell of toilet bowl cleaner. All of it so mundane, so normal.

She turned the water off and stood there.

"Are you okay?" Lorri asked.

Lydia looked at her and opened her mouth to speak, but nothing came out. How did she put into words everything she was feeling right now?

She shook her head. "No. No, I'm not."

Lorri nodded and pulled Lydia in for a hug.

Part of Lydia was disgusted by the physical contact, the blood that was still on her sister and was probably on her again. But she pushed that feeling away. That was the mastem in her, she knew. This was Lorri, her sister.

"What's going to happen now?" Lydia whispered.

"I don't know," Lorri said. "We've got to hope the doctors can help Jamaal."

Tears streamed from Lydia's eyes and she pushed back from her sister. "And then what? Even if they do and Jamaal makes it through, what then? What if all this fighting turns into war and we can't stop it?"

Lorri shook her head. "We're going to handle it." She grabbed Lydia's shoulders. "Arturo and McLeod and us. We'll figure this out."

Lydia stared at her. Something was different in her. Or was she just telling Lydia what she wanted to here?

"Whatever it takes, we've got this. We can handle it." Lorri touched her cheek. "I'll take care of you. I swear."

Lorri, despite all her bluster and bravado, was always the one to step up. Even when they were younger, Lorri had defended her when other kids picked on her at school. But this was all so much more.

"Look, get some rest," Lorri said. "Get it while we can. Who knows when we'll get another chance."

Lydia nodded.

"I'm going to go find some food, okay? I'll bring something back for you."

Lydia just nodded again. She didn't know what else to say.

Lorri patted her on the shoulder and left the bathroom.

Lydia turned and stared at herself in the mirror. Her skin was all splotchy now, but the blood was mostly gone. It would have to do. The craze that had overcome her had faded at least.

She walked out of the bathroom and looked across the waiting room, over to Arturo. He lay with his head back against the wall, his eyes closed, and his mouth hanging open ever so slightly. He must have fallen asleep.

Blood covered him from head to toe, and if she hadn't been fighting right next to him, she'd be worried most of it was his.

She couldn't imagine how he was handling all of this. He'd slipped and fallen, was about to die, when Jamaal had jumped in the way. What must be going through his head right now?

Jamaal and Arturo were practically brothers. She couldn't imagine seeing Lorri sacrifice herself, just to save her life.

Lorri was right though. No matter what, they were going to get through this, all of them, together. They couldn't do it alone. There wasn't anything they could do for Jamaal right now, but they still had to take care of each other.

Lydia went back into the bathroom to grab some wet paper towels. Arturo needed his rest but he couldn't be left covered in blood.

Arturo opened his eyes a heartbeat later and shot straight up out of his chair, the same chair from the waiting room. A burned wasteland surrounded him instead of the pink wallpaper and tiled floor of the hospital. Smoke and steam rose into the sky and the odor of charred wood and scorched flesh filled his nostrils.

Blackened bodies lay all around him, blown outwards like he'd stood at the center of an explosion. A single tree stood ten feet from him, its skeletal frame crumpled and broken. The remains of a house popped and snapped as embers continued to smolder.

Light glinted off a piece of metal that hung around the neck of the body nearest him.

Recognition dawned on him. How couldn't it? He'd dreamt of this place nearly every night since his thirteenth birthday. It was the house he grew up in, or what was left of it. The bodies were his childhood friends. His little brother, his parents, his entire family, they were the ones closest to him. They were all dead because of him and the power he'd unleashed.

He'd dreamt of the moments leading to his powers emerging more times than he could count, never changing anything no matter how hard he tried. But he always woke up when those powers emerged. He never relived waking up, Oriphiel finding him and taking him to the sentinels.

And now, he was acutely aware that this had to be a dream. He smacked himself but couldn't wake up.

"What did you do?"

He spun on his heel. Jamaal stood at the edge of the ring of bodies around him, completely fine. No wounds, no blood. But he stared at Arturo with such a look of fear, of terror and distrust. Jamaal had never looked at him that way.

Arturo tilted his head. What was Jamaal talking about? All sentinels experienced this kind of destruction.

"I didn't mean for this to happen. You know that. None of us do."

Jamaal had caused a dozen tornadoes to drop on his apartment building, destroying everything for a few blocks.

"You could have at least—"

He stopped and scrunched his face. He arched his back and screamed as the tip of a sword ripped through his chest, covered in overly bright red blood.

"Jamaal!" Arturo lunged forward but stopped as Oriphiel poked his head over his friend's shoulder.

The mastem cracked a maniacal grin. "This is your fault, too, sentinel."

No. It wasn't his fault. This was all a dream.

The bodies around him moved. First an arm here, then a leg there. In a few heartbeats, the remains of his family and friends rose to their feet and shambled in around him. Their grotesque, half-cooked bodies cracked and flaked with each step.

Oriphiel spread his wings to encompass Jamaal, who gasped for air and shuddered in the mastem's grip. As Oriphiel grinned, his face shifted. A beak extended from his face while horns sprouted over his head. Scales and feathers mixed across his features. One eye brightened to blue and the other darkened to red.

"It's always been your fault," Oriphiel said, his voice taking on a mixture of deep bass and the screech of nails on a chalkboard.

"No, I didn't mean to hurt them," Arturo said. "I didn't mean it, Jamaal."

Jamaal raised his hand out to Arturo. "Help... me..."

The shedim-mastem-monster-Oriphiel cackled as his skin glowed. Power built in him and then he exploded, enveloping Jamaal in light.

The light faded and Jamaal's smoking corpse collapsed to the ground.

Arturo fell to his knees with a cry of pain.

Behind Jamaal, the explosion that was Oriphiel split into two entities, one of fire and one of water, swirling and roaring. The two screaming furies launched into the air, spreading from each other.

The corpses around Arturo closed in, moaning.

The elements circled Arturo and their screeches grew louder and louder, like a thousand cicadas. He covered his ears as blood trickled from his burst eardrums. The entities stopped and flew straight at him.

He screamed as they collided in a bright flash of light.

Arturo jerked awake in his chair, his hand clutched around a knife sheathed on his forearm. The hospital waiting room surrounded him again, quiet and mostly empty. A security guard stood by the doors and watched them, his hand on a taser. Arturo let go of the knife and flexed his fingers, which tingled like little ants crawled below his skin.

Lorri slept on a couch across from him, her arm thrown over her face to block the light. The cuts and scratches on her arms flaked and peeled, almost healed. She snored lightly.

The clock above her head read 11:23 p.m. He'd slept almost twelve hours.

"Are you okay?" Lydia sat next to him, a tissue held out.

Arturo grabbed it and wiped his face, particularly the tears that dripped down his face. "Yeah, I'm fine." The tissue came away clean. The skin on his hands and arms were clean too. But he'd been covered in blood from the battle before.

Lydia smiled. "When we got back from the bathroom, you were already passed out. I didn't think you'd want to stay covered in blood."

Arturo stared at her. It was a kindness he didn't deserve. "Thanks."

"No problem," she said. "I couldn't do much for your clothes unfortunately. Or for ours." She hesitated. "Are you really okay? You don't sound like it."

"Just a nightmare, that's all." A chill crept up his spine as the dream replayed in his head.

"Want to talk about it?"

"No, I'm fine."

Lydia touched his shoulder. "Come on, I can help."

Who else did he have to talk to? He'd already lost one friend and mentor today, and a second was on the operating table. And Lydia was definitely the kinder of the twins.

"Okay. I'm standing where my power emerged when I was thirteen. My family is dead all around me, burned alive."

Lydia cringed. "Lorri was fire, too. I was ice. Thank God we had separate birthday parties."

Arturo nodded but wasn't really listening to her. He was enveloped in the memory, both of the dream and that day nearly fifty years earlier. "I've dreamt it so many time. But never what came after. And this was different."

Lydia tilted her head. "What did you see?"

Arturo took a deep breath. Maybe he shouldn't talk with an apprentice. Professionalism needed to be maintained, and to be talking about his own fears seemed a bit too much.

Before he could decide to share the rest of his nightmare, the door to the waiting room swung open and the doctor who'd taken Jamaal back walked through, drying her hands on a towel. She whispered to the security guard and shooed him away, then pulled up a chair by Arturo and Lydia.

"Hello, my name is Doctor Lawson."

"Arturo. And this is Lydia."

"A pleasure. I just got out of surgery with your friend, I believe you said his name was Jamaal?"

He was still alive. Arturo felt his hopes rise but knew better than to depend on those. "Yes. How is he?"

"Sedated and in critical condition to say the least. A sword through the gut will do that. But before we can move any further, I need to know what he is."

Arturo met Lydia's gaze for half a heartbeat before he spoke. "I'm sorry. What do you mean?"

Doctor Lawson raised an eyebrow. "I know he isn't a shedim. We tested his blood with ice before the procedure. And the heat from our lasers didn't have any effect, so he isn't a mastem either. So I'm asking you, what is he?"

The room spun a little. How did she know about the shedim and mastem? Humans weren't supposed to have that kind of knowledge. And certainly no mastem or shedim would want a human to know their weaknesses.

"We don't know what you're talking about," Lydia said.

"Please. I know you all aren't human. Why do you think I cancelled the call for the police? I just need to know of anything to avoid so I don't accidently kill my patient. He's already healing faster than any normal human has a right to, but slower than the other species. But he also doesn't have any of their weaknesses."

She paused, waiting for them to respond. He'd broken enough rules today. He didn't need to keep doing it. She didn't need to know what they were in order to treat Jamaal. He shook his head.

"All right, if you don't want to tell me what he is, fine. Just tell me if there's anything I should stay away from when treating him."

The doctor was smart, he had to give her that. And they owed her for not calling the cops on them, which was probably hospital procedure for a violent crime. This information wouldn't hurt.

"No, there's nothing you need to avoid," Arturo said. "Treat him like you would any human. Just speed up your timetable."

"Good. Then assuming he doesn't develop any sort of infection or other complication from the surgery, the next twenty-four hours will be the most crucial in his recovery. I wouldn't say any longer. But if the wound does become infected, our options are going to become extremely limited. Our treatment will need to be quick and quite aggressive. Are there any family members we need to call? I need authorization to treat."

"No," Arturo said. "We're his family. Do what you have to do."

Doctor Lawson hesitated, then nodded. "All right. Do you have any questions for me?"

"How do you know about the shedim and mastem?" Lydia said.

Doctor Lawson waved a hand around the hospital. "When you've worked in the ER as long as I have, you see cases that can't be explained. I've seen some of the worst trauma wounds imaginable heal miraculously. It took a bit of snooping but I've seen my fair share of shedim and mastem, especially here in Dogtown."

Did Belial know about her? Was that why he sent them to this particular hospital, not just because of how close it was to the neighborhood? Arturo doubted Belial was that oblivious. But the sentinels didn't think the average human knew about ganastu, so maybe the Bosses were the same.

"So you always check your patients before treating them?" Lydia said.

"No, but after the explosions and the sword wound, I figured you probably weren't human. I'm still curious about what exactly you are though?"

"We're something else," Arturo said. He shook his head at Lydia, who had the grace to defer to his decision. "Can we see our friend now?"

The doctor narrowed her eyes and stared at him. But he didn't look away and she sighed. "He's being moved to the ICU. You can see him in about an hour, but he'll be sedated for most of the night."

"Thank you," Arturo said.

"You're welcome. I'll send a nurse out when he's settled." Dr. Lawson left them in silence.

Arturo shuddered at how close Jamaal stood to death's doorstep. He'd seen a lot of people die from similar wounds, some of them sentinels. The risk of infection and complication was smaller for them than humans but it still posed a real threat. But there wasn't anything he could do about that save trust Dr. Lawson's skills as a surgeon.

Lydia laid a hand on his arm. "What's wrong? It's great news."

"He isn't out of the woods yet."

"You heard her," Lydia said. "Have some faith that he'll pull through."

Arturo shook his head. "He shouldn't have to. He wouldn't even be in this situation if it wasn't for me."

"No, he tried to fight Oriphiel off because he was going to kill you. That's what friends do."

"It was my fault. I shouldn't have even been in the field." It was all his fault. The Oriphiel of his dream had been right.

"No," Lydia said. "It was an accident."

"Yes," Arturo snapped. "Jamaal got stabbed because I couldn't make up my damned mind. And because I couldn't decide, he might be dead tomorrow. Everything that's happened has been my own fault, my own inability."

"Arturo, that's not true."

What did she know? She was still so young. She'd picked her own nature early and didn't have any worries about control. Not like he did.

"It is true. I wasn't in control at the park and that's why I butchered that shedim. I almost lost it with Marut. Hell, even at The Trolley, Anzu almost killed me because I wasn't focused enough."

"Any of us could have made those mistakes."

Arturo took short breaths and his hands trembled. "I can't afford mistakes. Not when your lives are at risk. I'm not in control anymore. Not at all. My natures are getting stronger and they're going to get someone killed. They might have already killed Jamaal. I can't be responsible for killing one of you two—"

Lydia smacked him.

Heat bloomed across his face as pain radiated into his jaw and made his eyes water. He couldn't remember what he wanted to say, tried to stammer some kind of response or reprimand, anything. But he couldn't even think straight. Did she actually just hit him? He blinked a few times and stared at her.

Lydia rubbed her hands together. "I'm sorry." Her own voice was quiet and shaky. "But you need to keep it together. You can't lose it, not now when the mastem are on the brink of starting an all-out war. We need you."

"But I can't choose—"

"Who cares? You've made it this long controlling them. You can do it a little longer."

"No, I can't. That's what got me into this mess, thinking like that. Things are just going to spiral from here."

Lydia threw her hands up. "Let me give you some advice. We're sentinels, part shedim, part mastem, *and* part human. Our humanity makes us stronger than either of the others. Which means we can control those tendencies that rule ganastu. We make our own decisions and use our inner shedim or mastem. They don't use us. So choose a nature, don't choose a nature, it's not going to change things. You need to realize that."

Arturo shook his head. "It's not so simple."

"It is. You're just too scared to see it." Lydia stormed out of the room.

Arturo stared after her, his mouth hanging open.

She was right. He was scared. He'd spent almost four decades without being able to pick what came so easily to most sentinels.

Every time he'd get close to a decision, the nature would rear its head and force him to act irrationally, to second guess himself. Or he'd see a young sentinel change when they chose, start to exhibit the chaotic or ordered tendencies of the nature that now influenced them. It wasn't always a strong effect, but he'd seen it. He didn't want to risk that kind of lack of control.

So he'd settled on controlling both of them. But after all these years and without him even knowing it, both had grown stronger. If he embraced one now, what kind of effect would it have on him?

"She's right, you know?" Lorri stood from the couch. How long had she been awake? "I've hated the fact that you are my instructor since you showed me you hadn't chosen a nature. I wanted to have someone who knew everything there was to know about the shedim inside me." She took a deep breath. "You have no idea how infuriating it is to not get that."

Arturo opened his mouth but Lorri raised a hand.

"But that doesn't matter anymore. As much as I don't want to admit it, Lydia and I can't beat Oriphiel and the other mastem on our own. Especially since Jamaal's hurt. Whether or not it was your fault doesn't really matter now. We need you."

With that, she walked out of the waiting room too. Arturo stared at the wall but he might as well have been a million miles away. He didn't know what to do anymore. Better that he'd been stabbed by Oriphiel rather than Jamaal. At least then someone could be strong enough to lead the hunt for the mastem.

CHAPTER 26

Arturo stood outside the hospital room the nurse had led him to. Lorri and Lydia hadn't returned when the nurse came to find him, and even if they had, she'd said only one person was allowed back at a time, with it being so late and visiting hours over.

Arturo took a deep breath and opened the door.

Jamaal had a private room and breathed deeply in his drug-induced sleep. His eyelids fluttered every few moments but didn't open. A bandage covered his abdomen and almost blended in with the cream sheets and blankets that covered his lower half.

Monitors beeped with the rise and fall of his chest. His heartbeat held steady and strong, much stronger than before the surgery but not quite where Arturo thought it should have been. But he said a silent thanks nonetheless. At least his friend didn't need any breathing tubes or machines. Arturo had expected to see so much worse when he entered.

He approached the bed and eased himself into a chair next to it. Its corners were frayed, like the sheets on the bed, a reminder of how little funding a hospital in this neighborhood actually received. But the room was clean, which would minimize the chances for infection. It gave Jamaal that much more of a chance.

But his dark skin still held an ashy tone to it that hadn't disappeared with the increase in his body temperature. He'd lost so much blood and he had a long fight ahead to heal himself.

"I'm sorry, my friend." Arturo squeezed Jamaal's hand. "I wish I could go back and change all of this, just choose a nature and stick with it. Maybe then you wouldn't..." A lump caught in his throat and he swallowed a shudder. "I'm sorry I let you down," he whispered.

Sure, it was easy to say it now. But the truth remained that Jamaal was laid out on a hospital bed while he walked around fine. The nurse said he'd be unconscious for several more hours but his recovery looked promising. All they could do was wait. Was that enough though?

And time wasn't exactly what Arturo wanted. He replayed the battle over and over in his head. The moment his powers surged forward and blinded him. Lydia's scream. The sickening sound of Oriphiel's blade as it slid out of Jamaal.

Oriphiel. Arturo squeezed Jamaal's hand harder. Arturo had never been betrayed like this. The sentinels were a close-knit community, rivaling the familial bonds of even the shedim. And Arturo had always been able to rely on Oriphiel like a pseudo-grandfather.

Arturo would kill him for all of this. For causing so much destruction and chaos. For hurting Jamaal.

And the mastem preached about order. This was pure chaos. And it was all Oriphiel's fault.

But was it really? Arturo couldn't blame Oriphiel for everything. The blame was in part his. He couldn't shirk that. He should have chosen a nature by now. He should be the one on the hospital bed. Jamaal should never have needed to save him from Oriphiel.

He went round and round in circles of blame and guilt.

"What do I do, old friend?"

A knock sounded at the door and McLeod entered. Dark bags hung under his eyes and his shoulders were hunched more than usual. He wore a loose jacket with black pants but there were a few bulges here and there, no doubt knives placed for easy access.

McLeod walked up to Arturo and clasped his hand, then pulled him in for a hug. Arturo leaned into that hug for a moment, appreciating the support more than he could explain.

"How is he?" McLeod asked.

"Stable," Arturo said as he stepped back. "Just drugged. The doctor says if he can get past the chance of infection, he's got a good shot."

"Good. Good." McLeod patted Jamaal's arm. "Sorry it took me so long."

Arturo glanced at the clock on the wall. It was well after midnight. "Where have you been? I mean, there isn't much you could have done, but..." He glanced over his mentor's shoulder out the window by the door.

A woman with stark white hair, high cheekbones, and a nose like a hawk leaned against the opposite wall with a cell phone held to her ear. Her gaze met his with a piercing intensity until he looked away.

"Who's she?"

McLeod's shoulders sagged a fraction of an inch more. "That's Dahlia. She's the reason I didn't get here sooner." He paused. "She's our rep on the Sentinalia."

Arturo snapped his attention back to McLeod. "The Sentinalia? What's going on? Has there been another attack?" Oriphiel had said they had a day.

McLeod urged for Arturo to calm down with raised hands. "Easy. There haven't been any more attacks since Dogtown. Several teams of sentinels have flown in from Chicago, Kansas City, and New Orleans to help contain the conflict. They arrived about ten minutes after we spoke earlier."

"So you got them settled in. Perks of the job." It explained why McLeod had only just gotten down to the hospital but didn't explain why one of the Sentinalia had shown up in the field.

"They've already deployed into the city and made contact with the Lords and Bosses," McLeod said. "Both sides have agreed to meet to discuss a truce."

"But Oriphiel was behind the attacks. And he had a pretty decent size force backing him."

"And both races realize that. Oriphiel might not be a Lord, but he spread the lie that the shedim were responsible for the attack and convinced many to strike who wouldn't have otherwise. They didn't know they were acting against the orders of the Lords. He's always been loyal. The betrayal's a surprise to everyone."

That was an understatement.

"Both groups have agreed to talk but only with sentinel supervision at an undisclosed location. That's why Dahlia's here. We'll be providing security for the talks along with a handful from both races while she mediates the negotiations."

"And while they're meeting, we can find Oriphiel?"

Dahlia stormed into the room and McLeod's shoulders tensed. The heat rose several degrees and a bead of sweat trailed down Arturo's neck. His shedim recognized its kindred spirit and tried to rear its head but Arturo knocked it back. Now wasn't the time.

"You will not, sentinel," she said, her voice as sharp as her stare. "You are relieved of your duties, effective immediately."

"Excuse me?"

McLeod shook his head but Arturo ignored him.

"You can't—"

"Don't presume to give me orders, boy. You heard me. It's too much of a risk to put you back in the field. You may already be compromised after your connection to the mastem Oriphiel. You can't be allowed to cause more damage."

Arturo's shedim and mastem both snarled at the insult, then at each other as they sparked with more white lightning. He lifted a hand to his temple as he focused on each to push them back down. "I'm not in league with Oriphiel."

"Maybe not, but you have no control of your natures."

"I'm fine."

"Clearly not. You can't even take this reprimand without fighting for control. How do you expect to deal with the stress of the field?" She glared at McLeod, who to his credit held her gaze. "You should've been removed from duty the moment it became apparent your control was compromised."

"He hasn't had any problems like this before," McLeod said.

"When *exactly* did you first notice he was losing control?"

When McLeod didn't immediately answer, Arturo turned to him and McLeod cringed.

"Well?" Dahlia demanded.

"Three weeks ago."

Arturo couldn't believe it. McLeod hadn't approached him until three days ago, but he'd known for weeks that Arturo was struggling? Arturo hadn't even realized something was off until a week ago and even then, he'd chalked it up to exhaustion. How could his old instructor have stayed quiet, knowing what it could lead to, what it had led to?

"Exactly," Dahlia said. "Arturo Morales, once the current crisis you have failed to abate is taken care of, you will be returned to the Academy to be evaluated for your feasibility as a sentinel. We will also assess your threat to others. Until then, you will not partake or interfere with any sentinel operations. Do you understand your orders?"

Arturo clenched his jaw and bit back a comment about where she could shove her orders. "Yes, ma'am."

"Good, now I have other preparations to attend to so that we can get all of these hostilities under control." She left the room without so much as a glance at Jamaal.

How could this all go wrong now? He'd lost control and gotten Jamaal hurt, nearly killed. And now, he was pulled from the field, denied the opportunity to hunt Oriphiel down and stop him from hurting anyone else.

"I'm sorry," McLeod said. "I should have said something sooner."

And him. McLeod knew he'd been slipping for so long and hadn't said anything. If he'd said something before a crisis had been upon them, could he have avoided this altogether? Could he have kept Jamaal from getting hurt, found Oriphiel out before he'd caused so much pain? But McLeod had just stayed silent.

"Why?" Arturo said. "Why didn't you help me?"

"I had faith in you. Faith you'd figure this out on your own. You're the best sentinel I've ever seen. I didn't think you would let it go this far without making a choice."

"Do you think I wanted this?" Arturo pointed at his best friend sedated on the bed. "Do you think Jamaal would've gotten hurt if I could have chosen? Dammit, McLeod, I can't choose. I can't. Neither option is the right one for me."

"But you have to choose," McLeod said. "If you don't, they'll lock you up, let your warring natures drive you mad, and when the power explodes out of you again, it won't be able to hurt anyone else."

Both his shedimic and mastemic natures called out to him, urged him to choose. Their songs were sweet and seductive. If he chose one, it would rule his mind and thoughts. He'd lose the balance he'd fought for and forever lean towards chaos or order.

No matter what anyone said, he wouldn't let that happen. To lose himself in one side over the other scared him more than anything. "I can't. I just can't."

"Then I can't help you. I have my own orders that I have to follow. Once the negotiations are over, the Sentinalia will decide what to do with you. Decide by then."

So that's the way it was then. It came down to this. A day or so of freedom. Even if he wanted to, he didn't think he could make a decision this life-changing in a single day.

"What about Lorri and Lydia?"

"Their orders are to remain in the hospital for the time being. They'll watch over Jamaal and you."

Arturo smirked. "You mean they'll make sure I don't do anything I'm not supposed to."

"Their orders are to make sure both of you are kept safe. If Jamaal pulls through, Lydia will resume her training with him, but Lorri will be reassigned, likely to whoever is sent in as your replacement."

It was standard protocol, one he had dealt with in the past. He'd taken on a couple apprentices who had lost their instructors but it was usually after they were killed in the field. They didn't go mad first.

A loud tap shook the window. Dahlia glared through it and McLeod held up a hand.

"Are all the Sentinalia so cold?" Arturo said. What he really meant was, were they so cruel?

McLeod pursed his lips. "No, Dahlia and I, well, let's just say we've worked closely before."

Arturo raised an eyebrow. There were so many layers to that statement he wasn't sure where to start.

"I have to go," McLeod said. "I'm sorry. Stay here and wait for the negotiations to conclude. I'll do what I can to keep you out of trouble."

"It's all right." Arturo sat back in the chair by Jamaal's bedside. "I did this to myself."

McLeod patted his shoulder once before he left the room.

Arturo's gaze fell on the rise and fall of Jamaal's chest but his mind drifted.

He'd been a sentinel since he turned thirteen, over forty-six years now. Practically his whole life. Not that he'd have much of a life once the Sentinalia locked him away. He'd thrown himself into being the best he could be, in perfecting his control and saving lives whenever he could. He'd dedicated himself to balance, both the balance sentinels protected and balance within himself.

Where had he gone wrong? What more could he do?

He could choose.

His shedim and mastem both perked up.

He could flip a coin and choose one over the other, fully embrace it. Anything would be better than going mad and forever losing his place as a sentinel. Arturo pulled a quarter out of his pocket.

Heads, shedim. Tails, mastem. Whatever landed, that's what he'd choose.

He flipped the coin. It soared in the air and as it fell, he caught it and slapped it on the back of his hand. This was it.

He pulled his hand away. Heads. The shedim it was.

Arturo closed his eyes, felt his natures. This was it then. No turning back. He took a deep breath and opened his mind for his shedim to leap forward. It roared upwards, spreading into his body, then screamed as his mastem slammed into it. The two spun and clashed, striking into each other.

Pain flashed in his head, cutting through his mind. He tried to push the mastem back down, give the shedim he'd chosen the space to assume control. But the mastem bucked his control off and bit into the shedim. It jerked away as the white hot pain seared through both natures and Arturo.

He grabbed them both and pushed them away, back down to his center. They reluctantly settled away from each other. He opened his eyes and took several deep breaths. Sweat coated his brow and he unclenched his fists from the arms of the chair.

He literally couldn't choose now. Both had grown to such power, such strength that it wouldn't give way to the other. What was he going to do? He'd waited too long. He couldn't be here when he finally lost all control. But he'd been ordered to stay.

He stood to leave but stopped in the door frame and looked back at Jamaal. "I'm sorry, my friend. Stay strong."

Arturo wandered into the hallway. Nurses and doctors working the nightshift drifted past him, paying more attention to their work than him. He envied them, like he envied Kelly. They didn't know what was going on, the war that was so close to spilling over into their lives. They didn't care if he lost his mind trying to save them all or if the Sentinalia tucked him away for the safety of society.

He couldn't fault them for that. What right did he have to do that? All he could do now was follow his orders, stay in control long enough for the Sentinalia to get him as far away from the people he cared about so he didn't hurt anyone else.

CHAPTER 27

Arturo made his way out to the waiting room a few hours later. He'd wandered the hospital floors, passing Jamaal's door several times but unable to bring himself to go in again. Now, he stood at the waiting room door, watching Lorri and Lydia. They sat on a couch together, each with their cell phone out. Lorri played some video game, tapping away with abandon, while Lydia flipped through pages of text. Even when they were relaxed, the two sisters were so radically different. Was it because they chose opposite natures, or had they ever shared any interests?

He moved around the couch and sat in a chair. "Hey."

The twins jumped and immediately put their phones away.

"How's Jamaal?" Lydia said.

"He's fine for now," Arturo said. He hoped that wouldn't change.

"What about you?" Lydia cocked an eyebrow as Arturo rubbed his face where she'd smacked him.

"I've been better," he said.

"We heard our orders," Lorri said. "We're stuck here instead of out tracking that bastard mastem down."

"It's protocol. Look, both of you, I'm sorry for what happened. I didn't mean for any of this." He met Lorri's gaze. "At least now you'll get a new instructor. It's what you've wanted since you got here."

Lorri stared at him for a moment then looked away, her brow creased. She fingered one of the knives on her belt. "It is what it is."

Arturo nodded. She didn't need to hide her disdain for him any longer.

"It's not fair," Lydia said. "You made one mistake and they're going to punish you by taking your command? In the middle of all this?"

"It was more than just this one mistake. I've been slipping for a while now. I just haven't wanted to admit it, not even to myself."

"Well, they could have at least waited until we found Oriphiel to take you out of the field," Lorri said. "If anyone could find him, you could. You know him pretty well, right?"

Arturo chuckled. "I appreciate the vote of confidence. But the Sentinalia are doing what's best for everyone. There isn't any more we can do."

Lorri rolled the ring in her eyebrow and Lydia pursed her lips. Neither of them wanted to hear it. He wasn't too thrilled himself but as he'd wandered the hospital halls, he'd accepted it. He'd lived his life by the Sentinalia's orders and rules, or as close to them as he could. And while he didn't always agree with them, he tried to mostly follow them, or at least use any loopholes to get around them. And there wasn't much wiggle room here. He'd dug this hole, and there was no way to climb out of it.

Lydia pointed over his shoulder and Arturo glanced back.

Kelly caught sight of them as she entered the waiting room and lifted a hand. Her face and clothes were stained with soot. She had a small bag slung over her shoulder and her left hand was wrapped in gauze.

"I was told you guys might still be here," she said as she joined them and sat on the arm of the couch. "I heard Jamaal got hurt pretty bad."

"Told by who?" Arturo said. McLeod was the only one who knew where they were.

"A guy down in Dogtown. Said his name was Elial. I feel like I've heard it before."

Lorri laughed. "That's unoriginal."

"His name's Belial," Arturo said at Kelly's confused glance. "And he's another Boss."

"Belial?" Kelly said. "Are all the major crime bosses in the world shedim?"

"Pretty much," Lydia said. "They can't help it."

"What's that supposed to mean?" Lorri shoved her sister.

"Oh, you know what I meant." Lydia shoved her back.

Kelly ignored them. "Anyways, I wanted to come down and see how Jamaal was doing?"

"The next twenty-four hours are the most crucial but things look promising." Arturo pointed at her bandaged hand. "Have a bit of trouble yourself?"

Kelly glanced at her hand. "Oh, this? It's nothing. Burned it on a piece of metal."

"How's everything out there?" Lydia said.

Arturo bit his tongue. They weren't supposed to be involved in the investigation anymore. They didn't need information on the neighborhood, but he was curious too. And this didn't strictly pertain to the investigation.

"We were finally able to get the flames under control," Kelly said. "It was rough going but then they just started receding. I assume the shedim helped."

"A good assumption," Lorri said. "Especially if all the fires died down together."

"Yeah, it was pretty much all at the same time. We got the perimeter under control and moved into the neighborhood, but didn't find many bodies. The ones we did find all looked human enough."

"The Bosses would've made sure to get the ones who couldn't pass as human off the street as soon as they could," Arturo said. "I wouldn't count on holding onto any of the other bodies either though."

"Like our friend Mr. Duodu?"

Arturo nodded.

"Well, that's fine I suppose." She reached into her bag and pulled out a plastic bag. Inside it were a few pieces of scorched metal. "We salvaged more debris from the bombs, like at the airport. Initial reports say it's the same construction, same materials, just more of them. But we still haven't placed where they were made or where the components came from."

Arturo pulled a piece of metal from the bag. It was heavy, denser than he'd expected. Probably helped the shrapnel survive the intense heat of the blast. A faint, familiar blue tinge reflected off its surface in the light. He passed the bag to Lorri.

She pulled out another piece and sniffed it. "Potassium chloride, gasoline, some other flammable liquids. Homemade but definitely professional. Whoever made these must have known exactly what they were doing to create the types of explosions and heat we saw."

"Our analysts have identified the explosive compounds. But most of the materials could be found at several locations here in the city. Although, like you said, it'd take a professional to know what to use to make a bomb like this. The only unknown is the metal."

Arturo tuned Kelly out as he rubbed his finger over the metal. He grabbed a paper cup of water that one of the twins had been drinking from and poured a little water onto it. The soot wiped away and showed bright blue metal underneath. It was a very specific shade of blue between cobalt and navy.

"I know where the metal's from," he said.

Kelly stopped mid-sentence. "What?"

"Oriphiel's brooch, the one you have in evidence, is made of the same metal. It was designed and manufactured at an old foundry in South County. Oriphiel used to have stock in the company but it's been shut down for ten or fifteen years now."

"That has to be where they're making the bombs," Lydia said.

"Then let's get down there and stop them." Lorri grabbed her jacket from the couch. Lydia and Kelly got to their feet, ready to go.

"We can't." It hurt to say it but he couldn't let the apprentices go.

"We can't afford to wait. We need to stop them before anyone else gets hurt," Kelly said.

"I want to help you, but we have our orders," he said. His palms itched with the desire to leap to his own feet and head out.

Lorri and Lydia glanced at each other, then to Kelly.

"Arturo was removed from command for losing control in the

field," Lydia said. "Our orders are to keep him and Jamaal safe until we're summoned."

Kelly stammered as she looked at each of them. "So you're going to sit here even though we have a real lead?"

Was that what he was going to do? He'd been told in no uncertain terms to stand down. He hated to admit it but he understood why Dahlia had issued this order. Jamaal was proof enough. He'd tried to gain control by choosing one nature and even that hadn't worked.

"I'll call McLeod and let him know," he said. "He'll send sentinels to investigate once the negotiations are done."

"That'll take too long and you know it," Lydia said. "They're focused on the negotiations and nothing else. We have to stop Oriphiel. He can't be allowed to escape and you're the only one who can put an end to him. Lorri and I don't have the experience to take him on. We need you."

"We have our orders," he said. Both of his natures rolled around each other, sending off little sparks. They wanted to go, to be used, but he couldn't trust them anymore.

"To hell with our orders." Lorri stepped up to him and jabbed a finger into his chest. "I may not think you're the best instructor in the world but you've taught me that we don't quit on a mission and we definitely don't quit on each other, no matter the risk. We see it through to the end. And we're going to do just that. For Jamaal."

Arturo met her gaze, stared past the brilliant blue of her eyes, and knew she wasn't going to be stopped. With or without him, she was going to hunt Oriphiel. And she wanted him with her. He raised an eyebrow.

Kelly pulled out her badge. "Arturo Morales, I'm hereby detaining you for questioning regarding the attacks in Dogtown. You are to come with me to FBI headquarters immediately."

"What?" What was she talking about?

"But before we go downtown," she continued, "we have to make a stop at a certain foundry to follow up on a lead. You will remain in my custody until we're done questioning you. Understood?"

The human was crazy but Arturo nodded.

"All right. And seeing as how these two young ladies have orders to follow you, I guess all three of you will have to come with me."

Arturo chuckled. Loopholes. That was all they needed. "Well, I wouldn't want to argue with law enforcement and risk an incident." This could work. It was a longshot but maybe something could come of it.

At least if it didn't work out, the twins had a legitimate excuse as to why they hadn't stayed at the hospital.

"Good," Kelly said. "Because I'd hate to have to cuff you again."

Arturo grinned. "Let's go."

His shedim and mastem both sparked again off each other as Arturo followed Kelly out of the hospital. They sensed battle and both were ready to leap at another chance to dominate him. He soothed each, pressed them back down. He needed a little more time. Just enough control to find Oriphiel, to stop him. Then he could let it all go.

Arturo drew his sword. Lorri beckoned from across the street behind the abandoned foundry. It was a large, squat brick building with boarded windows and graffiti sprayed over nearly every surface. Arturo darted out from the alleyway, Lydia and Kelly right behind him.

In the low light of dawn, the neighborhood appeared to be in worse shape than the foundry itself. Abandoned homes were covered with condemned stickers. A lamp post lay across the driveway of the building, hit by a vehicle at some point. The grass grew wild and threatened to conquer the sidewalks and streets. It wouldn't be long before nature reclaimed this part of the city.

Arturo stopped at the edge of the building. Oriphiel had chosen the perfect place to hide making the explosives. The chaos of the neighborhood masked any mastemic activity. No one would ever have thought to search here.

He poked his head around the corner to the front of the building. One of the two large doors at the loading dock stood open but it was dark inside. A white delivery truck sat parked in front of the second door, leaning to the side on flat tires.

"Looks quiet," Arturo said. He glanced down at his watch.

"They could be inside making more bombs," Lorri said.

True. All the windows were covered so there wasn't a way to sneak a peek. But surely they'd see some light from anyone inside. "Let's check it out."

Kelly pulled her bag off her shoulder and strapped on a large pistol and several ammo magazines.

Arturo laid a hand on her shoulder. "You'll wait here."

"I don't think so," she said. "You aren't leaving me outside this time."

He shook his head, but she barreled on.

"I don't need your protection. Not this time." She ejected the magazine from the pistol and pulled a bullet off the top. "Forty-five caliber hollow point. I'd like to see them heal after getting hit by one of these." She tossed it to him.

Arturo caught it and rolled the bullet around in his hand, rubbing the dimple on the end. It weighed more than he expected. The bullet could do serious damage, maybe get stuck in the body, but put a mastem down permanently? Hardly. All it'd do is make for a slow, painful healing process.

Lorri tapped his arm. "Let her come. If nothing else, she'll make good fodder."

Arturo glared at her, then handed the bullet back to Kelly. "Fine. But stay close and make sure you have a clear target before you go shooting anything. All we need is for you to hit one of us in the back."

"Don't worry." She slid the magazine back into the pistol. "I've only been shooting for most of my life."

Arturo smirked. Cocky. If she didn't get herself seriously hurt, she was only going to get worse. "You've still got the knife I gave you, right?"

"I've got it, but I won't need it. Let's go."

Arturo hoped she wouldn't.

The loading dock was still quiet. Where were all the mastem? Oriphiel commanded hundreds in Dogtown. If even a quarter of them actually supported him from the beginning, that still left him with enough to keep a constant watch over their supplies here. And if they really were in full production of bombs, there could be dozens of mastem inside.

"Lorri, I think we need a new door."

"What?" Lorri looked from the loading dock to her instructor.

"We need to get in without being noticed. Use your shedim and open the wall."

"You do it," she said.

Arturo sighed and shook his head. He couldn't. He was on borrowed time. His natures were restless but if he drew on one of them too much, he risked losing control again. Better to push it off as long as possible. "Open it."

Lorri examined the wall. "I don't know how."

Arturo hesitated a moment. She'd never truly admitted she wasn't able to do something. Usually she just bluffed her way through the training or had to be exposed for being unable. But she could do this. "Don't think of the bricks as solid mass. Think of them as more malleable and split them down the middle. You can do this."

Lorri squared her shoulders, then stood in front of the wall with her palms placed flat against it. She closed her eyes and for a moment, nothing happened.

Then the brick grew slick and smooth, like it was clay. She had it, as simple as that. Lorri brought her hands to the center of the wall and stuck them in, then pushed them apart like drawing curtains. In a way no architect could have managed, she pulled the bricks apart to reveal an opening nearly three feet wide.

"Well done." Arturo patted her shoulder as she backed away.

"Piece of cake," she said, slightly out of breath.

Arturo stepped up to the rip and listened. No sounds of movement or alarm emerged from inside.

He climbed through, sword ready, then waited for everyone else to get in. They were in some kind of storage room but natural light spilled in from their new doorway. Arturo walked to a closed door and eased it open on the foundry floor.

Silence and darkness filled the foundry. No mastem anywhere. The only light came from the dawning sun through a couple skylights and the open loading dock door along the far wall. Several long tables stood in the center of the room and empty boxes and jugs lined the walls, arranged from smallest to largest.

Arturo stepped out of the storage room and onto the main floor, alert for any movement. Every thirty feet or so, a large crucible for molten metal hung on a movable rig. He glanced in the closest one. It was clean. No dust that he would've expected from an abandoned building. They'd been used recently.

Lorri strode to the jugs. "Ether, gasoline, potassium chloride. This is definitely where they were making the explosives. They're alphabetized and sorted by size. But everything's empty."

A tarp covered a large pallet off to the side and Arturo pulled it back. "Here's the metal."

Blue metal cast in two-inch thick rods were neatly stacked three feet high. They held the same blue hue as Oriphiel's brooch and the metal shards recovered from the bombs.

"But where are the mastem?" Lydia said.

Kelly opened a couple more boxes. "And the bombs? Did they use all of them when they attacked Dogtown?"

Arturo threw the tarp back over the metal. "No, the attack failed in the end, even if it was Oriphiel's order. They'd need to make more."

"Or they already had more and are out planting them now?" Lorri said.

"Let's hope not." Arturo said the words aloud, but it was the most likely possibility.

A shard of ice shattered a crate six inches from Arturo's head. He rolled away as splinters scratched his face and wood chunks scattered across the ground. Five mastem ran onto the foundry floor, dressed in plain clothes but holding wickedly curved swords.

Arturo threw a fireball as he regained his footing and Lorri did the same. They both smashed into the lead mastem before she could dodge and lit her up. She screamed as the flame rushed across her skin, burning her with an angered fury.

Arturo's mastem snapped at the shedim for being used and he

quickly pushed both back down. He needed to avoid relying on his power, something that had been second nature for him all his life.

The other mastem closed the distance with the sentinels in a heartbeat and Arturo didn't have time to worry about his natures anymore.

He raised his sword to meet the first mastem. She swung her blade and he blocked, then slid to the side and reversed his momentum to cut at her chest.

She spun away from his attack, her long blonde hair fanning out behind her. As she came back around, she led with the tip of her sword in line with Arturo's throat. He raised his blade just fast enough to block but the mastem punched him in the jaw with her free hand.

He reeled back, his head spinning, then set his feet. She stabbed forward and he batted her blade down with his own, more on instinct than anything as the room's spin slowed. He shook his head and she grinned. He threw his hand forward and called on his shedim for a ball of fire. Arturo cringed as his mastem leapt atop the shedim, striking it back down, and nothing emerged from him.

His opponent jerked away from him though, avoiding the fireball that never came. She lowered her sword, then glanced up, her face filled with confusion.

Arturo didn't let the opportunity slip by and pushed through his icepick headache. He slashed across and cleanly removed her head. She tumbled backwards. He'd have to remember that move later, if he ever got a later.

Lorri lit her opponent on fire and his corpse smoldered on the foundry floor. Arturo turned as Lydia knocked the third mastem's blade from his hand and stabbed a knife into his skull. Silence filled the foundry.

"Where's the last one?" Arturo asked.

"Put your weapons down, sentinels."

He spun on his heel, sword at the ready. The last mastem held Kelly by the hair and pressed a knife to her throat.

Dammit. Kelly should've waited outside like he told her to. Arturo inched forward, Lydia and Lorri spreading out around him.

"I said drop them." The mastem pressed the knife harder to Kelly's throat and she squeaked a little. "You too, human."

She dropped her gun. Arturo clenched his jaw, then nodded and set his sword on the ground. Lydia and Lorri did the same.

Kelly eased her hand into her pocket.

"Now, you're going to stay right here while I leave with the human." He lifted his knife from her throat and pointed it at the sentinels, but still kept his other hand wrapped in her hair. "Try and follow us and she—"

Kelly pulled the knife Arturo had given her and rammed it into the mastem's extended arm. He screamed as he dropped his knife and let her go. She crouched forward and grabbed her gun.

Arturo lunged for his sword as Kelly rolled away and fired. The mastem's left kneecap exploded backward and he fell to the ground, his lower leg attached by a thin flap of skin and muscle.

The sentinels joined Kelly as she kicked the mastem's knife away.

"I take it back," Lorri said. "You can handle yourself just fine. Don't let me piss you off again."

Kelly rubbed her throat but kept her gun trained on the mastem's head. "Thanks, I guess."

Arturo knelt and grabbed the mastem by the front of his shirt. The creature gasped in pain, not surprising considering his leg was basically in two pieces. His day wasn't about to get any better.

Arturo pressed his sword to the mastem's Adam's apple.

His shedimic nature rose, urged him to press the blade a little harder, and for once, his mastemic nature agreed. Streaks of white lightning surged where they touched but when working in conjunction, it didn't hurt as bad. Arturo pushed both down with a hard shove. Now wasn't the time for that.

"Where's Oriphiel? Were there any more bombs?"

The mastem focused on his face and laughed, a wheezing, forced thing. "I won't tell you anything."

Arturo pressed the blade a little higher and the mastem lifted his chin.

"Okay, okay," he said.

Arturo pulled the blade back a little.

"Go to hell!" The mastem spat in Arturo's face, then cackled.

Arturo wiped the spit on his shirt sleeve as cold anger filled his veins. He punched the mastem in the face. He thought this was funny, did he? People were dying out there, innocent people. He punched him again and the mastem's nose snapped.

Kelly gasped and Arturo stopped. Surely she wasn't upset with roughing up the mastem. She'd been ready to kill him when she thought he'd been responsible for the attacks. He glanced up at her.

She wasn't looking at him though. She stared at the mastem's knee.

The flesh above and below the knee reached out to each other around the wound. Little tendrils of skin and muscle and bone crept forward like the roots of a plant. They wobbled in the air, searching, and where they touched the opposite side, they locked together and started to close the hole back up.

Keeping his sword at the mastem's throat, he drew a knife with his free hand. The pain kept the mastem focused. Couldn't let that change. He sliced through the fresh muscle and sinew, the bone that hadn't solidified yet but was still very full of nerve endings.

The mastem screamed as the knife severed the newly grown flesh. Arturo twisted the blade to secure it in the middle of the kneecap and slammed it in the ground. The flesh might grow around it but his knee wouldn't function. And a few twists would cut it all back again.

"That's why we use knives," Lydia said.

Kelly's face paled.

The mastem took several quick, sharp breaths, his face bright red.

Arturo had his attention now. "I'll ask you nicely. Where's Oriphiel? Please."

"I can't tell you. I can't. He gave me orders."

The wound had healed further around the blade. Arturo twisted his knife and it grated against the solidifying bone like a mortar grinding in a pestle. The newly grown muscle and tissue tore again.

Arturo's natures both reveled in the thrill of the creature's pain but he blocked them out. He couldn't give in to emotion right now.

"This is torture," Kelly said. She stepped toward Arturo but Lydia and Lorri each grabbed one of her arms. "What're you doing? This isn't right. We don't get information like this."

"You don't," Lorri said.

"We don't like it any more than you," Lydia agreed. "But we don't have time to waste."

Arturo stared at the mastem. They were right. This was the only way. They couldn't play it safe or subtle and when talking wouldn't work, all sentinels were trained to extract the information they needed with more creative means.

"Tell me," he said.

"I can't."

"We'll have to be a little more persuasive then." He eased his sword away from the mastem's throat. "Lorri."

The crackle of flame emerged behind him and light and shadows danced. Lorri stepped around Arturo, flames covering her index and middle fingers.

"The eyes first," Arturo said. His stomach turned and he hoped the mastem wouldn't push them any further.

Lorri knelt and reached forward.

"Wait, wait."

Lorri stopped.

"I'll tell you," he moaned.

Arturo nodded and Lorri stood, letting the flames gutter out.

"We didn't know where Oriphiel was going. All we did was load the bombs into one of the trucks. He took two dozen with him in the middle of the night."

"That's it?" Arturo twisted the knife again and the mastem screamed. Arturo let go and the mastem drew in a deep, ragged breath.

"No... He told us they were going to light the... the match on this war. After today... there would be new leaders who would guide us to victory. That's all, I swear."

Arturo stood and sheathed his sword.

"Light the match?" Kelly said.

'New leaders' was the key. "The negotiations," he said. "The leaders of both races are supposed to meet to discuss a truce. We need to stop them."

"It's too late for that," Lorri said. "They started at dawn. Didn't want to waste time."

"And McLeod didn't tell us where either," Lydia said.

"Dammit." It had Dahlia written all over it. She didn't seem the type to wait for anyone. They needed to get ahold of McLeod, warn him—

Kelly's hand snapped up like a cobra and she fired off a single round past Arturo's head. The wind brushed his ear as the bullet flew by. He jerked to the side and drew his sword.

The mastem stood for half a second with the knife that was embedded in his knee held up to attack. Then he fell backwards, the top half of his skull blown out the back. Blood and brain matter splattered across the floor.

"Nice shot," he said.

"Thanks."

Arturo reached down and grabbed the mastem by the chin. With a swift chop, he cut the creature's head off.

"That's disgusting," Kelly said.

"Has to be done." He turned to Lorri. "Burn the bodies before they heal."

Lorri lit the first body on fire, then glanced over at Kelly's still pale face. A smirk crossed her face. "Calm down. Take a deep breath before you pass out."

"No," Arturo said but too late.

Kelly took a deep breath and inhaled the sickly-sweet smell of burning flesh. She gagged and stumbled away behind a table where she threw up. Lorri laughed and flicked her wrist twice, igniting the other two mastem. They burned like they'd been doused in kerosene.

"That was mean," Arturo said. And uncalled for. He sighed.

"Yeah, maybe. But still funny."

Kelly glared at Lorri as she wiped her mouth on the back of her hand. She holstered her gun and walked outside to the dock.

Arturo pulled out his cell phone and dialed.

McLeod answered almost immediately. "Arturo, what's the matter? Is Jamaal okay?" The chattering of multiple voices filled the background but Arturo couldn't understand them.

"I don't know, sir." He certainly hoped so. "I'm not at the hospital."

There was a pause, then the sound of a door closing and blocking the voices. "Where the hell are you then?"

"We're at St. Louis Metal Casting in South County. We've found where Oriphiel built his bombs."

"You were ordered to stay at the hospital," McLeod shouted. "Wait, did you say we? Tell me Lorri and Lydia aren't with you."

"They came with Kelly and me. We—"

"Look, I know you want to help. But do you realize how much this could jeopardize their futures?"

Arturo winced. He knew exactly how much. Disobeying a direct order from a member of the Sentinalia was a capital offense.

"They're following their orders to protect me. Kelly took me into custody for questioning." It was a stretch and he'd known it from the beginning.

"That's a damn fine line," McLeod said, then chuckled.

Arturo grinned. "Yes, sir. But it paid off. The mastem cleared out all the bombs they have left. And from what the one we interrogated said, they know about the negotiations and are planning to attack."

"The location of the negotiations has been kept strictly need-to-know. Only the Lords and Bosses know, along with those they brought to participate in the security detail. Oriphiel doesn't know where we are."

"You've met him before," Arturo argued. "He plans for everything. You need to delay the negotiations until we can guarantee everyone's safety."

"Arturo, even if Dahlia would believe you, I can't stop the negotiations. They've already gone behind closed doors and no one is allowed to interrupt them until they reach some form of an agreement."

That wasn't good enough. "Oriphiel isn't going to miss an opportunity like this to destroy the Lords opposing the war he wants to start. Not when he can put all the blame on the shedim. It's the perfect chance for him."

"I believe you. I do. We'll do a sweep for any bombs." The weariness was obvious in his voice. McLeod had probably gotten even less sleep than he had.

"We'll be there in ten minutes to help. Just tell me where."

"No," McLeod said. "You have your orders. Go back to the hospital and I won't tell Dahlia you tipped us off. It's better this way. You don't want to get any further up her shit list."

"But we can help." Searching for explosives didn't require any usage of his natures. He'd be fine.

"I'm sorry. I've got my orders too. I'm going to follow them."

Bells chimed over the phone to a familiar tune, muffled like it was coming from outside the room McLeod was in. Arturo recognized it from somewhere. But where?

"I've got to go now," McLeod said. "I'm going to lose my signal. Just go back to the hospital and stay there." He hung up.

Arturo stared at his phone. That tune. He knew it. Arturo checked his watch. Noon. Where did it play at noon? Not the Basilica. They just rang their bells. Another church.

Or a chapel. A chapel sitting on grounds where the sentinels could secretly host the leaders of both races. "I know where they are," he shouted.

"McLeod told you?" Lorri said.

Kelly ran back inside. She'd regained most of her color. "Where?"

"He didn't tell me. But I heard the bells of the chapel at Washington University. They're the only ones I know of that play that particular chime every hour, on the hour."

"Jamaal and I got the file on Marut from an old mastem at the library there," Lydia said.

Of course. "Kaya," he said. "Oriphiel and Kaya are ancient friends. She was a bit of a mentor to him."

"She set us up," Lorri said.

Arturo nodded. She'd kept them off Oriphiel's scent from the very beginning. And they'd played right into it all along. Arturo jogged out of the foundry.

"Would she know about the negotiations taking place on campus?" Kelly asked.

"Oh, yeah," Arturo said. "She'd know all right. She'd be their ticket to getting the bombs into the negotiations. She's a Lord."

Lydia stumbled over her feet. "Seriously?"

Arturo nodded. "We need to get down there now."

CHAPTER 28

The tunnels that ran under Washington University were narrow and cramped. Piping and electrical cables ran the length of the ceiling. The walls were crafted of limestone and dripped with condensation like any cave tunnel. A thin layer of mud caked the floor. Naked incandescent bulbs were evenly spaced and gave enough light to not trip over anything. A musty odor tinged the air.

"Most of the students and faculty know about these and use them to get around, especially when it's snowing or raining," Arturo said as he led them through the tunnel, keeping his hands on the walls. "It's rumored among the undergrads that there are more tunnels no one knows about though."

A strong charge shot up his right arm, like he'd touched a live electrical wire.

"The rumors are true. The sentinels originally had an underground complex here when the city was still young. It's old and hasn't been used since World War II, when the shedim and mastem moved to larger cities."

Arturo placed both his hands on the wall and focused. He reached with his shedim and mastem in either arm. They resisted for a moment but he clamped down on them like a vice grip.

There they were, four long tubes built into the masonry like at McLeod's house. A lock only two sentinels of opposing alignments could open. Or one who hadn't chosen yet.

"Bingo." Arturo pushed his power forward. They leapt out with wild abandon and all four elements expanded, disengaging the lock. A click resounded and a segment of the tunnel slid backwards and to the side, revealing a tunnel that ran straight ahead of them.

Lorri and Lydia each held a knife at the ready. Arturo drew one of his own and led them inside. They needed to find the bombs before they blew. It would be easier if they could find McLeod and recruit any sentinels to help with the search.

The tunnel they were in was unused, with a thick layer of dust on the floor. Little alcoves were carved into the wall every few dozen yards or so. When the complex had been in use, they probably would have served as storage areas for supplies.

They kept walking for what seemed like hours but couldn't have been more than a few minutes. Time was funny in the darkness. Arturo picked up the pace. They really didn't have the time for this. If Oriphiel planted the bombs hours ago, it meant he'd set them on a timer. A remote detonator wouldn't have worked. Sentinel bases were shielded from radio signals.

As they passed a set of alcoves, three figures jumped out. Blades flashed in the dim light. One of the figures stabbed out at Arturo and he blocked, but hit his elbow on the tunnel wall. It was too cramped to maneuver. He slashed forward but his opponent parried and pushed his arm to the side.

He pulled his knife back and darted forward to use the close quarters to pin his foe against the wall. Tightly coiled red hair fanned out as she spun away from his charge and brought her blade across.

She stopped as her knife pressed against Arturo's throat. "Tell your comrades to drop their weapons," she said with a slight Irish accent.

Arturo glanced at Lorri and Lydia. They had a shedim cornered with their blades held ready. A mastem bent Kelly's arm back and pointed her gun at her head.

"Come on, Neena. We don't have time for this," he said. He tapped his knife against her chest where he was poised to plunge it into her heart.

"Arturo?" Neena lowered her knife and raised her hand. A fireball appeared in it and lit the tunnel.

"Stand down," Arturo said. Lorri and Lydia lowered their blades. The mastem let Kelly go and she stretched her arm, then holstered her gun.

"It's good to see you," Neena said. She clasped hands with him.

"You, too," he replied. They'd graduated from the Academy at the same time. She'd gone on to be stationed in Chicago when he'd moved to St. Louis. Over the decades, they'd worked a few missions together and tried to stay in touch as much as they could, but it was rare.

"You're not supposed to be here," Neena said. She studied Kelly. "Not to mention bring a human."

"Agent Nickolaus with the FBI." Kelly extended her hand.

Neena just stared at her until she lowered it.

"We came to help find the bombs Oriphiel placed," Arturo said.

"Join the club. McLeod has anyone who isn't on guard duty searching. But so far I don't think they've had any luck."

Arturo sheathed his knife. "Where is he?"

Neena pointed down the tunnel. "The command center is only a little further, just outside the main meeting room."

"Thank you," Arturo said.

"You know he's not going to be happy to see you," Neena said.

Arturo smiled as they walked on.

"Old girlfriend?" Lorri asked.

Arturo chuckled. Going through the Academy with someone was like growing up with them, especially when that someone was always the main competition for top of the class. "No, just a classmate."

The tunnel finally opened into a large room filled with a half dozen shedim, mastem, and sentinels. Pale florescent lights that flickered every few minutes hung from the ceiling. Everyone spun as Arturo and his team entered the room, knives and elements called on to attack.

McLeod cursed when he saw Arturo. "Stand down. They're sentinels." He beckoned them over to the table he stood at as everyone relaxed and resumed their conversations. "Dammit, what are you doing here? I ordered you to go back to the hospital."

"With all due respect, you need us more than Jamaal does," Arturo said. The map on the table outlined the tunnel network around them. The large wooden doors on the other side of the room led to the meeting chambers, where the negotiations were well underway. Four overlapping circles with illustrations of the elements were carved into the doors, a more stylized version of the sentinel symbol stamped into their weapons and gear.

"What about the bombs?" Arturo asked.

"We haven't found anything yet. And we've searched the entire complex."

"But you could have missed them." Lorri pointed at the map. "There are at least half a dozen entrances into the complex from different areas of campus. How do you know Oriphiel didn't bring the bombs in after you searched?"

McLeod leaned forward on the table. "I've got a sentinel, shedim, and mastem positioned at every entrance to make sure no one brings anything in."

Like Neena and the two guards with her. It was a sure way to make sure no one race got past the guards.

"What about detonating above us?" Kelly said.

McLeod looked at Arturo, who just nodded. Having a human there was unorthodox to say the least, but she was the least of their worries at the moment.

"The facility is reinforced above to prevent any damage from a topside attack."

"But we aren't that deep. Surely a big enough blast could cause some damage. I saw the explosions in Dogtown."

"We have our own ways of protecting our base, Agent Nickolaus," McLeod said. "Don't worry."

"Then where are all the bombs?" Lydia said. "Were we wrong?"

It was possible. Arturo assumed this was where Oriphiel had planned to attack next. It was the logical next step to escalate tensions between the races. It fit with what they'd learned at the foundry. But what if Oriphiel planted that information to throw them off yet again?

No, that couldn't be it. Oriphiel had no way to know they'd find the foundry. He knew protocol would've dictated the Sentinalia remove him from the field for his screw-up.

It still didn't answer the question though. Where were the bombs? McLeod said they'd searched everywhere.

"Wait," Arturo said. "When I called you, you said the negotiations had already started."

"Yes, they've been in there for about an hour and a half."

"So you didn't search the room?"

McLeod opened his mouth, then closed it. He spun and stared at the double doors. "Dahlia locked the doors when they entered, per negotiation protocol," he said. "But we secured it before the negotiations began."

"You weren't specifically looking for bombs then," Arturo said as he walked past him. He lifted his hands and with a great mental shove, he snapped the metal lock. A gust of air slammed the doors open.

He stepped inside, his team and McLeod right behind him.

Dahlia stood at the head of large oak table, apparently in the middle of some speech. Her face reddened as Arturo led the sentinels in. The others out in the command center clustered around the door.

"Get out," Dahlia ordered. "You have no right to be here."

Arturo ignored her and instead bowed to acknowledge the true powers in the room.

On one side of the table four mastem sat on stools – the Lords of St. Louis. Three of them had eight wings of the deepest blue. The fourth had ten wings of dark purple. They were only half changed and still retained their human faces.

On the other side were four shedim. They were the same Bosses from the other night down on the landing. Belial was chief among them and he nodded to Arturo.

Electric light filled the room from sconces built into the wall and a large chandelier hung over the table. It was molded with red and blue metals of fire and water, woven together in a great writhing mass. The lights flickered like those outside, giving the bulbs an almost candle-like appearance rather than electricity.

Arturo beckoned to Lorri and Lydia. They spread around the room to search the cabinets and shelves along the walls. The shedim and mastem stood from the table and watched them.

Belial approached Arturo and McLeod from the shedim side.

"What's going on?" he asked as he looked Kelly up and down. An odd gleam lit his eyes, like a cobra that had cornered a mouse. She shivered and stepped away.

"McLeod," Dahlia shouted. "Get them out of here. This is not appropriate."

Arturo didn't have time to deal with her.

"Hear him out," McLeod said.

"I will not—"

"We found where Oriphiel was building his bombs," Arturo said to Belial. Dahlia's mouth clamped shut. One of the mastem, the one with the purple wings, stepped closer. "But they were already gone. A mastem told us they planned to attack these negotiations. We've checked everywhere in the complex except this room."

"*You* were ordered to stay out of the field," Dahlia shouted. Amazingly, her face grew a shade darker.

"Would you please be quiet, sentinel," the mastem with purple wings said. Her tone indicated it wasn't a request. "I would like to hear what he has discovered."

Dahlia pursed her lips but didn't say anything further.

Authority filled the mastem's voice, authority gained from millennia of existence, the same authority Belial commanded. Evidently enough to silence a member of the Sentinalia too.

The mastem stood six inches taller than Arturo, much taller than anyone else in the room. She had dark skin, defined cheekbones, and a piercing stare from shining sapphire eyes. A feather and several beads were woven into her pitch-black hair.

"I don't believe we've had the pleasure," the mastem said. "My name is Uriel."

That certainly explained the power in her voice. Uriel was the oldest Lord in St. Louis, at least as far as the sentinels knew. She wasn't seen in species politics any more than Belial, but her influence could be felt in dealings with the mastem.

"Arturo Morales, at your service." Arturo bowed again.

"Is the word of one rebellious mastem really the reason you have interrupted us?" Uriel said.

"Hardly evidence to cause concern," another mastem agreed.

"Exactly!" Dahlia said. "You need to leave."

"I said enough," Uriel snapped. Her eyes glowed for a moment but she blinked the fury away. Dahlia sat down in her chair.

Arturo swallowed. "No, that's not the only reason. We believe one of the mastem who works as a librarian here on campus is working with Oriphiel too. She fed us some misleading information."

"You mean Kaya?" Uriel shook her head. "She is a Lord. She would not betray our cause."

"How else would they get the bombs in here?" Arturo said. "Or even know this was the location for your negotiations?"

Belial scoffed. "You should keep better track of your kind, mastem. It's no wonder they're all disobeying."

"*Dellioch*," Uriel said as she shot a glare at the shedim. "What would you know of loyalty?"

"*Kr'chent*," Belial spat back.

Arturo didn't speak much of either species' language but those words weren't particularly friendly. They needed to redirect that aggression elsewhere.

Lorri shut a cabinet. "Nothing."

The bombs had to be here. It was the only option that made sense.

"This is why you shouldn't be in the field," Dahlia said, surging from her chair. "You're hardly thinking straight. McLeod, get them out of here. His idiocy is an embarrassment for all of us."

"Now hold on a second," McLeod said. "There's no reason to insult him like that."

Arturo didn't really care what she thought of him. He glanced around the room as McLeod and Dahlia argued. Lorri and Lydia had checked every shelf, nook, and cranny. He trusted they could spot anything out of place, especially Lorri. She knew more about explosives than any of them and had gotten top marks for her work with them at the Academy. Anything out of the ordinary would have stood out to her like a sore thumb.

Where would Oriphiel have hidden them? He wouldn't let an

opportunity like this slip by. If he could kill a mastem as powerful as Uriel and make it seem like the shedim were responsible, he'd rally all the support he'd need to launch his war. But he'd have to hide them somewhere they'd never be found.

One of the lights in the chandelier flickered for a fraction of a second again. "How long have they been doing that?" he asked.

Everyone looked up as the lights flashed again.

"Ever since we got here," McLeod said. "This complex is getting old, could be anything."

"You taught me better than that," Arturo said as he climbed onto the table and ran his hand along the chandelier. The flames were forged from a deep red metal to appear lifelike. The water was formed with a vibrant blue metal, the same as the bombs. Arturo jiggled the fixtures. They were solid and tight, which meant someone had recently adjusted them. A chandelier like this would have loosened and shifted over the decades.

He ran his hands along the different portions of the light. The individual pieces were actually two halves sealed together, the red metal being one part and the blue another. Arturo pulled a knife and ran it along the seam of the blue metal. A line of epoxy was all that held it together.

The seal opened a little, exposing the wiring for the lights. Something lay behind and underneath it but he couldn't tell what it was yet.

Lorri climbed up next to him. "Find something?"

"We'll see," he said. "Grab the base of this section."

He twisted his blade in the seal and with a pop, the whole piece dropped into Lorri's hand. He whistled as everyone in the room got a good look at what was inside. Tubes of liquid ran the entire length of the chandelier and wiring tied it all together.

He pulled the cover off another water segment and Lorri caught it as it fell. More explosives lining the entire length too.

Oriphiel was ingenious. He'd replaced all of the water segments with bombs. And the molding had been perfect. He had to have planned for this all along.

All the wiring led back to the base of the chandelier, which was bolted to the ceiling. Lorri popped the covering off the base. A digital timer counted down, with a little over five minutes left.

Belial and Uriel each cursed in their own languages.

"What are we going to do?" Kelly said. "There's a whole campus full of people above us and we don't have time to evacuate them."

One of the other mastem leaned over to Uriel. "We need to get out of here before those bombs detonate. They will certainly take out a large portion of the campus."

Belial scoffed. "Coward."

Arturo was inclined to agree.

"We're not fireproof," the mastem spat.

Uriel grasped the mastem's shoulder. "No. That's not who we are. I will fly the bombs to a safe distance. Cut the chandelier down."

One of the other shedim with horns wrapped in barbed wire slapped her hand on the table. "And then the rest of your kind'll put the blame for your death on our heads. Then there will be war."

"It's no good," Lorri interjected as she examined the detonator. "Oriphiel wired the explosives to detonate if the power's cut."

"There's no need for loss of life," Belial said. "Fire is our element to command. We'll contain the blast." The Bosses glanced at him with not entirely confident looks.

"What?" the mastem who wanted to flee said. "More like you'll let it kill us, since you won't get hurt."

"We don't want war any more than you do!" Belial shouted. "Remember, it's shedim who have suffered so far. Perhaps you're in league with Oriphiel? One of your Lords has already proven to be a traitor!"

The room erupted into chaos. Shedim and mastem shouted accusations back and forth. With countless millenia of memories in the room, it didn't take long for ancient history to get dredged up. Someone mentioned the Black Plague while another spoke of civil war, although which country wasn't mentioned. McLeod and Dahlia stood between the opposing sides and tried to talk some reason into them.

"Three minutes," Lorri whispered to Arturo.

His inner natures circled each other as the heightened emotions in the room resulted in surges of power from the Lords and Bosses, fueling their desire to dominate. They pressed against each other and a twinge of pain bloomed behind his eye. He grasped each to calm them down but they threw him off.

"Enough!" Arturo shouted.

Everyone in the room stopped arguing and stared at him. His own halves receded back into their places again, but his headache stayed constant. It was getting harder to keep them back.

He hopped off the table. "Belial, can you control the blast?"

Dahlia stepped closer to him. "You don't have any say—"

"I wasn't talking to you," he snapped. He'd pay for his insubordination later but he didn't really care. If they didn't act, later wouldn't be a problem.

Belial looked from Arturo to Uriel then back to Arturo. "We can try."

"That'll have to be good enough. Lord Uriel?"

She nodded. "Do it."

Belial spoke in shedimic to the other Bosses, who each nodded. They spread around the table to take positions several feet back on each side. "You and your mastem are welcome to leave if you're worried," Belial said to Uriel. "If this doesn't work, there's no telling how far away is far enough."

One of the mastem opened his mouth, but Uriel spoke first. "We will stay and see this through as well. To prove our worth."

Belial shrugged. He raised his arms out to his sides in unison with the other Bosses and closed his eyes.

Lorri jumped down from the table and moved to the edge of the room. "Ten seconds."

Arturo braced himself as he counted down in his head. This had to work.

Nine, eight...

If it didn't, at least he wouldn't have to worry about going mad.

Seven, six...

Or what the Sentinalia would decide to do with him.

Five, four...

Jamaal would have to find Oriphiel for them.

Three, two...

He glanced at McLeod and nodded. There were worse ways to die. One.

A bright light flashed into the room and Arturo raised a hand to block it. Heat washed over him and the ground shook. For half a heartbeat, he doubted Belial's abilities. Kelly screamed next to him and he instinctively turned to shield her, not that it'd do much.

The heat faded first, followed by the light. Spots filled his vision and he tried to blink them away. After a few moments, his vision cleared.

The shedim stood their ground, their feet planted to the stone. The center of the room roiled as a large fireball churned, contained solely by the power of the Bosses. Arturo remembered the flames from the attack on Dogtown and the way they fought against him. The sheer strength they commanded in order to stop the blast immediately was mind numbing.

Each shedim's face was set in pure concentration and their muscles bulged in their arms.

"*Rihs*," Belial shouted and pushed forward.

The other Bosses did the same and as one, they took a small step in. The fireball swirled slightly faster and brightened as it shrank by a couple inches.

The shedim took another step and drew the flames inward again. Then they took another step. And another. Inch by grueling inch they tightened their circle, brought their hands closer, and compressed the explosion between them. The heat receded and the flames grew smaller and brighter. But with each step, their faces contorted. They grunted and strained as they held on truly for dear life.

The shedim finally stood within a few feet of each other and brought their arms forward. The inferno shrank from six feet to four. Then three. The flames glowed a bright yellow. They were actually containing the blast. They were going to do it.

Then the Boss to Belial's right, the one with the barbed wire in her horns, screamed. She collapsed and the flames erupted outwards like water from a popped balloon, straight for Uriel and the other Lords. Belial shouted and side stepped but not before Arturo rushed in front of them.

Arturo threw his hands out and grabbed hold of the flames with everything he had. They bucked and thrashed against him but he kept a firm hold. He couldn't let go. Not this time. It wasn't his life alone on the line. His shedim roared as it pushed itself to help him control such fire.

"Step up, Arturo," Belial shouted. The other three Bosses held their ground and waited for him to move up and join them.

Arturo nodded and pushed. The flames twisted, trying to get free from his grasp. He sharpened his power like talons and slammed them into the flames, which screamed out in his mind.

Arturo took a step.

Inch by inch he moved forward and the flames screeched as they were brought back under control.

Sweat slicked his body and his muscles ached but he kept his arms out. Heat washed over him in waves. He was only a few steps away from the others when his mastem lashed out. It struck and bit at the shedim's connection through him and into the flames.

He winced. No, not now. He wasn't choosing the shedim, just using it.

Arturo hurried and took two more steps to get in line with Belial. "I can't..."

Belial stepped over in front of him. "I've got it," he said. "You can let go."

Arturo nodded and withdrew his power. His shedim cried out as he forced it and his mastem back down. They snapped and wrestled against each other, throwing up sparks of lightning in his brain.

He stumbled back from the flames but steadied himself enough to grab the Boss who'd collapsed and drag her back. Lydia and McLeod grabbed her shoulders and took her the rest of the way to the edge of the room as Arturo sat hard on the ground.

He took several deep breaths while the Bosses finished their work, his natures still fighting in the recesses of his mind. Lorri knelt next to him and handed him her canteen. He took a drink but kept his eyes on the shedim.

They brought their hands closer and closer. The fireball shrank to the size of a beach ball, then a basketball. It now blazed a brilliant white, all that energy contained within such a small area.

The shedim's hands touched and the fire winked out. Energy flowed up their arms, disappeared into their chests, and then flowed down around their legs into the ground. They'd channeled the explosive force through themselves and back into the earth.

A single ball of scorched metal clanged to the floor as the Bosses relaxed. They'd done it.

Please stop, Arturo whispered to his natures.

They slowed their fighting, then simmered away from each other, leaving off their fight for now. Arturo sighed.

Belial's shoulders slumped as he turned around. "See, told you so." His knees gave out and Uriel stepped forward to grab him. "I'm all right. I'm all right."

She steadied him, then let go. "Thank you." She extended her hand.

Belial stared before clasping it. "Our pleasure."

"We do not want war any more than you do," Uriel said. "And so there will not be war on our parts today. We will hunt for Oriphiel and his supporters with the same zeal you do. When he is found, we will see to it that he meets justice."

Belial nodded. "Thank you."

"Just hope you find him before we do," Arturo said.

Uriel chuckled, then extended her hand to Arturo. He grabbed it and she helped him to his feet. "You are a fine young sentinel, Arturo Morales." She glanced at Dahlia. "The Lords are comforted knowing you represent your people in the field. You no doubt have a bright future ahead of you and will become a strong leader in time. I look forward to our next meeting."

Dahlia cleared her throat as she stepped up to them. "Shall we take a short break before we conclude the negotiations? We can get another table and chairs brought in."

Uriel inclined her head and left the room, followed by the other mastem. The sentinels and ganastu crowding the doorway split to let them pass.

"Well done," Belial said. "We'll be seeing you around." He left with his Bosses, the one who'd collapsed slowly coming around.

Dahlia crossed her arms, her hands clenched into fists. She looked past Arturo to the door and he glanced back. The crowd trickled away, the excitement over for the moment.

"You disobeyed direct orders," Dahlia snapped. "You're lucky you were correct this time. As it is, you kept this from devolving into an even bigger mess. You won't be punished today but the Sentinalia will deliberate on what to do with you next. Rest assured, there will be consequences."

She turned on her heel and stormed out of the room.

"Bitch," Lorri said.

"Lorri," McLeod warned, but his heart wasn't in it. He slapped Arturo on the shoulder. "I'm sure I won't hear the end of this, but I'm glad we didn't all get blown to hell."

Arturo smiled. "Things could've gone a lot worse."

"Like the Bosses and Lords deciding they still wanted war?" Lydia asked.

"Yeah, like that," Arturo said.

"What about Oriphiel?" Kelly asked.

"Who cares?" Lorri said. "We didn't blow up. One thing at a time."

True, they still needed to find the mastem but it would take time. He'd failed to kill the Lords and start a war. In fact, his plans had backfired. Rather than divide the races, they'd set aside some of their differences against a common enemy – him.

"With all three groups hunting him, it's only a matter of time," Lydia said. "Not much more we can do."

Kelly's face showed her exasperation. "What am I going to tell the FBI?"

Arturo laughed. Humans always moved so quickly. "I'm sure we can help with that."

CHAPTER 29

Arturo crossed the street in from of Limbo. All the bars and restaurants around the city were alive with activity tonight, a far cry from what most people might have expected. Brilliant blues and reds burst in the sky as fireworks exploded overhead. Laughter and music echoed up and down the sidewalks.

After the negotiations for a truce were finalized, orders to stand down had spread through the ranks of shedim and mastem. With war abated for now, everyone could settle back into their regular routines. But not without a huge celebration. Both populations were out tonight enjoying the elation of a diverted disaster and the human population was happy to go along with it. As far as they knew, the fireworks were celebrating the FBI's capture of the terrorists and serving up good old American justice.

As Arturo descended the stairs to the basement, he noted the good spirit and cheer that saturated the air. For the rogues in particular, it was always a step in the right direction when the Lords and Bosses could see eye to eye. Everyone in the room lifted their glasses for a toast to the future.

Everyone except him. He smiled and was happy for them, but until the Sentinalia decided what to do with him, his options were pretty limited. He couldn't operate in the field without risking the wrath of Dahlia and the Sentinalia. McLeod had ordered him to stay low and if he felt his natures growing out of control, to get away from everyone.

He sat at the end of the bar and called for a beer. The mastem bartender, a woman he didn't recognize with bright orange wings, glanced from her newspaper and waved a hand. A bottle of beer flew from the cooler to his hand. The top popped off and flipped over the edge of the counter into a trashcan. Neat trick.

Of course, McLeod had told him the way to fix everything. Just pick a nature. But he didn't have the heart to tell McLeod that even that option was off the table now.

His natures hadn't tried to take control since he left the university but he also hadn't tried to use them either. Their restlessness weighed on his mind like a heavy cloth. It wouldn't be long before they were at it again for dominance. And neither one was going to go quietly into submission.

Raum sat next to Arturo. "The next round is on the house."

"Who said I was staying for another?"

Raum laughed, more at ease than Arturo had seen the old shedim in years. "Oh, call it a hunch. Where else could you get a drink without hiding what you are? Besides, you deserve it. You almost single handedly stopped a war."

"Well, when you put it that way, I think I'll have another. But something a bit more sophisticated than beer."

"Anything you want." Raum raised a hand and the bartender brought him a glass of dark red liquor.

Arturo sipped his beer. "So what's the word?"

Raum shrugged. "Everyone's watching for Oriphiel and Kaya but no one's seen them since before the negotiations. Oriphiel cleared out his room at the Basilica, same with Kaya's office at the university. Any sightings of them are to be reported through the respective chains of command. Honestly, though, I don't think they'll show themselves any time soon."

If only that were true. He wasn't sure about Kaya, but he'd known Oriphiel most of his life. The mastem would find another way to get what he wanted. It was only a matter of time. But time was different for the mastem and shedim. When they measured lifetimes in thousands of years, waiting a few decades was like the blink of an eye. Oriphiel could stay hidden until well after Arturo was dead and buried.

"After your interruptions, I hear the negotiations went pretty smoothly. The Lords agreed to most of the terms the Bosses set and are making reparations over the next few years. Not that it'll bring back anyone who died, but it's a step in the right direction. I'm told my son was pretty pleased with the outcome."

Arturo jerked his head up. "Your son?"

Raum chuckled and glanced down at his glass. "I've really had too much to drink this evening. Yes, my son, Belial."

Belial was Raum's son? Arturo's mind spun at the implications. Raum was old, he knew that, but to be old enough to be Belial's father put him even further back. It did however explain why the attempts on Raum's life stopped after Arturo had saved him. Belial must have interceded.

Raum spun around in his seat and leaned back to watch the busy bar. "What about the FBI? They say they've caught the terrorists, but that's all that's being reported."

Arturo focused back on Raum. "The Sentinalia's worked the cover. It'll hit the press in full tomorrow morning. Some kind of suicide terrorist organization using hallucinogenic gases to make the victims see monsters. They'll plant a few of the dead bodies from Dogtown at St. Louis Metal Casting, then make them disappear after the case is closed. Kelly'll get a commendation, maybe a promotion."

"Ingenious. Your kind have really perfected the art of cleaning up our messes."

"A few thousand years of practice helps." Arturo drained the last of his beer. The bartender swept it up and replaced it with an old scotch. He sipped it and warmth spread through him like sitting by a fire after coming in from the snow. "If I save the city more, will I get more free drinks?"

Raum raised his glass. "That'd get old quick. And expensive."

Arturo had to agree. Too much had been lost already.

"Besides, balance is always better." Raum stared into his drink, then downed it. "Speaking of balance, rumor has it you're no longer on active duty?"

Arturo coughed on a swallow. "How did you find out?"

"It's true then."

Arturo nodded. "Yeah."

Raum waited a moment but Arturo wasn't going to give him any more information. He really didn't want to talk about it with the old shedim. They had never been that close.

Raum shrugged. "There are many individuals on both sides who will be glad to hear you won't be in their way anymore. Personally, I hate to see you suffer or lose what little sanity any of us are given. But that's what happens when you ride the fence."

Arturo smiled. He didn't need to say anything. The shedim knew what was going on all along. His sources were that good.

"A bit of advice. Riding the fence inevitably ends in a fall. So why not tear the fence down?"

Arturo stared at him. What the heck was that supposed to mean?

Raum stood and stretched. "Stay as long as you like. Whatever you want is on the house."

Raum walked off to make his rounds. He amazed Arturo every time they were together. The old shedim played the warm and welcoming bar owner so well, like he truly had forgotten the struggle between the races and accepted anyone who walked through his doors. If more were like him, they'd have less problems in the world.

Arturo took another sip of his scotch. They'd gotten lucky this time. So many things could have gone wrong. Jamaal could have been killed. They could have been too late to stop the bombs.

He could have gone mad.

Although that one was inevitable, it seemed. Being out of the field hopefully bought him a little more time.

Thirty-six years in the field. Less than a tenth of a sentinels average lifespan and now he was going to lose it all. He'd controlled his natures so well for so long. His own discipline had always been enough. But now?

"You know, the last time I snuck up on you was in a bar," a man said. "And if memory serves me right, it didn't turn out so well for either one of us."

Arturo glanced up as Anzu sat next to him. He grasped a knife but didn't draw. How did he let the damned shedim get this close to him again?

Anzu looked down at Arturo's hand. "Oh, ease up, sentinel. I'm not here for any trouble. Raum would kill me where I stood if I outright disobeyed the rules of his house."

"Then what do you want?"

"Honestly?" Anzu raised his hand and called for a whiskey. "I just wanted a drink before I left town. And the only place I can do that is here with the rogues."

"You're leaving?" Arturo said.

"Yeah, Belial's ordered my exile or death." Anzu's glass floated down in front of him. He drained half of it and dropped the duffel slung over his shoulder to the floor. "Seems he didn't like me trying to kill you."

His shedimic nature growled. It wanted Anzu dead but Raum's rules were absolute. No fighting in his bar and certainly no killing. "Where are you off to?"

"Not sure yet. Probably out east. Maybe New York or D.C. I have family running a few rather profitable rackets." He looked at his hand, where the scars from their first meeting remained. "Don't worry, I won't forget you."

"Going to be taking any more souls early?"

Anzu grinned, malice in his eyes. "I wouldn't rule it out. But that'll be someone else's problem, won't it? From what I hear, you're in big trouble."

"Does everyone know?" Arturo let go of his knife and leaned onto the counter.

"Good news travels fast in this town. Don't worry about it. I mean, I'm happy you're getting punished. Even if it isn't death. But at least you stopped the war."

"People keep saying that."

"It's true. I'll be the first to admit I'm an evil son of a bitch, but I didn't want war. Not all shedim like to fight like me. I'm also big enough to thank you for what you did for my kind. I'd say we're even now."

Arturo's phone buzzed on the bar.

"Best of luck to you in retirement. Maybe I'll see you around some day." Anzu drained his glass and hefted his bag on the way to the stairs.

Arturo checked the caller ID. Kelly. Probably more questions from her superiors. She'd called him three or four times already for details to pass along.

"Hello," he said.

"Hello, Arturo," Oriphiel replied.

Ice ran through his veins, followed by heat in his cheeks and fists as both his natures snapped at each other. The hustle of the bar faded to a soft murmur around him. "Oriphiel. What are you doing? Where's Kelly?"

"Oh, you mean the human? She's fine."

Muffled screams echoed over the phone, along with the howl of rushing wind.

"She put up quite the fight for me."

"What do you want?"

Oriphiel chuckled. "Very good. Perhaps you weren't a total waste of time. You realize you cost me my war, old friend." He bit off the last words.

"A war that would have caused too many deaths on both sides. That isn't worth it."

"There is no price I wouldn't pay to see all shedim dead," Oriphiel shouted. "But back to what I want. I need to speak with you. I expect to see you soon, for old time's sake. Come alone. You know where. It's a lovely night."

The line went dead. Arturo stared at his phone. Oriphiel had never acted like this before. He didn't give in to emotions, especially not vengeance. And he didn't harm humans. Or at least he didn't used to.

It didn't matter. Arturo needed to get Kelly away from Oriphiel.

He heard the wind and Oriphiel's words again. For old time's sake. They'd been meeting at the same place for years. Arturo knew exactly where they were.

CHAPTER 30

Arturo stared up the steel frame of the Arch. A thick fog spread from the river and obscured the top in a circling mist, like he stood at the center of a great storm. Wind whispered through his hair and power clung to the air, soaking into his skin. The hair on the back of his neck stood on end.

Oriphiel was there. And he was waiting.

Arturo drew his sword and took a firm grip on his mastem. It bucked him off, even though he meant to use it rather than push it away. His natures were tired of his indecision. He didn't care. He had to stop Oriphiel tonight, had to get Kelly out of there. If he could get through this, he'd deal with the madness later.

He grabbed his mastem and yanked it up, calling on the air around him. It pooled under his feet and buoyed him up through the darkness. Weightlessness was usually a thrill but not now. The only thought on his mind was what awaited him, this fight that he'd never before won.

He reached the top of the Arch and stepped onto it, feet planted firmly.

Oriphiel stood across from him with his sword drawn and held at his side. He'd traded his armor for his favored white suit, which was immaculate, save for a ripped sleeve. His hair was brushed perfectly to the side, every strand in place even with the strong breeze. Moonlight reflected in his eyes as he watched Arturo, a spark of mania the only thing out of place on this once gentle mastem.

Kelly lay a few feet to his right, arms and feet tied and her mouth gagged. Her hair was frazzled and a bruise welled on her cheek but she otherwise looked unharmed.

"Well, now, what took you so long?" Oriphiel smiled. "I was beginning to worry you wouldn't show."

"What are you doing?" Arturo said.

"What am *I* doing?" The mastem balked and lifted his hands in the air. "You've got to be joking. I'm doing what I've always been doing – what needs to be done. *I* was going to stop the shedim once and for all. But you wouldn't let me do that." The mania in his eyes bled away to pain and his voice pulled at Arturo. "Why wouldn't you let me?"

Oriphiel looked to the sky and Arturo slid towards Kelly. But before he could get even a foot closer, Oriphiel sidestepped and flicked his sword down to her throat.

Arturo lifted his hands. "Okay," he said. He needed to buy time, try and use logic against Oriphiel. The mastem believed in reason, he always had.

"The balance has to be maintained," Arturo said. "That's what sentinels do. We don't let either side go against that. You taught me that as much as they did."

"No, I taught you the shedim needed to be controlled lest they take over."

"The same could be said for your kind."

Oriphiel scoffed. "We don't deal in murder and mayhem on a whim. Our moves are calculated to cause the least harm possible."

"That's what you call what you've done?" Arturo said. Nothing was further from the truth.

"It was for the greater good! With the shedim dead, you could have lived a normal life. You could have happily chosen your mastemic nature and never worried again."

His mastem perked up at Oriphiel's words. To have an ordered existence without the chaotic day-to-day unknown of sentinel life.

Bend, it urged. Choose. That path led to madness. No choice was possible now.

Arturo shook his head and pressed the nature down before it could speak further. "I know what you're doing." Just like in Dogtown, he wanted Arturo to either choose a nature and fight or get incapacitated when both natures tried to take control. Only this time, no one would be there to take the fall for him.

Oriphiel pointed at Arturo with his sword. "I see it in your eyes. You know what I'm saying is the truth. Why won't you accept it?"

"No," Arturo said. "Even if I thought you were right, I would never agree to the slaughter of innocents." His shedim pressed outwards to take advantage of his sympathy. Its kind had done nothing wrong, had never asked for Oriphiel's attacks. It was in the right. It deserved to be in control.

"There are no innocent shedim. Each and every one of them is driven to corrupt human souls."

Arturo's mastemic nature nipped at the rising shedim. The two sparked white lightning off each other as they collided and a sharp ache bloomed at the back of his skull. "No," Arturo said to Oriphiel and his natures. He closed his eyes and rubbed his temple.

"You are being foolish," Oriphiel whispered in his ear.

Arturo jerked and slammed his natures aside as he spun, his sword leading in a cross slash. But the only thing he caught was fog. Oriphiel wasn't there. Arturo turned to block the real attack but he wasn't nearly fast enough.

Oriphiel kicked him in the back and knocked him across the slick metal of the Arch. Kelly screamed through her gag as Arturo slid to a halt at the edge. Far below him, the tops of the trees barely stuck out over the fog.

The mastem had thrown his voice on the air while Arturo's inner battle distracted him. A stupid trick to keep him off balance.

A puff of wind fluttered across his skin and he rolled over, his sword held up. Oriphiel's blade smashed down on his block and Arturo grunted. Pain radiated down his wrists and into his arms, like a load of bricks had landed on him.

He kicked at Oriphiel's legs before the mastem could strike again.

Oriphiel leapt back and his wings sprouted from his shoulders. He whipped up the fog around them as he flapped once and landed on the other side of the Arch.

Arturo flipped into a crouch, then rushed through the fog. No more distractions. He slashed across, then jabbed, his arms tingling as feeling returned.

But Oriphiel was ready and batted his blade aside with ease. With his arm out wide, Arturo's defenses were open. The mastem stabbed inside his outstretched arm and Arturo drew a knife to block.

The mastem never connected though, pulling his blade back at the last moment and spinning away.

They fell into a rhythm of attack and block, strike and parry and dodge, a dance they'd played out so many times over the years. Arturo always found comfort in those sparring sessions, where he could lose track of thought and time in the movement of muscles and metal. Oriphiel was one of his greatest instructors in hand-to-hand combat. With every missed block and poorly executed strike, the mastem taught him with cuts and bruises.

But this time one of them wouldn't survive, couldn't survive. This time, Oriphiel wouldn't go easy on him. He wouldn't stop the moment before the killing blow.

And neither could he.

Sweat beaded on Arturo's brow and his back muscles ached. He couldn't keep this up, not as long as Oriphiel could. Where Arturo had held a sword for decades, Oriphiel had thousands of years of experience with that many years' worth of collected souls to draw on for energy.

Strength and skill alone couldn't keep him alive.

He blocked a second too late and Oriphiel sliced his forearm, causing him to drop his knife. Blood welled along the painful line as Arturo backed away.

"First blood," Oriphiel said. He kicked Arturo's knife over the edge of the Arch.

Focus. Stay focused. Don't get complacent.

"You can't win. Just give up. I don't want to kill you."

Arturo looked up into his friend's eyes. "You don't have to. Turn yourself in. Let this thirst for war go."

Oriphiel shook his head. "I cannot, my friend. The shedim have been allowed to survive for too long. We must stop them now."

"I won't let you," Arturo said and he meant it. Oriphiel would have to kill him because Arturo would never stand aside.

Oriphiel cried out and pressed forward to attack again. A line of tears slid down his cheeks. Arturo's heart broke at the sight of them.

He rolled to the side as Oriphiel slashed at him. As he came back to his feet, he called on his shedim and threw a small ball of flames at his foe. Oriphiel darted to the side and the flames missed by mere inches. He threw twice more at different angles.

Each flame fizzled in a puff of vapor as Oriphiel condensed the fog in the air. Arturo kept throwing, hoping he'd be fast enough to get past Oriphiel's defenses but knowing he wouldn't. The mastem had expected this, planned for it like he always did. The fog in the air was no accident, but rather all the moisture he'd ever need to keep Arturo's flames at bay.

He had so much power, how could Arturo beat that?

Arturo's shedim reveled in its repeated usage but his mastem wouldn't stand for it. Repeated use meant it was losing ground and it fought its way forward, pushing the shedim away from Arturo and worming its way in. The next attack he threw wasn't fire. A globe of water mixed with Oriphiel's counter and splashed in the mastem's face.

Oriphiel sputtered, then wiped his face with the back of his hand. "You are losing your grip, sentinel."

Arturo's natures collided with a screech and pain tore through his head, worse than any he'd felt. He tried to grasp them both but they wouldn't have it. They shoved him away. Flashes of memories clouded his mind. His dead family scattered around him. His first training with other sentinels. His field assignment to McLeod.

Through the visions, he swung his sword, hoping to keep Oriphiel at bay. Another bolt of pain ripped through him. Lydia's scream as Oriphiel plunged his sword into Jamaal while Arturo's natures clashed with lightning flashes. Their constant struggle as they bashed against one another over and over, trying to gain control of him.

No, he needed more time. He couldn't lose it, not now.

Arturo pushed the memories aside and lunged forward. His foot slid out from under him and he fell on cold metal. His sword skittered over the edge of the Arch, sped up by the patch of ice Oriphiel had frozen along its surface.

Arturo drew his last knife but Oriphiel waved a hand. A strong gust of air blasted into his chest and he flipped over the edge. The knife clattered away as he clamped his hands on the lip. Without his mastemic nature, nothing would stop him from falling.

Oriphiel leapt into the air and landed above him, sword at the ready. "I didn't want to hurt you, Arturo. You are my family. I've tried to guide you all these years. But you couldn't get out of your own way."

Arturo glanced at Oriphiel. His mother and father stood next to him, their eyes clouded and lifeless. He blinked and his parents disappeared.

"You half-breeds can't defeat us," Oriphiel said. "Especially not when you're too busy fighting yourselves. You're only part mastem after all."

Not when he fought himself. His dream flooded back into his vision, his shedim and mastem separated. McLeod told him he couldn't fight both natures. Jamaal asked him why he kept fighting them. This single truth, that sentinels inevitably must choose one nature over the other, was drilled into every one of them.

And now, Arturo's life hung by a thread because he refused to choose one over the other. His natures rose in a last-ditch attempt for control. If one could claim him, they might survive this. His mind spun as they collided again and again.

White light flashed every time they connected. But something was different. A bright seam sealed them together inside the lightning, then ripped apart, leaving darkness. The lightning still hurt, but it was almost like his natures slammed into each other only to have to fight to get apart. Had they always done that?

He couldn't win if he fought himself. What if he didn't have to fight, if his natures didn't have to fight anymore? What if he didn't have to choose just one?

So why not tear the fence down? Raum had said.

His natures slammed into each other again and instead of letting them pull apart, Arturo clamped down with every ounce of willpower he could muster and held them together.

Oriphiel raised his sword. "I'm sorry."

Time slowed as Oriphiel brought his blade down. Arturo pushed reality away and focused on his natures.

They hissed and sparked at each other, one blue and one red. Each clawed for domination, demanded to be accepted in full. He extended his hold further along their lengths, bringing them together. The white seam linking them expanded like living lightning, growing faster. The pain in Arturo's head receded with the spread of the connection.

The mastem and shedim stopped fighting him, instead focusing on where they'd combined and trying to break apart. But it was too late.

Arturo stopped fighting. No more fighting, no more struggling over which was better. He wanted both, needed both.

His natures rode him and spread their power throughout his body. Every fiber of his being held a part of each of them and now, instead of keeping them apart, Arturo pushed them together. He claimed them both. And where his power had existed separately, they shifted, intertwined, sealed. His veins burned with frozen fire.

They blended closer and closer. More lightning connections leapt out between the natures, latching and drawing red and blue together to glow brilliant white. Every bit of the two natures throughout his mind and body and soul were drawn inwards to this white light, brought together rather than kept apart.

Oriphiel screamed and Arturo opened his eyes. The mastem's sword fell over the edge, nicking his cheek as it sailed past him. Oriphiel spun and grabbed Kelly by the throat, lifting her off her feet and squeezing her neck. She slapped at his hands as her face turned red.

The knife Arturo dropped protruded from Oriphiel's shoulder. Kelly must've used it to free herself, then struck for his heart. Clearly she'd missed.

Arturo yanked himself back on the Arch. He kicked the mastem in the back of the knee, his movement faster than ever, spurred by the power of his merging natures. Oriphiel grunted and dropped Kelly, who fell to the metal and sucked in a ragged breath.

Arturo punched Oriphiel in the kidney before he could recover. The mastem stumbled away, turning to stare at him with wide eyes. Arturo rushed him and punched. This time, Oriphiel was the one to barely get his arm up in time to block.

To Arturo, it was like the mastem moved through mud. He swung with his other fist and landed a punch on Oriphiel's wounded shoulder. The mastem cried out and reeled to the side.

The last parts of Arturo's mastemic and shedimic natures spiraled into his center.

Oriphiel straightened, yanked the knife out of his shoulder, and threw it over the edge. "About time," he said, then rushed forward.

Arturo batted his punch away and stepped in. He connected with the mastem's gut. Oriphiel doubled over and Arturo rammed his knee into the mastem's face. His nose crunched and he stumbled back.

Arturo moved to throw a fireball, to finish this once and for all, but he stopped. The blinding light at his center pulsed, then erupted, shooting out hundreds of tendrils of power that spread back through his body and filled him to the brim. It thrummed with strength and vitality, pure power that he somehow knew could call any of the elements he'd want. But something was different. This new power called out, sang for another energy source outside his body.

A convergence of power inside Oriphiel answered his call, like a blip on sonar. An immense pool, strong, vibrant and deep, but one that didn't belong to the mastem. The power called back to Arturo and sent a shiver up his spine with its longing.

The power spreading through Arturo's body reached his eyes and light bloomed inside his opponent as Oriphiel stood and wiped the blood from his face. Thousands of bright lights swirled around inside the mastem.

Arturo glanced to Kelly, still struggling to catch her breath, where a single smaller light pulsed.

Souls. Arturo could see the souls Oriphiel had collected over his lifetime. He gazed out over the city, and the souls of each human in St. Louis beat with every pulse of his power.

He focused back on Oriphiel and reached out, brushed his power against those souls. They sang back with a stronger longing.

Oriphiel shuddered and the souls rippled like a pool of water disturbed by a stone. "What was that?" Oriphiel shouted.

"You were wrong," Arturo said. "Sentinels aren't weak." This wasn't weakness at all.

Oriphiel's eyes widened. "That's impossible. You didn't... You couldn't..." He raised his hands. His power, his souls, screamed in agony as they channeled up through his arms.

"No," Arturo said. His power clamped down on Oriphiel's souls, pinched them off like the end of a balloon.

Oriphiel drew his arms to his chest and slumped. His whole body shivered. He glared at Arturo, then lifted his hands and tried to call his power again, but Arturo kept his grasp firm. No matter how hard he tried to draw, the pool was closed off.

"Arturo, let me go," Oriphiel said. His eyes held a quality Arturo had never seen before. Fear.

Arturo yanked down on Oriphiel's power and the mastem fell to his knees. The souls whispered to Arturo's mind. They pressed and prodded and begged to be freed. His own power obliged, thinning to a razor's edge and slicing through Oriphiel's hold on them.

The mastem screamed as the souls flooded out of him. They twisted around Arturo's line of power and funneled into him, pooled into his core, then spread outwards. Every pore, every cell, every inch held more and more power than he'd ever known as the souls, the single strongest source of power coveted by shedim and mastem but never sentinels, filled him.

He shivered and his skin prickled like he would pop at any moment. The flood slowed to a trickle as the last of the souls left Oriphiel.

"What have you done?" Oriphiel cried. His hands trembled and his face was pale. "Give them back."

He'd stolen Oriphiel's souls. No sentinel was capable of taking souls. That's why they were entrusted to keep the balance. They had no interest in souls as power, only in keeping the lives of humans and ganastu safe.

But Oriphiel's souls churned and bubbled inside him, ready to be used while the mastem looked frail now, empty. No bright lights filled his body, just an empty black pit. He was powerless.

"Oriphiel, you're done. Give it up and I'll make sure you are judged fairly by the Sentinalia. Please, my friend. I'm begging you."

Oriphiel watched him. There was no hope now, surely the mastem saw that. Arturo had the upper hand.

Oriphiel screamed, drew a knife, and launched himself through the air.

Arturo slammed his arms up and the souls channeled through him. Pure power, not fire or water but white energy, erupted like a typhoon. The night flashed like day and for a moment, all Arturo saw were Oriphiel's eyes glaring at him.

The light engulfed his friend and arrested his movement in mid-air. Wind whipped the fog into a hurricane around them. A shrill scream pierced the night, like a train screeching to a halt. The last of the souls left Arturo's body and swirled around Oriphiel, holding him in place a few feet above the Arch. He shouted and swung his knife but it passed through the souls without any resistance.

Then as one, they saturated into his body and bit into the black pit that was the mastem's soul. He fell to the hard metal as his muscles spasmed. He rolled onto his hands and knees and reached out to Arturo, pain and anger creasing his face. The darkness inside him disappeared as it was overwhelmed by the collective power of his souls. Light bloomed across his skin, so bright Arturo had to shield his eyes.

As the light faded, it left behind a cracked husk of a corpse. Burnt ozone filled the air. A gust of wind rushed across the Arch and Oriphiel's body collapsed in on itself, carried off into the night sky.

Arturo fell to his knees, drained as though every bit of power had seeped out of him. He took several deep breaths to stop his vision from spinning. The souls had left him empty and alone.

Kelly scooted over next to him. "Are you all right?"

He nodded. "Yeah, I think so. You?"

"Yeah. What the hell was that?"

Great question. What had he just done? He looked inside, searching for his own power that had been overshadowed by Oriphiel's souls. There it sat, pure white energy where shedim and mastem had been his whole life.

Arturo lifted his hand. A flame appeared, then fizzled to be replaced with a ball of water. Then an orb of pure energy, an extension of his new nature like what he'd killed Oriphiel with flickered into existence.

"I think I embraced my natures," he said. That was only part of it though. He'd embraced his shedim and his mastem, sure. But it wasn't just them. Something Lydia had said in the hospital rushed back to him. Their humanity made them stronger than the mastem or shedim alone. He stared out over the city.

"I embraced all three natures," he said. He didn't know how he knew that. He just did. He couldn't deny it.

"Three?" Kelly said. "I thought sentinels were shedim and mastem."

"We're also part human," Arturo said. "It's our human blood that lets the two other races mix in us. We've just never realized how powerful that human nature could make us."

EPILOGUE

Arturo couldn't just stand out here. He eventually had to go in. He took a deep breath before he pushed open the door.

Jamaal sat in his hospital bed with an IV in his arm. The monitors were all off and he watched a cartoon from the eighties on the little television in the corner of the room. A lunch tray that was clean except for the Jell-O lay on the counter.

He smiled and muted his show. "Well, look who it is. Took you long enough to get down here." He motioned to the chair next to him.

Arturo took it as he studied his friend. His skin had lost its gray pallor and returned to normal, a great sign his recovery was well on track.

"Yeah, sorry." Arturo hadn't wanted to disturb his friend's healing process. He also wasn't entirely sure how Jamaal would react with having nearly died because of his indecision.

"Eh, whatever," Jamaal said.

Arturo stared at Jamaal, not sure how to take that. He had every right to be angry for having to take a sword for him.

"I hear you killed Oriphiel," Jamaal said. He cracked a smile. "Kind of a jerk move, don't you think? I really would've liked a bit of payback. I've got a nasty scar from that asshole."

Jamaal lifted his shirt. A jagged six-inch line ran across his stomach, already pink with new grown skin. He poked at it. "I've got a matching one on my back where it went through, too. Doctor says it's a good thing I'm not human or this probably would've killed me. Or at least paralyzed me where it nicked my spine."

Arturo winced at how close his friend had actually come to losing everything. Doctor Lawson had left out the part about potential paralysis.

"I... I'm sorry. About slipping like I did. If I'd been in control, none of this would've happened to you."

"Stop," Jamaal said, his voice serious.

"I lost control and—"

"Arturo, enough." Jamaal grabbed his shoulder. "I would've jumped in whether you lost control or not. It's what friends do for each other. Don't tell me you wouldn't have done the same for me if I was lying on the ground."

Arturo opened his mouth, then closed it and nodded. Jamaal was right. "I promise it won't ever happen again. I won't lose control."

"You can't promise that," Jamaal said. "Not until you choose..." He caught Arturo's gaze and his eyes widened. "You chose? I knew it. That's how you defeated Oriphiel."

"Yeah." Arturo reached inside for his new blended nature. "I chose."

"Well, fess up. Don't keep me in suspense. Which one did you go with? I mean, after all these years, this is kind of a big deal. It must have been your shedim if you killed him."

"Not exactly," Arturo said. "I chose all three."

Jamaal scrunched his forehead. "What?"

Arturo called on his power and it rose to answer him. It came to his bidding faster than ever before, fully committed to his will. He smiled at how much easier he would be able to complete even the simplest tasks now. He didn't have to balance control any longer.

His power spread through him and with a blink, the room lit with the same light as the first time his power melded. When he turned his gaze to Jamaal, he saw his friend's soul. It was a bright, vibrant mixture of power totally unlike Kelly's soul, or any human's. It pulsed bright blue but with streaks of white and red mixed in, the mastem's dominance and the shedim and human underneath.

He raised his hand and two balls of flame and water appeared and circled each other. With a little thought, rather than the focused command he would have normally used, the two merged into one of pure energy. "This was how I killed Oriphiel."

"What the hell?" Jamaal sat up further in his bed. "What is that?"

"I embraced all of myself and they melded into this. It happened while I was fighting Oriphiel. My new power let me take all the souls he'd collected and turn them against him."

"Woah, wait, wait." Jamaal raised his hands and shook his head. "You used other souls as power? Like the ganastu? How did you do that?"

Arturo knew what Jamaal was thinking. Sentinels didn't do that. Their shedimic and mastemic natures didn't give them that power. He flicked his hand and the energy dissipated.

"I'm not sure how it works. But I don't have a shedimic or mastemic nature anymore. They joined with my human nature to make something new. And it lets me control all four elements and soul energy."

"Soul energy?" Jamaal laughed.

Arturo smiled. It was like old times, like Jamaal hadn't almost died for him. Like they were discussing the latest ruling from the Sentinalia or a craft beer.

"Yeah, I don't know what else to call it. I haven't told anyone else yet. But it was how the power manifested when I took his souls."

They sat in silence together.

"So you don't have to worry about fighting for control?"

"Not even a little," Arturo said. "I really didn't believe you when you said it would be easier after I chose. But now, it wants to be used without me forcing it.

"Exactly. I told you so."

"Yeah, yeah."

A knock sounded on the door and McLeod walked in. He smiled when he saw Jamaal awake and alert. "The doctor says you should be able to leave after a few more days."

"Sooner," Jamaal said. He clenched his fists. "I'm already getting my strength back and the walls are getting a little too tight for me. Plus they have the worst Jell-O ever."

Arturo and McLeod laughed but Jamaal just stared at them.

"I'm serious," he said.

"First world problems," Arturo said.

McLeod patted Jamaal on the shoulder. "I never could stand hospitals myself. You already look better than when I stopped in earlier."

"Thanks, sir."

McLeod turned his attention to Arturo. "I'm glad you're here. I was going to call later."

Arturo's stomach clenched. He'd reported Oriphiel's death as soon as he'd gotten Kelly back to her apartment. But he hadn't mentioned his new power. Not yet at least. McLeod would be obligated to tell the Sentinalia and Arturo wasn't ready to be interrogated like that yet. This new power was unheard of. He needed some time to understand it for himself first.

"Even though you disobeyed direct orders to stay out of the field, the Sentinalia have agreed to reinstate you."

Arturo stared at McLeod, his mouth slack, until Jamaal smacked him with a pillow.

"Thank you, sir," Arturo said.

McLeod raised his hands. "They've got a few conditions though. First, you are on probation for the next year. It means reduced pay."

"Bullshit," Jamaal whispered.

McLeod glanced at him but ignored the comment. Arturo did, too. It was a small price to pay.

"You will undergo random testing for your control, to be administered by myself or any sentinel they send. If you fail, or if any concern is raised over you or your abilities, they will pull you from the field and imprison you until you choose or your power consumes you."

Silence filled the room. Arturo could handle that. He wouldn't be losing any kind of control anytime soon. So passing the tests wouldn't be a problem.

"What about Lorri?" Arturo asked.

"She will continue to train with you until she is ready to test for full field status."

"Oh, she's going to love that." Jamaal slugged him in the arm. "She was probably excited to get a new instructor."

"Jerk," Arturo said. Jamaal might have been right, but he wasn't so sure anymore. "How did Dahlia feel about it?"

"Who?" Jamaal asked.

"Dahlia is our rep for the Sentinalia," McLeod said. "She came to town while you were out. And she wasn't too happy at all. My understanding is the decision was nearly unanimous, with only her voting against you. You're lucky Belial and Uriel both put in statements on your behalf. Most sentinels would at least get a suspension for disobeying direct orders."

Jamaal scoffed. "A vacation wouldn't have hurt any."

"Consider this your vacation," McLeod said. "Arturo, I don't know how you defeated Oriphiel but it might not work next time. You need to spend time thinking about what nature you want to follow. It's the only way to make sure we don't end up in this position again."

Arturo glanced at Jamaal and then back to McLeod. He'd have to tell McLeod eventually. But not now. For now, he'd learn what he could on his own, explore this new power.

"It won't be a problem," he said.

* * *

Arturo dangled his feet over the edge of the Arch. It was early in the morning, before dawn. Five days had passed since the attack on the airport. Five days and they'd averted a war between the shedim and mastem and he'd killed Oriphiel. And in that time, he'd nearly been kicked out of the sentinels and almost lost his best friend.

He'd also embraced his natures.

He called his power to his hand, the shimmering white globe flickering as it spun in his palm. What did this new power mean? No other sentinel had ever embraced all three natures, at least as far as he knew. What could he do with this?

He released the energy and stared over the river. He rubbed his hands over his pants to warm them and his fingers brushed a lump in his pocket. He fished out Oriphiel's brooch. Kelly had given it back to him after the fight.

This was his and Oriphiel's safe space. They'd spent hours sparring or just sitting and talking right here. A pang of loss twisted his gut. Oriphiel had been there for him when he killed his family, taken him to safety. He was a surrogate grandfather and it was here that Arturo had killed him.

He was really gone. Oriphiel had been responsible for all those deaths, but he'd also saved many lives in his long life. Without him around, who would Arturo turn to when everything became too stressful, when the guilt of his own past threatened to overwhelm him?

A clang resounded from behind him, followed by a screech as the maintenance hatch swung open. He glanced over his shoulder. Lorri's head popped up, looking around. She caught sight of him, pulled herself onto the Arch, and flipped the hatch shut.

"Jamaal said I might find you up here," she said. "Do you have any idea how hard it was to get up here without being able to control air?"

Arturo smiled. "Yet you managed to figure out a way."

Lorri plopped down on the metal a few feet back from the edge. "Of course I did. I've never seen the Arch and now seemed as good a time as ever."

A barge drifted by on the river below and sounded its horn. Life would return to normal, but would normal be the same without Oriphiel.

"McLeod said you were reinstated."

"That's right," Arturo said, not looking at her. "How do you feel about me being your instructor again? You could always request a transfer."

She tapped her toes. "Well, that wouldn't be smart, would it? You beat an ancient mastem, a feat I couldn't even come close to doing yet. *Maybe* there's a thing or two I could learn from you."

Arturo laughed and glanced over his shoulder. Somehow, over these last few days, he'd gained some measure of her respect. It might have been just killing Oriphiel, but something told him it was more than that.

He tossed the brooch back and forth in his hands. Oriphiel might be gone, but Arturo was still here. And the lessons the mastem had taught him, the drive to protect humans and balance, those he would remember.

"Want to spar?" Arturo said.

Lorri grinned. "Okay."

She stood and drew a knife.

Arturo got up and looked at the brooch in his hand one last time.

"Goodbye, Oriphiel."

He threw the piece of metal as far out into the river as he could, losing sight of it well before it hit the water.

He pulled a knife and took a deep breath. Time to work.

"Come on then," Arturo taunted. "Show me you learned at least something useful these past few days.

She darted forward and their blades clashed with a spark of metal.

THE END

ACKNOWLEDGMENTS

There are so many people who have played a role in the development of this book, and I'm sure I will forget someone. Know that even if your name isn't here, I thank you all for your support and encouragement. I want to first thank God, my creator, for instilling in me my creativity and determination to complete this book.

Thank you to the Seton Hill University Writing Popular Fiction Program, for teaching me so much that was necessary to write this book. A special thank you to Nicole Peeler and Paul Goat Allen for advising and mentoring me during my time in the program.

Thank you to the many people who have read and offered feedback on any scenes, chapters, chunks, random thoughts that became Sentinel's Soul, from my critique partners in graduate school to beta readers, more people than I can count. Thank you all.

A special thank you to my writing group, former students and now trusted colleagues and friends - Lia Garofolo, Sawyer Smith, and Paul Schnabel. You three were crucial to me finishing this book and helping me have the confidence to publish it.

Thank you to my editor, Amanda DeBord, for pushing me to make this book better. Couldn't have done it without you. Thank you to my amazing cover artist and friend, Grace Preston.

Thank you to my family. My mom who encouraged me to read and happily (I think) funded my obsession with books. My wife, Shey, who puts up with my need to write and create, who encourages me to pursue my passion and take the time I need to get better at my craft.

Finally, a special thank you to the late Dean James E. McLeod, a mentor for many, especially to me. Thank you for your words of wisdom and encouragement to never stop writing.

ABOUT THE AUTHOR

Photo by Kate Whitaker Bland

Kristopher L. Campa received his Bachelors of Arts in English Literature from Washington University in St. Louis and his Masters of Fine Arts in Writing Popular Fiction from Seton Hill University. *Sentinel's Soul* was his thesis novel for the program. He is an avid reader and writer of Fantasy, Science Fiction, and Horror and has the distinct pleasure to teach creative writing courses in all three genres at Washington University in St. Louis's University College.

He lives in St. Louis, MO with his wife, two sons, and two dogs. When not writing (which happens more than he likes to admit), he enjoys playing D&D and board games with the whole family and friends, practicing pyrography, and working with his students.

Find and connect with him online (kristopherlcampa.com), on Facebook (www.facebook.com/KristopherLCampa) and on Instagram (@kristopherlcampa).